DREAMS ON THE C&O

ROBERTA L. GREENWALD

This is a work of fiction. Names, characters, places, events, and incidents are either the product of the author's imagination or are used fictitiously. Any resemblance to persons living or dead is entirely coincidental

All rights are reserved. Reprinting of this book or sale is entirely unauthorized. No part of this manuscript may be reproduced, stored in a retrieval system, or transmitted in any form or by any means – electronic, mechanical, photocopy, recording, or any other – without the prior permission of the author.

Dreams On The C&O

Book 2

Copyright © 2021 Greenwald, Roberta L.

All rights reserved.

ISBN: 9798777536563

I dedicate this book to all the *dreamers* out there who have always wanted to change something big in your life. Maybe with your career, a partner, going on a diet or maybe starting an exercise routine, traveling to a far off land, and so much more – only you know what the dream is for you! Don't be afraid, just be courageous and take the next step to make it happen! With the dream, there will be frustrations, doubts and setbacks, but until you become determined to attempt it... you will never know what could have been. *Just never give up and keep on dreaming!*

DREAMS ON THE C&O

BOOK 2

CHAPTER 1

"I'll be back real soon! Hopefully, I will see you again the next time I stop by!" Mason yelled out over the top of his head, as he pleasantly smiled at Zoe and waved a fond goodbye, leaving her to stare after him without a word in return, departing the now empty restaurant by the name of *Luna's*.

"Who was that hunk?" Ava pried and curiously asked, as she stood beside of Zoe at the front counter, trying to get on the same page with her and take it all in.

"Umm… someone new in town… that works at the C&O Canal corporate building down the street," Zoe distantly answered, still somewhat in a daze, not desiring to be questioned about Mason Jones any further.

Ava paused to study her friend, knowing how Zoe currently felt about men after her painful break up with Noah Clark, even though three months had already past. She had built up a secure wall around herself that focused entirely in on the restaurant, her father, her beloved dog and a few close acquaintances. It would take a miracle for any guy to break down that fortress now.

"He seems pleasant and he's definitely handsome!" Ava guardedly interjected, knowing she was treading on thin ice with her boss and close friend.

Zoe snapped to, tightly pursing up her lips. "He may be just that, but I don't have any time for this nonsense, Ava! I won't be making that same stupid mistake all over again!" she declared, turning on her heal and heading towards the kitchen at a rather fast pace. "I have potatoes to peel and I could use your help rolling the silverware, now that the *lunch crowd has died down."*

"*Sure thing!*" Ava responded back, as she shook her head, trying not to make too much out of the situation. All she thought about, when it came to Zoe Carter, was how tragic for her that she had lost the love of her life. Why did *Noah have to go off to grad school in London, England, instead of staying local and getting his master's degree here? And if he really wanted to attend school in a foreign country, what is his problem that he couldn't have kept seeing Zoe for the two years he was away in college?* Ava considered as she finished filling up an empty tub with rolled silverware, finding it totally ridiculous and shameful that they had split up after being almost inseparable while they were dating.

The breakup had been sudden and unexpected after four years of being together as a couple. They had weathered the distance between them, during their undergrad years of college, with a two-hour drive being necessary if they wanted to see the other one. Zoe did the majority of the traveling - going from Williamsport, Maryland to Frostburg State University - committed to seeing Noah on most weekends, no matter what.

They were in love – at least Zoe thought so – and in her mind an engagement would be forthcoming after they graduated from college, instead of a breakup. But Noah had other plans, after his unexpected acceptance into Imperial College in London, England. He felt that it was unfair to stay together with the unavoidable distance that was now between them - an obstacle that was no longer easy to overcome.

Zoe was crushed! Noah had made the decision for both of them without any regard to her feelings, even if she would have remained loyal and faithful and had waited on him until he had returned. *The trust that I so reluctantly gave to him early on in our relationship is now nothing but a lie!* She had concluded, feeling totally washed over and tossed aside unfairly.

Emma Baker - Zoe's best friend and business partner – had warned her that Noah could potentially turn off the charm one day and hurt her, but she never wanted to believe it. Emma had known Noah for most of her life, growing up in the same small canal town of Williamsport, Maryland, aware of his past track record with his girlfriend Sophia and his other female conquests that he had entertained on the side. Zoe blamed his sorted and questionable behavior on his youth, being convinced it was now a thing of the past since he was dating her. *The Noah of the present is a mature adult who only wants and desires a relationship with me,* at least that is what she voiced, protesting a little too loudly, trying to convince herself as well as others.

The reality struck home when Noah had asked Zoe to meet him at the C&O Canal two weeks before leaving for London, giving her the horrific news that he wanted to end things and go on now without her in his life, as they stood together looking out over the Potomac River from the newly restored, historic Conococheague Aqueduct. Noah reassured her that they could pick up where they had left off, once he returned home after two years, if they were both single and not with someone else at the time. Zoe, who was typically shy and reserved, found her voice that day, giving Noah the *"middle finger"* as she turned and walked away angrily, letting him know with a choice swearword prefacing her statement of *"...that is never happening!"*

Noah was caught off guard, not expecting such a dramatic reaction out of Zoe, as bystanders stopped to take it all in, wondering what was taking place. He considered going after her - just to calm her down - but realized it wasn't going to accomplish anything in the end, since he wasn't changing his mind about the breakup or going off to England for grad school. The plans and preparations had already been made and confirmed, and once Noah departed for London, he never intended to look back at what he had left behind in Williamsport – be it with Zoe, or any other former part of his life.

Zoe was forced to go forward in a new direction alone, after temporarily stumbling, feeling like she couldn't go on without Noah.

She picked up the pieces nicely with the help of her father, grandparents and good friends, going on with her plans to open up her restaurant *Luna's* – that was coined after her beloved shelter dog of the same name. Emma and Ava stayed loyal to Zoe, working in the restaurant right beside of her, trying to keep her strong and determined after the breakup. *Luna's* became an overnight success story, being frequented not only by the locals of the town, but also by the numerous tourists who visited the C&O Canal on a daily basis, giving new purpose and meaning to Zoe's life and existence.

    The dining establishment was situated close to the canal and the newly built C&O Canal corporate building that was now the headquarters for the entire 184 miles of the canal, running from Georgetown – near Washington DC - to Cumberland, Maryland. The Parks Department federal workers brought in a steady stream of customers to *Luna's,* mainly over the bustling lunch hour, but also after work for dinner or even for some light-hearted entertainment. It was a popular *"go-to"* destination for listening to some music, putting a puzzle together at the large *"puzzle table",* playing a board game, or even reading a book or magazine that was freely offered.

    The concept of *Luna's* had changed in the short time the restaurant had been opened. Zoe had remained firm that there would be no installation of TV's throughout the place, probably because of Noah's insistence *that they would draw in more people who would be hanging out and watching sporting events.* She didn't want *Luna's* to breathe *"sports bar",* knowing that there were several other establishments close by who catered to that sort of thing. Her vision was geared to a different sort of crowd who desired good food and *"hands-on"* activity, over the sterile viewing of a television screen. A liquor license had been obtained, and wine and beer were now also offered, along with a variety of dinner specials that had been created especially by her grandmother - from *"passed down"* family recipes. Overall, the atmosphere of *Luna's* was warm and inviting, with no shortage of patrons, who were willing to wait on a table when it was deemed a *"full house".*

Her grandparents – Pappy Joe and Nana Ruth Carter – lived in Fort Wayne, Indiana, and had been a stable force of support both emotionally and financially for Zoe, providing the necessary funding to back the restaurant from the start. Zoe was pleased that she was finally seeing her way through the haze of the first few months of operations, letting her grandparents know that it shouldn't be long until she didn't need their monetary assistance any longer. It came as quite a surprise to all parties involved, when a substantial profit was turned over almost on day one of the grand opening, far surpassing the goals and expectations that were anticipated.

With *Luna's* immediate success, Emma was thrilled with her decision to stay local and help Zoe out, instead of departing to another area away from Williamsport, where she had seriously considered taking another job after her graduation from Loyola University. Although Emma wasn't asked to financially back the venture, she was still hesitant about getting involved, but in the end her friendship with Zoe won out and was the deciding factor to stick around. In her mind, it was worth the risk, even if the restaurant didn't survive, just to take a leap of faith and see how things played out. She was driven to succeed, equally as much as Zoe was, striving daily to give it her all, hoping that everything would turn out okay in the end.

Bryan Carter was Zoe's father, and the plant manager at the local power company for over five years now. He was still dating Kelly who he had met on an online dating site, being almost inseparable from her after work and on the weekends. *Luna's* was a dinner destination for them at least several nights a week, wanting to support the *"all-out"* efforts of his daughter and Emma both. Zoe approved of Kelly, for the most part, which wasn't easy after her mother's abandonment when she was only five years old, disappearing to Oregon with a love interest that she had worked with at a furniture store, leaving Zoe and Bryan and never returning again afterwards. Bryan hadn't been with anyone for years after that, only taking the plunge once Zoe had encouraged him to do so, while she was still actively dating Noah. The twist of fate was they were no longer together, but Bryan and Kelly had continued going strong.

Luke Taylor had remained in Williamsport, working at his father's car dealership — Taylor Toyota - where he was guaranteed a career and a generous income, as long as he always did what was expected out of him. *Luna's* was a place that Luke avoided, even though he had hung out with Zoe and Emma over the past four years along with Noah. Unfortunately, it was his best friend who was at the heart of the divide, feeling like his loyalty needed to remain with him, since they had been like brothers for most of their lives. It was awkward avoiding the popular restaurant where everyone else in town had already ventured, but Luke saw no other choice, feeling conflicted and sad that the *"group of four"* was no longer together.

His pals would meet up at *Luna's* quite frequently, claiming, *"that it was the best new place to go to for a decent meal"*, making it a regular dining spot first before going on to a bar or doing something else later - where they would typically then run into Luke. No matter how many times he was asked why he *wouldn't just try Luna's out*, he resisted and made excuses, being resolved to stay away no matter what they said. Being from this small town, gossip could run rampant, but Luke had remained quiet about the breakup between Noah and Zoe, not revealing what he knew when he was pressed repeatedly for the details. He came to the difficult realization that his social life had greatly been affected by what had happened, and there wasn't a damn thing that he could do about it.

Lillian had gone on to become a hairdresser, working elsewhere for a few years, learning her craft and building a successful client base. With the opportunity to open up her own shop in Williamsport, she took the plunge, hiring two new beauticians and a *"shampoo girl"* besides. Zoe continued to be loyal, following her wherever she went, having made a promise to Lillian early on, while she was still in beauty school, *that she could always practice on her hair*, bringing it up jokingly during every appointment after that.

    Ava worked at *Luna's* as a server, being happy and content with the world around her. She had recently started dating Philip, who she had known from college, being reacquainted with him when he showed up unexpectedly at the restaurant for lunch one day. Zoe had mixed feelings about it all, happy that her friend had a boyfriend, but irritated all the same, since she easily became distracted now - lingering and talking at his table - not always doing her job to the fullest for the other customers present. A simple reminder was necessary from the female owners, that *personal could not affect professional,* resolving the issue quickly.

    Sophia, along with many of *"her squad",* had remained in Williamsport, stopping in from time to time to *Luna's,* which honestly surprised Zoe and Emma that these snobbish girls - who had done nothing but annoy them while they were still in high school and then in college - would actually be so bold as to enter their eatery. Sophie would act sheepish and totally unfazed by her past actions, dismissing the last time that they had encountered each other. She had been intoxicated, acting rudely and being overbearing, flirting openly with Noah, trying to pull him away from Zoe at a college graduation party that was hosted at Luke's parents' house back in the summer. Business was business, and if Sophia could put it all behind her, so could Zoe – even if they had both dated Noah at some point of their lives.

    Luna was Zoe's English Lab and rescue dog that she had adopted from the Washington County Humane Society. She was the truest and most loyal companion of anyone in Zoe's life - now that Noah was gone. She stayed at the restaurant while Zoe worked, having a bed and bowls with her name inscribed on each one, going home with her afterwards, once the place was closed. Luna was somewhat of a local celebrity, not only in the restaurant, but also in the town itself, with most seeing her constantly by Zoe's side as they took walks up and down the city sidewalks, and on the C&O Canal towpath, stopping to pet her any chance they got.

The past few months had been difficult, but Zoe had finally turned the corner, accepting the reality that Noah was gone and their relationship was over. For a time, she was angry, wishing she had never dated him, but now she allowed the memories of what they had experienced together, float pleasantly by in her mind from time to time, with a smile crossing her face for what had been.

Maybe not for Noah, but truly for Zoe, she had fallen in love with him - totally and completely – with all her being. Even now, and as much as she didn't want to admit it, he still held a special place in her heart. This cold and uncaring guy – Noah Clark – had without any regard, walked away from her and their relationship, *probably never giving her a second thought now*, she assumed, but for Zoe he had been more than that, he was a significant part of her life – her first love that had changed her world, as soon as she had met him in high school homeroom.

Chapter 2

    Bryan Carter made his way out to the mailbox of his house, after watching the mailman pull away with a low muffle of a tailpipe, stopping immediately once again, at his neighbor's residence that was right next door. He opened the mailbox to an assortment of letters and a few sales flyers, advertising the latest big sale at several local car dealerships in the area, as well as some furniture stores who were proclaiming *"free furniture"* as their hook to get *"would-be"* buyers to come in and shop. As he looked over each envelope and shuffled it to the back of the stack for closer observation later, a letter addressed to him with a return address from the state of Oregon, gained his undivided attention and focus. He ripped into the envelope quickly, pulling the enclosed letter from it, unfolding it to his view.

Dear Bryan,

    I know this letter is long time overdue, but honestly it was quite a challenge finding your current address. I even attempted to reach out to your parents, but never heard back from them with an answer as to where you are currently living. The intention of this letter is to see how you and Zoe are doing, but also written with the hope that you can convince Zoe to speak with me some time in the near distant future.

    On my end, I did want to catch up with you on a few things. After our divorce, I did go on to meet someone and remarry, and it wasn't my co-worker from the furniture store that I had left town with initially. My husband's name is Edward Davis. We have a child together, which would make Eddie Junior my son and Zoe's half brother. He is fourteen years old now and has begun to ask a lot of questions about my life prior to marrying his father. I am trying to give him the answers to what he seeks and deserves to know, but I have held off out of respect to you and Zoe.

So now I am asking, will you give me permission to tell Eddie about my life with you and Zoe in Fort Wayne? I would also like to speak with Zoe about all this and hopefully gain her approval to move forward, so that I can share with my son the details of my past.

I am sorry how things ended up with us, Bryan. I know I hurt a lot of people with my careless decision to leave, including our daughter and your family, but it also hurt my family members as well who were very disappointed in me for leaving you. I can only ask for your forgiveness and cooperation now to proceed forward and try to heal things between Zoe and myself. I know I am asking a lot, but life is short and I am not the same woman I was seventeen years ago when I foolishly took off and left our home.

I do hope you are doing well and I will anxiously wait to hear back from you. My return address and phone number are included on my letterhead at the top of this page, so please feel free to contact me either way. You can text me also to the number listed. Take care.

Sincerely,

Cynthia Davis

Bryan read the letter twice. The first time through - very quickly - and the second time - slowly and methodically - taking in every word and hidden meaning that he might have skipped over. He felt numb from the realization that Cynthia had *finally* reached out to him in a cordial sort of way. It had been his daily desire, early on when she first departed, but within a year, reality set in when she sent him divorce papers that he signed and mailed back without protest. She wanted nothing from him, which included their child. Zoe was no more the wiser, with Bryan keeping the whole exchange a secret to spare her already crushed feelings.

"Now she sends me this? After all these years?" he said aloud in frustration, as he continued to consider the delicate situation while standing outside of his rancher in the driveway, scratching his head and examining the letter yet for another time. Zoe was at work with her dog, Luna, and Bryan was glad for the time of solitude so that he could reflect and consider exactly how to handle the matter with his daughter. *She is way past the time of grieving over the loss of her mother while she was a youth, but maybe that pain could all come rushing back now? After all, Noah just suddenly up and left, breaking her heart, and now to add Cynthia to the mix? This may not be the best decision on my part,* Bryan concluded sensibly as he replaced the letter into the envelope, and then proceeded to walk back inside the house.

He entered his bedroom, scanning his personal area for a hiding place that Zoe would never stumble upon, even if she decided to put his clean laundry away which she did at times. The decision was made to hide the letter in his dresser, underneath the socks in his top left bureau drawer. Reconsidering, he moved the socks to the side, flipping the letter over so that she could not see the address on the front, replacing the socks to hide it well again. *"That should work,"* he concluded, as he walked out of his bedroom and back to the kitchen, feeling a sense of relief.

With another cup of coffee poured, Bryan flipped on the television and sipped deeply from the hot brew, attempting to focus in on the news of the day. *Why didn't I just throw the letter way?* He pondered silently, bringing it up for another time in his mind, with the announcement *"of only clear skies"* being heard in the background from the weatherman.

"Hello?"

"Hey mom, it's me."

"Bryan, so good to hear your voice!" Ruth exclaimed pleasantly, knowing it had been awhile since she had last spoken to her son. *"How is everything going with the restaurant?"*

"Just fine, mom. *Luna's* is killing it. No worries there."

Ruth looked puzzled. *"Good! Glad to hear, and is everything else okay?"*

Bryan paused and cleared his throat before beginning again. "Well, to be perfectly honest, there is something that just came up today that I thought I should speak to you and dad about."

"Your father isn't here right now, Bryan. He is up at the church mowing the grass, but I can have him call you when he comes home, if you would like?"

Bryan smiled, thinking about the kindness his parents were always bestowing to everyone around them, being so much different from his ex-wife, Cynthia, who was so self-serving and a *"selfish little bitch"* type in her personality.

"That would be great, mom, but I would still like to run this by you first, if you don't mind?"

"Of course, Bryan!" Ruth answered sincerely, taking a seat at her kitchen table, ready and willing to lend an ear and give some advice.

"I received a letter today that I never expected to have mailed to me in a million years."

"From whom?" Ruth asked, now feeling perplexed and curious.

"From Cynthia."

Ruth cleared her throat before answering, never considering that Cynthia would have taken it a step further, after making the initial outreach to her and Joe a while ago. *"You are saying that your ex-wife, Cynthia, contacted you?"*

Bryan shook his head. *"Mom, what other Cynthia's do we know?"*

She paused, knowing she was a woman of faith and shouldn't have kept the truth from her son. "Bryan, I must confess something to you. Cynthia contacted your father and I a few weeks ago by way of a letter, asking if we would provide her with your contact information. We decided not to answer her or inform you of what took place, since Zoe had already been through so much with Noah leaving the country. I guess we did the wrong thing by keeping this to ourselves."

Bryan sighed, realizing his mother was being overly protective, trying to look out for their best interests. "I understand where you are coming from, mom, but I am a grown man and need to make my own decisions about such things. If you are worried that I would have fallen prey to her cunning charms and schemes once again, let me reassure you of this, she is remarried with another child now, and I absolutely have no interest in her, whatsoever."

Ruth laughed nervously, feeling somewhat embarrassed. "Bryan, that never even crossed my mind or your father's mind. I just know how devastated we all were after what she pulled on you and Zoe, and we figured it was better left unsaid. Please forgive us for our poor decision making," she pleaded, feeling the tears welling up now in her eyes.

"It's okay, mom. To be honest, now it is I repeating what you just did."

"How's that?"

"I just hid the letter that she sent to me. I can't bring myself to tell Zoe about any of this. All Cynthia wants me to do is smooth the pathway for her to reconcile with Zoe at some level."

Joe Carter opened the kitchen door, realizing he had just stepped into tense situation. He could hear his son speaking out loudly on his wife's cellphone that was sitting on the table in front of her. He glanced at Ruth, seeing her discomfort from the obvious troubling conversation that they were engrossed in, taking a seat beside of her.

"Bryan, your father is here now. You may want to share with him what we were just discussing," she suggested, looking at her husband with a frown that was full of worry.

"Hello, dad."

"Hello to you too, Bryan," Joe said as he smiled reassuredly at Ruth, wiping his still-damp forehead with his handkerchief that was stuffed in his shirt pocket. He had just finished mowing the church lawn and felt slightly worn out, as he pulled out a chair at the kitchen table and sat down. *"What is on your mind today, Bryan, that seems to be creating some concern in your mother?"* he asked good-naturedly.

"A letter from Cynthia, my ex-wife," he announced, getting right to the point with his father, not holding back, or beating around the bush in any way.

Ruth looked at Joe with regret, grabbing for his hand. *"I told him about her reaching out to us a few weeks ago,"* she whispered, trying to get him updated and on the same page with them.

Joe grimaced, knowing Ruth had convinced him not to mention it to Bryan, even against his better judgment. *"I'm sorry, Bryan. It was a bad decision on the part of your mother and I to have kept that a secret. You had every right to know that we had heard from Cynthia."*

"It's okay, dad. I'm over it. I realize that you were just trying to spare my emotions, but as I just told mom, I am a grown man and I should have been informed of her contacting you, and then I would have dealt with it as I saw fit."

"I promise, we will never do that again!" Ruth interjected emotionally, jumping in to the conversation, feeling responsible for the blunder.

"What's done is done, but I need advice going forward. Cynthia wants my permission to tell her son – from her current husband - about the life we had together prior to her getting remarried and having him. She also wants me to speak to Zoe on her behalf about all this as well. I don't know if I have it in me to do either. Zoe is finally calmed down from the Noah fiasco, so why would I want to wind her up again about her mother and the past?"

Joe looked around his kitchen and then at his wife, whose heart was filled with only the best of intentions, breathing a silent prayer for profound guidance and wisdom before he answered. "Son, you said you were an adult and should have the right to make your own decisions, well the same holds true for Zoe. She is twenty-two years old now, and has the same right to make her own choices. Maybe the Noah situation has made her a stronger female than you realize, and she is better equipped to deal with the ups and downs of life, and unexpected situations such as this."

Bryan sighed, realizing his father always had a way of taking a broken situation and straightening it out, making sense of it all. "You win, dad. I will let Zoe know that her mother reached out by way of letter and wants to communicate with her. I may not tell her tonight, but I will tell her... when the time is right."

Chapter 3

It was Saturday morning and Zoe yawned and then sat up, stretching her arms high above her head, trying to shake the cobwebs from her mind. Luna yawned also and looked at her mistress, snuggling in a little closer to her side, trying to convince her to stay in bed a little while longer. "Sorry, sweet girl, but unfortunately I gotta get up and begin my day," Zoe cooed, as she gave her pet a comforting hug, sliding her feet into her slippers that were sitting close by on the floor.

Luna groaned loudly, protesting the obvious, as she jumped to the floor with a loud thump and then proceeded towards the bedroom door that Zoe had just opened. She walked down the hallway with her beloved pet plastered to her side, towards the kitchen where Bryan was cooking a hearty breakfast, which he routinely did most weekends. The smell of bacon and eggs and coffee whiffed pleasantly throughout the air, and Zoe felt suddenly hungry and was ready to eat.

It was her late day, which she rarely took, being constantly devoted to *Luna's*. Emma had promised to take on the early shift so that Zoe could come in at her leisure – insisting that she needed a break after not taking off for even one day over the last two weeks. Emma would open the restaurant, helping the cook with food prep and the rest of the team with whatever else that needed to be done, before the early morning crowd showed up and filled the place. Zoe had been encouraged to take off for the entire day, but that was never in the cards, always driven to stay busy so that she didn't have the time to think about Noah and the pain he had caused her. Anger for this guy was a driving force for both of the friends, even if it wasn't actually discussed. Emma detested him even more so now than she had before – since he had crushed Zoe's heart and spirit with his departure, leaving her a former shell of herself.

"Be right back, dad," Zoe explained sweetly, as she leashed up her furbaby and made her way out to the back yard. She shivered, realizing she had forgotten to put on her hoodie, as she crisscrossed her arms and hugged herself tightly, bobbing up and down, trying to stay warm, hoping that Luna would get her *"morning potty time ritual"* over with quickly. A hint of autumn could be felt in the air with the obvious coolness that had replaced the balmier mornings from just a few weeks earlier. The leaves on the trees were beginning to turn yellow, orange and red from a few nights of frost, with the days getting shorter and shorter - with far less daylight now.

Bryan smiled as he poured Zoe a cup of coffee after making her way back inside, placing it in front of her on the table, as she sipped from it deeply knowing that would do the trick of warming her up. *"Maybe you should grab your jacket the next time before walking Luna?"* he teased lightly, adding a piping hot plate of food in front of her next.

"Exactly," she agreed with a pleasant grin, taking a big bite of scrambled eggs that her father always added a dash of cream to that made them extra fluffy. "I love fall in Maryland, but I do prefer summer mornings when the air is a bit warmer," she confessed. "By afternoon it's definitely great, but the darn brisk start of the day right now, always gets to me this time of the year."

Bryan listened without relating, grabbing his own plate of grub and a large mug of coffee that he had already refilled twice, knowing the early mornings and the brisk air of autumn energized him, which was a distinctive difference between him and his daughter. Zoe's mother - on the other hand - never liked the cold, complaining about it any chance she could, which only served to remind him that his daughter did come from two very different people whose individual make up was a part of her.

"Are you going in to work today?" Bryan inquired.

"Yes... of course," Zoe answered, wiping her mouth on her napkin. "Emma wanted me to take the whole day off, but you know me, I just can't bring myself to doing that."

Bryan paused, to study his child. "We all need our breaks, Zoe. It revitalizes me to have off on weekends, making my work week that much better."

Zoe slid back her plate, making her own observations now. "Dad, you have Kelly in your life. You must admit that you worked a whole lot more before she was around. I am just trying to give *Luna's* my all right now. The success or failure of my restaurant is based solely on my efforts."

Bryan reached over to touch the top of his daughter's hand, giving it a comforting squeeze. "Not just your efforts, my dear. You have Emma and a whole staff of workers that are devoted to making *Luna's* a success."

"Yes, you are right," she agreed, getting up to clear the dishes from the table and place them in the dishwasher. "But everyone there relies on my guidance, and I can't let Pappy Joe and Nana Ruth down."

"Why do you think you would ever let them down?" Bryan pressed, being confused by her assumptions.

"The amount of money that they have invested in this endeavor. It is more than I ever dreamt they would have put forth to help me. I don't deserve such generosity!" Zoe declared humbly, returning again to the table.

Bryan smiled warmly at his daughter, knowing she had a soft and caring heart towards her grandparents. "If they didn't have the money and the ability to give it, they wouldn't have done so. Your pappy and nana have been richly blessed over the years with income, and it didn't hurt that Nana Ruth received quite a substantial inheritance when her parents passed away - being an only child."

"What exactly was her inheritance?" Zoe asked with keen interest, only knowing bits and pieces of the story.

"Her parents – or your great grandparents - owned the largest farm in the Fort Wayne area that provided fruit and vegetables for several major packing companies which they contracted with. At the time of their retirement, they sold the farm for quite a hefty profit, becoming overnight millionaires. They were modest people, never changing their lifestyle after that, living contently in a smaller home within a mile of the house that we lived in. Nana Ruth was shocked when the will of her father was read – being the last to die of her parents - never expecting to receive enough money to live on securely for the rest of her life. Beyond this fortune, Pappy Joe was a Civil Engineer for almost forty years, and he retired with an amazing pension. So to that point, they share what they have with us and others, and it makes their lives worth living."

Zoe was fascinated with the tale, never hearing it stated so vividly. *"I knew Nana Ruth and Pappy Joe lived a comfortable life, but I never knew they were independently wealthy, since they never talk about it."*

Bryan began to laugh and shake his head, surprised that his daughter was just figuring things out. "Your car and education, my car and this house, the restaurant – just to name a few – yes, money is never a problem with them."

"I guess I realize that now, but I still don't want them to ever think that I would intentionally take advantage of them. One day, I would like to pay all the money back that they extended to me for *Luna's*."

"They would never take the money back. Just always show them love and respect. That is what they desire and need the most."

Zoe eyes began to fill with happy tears. "Life hasn't always been easy, but with Pappy Joe and Nana Ruth I have been blessed beyond measure."

"Yes, we both have..." Bryan answered with some hesitation, knowing it was time to change gears and talk with Zoe about the *"uneasy part of life"* she had just made reference to. "Zoe, I need to talk with you about something else that is on my mind."

"Okay?" she replied, sensing his sudden change of attitude.

"I received a letter yesterday that I never expected to receive in the mail."

"From whom?"

Bryan breathed heavily, as he shifted in his chair, not sure he wanted to continue. *"From your mother."*

Zoe's eyes widened, feeling like she was not hearing him correctly. *"What did you just say?"* She asked intensely, sitting up a little straighter now.

"A letter arrived yesterday that was addressed to me, and it was from your mother. She wants to make contact with you and she asked me for permission to do so."

Zoe began to laugh nervously, feeling the same similar set of shocked emotions that she felt when Noah broke up with her just a few short months ago. *"I can't believe this is happening. Why would she want to speak with me now? It has been seventeen years since I have last seen her!"* she spewed out angrily, as she attempted to sort things out with pain-filled eyes. She couldn't even bring herself to speak of her as *"mother"* as they discussed the situation. Nana Ruth was truly the only mother figure that she knew of and accepted, since she was a little girl.

Bryan sighed heavily while looking down at the table, before continuing. "I am sorry, Zoe, that this is suddenly occurring. Your mother remarried and you have a half brother that is fourteen years old. He seems to be curious, all of a sudden, about his mother's life prior to having him. She wants to explain things to him, but not before gaining your approval to do so first. I guess she is also hoping you can put the past behind you now, and start again with her, while getting to know your brother in the process."

"*Sounds like a bunch of happy horseshit, if you ask me!*" she stammered out, getting up to lean against the counter across the room, being very much on guard now. "*She doesn't need my approval to do anything of the sort! I will never forgive her or see her or this boy – who, by the way, I will never consider to be my brother or sibling - so why all the effort? And how did she find us anyway?*" Zoe lashed out in disbelief, feeling frustrated and helpless.

Bryan stood up also, keeping his safe distance, as he leaned against the wall opposite Zoe, knowing he needed to provide her with an explanation. "Cynthia reached out to Pappy and Nana, but they never responded back, so it definitely didn't come about through them. *Who knows how she found us… Why don't I get the letter and you can draw your own conclusions?*"

Zoe's heart began to race, feeling her blood pressure rising. "Dad, I love you dearly, but I can not or will not deal with this woman or her son! She is dead to me! When she left me at age five, never returning home even though I begged God every night for her to do so, I closed that door to her and the past. Can you *please just understand how hard this is on me now?* Zoe begged with tears now flowing freely down her face, making Luna walk over to her side, in a protective sort of way.

Bryan approached his *"broken-in-spirit"* daughter, wrapping her lovingly in his arms as he held her close and whispered gently against her hair, kissing the top of her head and trying his best to comfort her. "It's okay, Zoe. *All she wanted to do was discuss this with you. Obviously, I know the answer is a definite "no" and the subject is closed. We don't need to give any of this one for more moment of thought… so let's just get it out of our minds… move on… and forget that it ever happened.*"

Chapter 4

Luke Taylor was six foot two, with sun-kissed blonde hair and sky blue eyes that were hypnotic. He was not only very attractive, but also athletically built with a soft-spoken personality, never flaunting what he was naturally blessed with in life. The thought never crossed his mind to do anything other than work at his father's Toyota car dealership in the area, being the third generation of his family to do so. High school and then college at Frostburg State University went by much too quickly for his liking, still missing the camaraderie that he shared with his teammates, while playing football and soccer.

Working as a salesman at the dealership, kept him amply busy and distracted, but he missed the days of hanging out with Noah Clark, his friend, fellow athlete and roommate when they were in college together. Not only did Noah break up with Zoe Carter after four years of being with her romantically, but he also cast aside most of his local friends that included Luke. Whatever Noah's current mindset, Luke felt that with the breakup, his friendship had been destroyed and lost too – barely hearing anything from him since he had left for London, England.

Typically, it was his mother, Theresa, who kept him abreast of Noah's exciting world abroad, whenever she would run into his mother, Jessica, at a shop in Williamsport. They would talk and gossip about everything and everyone else in the town, breaking for a cup of coffee at The Desert Rose just to discuss the latest and catch up. Luke honestly wondered if Noah had temporarily lost his mind after the breakup, with his current behavior being like nothing he ever seen before. Just the mere fact that Noah wanted to go off to London, England for grad school, without discussing it first with anyone – including him - was a shocking enough detail that he still couldn't wrap his mind around.

Outside of work, Luke did hang out with a few close friends who had remained in Williamsport, usually meeting up at the Third Base or the C&O Canal Bar several times a week, to watch a sporting event and grab a drink and a bite to eat if it was anywhere but *Luna's*. Females were also in the picture, but there was no desire to get serious with any of them, especially after what had taken place between Noah and Zoe. Luke thought it was a certainty that the pair would have been engaged and planning a wedding by now, since they seemed *"joined at the hip"* from the time they began dating right outside of high school. There was no doubt that there had been the occasional cheating that went on with Noah, but it was brushed off as a part of growing up and a rite of passage during the *"sowing your wild oats years"* that was somewhat expected out of all of them, before settling down with a wife and kids.

Luke pulled his Toyota 4Runner into the one available parking space in front of *Luna's,* squealing his tires to a fast stop. He checked his appearance in the rearview mirror before exiting, wanting to look his best as he smoothed back a strand of his misplaced hair. The credit manager, at his place of business, had asked him to stop by the restaurant and pick up a large tray of sandwiches, which she had ordered for a retirement party that they were throwing for one of the salesman who had been employed with the Taylor family for thirty years. Luke hesitated, but finally agreed to do so, knowing he was currently in the area, saving someone else the trip into Williamsport. Never stepping foot in the place before was strange enough, but seeing Zoe besides for the very first time since his college graduation party and the breakup with Noah, was nothing he could plan for or wanted to deal with. He smiled pleasantly as he opened the front door to the establishment, realizing it was Emma there to greet him instead of Zoe, which brought him an overwhelming sense of relief.

Emma's breath caught, as Luke approached, in all his handsome glory – just as good looking as she remembered, dressed in tan khakis and a white polo shirt with the Taylor Toyota company logo embroidered on the front. *"Luke?"* she muttered, honestly making sure it was the *"actual man"* standing in front of her.

"One and the same!" he playfully grinned. He never had a problem with Emma, but had come to accept the sad fact that she probably detested him now also, branding him *"guilty by association"* after what Noah had pulled on her best friend and business partner.

"What are you doing here?" Emma questioned in surprise, still in a daze from seeing him now, after not doing so for such a long time.

Luke began to laugh. "Missed you too, Em, but seriously, I came here to pick up a tray of sandwiches for work that an order was placed for."

"Oh... yes, they were just prepared. So they are intended for you?" she asked in confusion, still trying to connect the dots.

"A manager at my company placed the order and requested that I pick up the tray, since I was having breakfast at my folks' house this morning, which as you know is in close proximity to your restaurant. *That is okay, right?"* he prodded, always enjoying their former banter.

"Of course... it's okay... Luke," Emma intensely answered, as she stammered through the sentence, suddenly feeling the situation was rather awkward to say the least. She was embarrassed and her face reddened, which rarely happened, but Luke had a way of bringing that side out in her. "I will be right back. I need to go to the kitchen and get the tray of sandwiches for you."

"I'll be waiting..." Luke teased, smiling broadly and winking as she turned on her heel and quickly departed. He looked around the place, taking in each and every detail with a fresh set of eyes. Just as his friends had described, the restaurant was beautifully decorated with an industrial vibe that he liked, but lacking in televisions, which honestly surprised him since the competition nearby all had TV's displayed on their walls.

Emma reappeared with the large tray of sandwiches that was piled high and covering her face, as she proceeded to walk slowly and tried to keep it balanced, going in Luke's general direction. Two bags of potato chips were lying on the top of the deli tray, as she handed it all over to Luke. "The chips are on me," she casually offered, wanting to let him know she had done him a favor.

"Well thanks, Em. What do I owe you?" he smiled, placing the tray on an empty table close by, ready to extract his wallet from his pants pocket.

"The lady from your work, who called in the order, paid us already over the phone with a credit card," she explained matter-of-factly. *"So you owe me nothing!"*

Luke paused to study his friend of the past, feeling her words held a dual meaning. *"Emma, I am sorry about Noah and what happened between him and Zoe."*

A well-defined look of mistrust and bitterness was suddenly outlined across Emma's face. *"You owe me no explanations! You are not your brother's keeper!"* she gritted out angrily, totally overreacting to the situation.

Luke felt slightly taken back and stunned, realizing how upset Emma truly was concerning the sad ordeal that he had no control over. If there was one thing he was learning to be an expert in, was sorting out people's emotions, especially with being in automobile sales. "No, I am *not* my brother's keeper. Just so you know, I haven't spoken to Luke in weeks. He seems to have gone MIA on all of us... This whole thing has bothered me also, you know..." Luke confessed with a sincere, distant smile, trying to alleviate the tension in the room between them.

Emma sighed loudly, trying to gather her wits. *"I'm having a hard time believing that your best friend, since we were kids, just up and left the area and doesn't speak with you now? That is what you want me to believe?"* Please stop making a fool out of me!"

Luke locked his blue eyes with Emma's similar colored, azure blue ones, trying to convince her of his innocence in the situation. *"What can I say or do that will make you realize that I am telling you the truth? I have no reason to lie to you, Em,"* he whispered for her ears only. *"Every now and then my mom talks to his mom, but that's about it. Half of the stuff she tells me goes in one ear and out the other, because I'm honestly not convinced that it's even true."*

Emma gulped, suddenly remembering a kiss from years ago at the Williamsport carnival that Luke had passionately placed on her lips, recalling it was done in jest just to get a reaction out of Noah and Zoe. "Even if your friend has mysteriously abandoned you - which I still have a hard time believing - I haven't left my dear friend's side throughout this entire nightmare. Sometimes in life, we must say our goodbyes to people or things – which might not seem necessarily fair – out of respect to someone else. I think, Luke Taylor, you fall into that category. You are an unfortunate casualty caught in the crossfire of all of this, just like I have been. *I must admit, I was very sad when it was all over. I did enjoy hanging out with you from time to time,"* Emma confidentially admitted, surprising herself that she did.

Luke reached across the counter to grab Emma's hand that was resting there, not releasing its hold even though she resisted. "That righteous statement of allegiance you just made is absolutely ridiculous! Noah is an asshole for what he did, and I never was a part of any of it! I have stayed away from *Luna's* out of respect to Zoe, but now I'm honestly wondering why? *I haven't done anything wrong, Emma, and it's about time you realized that and stopped holding an unfair grudge against me!"*

Emma shook her head stubbornly, holding to her guns, as Luke abruptly released her hand and picked up the tray of sandwiches again and walked towards the door, ready to make his departure. The door flung open with Zoe almost bumping into him, looking shocked - as if she saw a ghost - with the large tray now being the buffer between them.

"Luke?"

"Yes, Zoe, my name is Luke. Not Noah Clark, but Luke Taylor. Hopefully, you and your friend over there, can keep the two of us straight!" he yelled out while pointing with his chin in Emma's direction, which was totally out of character for him with his mild-mannered disposition. The door closed with a slam, being kicked shut by Luke's foot, and within moments the sound of a car engine could be heard revving up, as it departed from the front of the building, accelerating down the street with a squeal of his tires.

"What in the hell is going on?" Zoe asked, feeling like the next chapter - in her already crazy day so far - was suddenly unfolding. Luna stood close by her side, as Zoe unleashed her, granting the dog permission to retreat to her soft bed situated across the room, as she plopped down with a loud groan, desiring to be removed from the current drama that was taking place.

"Luke stopped in to pick up a tray of sandwiches for a work party that his company is hosting for a retiree. We began to talk about what happened between you and Noah... and I guess things got a little heated and out-of-control," Emma confessed, feeling somewhat uncomfortable now for allowing it to go that far.

"Seriously, Em? You really didn't need to treat Luke that way. How many times have I told you that he didn't have anything to do with this situation with Noah and I?"

Emma crossed her arms defiantly, with her irrational mindset and strong determination sometimes getting the better of her, as it was clearly doing right then. *"He is guilty by proxy, if you ask me."*

"No he isn't!" Zoe insisted, proceeding towards the back office with Emma in tow, still attempting to make her point. "I would never want to be condemned if you did something horrible, just because we are friends."

"I would never do anything terrible like Noah did to you!"

Zoe shook her head in frustration, just wanting some *"normal"* to her day. *"Can we just get past all of this? I had a bad morning dealing with some personal stuff at the house, and now I show up at work and I have to hear about all this too? Please, Emma, just stop and give it a rest!"* Zoe begged, feeling totally depleted and not ready to *"run a floor"* until late into the evening with her current mindset.

Emma took a deep breath, trying to regroup. *"What happened at home? Something with your dad and Kelly? Did they break up?"*

Zoe sat at her desk, with the tears suddenly forming again, remembering the earlier conversation with her father. "Kelly and my dad are just fine… "

"Then what is it?"

Zoe stared at her friend, not quite sure she had the mental capacity to share the sorted details with her, but knowing she had no one else to turn to for advice at the moment. *"I feel like I am experiencing a bad dream. My dad received a letter from my mother yesterday. She wants to get in touch with me and she turned to my father first, seeking his approval to do so. She remarried and has another kid, and wants me to get to know my fourteen year old brother and probably forgive her for the past."*

Emma's eyes widened, forgetting that Zoe even had a mother most of the time. *"Didn't she disappear when you were just a little girl?"*

"Yes, Em, you are correct, she sure did. I was only five years old when she left, and now after all these years she wants to make an unwelcomed entrance back into my life," Zoe explained with a sad shake of her head. "I don't think I even have it in me to give her another chance."

Chapter 5

The crowd at *Luna's* was steady throughout the day, which was typical on the weekends. Zoe, for the most part, stayed in the kitchen, trying to keep her distance from the customers, just to breathe and get past all the intensity of the morning. The talk with Bryan about Cynthia was bad enough, but then to walk into the restaurant and find Luke engaging with Emma - obviously upset - and then leaving with a tray of sandwiches was quite unexpected.

Zoe loved to disappear into the back of *Luna's* as she helped out with the food preparation, and also took part in some of the actual cooking quite regularly now. Surprisingly, she had mastered the menu and had greatly improved in her cooking skills, creating each dish with the helpful instruction and advice of her master chef, Dennis, who freely offered step-by-step guidance any time she requested it.

The double doors to the back of the kitchen flew open, as Emma sailed through, approaching the stainless steel countertop where Zoe was finishing up a container of tuna salad. *"Someone is asking for you,"* Emma tossed out, pausing to grab a bottle of water that she downed quickly.

Zoe looked up at her after snapping the plastic lid in place. *"I'm prepping in the kitchen, as you can plainly see. Did you tell whoever is asking for me that it isn't a convenient time?"* Zoe questioned, feeling half irritated with Emma, as she blew a wisp of hair from her face and placed the container in the refrigerator.

Emma began to laugh. *"Pardon me, Ms. Zoe Carter! I didn't know I was your personal secretary.* Why not be pleasant and just say a friendly hello? The guy out there seems harmless enough," Emma added nonchalantly, munching on a few cherry tomatoes from a bowl that was sitting close by.

"The guy out there?" Zoe repeated, somewhat perplexed, now feeling like her suddenly calm demeanor of spending time in her *"go-to"* place of solitude was disappearing once again.

"Yeah, there's a *"stud of a man"* out there asking for you... A good-looking guy with a southern drawl, and he has on a pair of interesting looking cowboy boots too," Emma mentioned, trying to pique her friend's curiosity. *"You don't see boots like that every day around here!"*

Zoe smoothed back her ponytail, looking herself over in the mirror that was conveniently hung in the kitchen for times such as this, just to make sure she was presentable to the public. She untied her apron, hanging it on a hook designated for *"her use only",* glancing then at her blue jeans, her Luna's logo shirt, and her somewhat dirty black sneakers from a few food splatters, realizing her face lacked in makeup that she had forgotten to apply earlier. *"Do I look okay?"* she asked of Emma, as Dennis turned to do a silent and unasked for *"once-over"* glance himself, before turning back to deal with some almost done, crispy pork chops that were frying in a cast iron skillet in front of him.

"Um... yeah... but why do you care?" she teased, hearing a few of the details about this guy already from Ava, and then keeping the comments to herself to avoid Zoe's reprimand for prying.

Zoe shook her head and smirked, realizing Emma was just trying to get to her, even if it was purely for her own entertainment. *"He's new in town, if you must know!"* she snapped out, as she departed from the kitchen.

"That's what I heard... " Emma whispered under her breath, grinning in the direction of Dennis who was also privy to all the sorted details.

Mason Jones was seated at the same table that was chosen for him several days prior, looking even more handsome than Zoe had remembered. He smiled with a *"larger than life"* smile as he watched her approach, suddenly stopping by the table with her arms crossed defensively, waiting on him to speak. *"Hello, Zoe! I was hoping you were working today,"* Mason casually commented, with his pleasant sounding Texas twang coming through each word, which was somehow turning her on, even if she didn't want to admit it.

Zoe looked around the room, realizing each table was now full, hoping she didn't know anyone present and the conversation wasn't being ease-dropped upon. *"Yes... I am working... in the back... helping out with the prepping and cooking,"* she explained.

"What do you recommend tonight?" Mason asked with a smile, doing his best to lighten the mood and make pleasant conversation, as he studied her. He was dressed in blue jeans and a well-fitting, V-neck black sweater that showed off a slight fringe of curly brown chest hair, causing Zoe's heart to race from the sheer sight of it all. As Emma had so appropriately described, the cowboy boots were in place, but this time in black reptile skin, from an unknown variety that she couldn't quite identify.

Zoe gulped, not desiring the job of being his waitress, but finding it hard not to be civil with someone who had only been cordial with her thus far. *"It depends on what you are hungry for,"* she answered simply - trying to maintain a level of professionalism. Mason sat back in his chair, with the menu resting on the table unopened, with a constant smile etched upon his handsome face, just like it had been the first time she met him. It unnerved Zoe somewhat, as she took note of his relaxed and unhurried attitude about things, being very different from her own, but in a good sort of way.

"I'm not picky. I can eat anything!" Mason tossed out, trying to go with the flow and let her do the choosing for him.

"If you actually take the time to open the menu, you will see that we offer lighter fare, a regular dinner menu, and several daily specials as well."

"You've covered that all very nicely," Mason replied, trying to soften her up. *"Just so you know...I did already take a glance at the menu while you were detained."*

Zoe reddened, assuming he hadn't studied the different offerings yet. "If you like pork chops, I would suggest them. The cheesy scalloped potatoes and succotash are the side dishes this evening... that come with it," she hurriedly added.

"Sign me up!" Mason grinned, handing Zoe the still closed menu that was sitting on the table. Sweet tea with lemon had already been placed in front of him, which answered her question that someone else had already started his order, but it was now obvious he wanted her to complete it.

She turned without a comment in return, walking to the front counter and imputing his order into the computer as quickly as she could. Emma was there too, now distracted and busily explaining to several bikers, who had just left the canal towpath, that there would be at least a thirty-minute wait for an available table, which did not set well with any of them, after explaining how *starving they were* from their long bike trek that they kept droning on about.

"Did you notice the sexy cowboy boots?" Emma whispered, with a rise to her one eyebrow as she waited on an answer from Zoe.

"Are you enjoying all this?" Zoe responded with a scowl on her face, not appreciating her friend's twisted sense of humor one bit at the moment.

"Zoe, lighten up! I'm just teasing you!"

"Yes, Emma, I know you are teasing me, but I'm not ready for all this."

"What is *all this?* That a cute guy from Texas has just moved into town with no connections to your past or to the people that have grown up here? You should be rejoicing in the fact that this is the case. *This guy actually has no knowledge of Noah Clark or anyone else from Williamsport, for that matter! Hallelujah... Praise the Lord... Time to have a celebration!"*

Zoe shook her head at Emma's dramatic presentation, but then paused to consider what she was saying. *"You got a point there,"* she agreed, feeling a sense of relief from the revelation. *"But it honestly goes beyond all that. It's about me... and how I am still feeling... I'm not sure if I'm ready for another relationship with any guy – no matter how perfect he seems."*

Emma reached out to pat the top of Zoe's hand. "You know the saying – *"the best way to get over someone old is with someone new"*. Maybe it's time to try again. There is no timetable here, but you may want to consider getting to know this Texan just a little bit better. Why don't you try to take things slowly and see what happens? You may be surprised to find out that it may be a good thing."

Zoe walked away, back through the double doors to the kitchen again, pondering what Emma had challenged her to think about. *"How is that order coming along, Dennis?"*

"What order are you referring to?" he replied, being especially busy and distracted with the other tasks at hand, flipping a half-pound burger over on the uncooked side, and then juggling several other entrees all at the same time that he was trying to prepare.

"The pork chop dinner special that I personally put in?"

Dennis smiled, realizing now that it was intended for Zoe's *"special guest"* who had asked for her. "It will be *"up"* in five minutes!"

Zoe carried the tray high up on her shoulder, still being a pro at doing so after working at The Desert Rose for several years. She placed it on the tray holder that was positioned close by the table, presenting Mason with the pork chops that were still sizzling on the plate with a towel underneath, so that she didn't burn herself. *"Be careful, they are very hot!"* she warned, as she wiped off a splatter of succotash juice that was dripping off the one side of the oversized dish.

"Will do, little lady," he answered, as she positioned a steak knife beside of the other silverware for his use. The pork chops were cut overly thick and one of the specialties of the house, requiring something beyond a regular table knife to cut through them, even though they were tender and juicy.

"Can I get you anything else?"

"Nothing at the moment beyond your beautiful smile... and maybe a little more sweet tea," he pleasantly requested, as he took a big bite of the cheesy scalloped potatoes.

Zoe was caught off-guard by his words that warmed her, finding everything about him intriguing. *"I'll be right back with your refill,"* she announced shyly with downcast eyes, realizing he was flirting with her whether she was ready for it or not. She returned with the pitcher, topping off his glass without a word spoken, ready to walk away again before the conversation started back up.

"My compliments to the chef. These pork chops are exceptionally delicious! I don't think I've ever had them this good... even in Texas!"

"Well I'm glad you like them, and I will let him know," Zoe answered, turning back with a start, still with the pitcher in hand.

"It wasn't you who made them?" Mason inquired, somewhat confused.

"No... not me... but my chef, Dennis, who does the majority of the cooking here at *Luna's*. I just help him out with the preparation end, for the most part," she explained, "and sometimes do some simple offerings when things get especially busy around here."

"Oh, I see... You obviously have a lot going on, running both ends of the shop like you do," Mason noted, as he cut into another slice of the pork chop.

"Yes, it's always a full and busy day once I arrive for work. Matter-of-fact, I better be checking on some things now or I'll be hearing about it from my business partner that I'm slacking on the job."

"The one who is watching your every move over there by the counter?" Mason good-naturedly jabbed out, knowing Emma had barely taken her eyes off of the two of them since Zoe had signed up to be his server.

"That would be the one!" Zoe laughed, suddenly feeling glad that Mason had showed up again after all. He definitely was lifting her spirits, much to her surprise.

"Come back and check on me in awhile. I think I'll be having some desert afterwards - since I always have a sweet tooth!" He confessed, winking at her as she turned to definitely leave this time. *"You do have some tasty homemade deserts around the place, I hope?"*

"Yes, we do..." she timidly replied with a smile, suddenly wishing she could offer herself to Mason as his sweet *"after dinner"* desert sampling.

Chapter 6

Zoe sat at her desk in the back office area of *Luna's* trying to close out the books from the day's business. It had been another profitable day, which she was always grateful for, knowing how much confidence her grandparents had placed in both she and Emma, always encouraging them that they could be successful and pull off such a huge undertaking.

The two dishwashers were finishing up the last of the pots and pans, and the servers had already departed. Luna lay asleep at her feet, curled up and not giving her much room to move. Emma entered the swinging doors, staring at her friend with her hands planted squarely on her hips. *"How many times are you going to stare at that computer screen? The ledger is always balanced, Zoe,"* she chided playfully, while pouring a glass of Chardonnay and then sitting in a seat close by her business partner.

"Yes, I know..." Zoe answered, knowing what Emma said to be true. She rose and stretched her arms high over her head, trying to clear the kinks from her sore neck and back as she grimaced slightly from the pain she was feeling. "But I always need to make sure it stays that way on a daily basis."

Emma laughed and shook her head, sipping deeply of a new sweet variety of chilled wine that had been recently added to the menu, that she was extremely enjoying and fond of. *"Why don't you drop Luna off at your house and then come over to my place afterwards? My mom is out of town with one of her newest online boyfriends, and my brother and sister are with my dad. I don't know about you, but the hot tub in my backyard is calling my name,"* she offered, standing up and placing her empty wine glass in the sink for someone else to wash, ready to call it a day.

Zoe glanced at Luna, trying to read her dog's mind, knowing she rarely did as Emma suggested and leave the dog behind. Luna typically went everywhere with Zoe, now that Noah was no longer around to hang out with, but sometimes it was definitely easier just to be alone. The Lab had become her constant companion and almost like an *"emotional support dog"* throughout the worst few weeks after the breakup. *"I guess so... My lower back could benefit from a soak in the hot tub, and Luna seems to be tired anyway."*

Emma laughed. "Luna comes as close to a human child as one can get. Such a spoiled baby girl, that you have there!"

"Yes, she is," Zoe admitted, smiling warmly, while wrapping her arms affectionately around her pet's neck, with a shake from the dog and a few circles then to follow, giving all the signals that she wanted to be leashed and was more than ready to depart the place. "I will drop off the bank deposit, and then meet up with you as soon as I take Luna to the house and change into my bathing suit. I shouldn't be any longer than thirty minutes since my dad won't be at the house trying to have a conversation with me. He and Kelly are out doing something special, which at the moment slips my mind, but I doubt he will be coming home tonight either."

"That seems to be the trend now with those two," Emma casually mentioned, as she armed the security system and then locked the front door.

"Yes, you are right. He definitely likes her."

"Are wedding bells in the picture?"

Zoe paused to consider her friend's question. "Who knows... maybe... or maybe not, and they will just be lovers and date forever... "

Emma laughed. "Well, that sounds better than what the two of us have currently going on - with the lack of either one of us having boyfriends."

They walked to their cars, unlocking their doors respectively, with the beeps of each sounding off in unison. *"I'm fine alone… "* Zoe resolved, doing her best to believe it, slipping into the driver's seat after Luna jumped into the passenger's side first.

Emma leaned on Zoe's car window to make her point clear. *"I'm not fine being alone, and it's no way for you to live your life either. We are young and maybe its time to put ourselves out there and start dating. We should consider going on one of those dating sites just like my mother is doing."*

"You do whatever you want, Em, but I *will not* subject myself to guys on those ridiculous dating sites!" Zoe said sternly while starting up her engine. "Now get in your car, silly girl. I don't want to pull away until I know you are safe and in your vehicle," she insisted, always feeling concerned about being alone as a female after dark.

"Always the *"worry wart"*, Emma yelled out, obliging Zoe's request, as the two pulled away from *Luna's,* ready for some therapeutic relaxation after a busy day of work.

Zoe slipped into her one-piece, black bathing suit that was now the swimsuit style and color of choice, over her brightly colored bikini that she used to wear. The modesty and color of it seemed to match her current mood, no longer desiring to be the temptress that she once was, always trying to keep Noah attracted and begging for more.

She parked her car in Emma's driveway and walked around to the backyard, already finding her in the hot tub, bubbling away with two poured glasses of Chardonnay sitting on one of the whirlpool's oversized ledges close by. Music was playing at a moderate volume from the surround sound speakers, with the hopes of keeping the neighbors at bay with an acceptable noise level. Zoe pulled her shift dress from over her head and then kicked off her flip-flops, walking up the steps and slipping over the edge, finding the familiar *"seat of choice"* that was calling out her name.

"Feels wonderful, right?" Emma asked softly, being lost in the moment, with her head resting on one of the built-in pillows.

"A... maz... ing," Zoe whispered back, lavishing in the warmth and the immediate feeling of relaxation of the massage that was pulsating off of her lower aching back. She grabbed the stem glass of wine intended for her, and sipped a few times from it before replacing it on the ledge. "Thank you, Em, for suggesting this," she expressed sweetly, knowing her friend was always looking out for her best interests.

"Hey, it was a tough day at work, and I thought we both needed and deserved this!" Emma replied, joining Zoe in downing half of the wine.

The two sat quietly for several minutes, just unwinding and relishing in the enjoyment of the *"oversized"* hot tub with all the *"bells and whistles"* included. It featured six over-sized seats that were typically never filled to capacity, and an ever-changing, multi-colored LED light show that was controlled by a waterproof remote, along with a built-in sound system that *"pimped out"* the whole entire package.

Emma's mother, Margie, had recently purchased and financed one of the largest outdoor hot tubs offered in the showroom of the pool and hot tub store in the area. It was a ten thousand dollar model that came complete with a set of over-sized steps and a deluxe cover that was guaranteed to last for five years - even with the harsh Maryland winters that would cover it over with snow. Margie had decided to finance the extravagance that she really didn't need, for an extended period of time at zero percent interest, on the advice of an overly pushy salesperson that had encouraged her to *"get in on the sale of the year that was like no other!"* She couldn't resist and say no, being pulled in with his expertise. He was a handsome, charismatic guy who was probably twenty years younger than she was, being *"turned-on"* by his over-zealous, flirtatious personality - just to close the deal - with no intentions on his end to take it any further once she signed on the doted line, and the product was delivered and set up in her backyard.

Margie enjoyed playing the game with someone so young and desirable, but also knew the reality of the situation, that it was just a brief *"tete-a-tete"* for the sheer purpose of lining his wallet to pay his monthly bills, from the large commission check of her sale. The bigger goal was to impress her current love interests, that she discovered on her numerous dating sites that she was currently enrolled with, hoping that one of them would finally be hopelessly enchanted with her, wanting to propose and then marry her in a timely fashion.

Emma reappeared with the chilled, half-emptied Chardonnay bottle in hand, after using the bathroom and grabbing it on the way back out the door. She refilled each glass and then climbed back into the hot tub, sliding into her seat once again. *"I wanted to speak with you about something,"* she mentioned casually, as she looked at her friend and sipped from her topped-off glass.

"Okay. What's up?"

"We got side-tracked today with Luke showing up, and then the restaurant was busy with non-stop customers, but now we are free to talk."

Zoe shook her head in agreement. "Sure, I realize that, so tell me what's on your mind."

"You came in today, being upset with your mother's reach out to your father in a letter. Remember?"

Zoe sighed deeply, reaching now for her own glass of wine, suddenly looking painfully distraught. *"Please... don't call her my mother,"* she replied, barely being heard over the noise of the hot tub motor. *"I only consider Nana Ruth to be the mother who raised me."*

"Yeah, I get that, but biologically speaking, no one can deny the reality of the situation," Emma stated matter-of-factly, while stepping over the line once again and hurting Zoe's feelings - which was unfortunately done quite often over the years. "I don't talk about Owen and Reagan all that often, since they are a lot younger than I am, but I adore my brother and sister, and life wouldn't be the same without them. You always thought you were an only child and now you know that isn't the case. *Why wouldn't you want to open the door and get to know your only sibling? He may be a great kid and you may come to enjoy his company if you were around him some, or even talked to him on the phone now and then."*

Zoe's eyes opened wide, shocked once again by her friend's boldness and lack of couth at times. *"Emma, seriously? How can you even begin to suggest such a crazy idea? He is only a fourteen. If I am around him, that means I also have to be around Cynthia. I will never get over what she did to me and my father when I was a kid!"*

"I knew this was going to piss you off, but once in awhile, Zoe, you gotta take a damn risk in life! You always want to stay in this little *"bubble of a world"* that keeps you safe and secure, but what is the enjoyment in all that? Maybe something bigger and better is out there waiting on you, if you just give it a chance!"

Zoe began to cry, looking down at the foaming hot water that was rippling all around her. "Why don't you consider what has happened to me from coming out of my so-called *"bubble"* four years ago, trying to be in a relationship with Noah? The pain of that mistake is *still* much too recent. *I can't be crushed like that again... ever!"*

The wine was talking and Emma was slightly intoxicated. *"Zoe, it's time to get over fucking loser Noah Clark! I hate the bastard more and more each day! I warned you early on he wasn't to be trusted, but you just kept on loving him no matter what!"*

Zoe returned her wine glass to the ledge, climbing over the edge of the hot tub in the process, not bothering to take the steps. "Emma, I know we are best friends and business partners, but how dare you speak to me in this manner! I will blame your poor behavior on the wine, but you do not have the right – both now and in the future - to insult me like this and say that I was obviously naïve when it came to Noah! I was in love with him and he claimed to be in love with me too. The mystery will always exist why he suddenly changed his mind, but I do believe in some sort of fashion he was in love me."

"Of course he loved you in his own way! I'm sorry!" Emma yelled out, suddenly regretting her poor choice of words and actions, as Zoe hurriedly replaced her shift dress and slid into her flip-flops, trying to walk away at a rather fast pace.

"You seriously should be!" Zoe gritted out with a pained and hurtful expression of disappointment etched across her face, as she slammed shut the side gate of the fence that surrounded Emma's backyard, pulling out of the driveway a little too quickly, not caring what the neighbors thought, just determined to get away.

Emma slid from the hot tub herself, gathering up her things, and then finding the hand-held remote that turned off the speaker system, lights and the motor, with one final click. *"Jesus, me and my damn big mouth... "* She muttered out in frustration, knowing she would need to do a lot of *"ass kissing"* to get back into Zoe's good graces - yet for another time.

Chapter 7

Zoe rolled and tossed throughout the night, causing Luna to finally give up and jump off the bed to the floor, just to get some rest. *"Sorry girl,"* she comforted, knowing she was frustrating her precious pet now also. She lay in bed, just staring at the ceiling, considering Emma's words about her mother and brother, not wanting to think that she might be right. At times it could be aggravating, but Zoe knew she could always get a straight answer out of her best friend, even if she didn't want to always hear or accept the truth.

It was six-thirty in the morning, and Zoe had planned to sleep for another hour, but gave up the quest and made her way out to the kitchen instead, ready to put the sleepless night behind her. She made some coffee, hoping it would do the trick and give her some much-needed energy for the day. Bryan hadn't made it home yet, and obviously was still with Kelly at her house or in a motel - wherever they had decided to stay for the night. Luna had been walked and fed, and now a fast breakfast would be consumed before getting ready for work. She opened a few drawers in the kitchen as she downed the last of her cereal, not finding what she was searching for, feeling the need to text her dad just to make things easier.

I'm looking for Cynthia's letter," Zoe confessed to Bryan. *After giving it some thought, I think I would like to read it after all.*

It's in my top dresser drawer on the left, under some socks. No one is forcing you to do this, Zoe.

I know... but I decided that I wanted to see what she had to say for myself.

I understand...

Thanks, dad.

I will be back home later tonight. I spent the night at Kelly's house - in case you were wondering.

I assumed that.

Okay, my dear. Have a good day. See you later.

Zoe preceded back the hallway to Bryan's bedroom, pulling open the left dresser drawer, as he had instructed. Lying under a layer of socks was the turned over letter from Cynthia, with Zoe's home address handwritten out in blue ink. She carefully extracted if from the drawer, straightening out the socks afterwards in the process. She ran her hand over the printing, somehow seeing her mother writing out each number and word of the address, as she sat on her father's bed taking it all in. She pulled the letter from the envelope, transfixed by what she was ready to read.

Dear Bryan,

I know this letter is long time overdue, but honestly it was quite a challenge finding your current address. I even attempted to reach out to your parents, but never heard back from them with an answer as to where you are currently living. The intention of this letter is to see how you and Zoe are doing, but also written with the hope that you can convince Zoe to speak with me some time in the near distant future.

On my end, I did want to catch up with you on a few things. After our divorce, I did go on to meet someone and remarry, and it wasn't my co-worker from the furniture store that I had left town with initially. My husband's name is Edward Davis. We have a child together, which would make Eddie Junior my son and Zoe's half brother. He is fourteen years old now and has begun to ask a lot of questions about my life prior to marrying his father. I am trying to give him the answers to what he seeks and deserves to know, but I have held off out of respect to you and Zoe.

So now I am asking, will you give me permission to tell Eddie about my life with you and Zoe in Fort Wayne? I would also like to speak with Zoe about all this and hopefully gain her approval to move forward, so that I can share with my son the details of my past.

I am sorry how things ended up with us, Bryan. I know I hurt a lot of people with my careless decision to leave, including our daughter and your family, but it also hurt my family members as well who were very disappointed in me for leaving you. I can only ask for your forgiveness and cooperation now to proceed forward and try to heal things between Zoe and myself. I know I am asking a lot, but life is short and I am not the same woman I was seventeen years ago when I foolishly took off and left our home.

I do hope you are doing well and I will anxiously wait to hear back from you. My return address and phone number are included on my letterhead at the top of this page, so please feel free to contact me either way. You can text me also to the number listed. Take care.

Sincerely,

Cynthia Davis

Zoe read each word, stopping to ponder the true intent of what was written. It did appear that Cynthia was being sincere, whether she wanted to accept that fact or not. She studied the return address on the letterhead, along with the phone number, realizing Cynthia was making it easy to reach out if she chose to do so. Zoe centered her cell phone camera over the contact information, snapping a quick picture before replacing the letter back into the envelope, and then returning it to where she found it, under the layer of socks in her father's dresser drawer.

She showered and dressed, trying to chase Cynthia's pleas from her mind. *Why does she deserve even one ounce of consideration from me after what she did to our family?* Zoe pondered in frustration, as she leashed up Luna, ready to go to the restaurant for another hectic day of work. The short drive to her destination crossed by the familiar sites that she passed every day. The local library, the Bryon Memorial Park, the Sheetz convenience store, The Desert Rose and an assorted array of other shops that were now open and already bustling with customers, who were coming and going along the busy city streets.

As Zoe parked a short distance away from *Luna's*, she idled and studied the photo of the contact information of Cynthia's that she had taken with her cell phone's camera, memorizing the number now. "What the hell, maybe Emma is right and I should reach out to her. *If I am not comfortable with the conversation, I will just hang up,"* Zoe reasoned, finally getting up her nerve and making the decision to do so.

"Hello?"

Zoe gulped, hearing a female voice from her past and feeling paralyzed to respond, as she breathed heavily against her cell phone, and her heart beat frantically out of control.

"Hello... Is someone there?" Cynthia questioned.

"It's me... Zoe. You wanted to talk, so I'm here to listen."

Margie Baker sat at the counter of her kitchen island, perched up high on a barstool with her laptop open and in front of her, looking intensely over any new love interests that had popped up since her last perusal. It was a daily chore, almost like a full-time job, keeping up with all her potential, romantic conquests that either reached out to her, or vice versa, on the many different dating sites she was a member of -

which probably amounted to thirty. Some were paid for and some were free, but in the end none of them had provided her with that *"special someone"* she was so desperately searching for.

Emma entered the room, yawning as she took in her mother and what she was doing once again. *"Will you ever settle on someone?"* she moaned out in frustration, shaking her head at the constant frolicsome activity of her mother that she was always focused in on and involved with.

"Emma, that's a little cruel and insensitive," she curtly reprimanded, as she finished up and sent a lengthy email to a *"so called"* lawyer that could be masquerading behind the title just to gain her attention and approval. It wouldn't be the first or the last of the *"fake profile people"* who wanted to convince her of something that was nothing more than a lie. The sad stories of being *"bamboozled and misled"* were told afterwards to Emma, once the truth finally came out. She was sick and tired of hearing about all of the *"crazies"* and what they had pulled on Margie, wishing that she too finally *"had enough"* and felt the same way! Emma didn't want to be her mother's therapist, but unfortunately it was forced upon her since they were roommates, whether she liked it or not.

"Sorry, mom, it's just so unending and unnerving - you know. What happened to Robert? I thought he was finally *"the one"?"*

Margie shook her head sadly, side-to-side, realizing it was her opportunity to vent once gain. "I thought so too, until his wife reached out to me a few days ago and informed me that they are married."

"How did she ever get your phone number?" Emma curiously asked, willing now to hear another sorted tale of *"The Life of Margie",* which was her own personal soap opera, as she poured herself a cup of coffee and joined her mother at the counter for a further explanation.

"Do you need ask? His cellphone of course," she explained sadly, looking somewhat defeated.

Emma reached out to pat the top of her mother's hand. "I would honestly take a break from all this and focus in on other things for a while. I don't have a boyfriend right now, and I could care less - one way or the other."

Margie began to laugh. "Yes, I know this, sweetie. I may be chasing a broken dream, but you are young and you should be making it a priority to try to find someone. *Don't you desire marriage and having children one day?"*

"Mom, for heaven's sakes, you act as if I'm in my thirties! I have plenty of time to pursue all that! For now, I'm content with my focus being on *Luna's* and making a decent living."

"If you say so…. " Margie answered, looking slightly skeptical, closing her laptop and then placing her empty coffee mug in the dishwasher. *"I noticed an empty wine bottle in the trash. Did you have company here last night?"*

"Yes, Zoe stopped by and we got in the hot tub after work. Sorry that I grabbed a bottle of your Chardonnay. I will replace it," Emma promised.

"That is not necessary, Emma. You are more than generous with providing our household with free food from the restaurant."

"Well thanks, Mom," Emma smiled, knowing her mother at least had a grateful side to her for the most part. Talking about Zoe, she is not happy with me right now. We got into a big fight last night."

"I'm sorry to hear that. Anything you want to share?" Margie asked, always ready to lend some advice, as she turned her undivided attention towards her eldest daughter.

Emma hesitated, not sure she wanted to tell her mother about the letter and Zoe's mother reaching out. "I appreciate you being willing to listen, but I think I got to sort this one out on my own."

"Understood," Margie smiled. "But just remember, Zoe is your best friend, and it pays to clear the air and keep things on good terms with her since you guys work together and see each other almost everyday."

"Yes, Mom, I am very aware of all this," Emma replied, as she stood up and gave Margie a heart-felt, warm hug. "I got to get ready for work. The C&O Canal tourists are probably already lined up at the door, ready to fill the place. Zoe is working the early shift, and if I don't get in there soon, that will be the next thing we will be arguing about!"

Cynthia Davis was a thin and attractive woman, with hair and eyes resembling Zoe's. She was caught off guard by the unexpected call that had just come through. There was no doubt that she had requested it, but realized the odds were against her for it to actually materialize, trying her best now to regain her composure and proceed forward with the *"hoped for"* conversation. Cynthia walked from her average-sized, two-story home, leaving Edward inside alone, who was preoccupied and focused in on his video game, that he played way to often for her liking. She proceeded down the street, taking to the sidewalk, passing by numerous well-manicured yards in her neighborhood, trying to gain some space away from the listening ears of her son - in case he decided to walk outside and find her. She cleared her throat, attempting to find her voice that didn't want to come out that easily, and then smiled pleasantly, with a false pretense, with no one there to witness her actions.

"Well, it certainly is nice to hear your voice," she began cheerfully, trying to lighten the mood with a pleasant lift to her tone, as she clutched the cellphone close to her ear with two hands.

Zoe shook her head, purely taken back by her strange opening line. *"I guess it is.... after seventeen years of not doing so,"* she sarcastically retorted back, not cutting Cynthia even the smallest of a break.

A neighbor was mowing his lawn, and paused to nod at Cynthia as she hurried on by, walking at a rather fast pace to avoid the sound of the lawn mower engine in the background of the phone conversation. Her heart raced from the response that Zoe had just given her, knowing she deserved it and had it coming. Cynthia stopped dead in her tracks, taking a few deep cleansing breaths for several moments, considering what would be the best thing to say that she could reply back with.

"You are absolutely right, Zoe. I am a foolish, horrible person for leaving you and your father, and not reaching out to you for the past seventeen years! I deserve anything you say or feel that is directed towards me."

Zoe was not prepared for Cynthia's humbling reply, catching her off-guard, being the one now stumbling for a voice. "I know why you are reaching out. My father gave me the heads-up about your son and how you want to share your past with him. I get it, but I don't get it. What he doesn't know won't hurt him. I'm not trying to be rude, but *I don't desire a relationship with either you or him, so what is the point of all this?"*

"The point is that I am not the same woman that I was when you were a little girl. If anything, I am a total different woman who looks at life so differently now. Please, Zoe, just consider meeting the both of us in person one day. I will even be willing to come to your town to make this happen - if you will just give us a chance!"

Chapter 8

Zoe got up from the sofa, with Luna jumping down and following her out to the kitchen, right by her side. *"Wouldn't it make more sense to talk on the phone for a few weeks, and then we can consider taking it to the next step and discuss meeting in person?"* she reasonably suggested, while pouring another cup of coffee. *"And for that matter isn't your son in school right now?"*

Cynthia had made an entire loop around the neighborhood, approaching her house now from the other side. "Yes, Eddie is in school, but we could come for a weekend visit. Of course we can take things slowly and talk on the phone, if that is your preference, but we have already missed out on so much time together…. I guess I'm just anxious to see you again. That's all…. "

Zoe rubbed her eyes, finding the whole conversation like *"nails on a blackboard"*. "Okay…. If that makes you happy we will meet, but I want to go over all this with my father first. *Are you cool with that?"*

"Sure, Zoe. I am *"cool"* with that," she repeated back, finding her lingo somewhat unexpected but endearing.

"Mom?" Eddie yelled out, slamming the front door of the house behind him. *"I've been looking for you cuz I'm starving! Can you make me a grilled cheese or something else?"*

"Sure, Eddie. I will be right in, and then I will make you whatever you would like," Cynthia answered, with her hand now covering over the receiver.

For the first time, Zoe heard the sound of her half-brother's voice, and for some strange reason it made her feel a sudden connection to him without even knowing why. *"You are obviously wanted inside,"* she commented dully, not wanting to give Cynthia a reason to think that she cared even in the slightest.

"That was Eddie and he is hungry and wants lunch."

"I gathered. I will speak with my dad, and then get back to you."

"I hope it won't be too long until we speak again?"

Zoe shook her head, feeling pressured and not liking it. *"Cynthia, please be patient with me about all this! Too much too soon! Have a good day and I'll call you back when I'm good and ready!"* Zoe declared bluntly, before hanging up without warning, not waiting to hear her estranged mother's response. She suddenly was feeling the resentment building up inside of herself once again, and the best way to deal with it was to simply to end the call. She thought about the whole conversation and how things ended with Eddie demanding that his mother make him something to eat. Zoe couldn't even remember a single memory of her mother doing the same for her. She had suppressed so much after she had left. It was the only way she could go forward and have a normal life, replacing her five short years of life spent with Cynthia, with seventeen more with her father and grandparents. And then there was Noah, who was *"cut from the same cloth"*... walking away and leaving her, just as her mother had done likewise during her youth.

Suddenly, tears were forming and streaming down Zoe's face as she collapsed on her bed, trying to push the sad memories away from her mind that tormented her thoughts, that not only included her mother now, but Noah as well. A full day of work was ahead, and this was no way to begin it with puffy, swollen, red eyes and a blotchy face to match.

"Don't you have to get to work? Bryan inquired, as he leaned around Zoe's doorframe, concerned she was going to be late.

"I didn't hear you come in," Zoe admitted awkwardly, propping herself up on both elbows, looking at her father.

"What's going on? Have you been crying?"

Zoe sat up, wiping the back of her hands over her eyes and then her snotty nose, trying to clear away the evidence. "Yeah... I have been... Just got off the phone with Cynthia."

Bryan approached, sitting on the bed beside of his daughter, immediately feeling a sense of concern for her well-being. *"Did she upset you, Zoe?"* he asked with alarm now crossing his eyes, immediately needing the answer.

"No, not really. I just have so much on my mind right now, and she wants to see me soon. I'm not sure if I'm ready for that just yet."

Bryan empathized, reaching out to hug his girl protectively. "You are in total control of all this. Only you will know when the time is right, and when you are ready to take things to the next level with your mother."

"Dad, please don't call Cynthia *"my mother"*. I will never see her as such. You know that I only consider Nana Ruth to be *"like a mother"* to me!" she responded with the tears still clinging to her long eyelashes.

"I am sorry, Zoe. I get it, but the fact remains that she is your mother. Without her, you wouldn't be alive today. She left you many years ago, but always remember that she left me too. I haven't talked about it, to spare your feelings, but it crushed my heart also. I did love her... you know," Bryan added, with a far-off distant look.

Zoe studied her father, never hearing him confess his feelings about Cynthia so openly. "I guess it's me now that owes you an apology. I'm sorry, dad. I never really thought about things from your perspective. You just always seemed to take it all in stride."

"I had to put up a good show for your sake. But at night, I did my own share of crying into my pillow, wishing she were still around and back home with us. I kept playing the same tape over an over again in my mind, trying to figure out what I did wrong in the marriage that would make her abruptly up and leave like she did."

"Did you do something wrong in the marriage?" Zoe asked for the first time with uneasiness, never considering that to be even a remote possibility.

Bryan sighed and shook his head, feeling somewhat at a loss for words. He locked eyes with his daughter's beautiful light green ones, not sure how to properly answer her. "I worked a lot of hours back then, and was trying to establish my career. Maybe there were times I wasn't very romantic and the intimacy was lacking. I guess someone else that she worked with, gave her more time and attention, and she liked what he had to offer."

Zoe was somewhat shocked, not wanting to hear the details of her parents' sex life or the lack thereof. *"That is no damn excuse! She should have told you how she was feeling, and then you two could have gotten some marriage counseling and fixed things!"*

Bryan face froze, considering again the right way to respond, hating to admit his faults that he had kept well hidden from Zoe over the years. "She wanted to go to counseling and I told her we were fine. I didn't think it was necessary to pay someone to hear all of our problems. *I guess I was wrong to have said that to her,*" he confessed rather quietly, as he bent his head, recalling the regrettable memories now.

Zoe shook her head in disbelief and began to cry again. *"Maybe you were both wrong. Who knows! But all I know is that I was only a five-year-old little girl who lost her mommy, and I was never the same after that! Do you understand that?"*

"Yes, I do understand that.... all too well... and I'm sorry," Bryan whispered as he stood back up, looking down at his daughter's face that was filled with despair. *"I never meant to cause you or anyone else in this family any intentional sadness. I love you, Zoe,"* he concluded softly, leaving her alone with only Luna there to comfort her, after shutting the bedroom door behind him as he left the room.

Zoe showered and dressed in blue jeans and her *Luna's logo* t-shirt, pulling her hair straight back into a tight ponytail, and then applying a dab of makeup without overdoing it. Her sneakers had been left in the kitchen, where she had kicked them off while speaking to her mother, as she retrieved and laced them back up, while sitting at the table beside of Bryan. He was focused in on a football game that he was intensely watching, as he ate a ham sandwich and drank a beer, relieved that Zoe suddenly looked refreshed, and a better version of what he had witnessed earlier, no longer lost in self-pity.

"You off to the restaurant?"

"Yes, for the rest of the day. *Is Kelly stopping by?"*

"I won't be seeing her until tomorrow evening. She has some things she wants to get done around her house, since we have been together a lot lately," Bryan explained, matter-of-factly.

"Well, if you get bored, you can always stop by and grab dinner later at the restaurant," Zoe stated warmly, trying to clear the air and get back on track with her father, as she and Luna were ready to go out the door.

Bryan stood and followed the pair outside. "I think I will just lay low the rest of the day and probably even get to bed early tonight. I have a big meeting in the morning with corporate that I need to prepare for."

"I understand," Zoe replied, leaning in to give her father a tender kiss on the cheek. "I just thought I would make the suggestion, in case you started feeling lonely."

"Thanks, sweetie. And again, I'm sorry for upsetting you earlier. I hope you won't hold it against me now that you know your dad has a few kinks in his armor," he confessed somewhat regrettably.

"I'm fine, and to be honest, I'm glad we got it all out in the open. I guess I had to grow up and be an adult to comprehend what was going on to some level. You couldn't have told me those sorted details back then, but it all makes sense now."

"I am always here for you, Zoe."

"I know, Dad. You are the best!" she praised, as she got in her car and drove away, extending her father a pass – whether he deserved it or not.

Zoe considered the concept, realizing now that her father wasn't perfect in the marriage either. It had never occurred to her that maybe her mother had a reason for feeling conflicted and doing what she did, even if she could never see herself forgiving Cynthia for doing so. Zoe recalled that Bryan and her grandparents had come up with some worthless excuses that had never made sense, attempting to explain why Cynthia had left. She could still remember crying herself to sleep every night, feeling heartbroken and tossed aside, feeling like her mother no longer wanted her anymore.

Cynthia had married Bryan in her early twenties and had become pregnant with Zoe within that same year, going back to work full time in only six weeks after she was born - whether she was ready to do so or not. Nana Ruth had volunteered to be her granddaughter's childcare provider, allowing Cynthia to continue working at the furniture store, sometimes late into the evening, just to bring in some necessary money for the household. Bryan was putting in a lot of overtime, trying to make a mark with his boss and build his budding career, with the hope that Cynthia could finally quit her job and stay at home with Zoe again one day. Both were tired and exhausted when they finally got home at night, with a small child to take care of besides, ignoring their relationship that was now *"starving and dying on the vine"*. Cynthia desired counseling, but the idea was carelessly discarded by Bryan, turning now to another man instead, that she worked with for affection and understanding. *Would I have done the same?* Zoe pondered naively, after putting two and two together and finally figuring things out - as she pulled into a parking space close by *Luna's,* hearing a few more additional details for the first time that day from her father, which had never been shared before.

She entered the restaurant without answering her own challenging question, seeing a familiar handsome face beaming and smiling broadly at her from a table close by, obviously happy to see that she had finally arrived. He waved, motioning for her to come over in his direction, catching Zoe off-guard once again by his boldness that was so much a part of his personality.

"I've been here for thirty minutes, killing time, hoping that you would show up sooner or later, Missy," Mason Jones confessed with his captivating southern drawl, that left Zoe Carter weak in the knees - with his alluring, not holding anything back, to the point, statements.

Chapter 9

Zoe was at a loss for words, realizing this alluring southerner wasn't giving up that easily where she was concerned. She cleared her throat and shifted her feet, crossing one leg over the over in a defensive posture. "I came in when I was supposed to be here... right on time," she explained curtly, as he took her in from top to bottom.

Mason patted the table, making the silverware rattle. *"Can you join me for a spell and just con... verse?"*

Zoe began to act agitated, suddenly feeling flustered. *"No, I can't sit and con.... verse,"* she said with a slight shake of her head and lift to her voice, finding his lingo and the way he enunciated words so different from the locals. "We have a busy dinner crowd who will be showing up soon, and my full attention is needed in the kitchen as well as out here running things on the floor, as I have clearly mentioned to you before."

Mason began to laugh a little too loudly, finding her explanation comical, but understandable all the same. "Well you can't blame a guy for trying, Miss Zoe. I realize you are in high demand around the place. That has become quite apparent to me since I have started to dine here," he answered with a strong southern accent that caused her to silently stand by with a catch in her throat, for the second time.

Luna made her way over to Mason, sniffing him thoroughly in the process, as Zoe took it all in, surprised by her dog's actions that she rarely saw. Typically, she stayed glued to Zoe's side, never venturing away in the direction of a customer. *"Luna, come here now!"* She demanded sharply, trying to pull on the leash and retrieve her pet back by her side.

"It's quite okay," Mason grinned, reaching down to pet and then scratch Luna on top of the head and behind her ears. "At least I'm having a mesmerizing affect on one other beautiful female in the place," he winked playfully, before releasing Luna back to her owner.

Zoe's eyes widened with what he was inferring. She smiled, having a hard time resisting his charm. *"Can I get you anything before we depart to the back?"* she asked, on a mission to change the subject.

"Maybe another beer and your time and attention when you aren't so busy?"

"I will let your server know about that request for a beer," Zoe answered smartly and to the point, as she turned on her heels and walked away with a swing of her hips, that left Mason feeling aroused by the action.

"Hey, Zoe!" Emma yelled out over the loud booming of music being played in the kitchen, while the preparation of some key dishes was progressing.

"Hey, to you too," Zoe greeted back, unleashing Luna and placing her belongings on the desk near by. "Not sure who the server is for Mason Jones, but he needs another beer," she explained straightforwardly, as she tied her apron behind her back.

"That would be me," Ava jumped in with a hand raised, already on her way back out to provide the necessary alcoholic beverage.

"Do me a favor, Ava?"

"Yes?"

"Try to give Mr. Jones ample coverage. He seems to want to turn to me way too often when he is here dining, versus turning to his server for assistance. As you all know, I am way too busy to cater to one individual person when the place is busy," Zoe offered in way of a poor excuse, as the others in the room took a moment to glance at her and then at each other, after hearing her questionable explanation. As they returned to their given tasks – there was no doubt in anyone's mind that this *"hunk of a guy"* was simply getting to her whether she wanted to admit it or not.

"Sure thing, Zoe. Wouldn't want your very busy time and attention to be distracted by this guy in any way," Ava added while rolling her eyes, departing for another time to the *"difficult Texan"*.

"What was all that supposed to mean?" Zoe asked of Emma in a puzzled sort of way, considering that Ava's words held a dual meaning, as Dennis the chef was chuckling near by with his back turned, flipping a steak in the process.

"Umm... Could it be that he is a nice guy that you should take more time to talk with when he stops in here to eat - which by the way - is almost every day now? Or maybe, just maybe, he likes you - so that is why he is now a new regular."

"Oh, Em, that is ridiculous and just pure silliness!" Zoe countered, while looking over at her friend after repositioning her ponytail. "He is new in town and doesn't have any friends outside of his workplace. He is just probably bored, and not knowing about any other places to dine besides here."

Emma began snickering from Zoe's naïve assumptions that seemed to be a constant with her. *"Seriously? You can't possibly be thinking that is the case.* If he was transferred here from Texas with a government job, I'm sure he is smart enough to figure out where to eat and hang out, outside of *Luna's*!" Emma loaded up a tray of steaming hot entrees, ready to make an exit out to a group of tourists who had been waiting a little too long for their food. Once again the double doors opened and shut, leaving her alone to contemplate the matter.

Zoe made her way over to Dennis, watching him expertly plate up the medium rare steak with a side of scalloped potatoes and a generous helping of green beans that had slivered almonds sprinkled over the top as an attractive garnish. *"What do you think about all this talk?"* Zoe quizzed, knowing her cook wasn't totally out of the loop and unaware of things.

He began to shake his head and grin, pouring a spoonful of his *"secret recipe"* steak sauce over the center of the sizzling, hot beef. "If you are referring to the Austin guy out there, I would say he has pretty good taste."

Zoe was taken back, feeling flattered but somewhat embarrassed. *"Well, thank you, Dennis. That is very kind of you to say so… "* She acknowledged with a slight smile, being taken back by his unexpected compliment.

"Oh, my dear, I wasn't speaking about you, although you are something to be desired. What I meant was the steak," he said while pointing towards the beef, "that is what I was making reference to. *He obviously has good taste since he ordered the steak!"*

Zoe's face reddened, totally taken back by her blunder and assumption. Her hand went to her mouth, being silenced now by two men – one out front and one in the kitchen. Dennis picked up the plate with a towel in hand, being very warm to the touch, shoving it in Zoe's direction. *"Don't wait on Ava. Go serve the steak yourself! Mr. Austin is waiting!"*

Mason Jones appeared content, patiently waiting on his dinner, already downing half of his second beer, before Zoe showed up with the single plate in hand. "Here is your steak," Zoe offered as she lowered the plate in front of Mason, wiping the side of the plate clean with the towel. *"Be careful, it's hot!"* she cautioned, as she stepped slightly away, waiting on his response after taking a few bites.

Mason appeared pleased, warming Zoe's insides almost to the level of the heat of the meat. *"Looks delightful,"* he grinned, his eyes now slightly bloodshot, probably from the beer he was drinking. He cut a big bite, chewing it almost in a seductive sort of way that was difficult not to watch. *"Taste delightful too... "* He added, winking at her during the process.

"Good to hear. Enjoy your dinner," Zoe responded curtly, turning to leave rather quickly.

"Zoe?" Mason replied.

"Yes?" She answered, turning back around towards him, with the soiled dishtowel still in hand.

"One date... That's all I ask."

Zoe stood in place, staring silently at him, studying the yearning in his eyes. She shook her head side-to-side in exasperation, being annoyed and feeling like her emotions were being overworked and tested for another time, remembering a similar situation that occurred years earlier when someone else by the name of Noah Clark broke her reserves down and she accepted a date that she probably should have said no to. *"Okay... one date, and one day only,"* she resigned, feeling like her will power had weakened and she wasn't sure if she wanted it to.

Mason began to smile with his whole face lighting up in noticeable victory. *"That is all I had hoped for, sweetheart,"* he answered with his strong East Texas twang coming through even more so, with a throaty rasp that was intensified by the alcohol he was indulging in. Zoe gave him a look of disbelief over his *"puffed-up ego"* that was being put out there on display for her and everyone else in the restaurant to see, even more so than usual. *"When are we going to have this date?"* he called out loudly as she walked towards the back of the house, sashaying away in her tight jeans that left him *"semi-hard"* just by watching her.

Zoe turned and paused with one hand already on the kitchen door. "Finish you steak and then we will talk about it," she answered simply before disappearing, away from anymore of his comments and the stares and glares of the other patrons present, which were taking in the *"side show"*. She proceeded to the refrigerator, pulling out a bottle of chilled Chardonnay that she rarely indulged in while working, pouring herself a wine glass full, not stopping until it was nearly at the top, downing a third of it in one swallow.

"Is everything okay?" Emma asked, somewhat concerned, knowing this was out of character for her friend, as she stood and waited patiently on a few more orders that Dennis was finishing up.

Two more swallows and Zoe responded, suddenly feeling the desired, relaxed affect - that took off the edge. *"Mason just asked me out on a date..."*

"No way!" Emma laughed out in disbelief. *"Did you say yes? I hope you said yes!"* She pressed on, not waiting for her response.

"Yes, Em, I agreed to go out on one date with him. *Happy now?"* she gritted out, acting out the part that she was irritated, knowing honestly that Emma only had the best of intentions where she was concerned.

"Happy for you? I am over the moon happy! When is the big date?"

"Slow down, Emma! I'm not sure how *"big"* of a date it will end up being. We haven't even set a time yet."

"Well, when will you do so?"

"How about giving the man a chance to finish his dinner first?" Zoe giggled. I promised him I would be back afterwards to discuss things and make plans." Zoe refilled her wine glass with Emma pouring one for herself also, considering it to be somewhat of a celebration, whether Zoe could see that clearly yet or not.

"I will have to come over and help you get ready for your date, just like I used to do when we were in college. I can do your hair and makeup and help you pick out an outfit, if you would like."

Zoe rolled her eyes. "We aren't that age anymore. I think I can handle things on my own, quite nicely, thank you."

"Yes you can, but I enjoy being there and pampering you, my friend."

"I know… " Zoe replied with a caring smile, reaching over to give Emma a warm hug. "Maybe we can make that happen after I see what Mason has in mind. I will let you know. Okay Em?"

"Sure," Emma grinned, happy that Zoe was turning over a new leaf and suddenly taking a positive first step in a new direction.

Zoe walked from the kitchen, returning to Mason's table. "I'm back," she grinned, taking a seat beside of Mason, making him sit up and take notice of her unexpected move.

"I can see that…" he answered, studying her face intently that seemed a lot more relaxed, not realizing the amount of wine she had just consumed. *"So when can we meet up? And please tell me soon."*

"You know the restaurant keeps me very busy and a lot of the time I get out of here very late, and then there is my dog and also my dad to think about…"

Mason looked puzzled, trying to read her mind. *"And your point?"*

Zoe lowered her head for a moment, trying to gather her wits before stating her point clearly. *"Mason, I'm not very dateable. My life stays fairly busy and yet I try my best to keep it simple. I am not sure how dating will fit into all of this for me."*

He reached out to touch the top of her hand lightly, looking deeply into her light green eyes that touched him to the depths of his soul. *"What happened to only one date?"* he teased, not releasing his grasp.

"I was only saying..."

"I know what you are saying. You are worrying needlessly over things that shouldn't even be thought about for the moment. Let's just relax and have that *"one date"* and see how it goes. If we like that date then maybe we will go for a second, and if that goes well, maybe a third. By then, these insignificant details will feel like small hurdles that we can work through, if we are happy with each other. *Does any of that make sense?"*

Zoe looked somewhat concerned as she locked eyes with Mason, not pulling away from his hand that rested comfortably on top of her own. *"I guess it makes sense,"* she reluctantly conceded.

"So how about tomorrow evening? Will that work for you?"

One more eye locking moment with Mason was to be had before she answered, hoping and praying that things didn't turn out the same way as they did with Noah, giving her heart again to another man who she thought she could trust. "Yes, I can make that work. I'm here early tomorrow, so I will be available in the evening by 7 p.m.

"Then let's make it 7 p.m.! I can pick you up at your house if you would like?"

"Not necessary," Zoe replied firmly, rising from the table and releasing her hand at the same time. "Meet me here at *Luna's* and I will be ready."

"Dress casual!" Mason instructed loudly as Zoe walked away, making a few that were seated close by take notice to the spectacle they were creating.

"Sure! I can definitely do that!" Zoe yelled back, disappearing once again behind the swinging kitchen doors, hoping for just a few moments of silence.

Chapter 10

Zoe plunged her head beneath the bubbled-filled tub of hot water, trying to rinse the shampoo from her long locks. A few good swishes and she reappeared to the surface, and then stood and squeezed out as much water from her hair as she could. She stepped from the bath, wrapping herself in a big fluffy terry-cloth towel, placing a second one around her head in a turban-style manner. The room smelled of eucalyptus and cedar, from the pleasant smelling candle that Lillian had given her last year as a Christmas present, and the soft pleasant sounds of music could be heard coming from her laptop, positioned on top of the dresser in her bedroom, playing a variety of top 40 hits. Luna was napping on her bed, almost sensing that her mistress had other plans for the evening that did not involve hanging out with her, which was the usual routine most of the time now, when she wasn't working.

Zoe sat on the bed, rousing Luna from her sleep, addressing her almost as if she were a human. *"Do you think this is a bad idea?"* She quizzed, hoping for the miracle of a verbal response. Luna sighed heavily and then yawned, not seeming to care in the least about such nonsensical things. Zoe laughed and scratched her furbaby's head, being amused by her pet. *"Not sure how to interpret that, but I'll take it as maybe good, but maybe also bad? Your split on your decision?"* Luna licked Zoe's hand, making her giggle and rebound back off the bed.

She opened her closet doors, studying the contents therein. *"He said to dress casual..."* she mumbled, withdrawing some blue jeans and a long sleeve, black spandex shirt with the tops of her shoulders cut out, pulling both from the hangers. Her cellphone began to ring as she turned to answer it, losing her towel that dropped to the floor in the process, standing cold and nude - with only her phone now in hand.

"Hello?"

"How's it going?"

"Everything is going just fine."

"What did you choose to wear?" Emma asked.

Zoe began to laugh, looking down at her unclothed body, realizing that the lack of Emma being there was probably driving her nuts. *"You seriously can't stand it that you aren't here helping me. Isn't that true?"*

"Well, I am here. Look out your window. I'm parked in the driveway."

Zoe peaked from behind her blind, seeing the familiar car of her friend idling in the driveway. *"Who's covering at the restaurant?"* Zoe asked, somewhat with uneasiness, knowing it was Emma's shift to work.

"Ava and the others said they could handle it for a while. Don't worry, I will return later once you are looking fabulous."

Zoe retrieved the towel that was lying on the floor, repositioning and securing it underneath her arms. She walked to the living room, opening the door and beckoning Emma in from her automobile. "Well let's make the most of the time you have, since you obviously feel this is more important than seeing things are running smoothly at *Luna's*."

Emma retrieved two bags from the back seat of her car that were filled to the top with all the necessary tools, potions and lotions for making *"one beautiful"* for a special *"first date",* dragging them in and ready to take charge.

Zoe snickered and shook her head, honestly happy that Emma was going to all the effort – just like she used to when they were younger - even if she didn't want to confess that she felt that way. They walked together back to Zoe's bedroom, with Luna following close behind. Emma laid the bags on the bed, with Luna jumping up and nosily surveying the contents.

"*Do you approve?*" Emma giggled, as the dog's nose went halfway inside of each bag and sniffed, checking out what the mysterious contents was all about. Luna reappeared, sneezing several times in the process.

"Well, obviously something doesn't agree with her," Emma observed, making Zoe laugh.

"*Who wouldn't sneeze with the makeup, hairspray, perfume and every other thing imaginable you brought in here to attempt to beautify me?*"

"It isn't all that bad," Emma said with a shake of her head, plopping down on the bed in the process. "*So what did you decide to wear?*"

Zoe went over to her desk chair, holding up the blue jeans in one hand and the black top in the other. "*What do you think?*" she inquired.

"Hmmm…. Okay… I guess it's all right. You may have chosen different pants though - for a first date."

"Mason made a point of telling me to dress casual. Jeans are casual," Zoe justified, trying her best to stand up for herself.

"Well that makes sense," Emma conceded, taking one of the bags now in hand. Grab your clothes and get dressed, and then I will put on your makeup and help you with your hair."

"*Yes, Mom,*" Zoe teased, getting up with her clothes and disappearing into the bathroom. Several minutes later she reappeared, sitting obediently at the desk chair where Emma was patiently waiting. This was the location that she always chose to apply the makeup and then blow dry out her hair, with the question always being whether to straight iron or curl it afterwards.

Within forty minutes, Zoe looked like a different person - much prettier and sexier than before. A look she hadn't seen in several months, never desiring or caring to do so, since being single again.

"There is my beautiful friend," Emma gushed, grabbing Zoe by the shoulders at arm's length and admiring what she had created. Her hair had been flat ironed straight, with the makeup expertly applied, and her outfit hugged each one of her curves perfectly.

Zoe's eyes began to mist up, feeling somewhat bluesy and nostalgic. "This shouldn't be happening again so soon with someone new. It wasn't supposed to be this way, you know."

"Stop it!" Emma reprimanded softly, with heart-felt concern. "The past can't be changed. What's done is done! You deserve a future with someone else. I'm sure Noah isn't sitting around in England and not dating anyone. We both know how he is. It's impossible for him to be alone for very long - without a woman or sex."

Zoe bent her head, feeling the sting of her caustic words, realizing Emma was being somewhat insensitive but truthful all the same. It was an irritating trait in her that came out from time to time, which wasn't widely accepted by many. *"Emma, I don't need to hear this! Whatever Noah is doing in London is no longer any of my concern or business. He honestly can fuck whomever he likes."*

"Exactly! And the same back to ya!"

Zoe shook her head, knowing she wasn't that carefree in relationships or the bedroom. Her heart and soul wouldn't allow it. She stood up, trying to change the current mood and steer the subject matter away from Noah. "It's getting late. I only have twenty minutes to get to *Luna's* where Mason will be meeting up with me."

Emma's face brightened. *"So I get to see him too? This will be interesting seeing you two together, sitting at a table at Luna's, just hanging out."*

"We aren't having our date at *Luna's*, silly. We are just meeting there and then going somewhere else."

"So where is he taking you then?" Emma pressed, feeling the urge to pry a little while longer, as she placed the last of her *"girly"* items back into the two bags, ready to depart from the house with Zoe walking out also.

"To be honest, I'm not sure. He just said to dress casual and that was it. I guess I will find out soon enough."

"If he gets weird on you, call me."

"Oh Em, you are too much at times!" Zoe laughed, hugging her friend warmly. "I wouldn't have accepted a date with him if I thought he was capable of violence or was some sort of creep."

"Just know I always have your back, girl."

"I know you do, just like I have yours," Zoe reassured, as she slipped into her car. "I will see you in a few minutes, and please remember to behave yourself when you get back to the restaurant and Mason shows up. We don't want to scare him off already."

"I'll try my best," Emma replied with a playful grin, pulling out of the driveway with Zoe following right behind her. A note was left for Bryan on the kitchen table that was short and sweet, not giving out too many details. *Dad, I'm out for the evening on a date. If you could look after Luna until I return home later, that would be great! Zoe.* There was doubt in her mind that her father would be pleased that she was finally taking a chance and going out on a date, even if she wasn't totally convinced herself.

Zoe pulled into a parking space that wasn't directly in front of *Luna's*, always saving those few prime spaces for the customers instead. Emma had already arrived, driving at a much faster pace, and was parked and back inside, much to Zoe's surprise. She glanced around, not sure if Mason would be waiting on the outside of the building on her or not. *No sign of him...* she breathed, feeling her insecurities beginning to surface, considering for a moment that maybe he wasn't being sincere, and never really intended to show up after all. *"It was nothing more than just silly banter while he was drinking and flirting..."* Zoe glanced at her cellphone realizing that she still had five minutes to spare, knowing that it did not qualify for a *"no-show"* on a date yet. Her hand went to the door handle of the restaurant, turning it slowly as she took a few deep breaths first. *"If he's not inside, it's probably for the best,"* she resigned, almost hoping that it was true.

As Zoe opened the door and stepped inside, her vision went immediately to a tall handsome *"hunk of a man"* standing directly in front of her, conversing and being jovial with Emma. He too was dressed in blue jeans, but his black shirt that he also chose, clung to his muscular chest as if it were designed especially for him. His hair and neatly trimmed beard were meticulously groomed, and the black cowboy boots that he wore complimented the look perfectly. Zoe's breath caught as she took him in, almost too anxious now to even be around him. He smiled and excused himself, walking away from Emma, only having his eyes now fixated on Zoe.

"You look amazing!" he whispered into her hair, as he reached out to give her a light kiss on the cheek – much to her surprise as well as Emma's.

"Well, thank you," Zoe answered, slightly taken back, as her nosy co-workers stood a distance away and watched from afar, including Dennis who had slipped out from the kitchen, just to see what all the commotion was about.

"Are you ready to go?" Mason asked pleasantly.

She glanced in the direction of her employees, witnessing their approving smiles, silently encouraging her *to enjoy herself for the evening.* "I am ready, if you are."

"Most definitely," Mason replied with an alluring grin, reaching out to grab her hand and hold it possessively by his side. "By the way, I feel honored that you are going out with me tonight," he expressed sincerely, as he opened the front door of the restaurant for her, trying to act like a gentleman.

Zoe looked up at the attractive face of the man who was taking her to an unknown destination, wanting to believe him and his compliments more than anything else in the world for the moment. No matter how things turned out by the end of the evening, for now she would enjoy the special attention and the way he was making her feel special and appreciated.

"Well, thank you, Mason," Zoe offered with a demure flutter of her eyelashes, which looked especially nice from the mascara that Emma had applied. It felt somewhat awkward and strange to be going out on a date with someone new, but at the same time wonderful, as he escorted her out of the building and led her down the street - ready for the adventure of their first date together.

Chapter 11

Mason continued holding on to Zoe's hand as they walked down the sidewalk a distance, finally stopping in front of a silver-colored Land Rover with Texas plates. He opened the passenger side door, offering to help her up from the slight rise in height of the vehicle. *"Are you o...kay, getting in there?"* he inquired, as she attempted to climb into her seat.

"Yes," she smiled. "I guess I hadn't considered what you would be driving," she commented casually, making him laugh as he started up the engine.

"Not to your liking?"

"No, it honestly fits you," Zoe reasoned, finally allowing herself to relax around Mason.

"How so?" He inquired curiously, pulling away from the parking space, ready to head out of town.

"I don't know... the cowboy... with his Land Rover."

Mason took her in, thinking about her broad sweeping generalization. *"Is that some sort of stereotype that I'm not aware of?"*

"Come on, Mason, you must realize that no one talks or acts like you – around Williamsport."

"Maybe..." he playfully winked, not wanting to give her the satisfaction of understanding what she was referring to. *"Are you hungry?"*

"A little... *Where you are taking me, by the way?"*

Mason smiled. "I've been asking around, trying to get the *"lay of the land",* so to speak. I was told Frederick, Maryland has some good restaurants, so I thought I would take you to a different locale outside of where we are living. Hopefully, we will discover a new place that ends up being a first for the both of us. *Are you up for that?"*

"Of course! That's sounds like a wonderful idea! I'm always up for the challenge of finding a new place to eat in the area," Zoe beamed, touched by Mason's thoughtfulness to do some inquiring, hoping to surprise her.

The drive took them from 81 South to 70 East, with the Market Street exit being taken, leading to the downtown area of Frederick, Maryland. The streets were lined with brownstone, three-story historic houses, retail shops, antique markets and restaurants that were all kept immaculately pristine in appearance.

"Frederick is definitely a lot bigger than *Will...iams...port!"*

"Yes, *you* could say that," Zoe giggled, hearing Mason's strong East Texas accent over-enunciating the name of her canal town.

Mason glanced at Zoe, realizing she was having a *"hay-day"* with his accent again. "You know *sweet... heart*, your accent sounds very strange to me also. Not *"Western Maryland"* sounding, but somewhat different from what I have heard from the other locals in the town. I just can't quite put my finger on it."

"Oh really?" Zoe replied with her one eye arched high, enjoying the light-hearted exchange that was becoming more of a regular occurrence between them now. "Maybe that's because I grew up in the Midwest, so of course I won't be sounding like people from the Williamsport area," she giggled, as he continued to drive.

"That makes sense," Mason winked, trying to focus in on the task at hand. "It looks like we are passing a lot of good choices, so we need to make a decision where you would like to eat, once I circle back around the block for a second time."

"I honestly don't care what we choose. What are you hungry for?"

"Wanna know what I really have a hankering for?" Mason grinned, with his full set of perfect white teeth being on display.

"Of course I do," Zoe replied, finding this new *"mystery man"* very alluring and intriguing, giving him her undivided attention.

"Where I come from we eat a lot of *"Tex-Mex"*. I haven't had any decent Mexican food, to speak of, since I moved here. I don't know about you, but I could really go for some of that and down a pitcher of Margaritas right about now also."

Zoe started to search on her phone, pulling up *"Mexican restaurants in down town Frederick, Maryland"*, seeing if there was anything *"new"* that she hadn't tried out yet in the area. She had been to the majority of the *"better-known"* establishments with Noah, during the years of dating him, so being open-minded now about the choice – with the intention of not offending Mason – was the only thing on her mind.

"*La Paz* has been in Frederick for a very long time. Not new to me, but will definitely suffice for what you are requesting. They also make killer Margaritas!"

"You don't mind going to a place you have already been at in the past?"

"I would have never suggested it, if it weren't one of my favorites, with its outdoor seating and great menu selections," she answered sweetly, wanting to take the pressure off of Mason. She directed him back around the restaurant loop, showing him where the best parking was located, choosing a spot close by.

Mason paused to look at her, before they exited the vehicle. "Zoe, you look so pretty tonight. I'm sorry if I keep repeating the same theme, but it's undeniably true. I'm just so happy that you said *"yes"* and we are doing this tonight."

"Well thank you for inviting me, Mason... and I'm feeling happy too," she confessed somewhat guardedly, not finding it easy to express her feelings.

He fed the meter, coming around to escort her down off of the high step of the Land Rover, steadying her from nearly stumbling. *"You okay there, little lady?"*

"Of course!" she answered, feeling self-conscious from doing so.

Mason grabbed for her hand, as they walked towards the restaurant. It featured an all-brick façade with an assorted array of brightly colored umbrellas that were off to one side - situated in a wrought iron, fenced-in patio enclosure. Numerous patrons were dining outside and enjoying the beautiful evening, looking like they were pleased with their menu selections and the inviting outdoor atmosphere of the place.

As Mason and Zoe entered the front door of the restaurant, a male host was there to greet them. They took in the lively bar and additional inside seating spread out in front of them. "Good evening. Welcome to *La Paz. Would you like to sit inside or out?"*

"If it's okay with you, I think outside would be great!" Mason suggested, looking at Zoe and then at the host, making sure she approved first.

Zoe shook her head in agreement as the host jumped in with his response. *"Perfect decision on such a perfect evening!"* he offered, after grabbing a couple of menus and then escorted them to the outside patio area, looking around for any available tables that were present. The other diners that were seated in the overly crowed area, were taking in the newest arrivals, with a few over-zealous, females checking out Mason and how handsome and built he was, as their heads came together and they whispered and pointed in his direction. Zoe took notice of their brazenness, even if Mason seemed unfazed by it all, only desiring a peaceful dining experience away from their silliness.

"Why don't we sit over there," Zoe proposed, choosing a table a considerable distance away from her competition, hoping for at least some privacy to enjoy her meal and Mason's company without the *"stares and glares"* from the *"desperate"* chicks that were also present.

The host escorted them to the table of Zoe's choice, handing each one a menu. *"Would you like your umbrella up or down?"* he inquired thoughtfully. *"Some like it up just for ambience sake, even though the sun will be setting soon."*

"We'll keep it up," Mason winked, giving the host a silent signal that he was hoping for a little romance with Zoe over dinner. *"Hey bud, can we order a pitcher of Margaritas as soon as you get the chance?"*

"I'll send your server over right a way, sir."

"Thanks a million!"

Zoe laughed. "Well, you definitely make a bold statement when you enter a room!"

"How so?"

"Seriously? You didn't see the eyes of the *"salivating females"* staring a hole right through you when we walked out here to the patio? And then the host – he seemed ready to leave rather quickly, hoping to locate our server fast," Zoe teased.

"I guess so..." Mason smiled, not fully grasping the point or considering all the details. He began to reach for Zoe's hand just as the young, attractive, female server approached, retracting it as she introduced herself.

"Welcome to *La Paz*. My name is Hayden. *I heard you were*

interested in a pitcher of Margaritas? Any preference on the flavor?"

"Zoe, your call on this one," Mason conceded while trying to be polite, as he waited patiently for her to answer.

"Honestly, I like the traditional – unfrozen over ice - with salt on the rim."

"I totally agree!" Mason chimed in, grinning with his approval, glad to discover the first thing they had in common with the meal they were sharing.

"Would you like anything other than chips and salsa in way of an appetizer?"

Mason looked at the menu quickly, taking in the list of *"starts".* "I like Queso dip. You can add a hefty portion of that."

"Guacamole would be nice also," Zoe added.

"I'll be out with your pitcher of Margaritas and appetizers in a few minutes," Hayden promised, disappearing quickly so that she could put in their order, and then keep up with all the other customers and their demands.

Mason returned to his original intention of grabbing Zoe's hand, staring deeply into her light green eyes. I like this place. Reminds me somewhat of a few of my favorite restaurants back home in Austin, only it's a lot warmer there this time of year."

"I can only imagine. I've never been to Texas."

"Really? Well maybe one day I will take you there."

Zoe coughed nervously, removing her hand from his, not expecting that sort of offer to be made so soon. "I wasn't suggesting anything like that, Mason," Zoe explained, as her face reddened.

"I realize that..." he answered, just as Hayden returned with a tray that included the pitcher of margaritas and two salt-rimmed glasses filled with ice. Homemade chips and salsa - that the restaurant was known for – along with a double portion of Queso dip and a generous portion of guacamole - were also presented with the drinks, thrilling Mason and Zoe with the selections.

"Would you like me to place your dinner orders now?" the brown-haired beauty inquired, as she finished pouring the first round of margaritas from the pitcher into each one of the glasses.

"Give us twenty minutes, hon," Mason directed with a wink, as Hayden slipped away, being somewhat intimidated by the presence of the Texan also.

Zoe looked on, feeling her insecurities mounting. *He just called her "hon". Probably a big flirt and no different than Noah…* she noted sadly, as her mood became noticeably distant and pensive.

"You okay?" Mason questioned, sensing her sudden quietness.

"I'm fine," she lied, taking a big gulp of her drink, trying her best to relax.

Mason scooped a chip into the salsa, eating the whole thing in one bite. "This salsa rivals anything I used to get back home. I would say they know what they are doing here," he grinned, trying his best to be charming.

"That's why I wanted to bring you here. The ambiance alone gets top billing, and the food and drinks only adds to the over-all experience."

"Zoe, your place in Williamsport rocks too!" Mason praised, clinking his margarita glass against hers, just to re-emphasize his point. "Everything I've had at *Luna's* is top notch. You got a great chef working for you."

"I think so too," Zoe agreed, feeling her defenses suddenly melting away, determined to relax again.

Hayden returned in twenty minutes, just as she was directed by Mason, writing down the dinner orders that included a trio of enchiladas and one over-stuffed burrito filled with chicken and steak. *"Would you like another pitcher of Margaritas?"* she inquired.

"I think we are good!" Mason reassured warmly, seeing plenty left in the pitcher for them to drink.

The dinners arrived, with barely half of it being eaten by either one, already both being quite full from the appetizers. Hayden brought *"take home"* containers along with the check, depositing both on the table right in front of Mason. *"I thought maybe you could use these?"* she offered, waiting on his response as she pointed at the containers.

He withdrew one hundred and twenty dollars in cash from his wallet, placing it inside the black folder before handing it back to the server. "Keep the change!" he instructed, as Hayden took in her generous tip. "And yes, we will be using the *"doggie bags!"*

"Thank you so much!" she brightened, knowing she was rarely over-tipped. Zoe could tell the server was confused by Mason's strange phrase of *"doggie bags"* that she probably had never heard used before. She noted the exchange, finding him genuine and caring, definitely delighted with the overall dining experience.

Mason offered to carry Zoe's *"take home"* container, placing it in the back seat beside of his, once they returned to the Land Rover. *"Why don't we take a short stroll before we depart from these parts? I would like to see what else Fred...erick has to offer,"* he suggested pleasantly.

Zoe looked at her cellphone, realizing the time. "Maybe only a short walk? I honestly do need to get back home soon," she explained, feeling the need to be practical and err on the side of caution.

Mason shook his head, grabbing for her hand. *"The night is young, dar... ling. I want you all to myself for a while longer,"* he enticed, reaching in to give her a lingering kiss on the cheek that made her jump at the contact, as she leaned back away afterwards and felt her face where Mason's lips had just touched. *"Zoe... I didn't mean to startle you so,"* he whispered, trying to ease her apprehensions.

"I'm sorry, Mason. It's just been a while since someone has kissed me like that, and then it didn't end so well after my boyfriend decided to break up with me," she openly confessed, as they continued walking past a few retail shops that were still open for the evening.

Mason suddenly stopped, turning Zoe to face him, as the sounds of a band could be heard playing from inside a bar - that had its doors open nearby. *"His loss..."* He answered simply and honestly. *"The man must have been a total fool to have let you go."* The margaritas were talking and so were Mason's luscious lips, as he swooped down to kiss Zoe fully on the mouth - without her resisting this time or desiring that it should ever end.

Chapter 12

The drive back to Williamsport was somewhat quiet, at least on Zoe's end, as she stared out the window a good portion of the time, allowing Mason to do the majority of the talking. She felt somewhat guilty about the lengthy *"make-out"* session, enjoying it a little too much, realizing Mason was just as skillful at kissing as Noah ever was. *Why feel badly over this?* She pondered silently, still wrestling with her emotions, feeling like enough time had not transpired for grieving over the loss of the relationship she had just shared with her prior boyfriend of four years.

"Zoe, we're back at Luna's," Mason mentioned matter-of-factly, interrupting the silent argument she was having with herself, during the entire journey home.

"Wow, we are? Sorry, I was half dosing," she fibbed, making excuses and choosing not to engage with him and do anymore explaining.

Mason gave Zoe one last hug before handing over the *"doggie bag"* to her. "It was a very nice evening, and I hope it won't be the last," he concluded politely, not actually making plans and asking her out for a second time as she had anticipated, especially after the public kissing on the city streets of Frederick.

"Thank you, Mason, for dinner. I really enjoyed myself also," Zoe acknowledged graciously, being at a loss to say more, not even sure if they would go out again after the *"less than stellar"* ending to the evening that felt somewhat disappointing to her.

The phone began to ring as Zoe pulled into her driveway. She sat idling, fumbling in the dark trying to locate her cell that was buried somewhere deep inside of her purse. She missed the call, realizing it had been from Emma, as the phone immediately began ringing once again.

"Hello?"

"Zoe, I was hoping you would have called me by now! I was worried sick!"

"Oh, for heaven's sakes, Emma, I just got home. I turned my ringer back on after my date was over, and was surprised to see that you called me several times. *Three missed phone calls from you? Seriously?*" She whispered quietly into the phone.

"Sorry, for being overly concerned about your well-being. Mason seems nice enough, but I wanted to make sure he wasn't a serial killer or something."

Zoe began to laugh until her belly hurt, not expecting her friend's irrational paranoia. "Well, I'm glad that you care that much about me, but Mason is harmless and you need not worry about him."

"Good to hear… So how about you filling me in on some of the juicy details of your evening?"

"We went to Frederick and to *La Paz* for dinner."

"Wow, that's cool! Did he like the place?"

"I would say he loved the place and the down town area of Frederick as well!"

"Hopefully, not too much! You don't want him getting any ideas about relocating and moving there."

"Em, honestly, sometimes I can't figure out what to do with you. Mason works in Williamsport and leases an apartment here also. *Why would he just up and leave our town already?"*

"You're right... I guess I was just thinking that we can't compete with Frederick, that's all."

"Well, that's a matter of opinion. Frederick is definitely nice, but we have our canal and our small town charm to boast about. I think Mason agrees... he says *Luna's* is just as good as *La Paz* – in way of dining."

"So he said all that, did he? What a suck up!" Emma joked, making Zoe laugh all over again. *"How about the kissing? Did he make the moves on you before the night was up?"*

"You just won't stop, will you?" Zoe replied with a shake of her head, not wanting to give in and answer all of Emma's questions so quickly, wanting her to beg a little while longer for the details she was dying to hear.

"I would hope he would have given you a good night kiss, at least."

"Several... actually."

"Oh my word, really?"

"I would say it was a full-blown, public display of affection, right out on Market Street in front of Bushwaller's - for the whole darn town to see!"

Now it was Emma's turn to laugh, being fascinated with the vivid description. *"No way! And you didn't stop him from doing so?"*

"I don't think I could have, if I wanted to...." Zoe breathed, remembering the tender, lust-filled moments of the magical kissing, as they stood entwined, wrapped in each other's arms, on the sidewalk of the busy downtown city street, where passerby's were beeping their horns and hooting out the windows of their cars, getting an *"eye-full"* of the shameless *"make-out"* scene.

"It sounds as if you like him, Zoe."

"Yes, I do... and I'm scared, Emma. Damned scared!"

"There's nothing to be afraid of. This is just a normal progression of things after a breakup. For most people, they go on and date again... hopefully, sooner rather than later. I think it's healthy not to ponder about things too long after a breakup. The longer it goes on, you get used to being alone, and then some *"broken hearts"* don't ever want to take another chance at love and try again."

"Where have you gotten all this wisdom?" Zoe teased, realizing Emma wasn't seriously dating anyone herself currently.

"I'm not sure... maybe my mother... or maybe elsewhere... who knows. She feels I need to start trying to find a boyfriend."

"Why don't you?"

"Are we in a race now?" Emma exclaimed, poking back at her friend.

"I need to get off of here. I'm tired and this conversation can be resumed at another time. I will just end by saying, that I had a nice time with Mason, but I want to take things slowly with him at this point."

"Did he ask you out on a second date?"

Zoe paused, considering Emma's words. *"Not exactly."*

"Not exactly? He either did or he didn't."

"He said, *"I hope it won't be the last"*. How would you take that?"

"Hmm... I would say he was trying to throw out a hint, but not sound too pushy at the same time. If I were to guess, you were being the *"typical Zoe"* and throwing out some mixed signals."

"Emma! Why would you say such a thing?"

"Because I know you. You probably retreated into your shell after the *"make-out"* session in Frederick. Right or wrong?"

"You may be slightly right… I was sort of quiet on the drive home."

"Exactly! So he was just trying to be polite and not overdo things with you. Maybe he wanted to take it easy at the end of the date and just play it cool. I'm sure one day he will ask you out again, if you continue to act friendly towards him."

"I guess you're right… well goodnight, my silly friend. I hope all your questions are now finally answered about my date and evening. I will see you tomorrow at work."

"Nite, Zoe."

"Nite, Emma."

Zoe washed her face, amongst her other nightly rituals, climbing into bed with Luna snuggled in close by her side. She pushed on the alarm button, knowing six a.m. would be there way before she wanted it to, and then rolled over after turning off her lamp, ready to fall off to sleep. Her cellphone beeped out an alert of an incoming text message, making her flip on the light switch once again – wanting to retrieve the phone so that she could read it.

Zoe, great evening! Loved being with you and enjoyed La Paz and Frederick. The kissing was delightful. When can I see you again? Mason

She sat up staring at the message, rereading it several times over, allowing the words to finally settle into her brain. A gleeful smile crossed her face, as she basked in the reality that he seemed interested. *"I guess Mason does want to take me out for a second time,"* she said aloud, feeling content with the realization.

Yes, it was a nice evening and the meal and margaritas were great! As far as seeing each other again, I am not opposed, but as I warned you before, my schedule can be a problem…

Not for me…. we will work on that together. So when can I see you again?

Zoe began to giggle, honestly surprised by Mason's determination, but enjoying his persistence all the same. *When do you want to see me out again?*

Is tomorrow too soon?

I would say we should give it a rest. Maybe in a day or two?

If you insist…. but I will be counting the seconds until then, love.

Goodnight, Mason.

Goodnight, Zoe.

Zoe silenced her ringer, laying the cellphone on her nightstand and turning off the lamp for another time, resuming the sideways position that she always slept in, with Luna repositioning herself protectively up against her mistress. She thought of the exchange that she and Mason had just shared. *I guess he really does like me*, she sighed, feeling thrilled that someone finally found her desirable again. Her emotions were torn, considering that he had used the *"love"* word twice in the text exchange, not ready for that level of intimacy.

"More dates and then the expectation of sex will certainly be next, since every guy expects that sooner rather than later. Am I ready for all of this, Luna?" she moaned out in frustration, wishing her beloved pet could answer the troubling questions at hand. Luna sighed loudly and shifted her weight, only desiring silence now, being incapable of solving the unknowns of her mistress's future.

Zoe drifted off to sleep, with a sensual dream of Mason taking center stage. He was in his black leather cowboy boots. Being totally nude, except for those fascinating cowboy boots, approaching her with a wicked grin on his face - in a seductive sort of way. Muscular, toned and handsome – on a mission to *"have her"*, displaying a massive *"hard-on"* that was protruding straight out and quite impressive – equally as big and grand as the state of Texas!

Chapter 13

It was Emma's day off of work, and her only desire was to take her Camry to the dealership to see what the loud rumbling was all about. She was almost certain that it was coming from the engine, and unfortunately was growing louder by the minute. The car had some age to it, actually over twelve years now. It was her mother's vehicle originally, and then handed down to Emma while she was still in high school, after Margie had picked out a new one for herself.

Emma drove into Hagerstown, taking the Dual Highway exit, going in the direction of Taylor Toyota. She parked in front of the large bay doors that already had two cars waiting in front of her. *"Hi, I'm Emma Baker and I'm here to drop off my Camry for service,"* she explained politely to the middle-aged, overweight male attendant with his *"readers"* placed low on his nose, focusing in on the computer screen in front of him.

"Yes, I do have a 10 a.m. appointment scheduled for you today," Mr. Burger confirmed while finally looking up. *"Is someone picking you up or are you waiting here on your vehicle until it is ready?"*

"I plan to stay here until everything is finished," she smiled, as she looked around the room for an empty seat, with not even one being available.

"It may be a couple hours," he explained. "But that's your choice, and we do offer free coffee or bottles of water if you would like."

"Is Luke Taylor working today?" Emma inquired, wanting an excuse to kill some time.

"You know Luke? The owner's son?" Mr. Burger asked in surprise.

"Umm... he's a friend of mine," Emma stumbled, not totally sure of his status anymore where she was concerned. "From back in high school..."

Mr. Burger stopped to study her more closely, just to make sure she was being sincere. "You can probably find him in the next building. He's in charge of sales now."

"Wasn't aware of that..." Emma answered over her head, already leaving and on a mission to find Luke. She walked across the parking lot, taking in row after row of new cars, in every color of the rainbow, making a wish that one of them could be hers some day. She opened the glass door to a stylish, contemporary waiting area that featured a few vehicles that had been strategically placed inside, making her wonder how they had pulled off such a feat.

"May I help you?" A pretty brunette with a wedge-style haircut asked, as she approached from a reception desk across the room. She was dressed in a red suit that was way too revealing and tight, displaying a tad too much eye makeup that was difficult not to stare at. She stood a little too close for comfort, making Emma feel suddenly nauseous, from the over-whelming sick smell of perfume that had been intentionally over-applied, perched now in front of her and waiting on the response.

Emma smiled, not caring in the least that she was a smidgen underdressed in comparison, with only a simple pair of jeans and a *Luna's* t-shirt on. Her blonde locks had been pulled back into a high ponytail, with only a hint of makeup and a pair of slightly soiled white sneakers present that she had slipped into – minus any socks. *"Is Luke Taylor working today?"* she asked, for a second time already that day.

"He is on a call right now. May I let him know who is here to see him?" Serena pried and inquired in a squeaky voice.

"Let him know Emma Baker is here to see him," she replied dryly, with a somewhat sarcastic lift to her voice, finding the female equally as

nauseating as her cheap perfume.

Within minutes Luke appeared, cordially smiling with his *"surfer boy"* good looks of very blonde sun-bleached hair and blue eyes overwhelmingly present that Emma remembered quite well, never getting *"that kiss"* out of her mind from several years earlier. *"Emma, what brings you in today?"* Luke questioned pleasantly, as he reached forward and gave her an unexpected warm hug that caught her totally off-guard. *"Isn't it funny that we hadn't seen each other for several months, and now I'm running into you again so soon?"*

Emma quickly broke free, taking a somewhat defensive posture as she rested on one hip and had her arms crossed warily in front of her. "I'm getting my Camry worked on today and I was told that it could take some time, so I thought I would stop in and say hello," she explained, trying to justify things with a logical excuse.

"I see... So what's going on with it?" Luke quizzed, attempting to look out for her best interests, as he escorted Emma from the building.

"I'm not sure. It's been making a loud noise in the engine - when I drive it."

Luke stopped to consider what she was describing. *"Maybe it's time for a new one?"* he threw out, immediately causing her to become wary again.

"Jesus.... I can't afford a new car, Luke!"

Luke began to laugh, reaching over to squeeze Emma's shoulder. "Don't jump down my throat, sweetie. I was only trying to throw out a suggestion. I remember that car... It was your mom's at one point. Right?"

"How on earth would you know that?"

"My dad remembers the history of most of the cars that were sold here, and even more so if someone came here to the dealership from

Williamsport. Let's just say he is training me well and sharing all of his knowledge from over the years, and wants me to be aware of those small details too."

"*I see...*" Emma replied, taking in the fit and handsome male that was turning her on once again – just the same way that he always did every time she was around him. He was dressed in cream-colored khakis with a sky blue, button-down dress shirt, and a green and blue striped tie was added and complimented his other apparel. The brown loafers that he wore completed his professional polished look, with the whole picture making Emma feel suddenly awkward and underdressed.

"*How old is the car?*" Luke asked, locking eyes with Emma's azure blue ones, studying her a little longer than was necessary, as he waited on the response.

"*Twelve... years,*" she muttered, lost in his spell that she was suddenly under.

"*Twelve... years,*" he repeated back, as the two realized an obvious attraction and connection was occurring beyond the conversation about the car. "*Emma, why haven't we been out on an actual date?*" Luke probed as he continued to stare at her, suddenly changing the subject to something more personal, much to her surprise.

Emma began to laugh nervously, typically not being intimidated so easily. "Maybe because our best friends dated, and we went in other directions when it came to who we were involved with?"

"*How stupid was that?*" Luke exclaimed with a big grin, making Emma's heart skip a beat, as she reminded herself that she wasn't imagining the exchange and it was actually taking place. "*And the irony is they aren't even together anymore, so what is stopping us now from seeing each other?*" he eagerly challenged, as he walked with her towards a row of new vehicles.

"*You can't be serious?*" Emma retorted back, waiting for Luke to spring it on her that he was only teasing, but showing no intentions of doing so.

"Oh, I'm more than serious, Em!" he answered intensely, as he grabbed her hand and dragged her behind a large SUV, wrapping her completely in his arms and then planting a bold seductive kiss directly on her lips - that lasted a few seconds too long.

They broke free from the embrace, with Emma being the first to talk as she tried to regain her composure and catch her breath. *"Luke, is this such a good idea? What will Zoe think if we start seeing each other after her horrible breakup with Noah? She may end up being very upset with the both of us."*

"We can't control any of this stuff, Em. When I saw you at *Luna's* I wanted to say something to you then about how I was feeling, but I was in a hurry to get to work. I had every intention of coming back to your place and discussing the matter with you. I'm not seeing anyone serious right now, and we both are local, so why not give this thing a try? That is, unless you are seeing someone else? But after the way we just kissed, I can't imagine it would be all that serious," he teased, setting her heart on fire once again with his searching blue eyes that were locked with hers.

A feeling of uncertainty ran through Emma, considering the possibility of being with Luke as nothing more than an unobtainable fantasy, and he was only messing with her emotions. "I am not seeing anyone serious at the moment either, but look at me, Luke," she questioned, pointing at her attire. *"Why would you ever consider someone like me as being a person that you would want to date?"*

"Because you are beautiful and I have always been attracted to you... which I finally figured out when Noah and Zoe were dating. And by the way, *I am* looking at you, and that not *"over-doing"* it while *"still looking amazing"* thing about you, is what turns me on the most. I love your face, your hair, and your body; and honestly the way it feels when I kiss you," he sincerely expressed, lifting her chin to his own, reclaiming her lips once again for another *"go round"* as he grinded up against her, allowing his hands to suddenly wander and explore without Emma having the desire to stop it.

"Excuse me, Mr. Taylor," Mr. Burger from the service department interrupted with a loud cough, after coming up silently from behind and witnessing the last of the passion-filled moments that were not intended for his eyes. He was trying to get Luke's attention, hoping it would have ended first before announcing his presence. *"I've been looking for Ms. Baker concerning her Camry?"*

Emma broke free, adjusting her top and then her hair also, feeling somewhat embarrassed from being caught. *"What's going on with my car?"*

"You need an engine overhaul, I'm sorry to say," he explained with a sad shake of his head. "Your car's engine may last a while longer, but I can't tell you exactly for how long."

"You got to be kidding me!" Emma exclaimed, suddenly feeling less amorous and overwhelmed with the thought of a huge repair bill that she couldn't afford.

"Yes, it barely has any life left in that old engine."

"Oh no!" Emma moaned, while placing her hands over her face in disbelief, feeling like she wanted to cry from hearing the unexpected news.

Luke stepped in, freeing her hands from her eyes. "Em, it's really okay. I'm going to give you a super great deal on a new vehicle, and I'll even extend to you the *"friends and family"* discount. The good news is that since your Camry is still running we will give you a decent trade-in allowance," he added, while smiling reassuredly at her in a caring sort of way.

"How do I even begin this whole process?" She whispered, feeling totally helpless all of a sudden.

"Don't worry about that right now. I will help you pick out the perfect car for your needs," Luke encouraged, ready to begin the *"tour of vehicles"* that covered several of Taylor Toyota's car lots - desiring only to please her.

"Okay, Luke. Let's do this!" she agreed without wavering, taking the first step forward in more ways than one - not only deciding to buy a new car, but also taking a chance at love. The thought of starting a new relationship with Luke Taylor – the super *"hot hunk"* that she had only dreamt about for most of her life, was now an actual possibility *being offered by him!* She was pinching herself, still lost in the moment, but never-the-less believing in it now - that *dreams* really do come true.

Chapter 14

"Em, why don't you consider buying a 4Runner like mine or maybe even a RAV4? Those are the two I would recommend," Luke suggested with a kind smile, as they continued to peruse and take in each and every car that was lined up, row-by-row and over several parking areas, being quite impressive and all outstretched in front of them.

"So, do you think I should go for a SUV this time?"

"It makes total sense with your restaurant. If you and Zoe do a catering event in the future, you will have more room to haul things in a SUV."

"What's cheaper to buy?" Emma inquired, making Luke grin from her innocent nature, at least in this area where she apparently had limited knowledge.

"Well, I guess the RAV4, but why not get one to match my 4Runner?"

Emma rolled her eyes, planting her hands squarely on her hips. "I'm not into the *"matchy, matchy"* sort of thing, and my number one goal is to save some money at this point. *And anyway, we are not seriously dating, so why would I want to buy a vehicle that matched your 4Runner?"*

Luke grabbed Emma's hand, not bothering to answer her question, knowing how edgy she could be. He dragged her to a royal blue RAV4 that was loaded with all the desirable upgraded features. "Take a look in here," he suggested, opening the door and allowing her to peak her head inside.

She took a whiff of the air. "It's definitely smells brand new with that *"new car smell"*.

"Yes, it does!" Luke grinned, delighted by the way Emma looked at things.

"How about we take a test drive? It will give me an excuse to be alone with you for at hour without anyone questioning why. What do you say about that?"

Emma could feel her heart suddenly racing, at the anticipation and possibility of it all. She realized Luke wanted to take her on a *"test drive"*, but it wasn't just with the SUV she assumed. *"Get the keys,"* she whispered, almost surprising herself, as she flashed her eyelashes seductively at him, giving him the answer that he had hoped for.

"I'll be right back!" Luke yelled out over the top of his head, as he sprinted towards the showroom, anxious to be alone with her now. He pulled back on the glass door and hurried inside to retrieve the keys and other documentation that Emma needed to sign-off on, knowing that it was necessary for her to drive the vehicle off of the lot.

"You leaving?" Serena asked, surprised by Luke's willingness to take the *"test drive"* personally with a potential customer, since he was now the new sales manager. With his recent promotion, it was expected that he would hand off all customers to any available salesperson in the showroom who was working that day, so that he could keep things running smoothly, dealing with any administrative tasks and financial issues that might arise.

"Yes, I am, Serena. Emma's a personal friend, and I will be gone for a while on a *"test drive"* with her. Please hold all my calls," he instructed with a brief, polite smile, walking at a rather fast pace from the showroom with the keys and a clipboard now in hand, ready to get the forms signed off on quickly, with no more reasons after that not to drive away from the dealership.

Serena looked somewhat defeated, hoping Luke would one day ask her out, but also realizing he was *"all business"* and had made that point quite clear to all those that were working there that *inter-office dating* at Taylor Toyota was frowned upon. He had warned the sales department in a meeting, which she was also a part of, that *if a problem ever arose because someone chose to get involved, affecting any business aspect of the company, that the guilty parties would be terminated from employment immediately.* This was enough of a warning to keep most from venturing there, even though Serena still held out hope that it could be possible with she and Luke.

Emma leaned against the RAV4, scrolling through her social media on her phone, waiting patiently on Luke to return. She smiled, as he jogged over to her side, panting a little as he tried to catch his breath. "I made a copy of your license and you will need to sign here," he explained, pointing to the signature line. "Then I will drop off the paperwork back in the office, and we will be free to leave!"

"So much to do just to *"test drive"* a vehicle."

"Yes, you are right, but with the wrong person - and if we didn't do this - a car could be stolen right out from under us," Luke explained succinctly, as he attached the *"dealer"* license plate to the front of the vehicle. "Time to climb in," he added with a grin, as he unlocked the door and waved in the direction of the front seat.

Emma obliged, as Luke took the passenger's seat beside of hers. *"How does the seat feel to you?"*

"Okay, I guess," she replied timidly, looking at her handsome instructor that was now sitting next to her.

"Maybe move it a little? You look as if you could come forward a bit. And I would adjust your side mirrors and rearview mirror too, until you can see everything clearly and without obstruction."

Emma did accordingly, hanging on to Luke's every word. *"Where is the ignition located at?"*

"This is keyless. Just push this button here," he pointed out and then pushed it for her, which started the engine right up without hesitation, much to Emma's surprise and fascination. "Wow, my Camry didn't turn over that easily. I definitely like that feature!"

"It is nice!" Luke agreed. "Pull up to the front of the building and I will be right back," he explained with a smile, dropping the papers off to Serena, as she gave him one last look of hurt. He jogged back outside, climbing into the passenger's seat, anxious to get on the road. *"Ready to take it out for a spin?"*

"I think so..." Emma answered hesitantly, feeling somewhat scared now.

"Then buckle up and let's get out outta here!"

Emma did accordingly, heading east on the Dual Highway and then climbing up over South Mountain on US 40 towards Myersville, Maryland. *"Where exactly are we going?"* she asked, as she glanced over at Luke.

"You will see," he announced playfully. "Take a left here."

Emma followed his directions, steering the car accordingly, taking them down a winding country road that had no other visible traffic on it.

"What do you think of the handling so far?"

Emma considered what he had just asked as she continued driving on the scenic road. *You or the car?* She thought to herself, hoping to answer both before they returned to Taylor Toyota. "I definitely feel comfortable in it, and I like the way it drives and takes the curves."

"So let me tell you about a few other features of the RAV4. The back seat lays flat, so you have plenty of room if the need arises."

The need is arising... Emma pondered, having her mind definitely on other things other than purchasing a new vehicle, wanting only to pull off the road and *"make out"* with Luke some more, just as they had brazenly done in the parking lot behind some cars. "Good to know," Emma answered aloud, still hoping he was insinuating more. "Especially, if the catering thing at *Luna's* ever happens."

"So what do you think, Em, can you see yourself driving this SUV?"

"Yes, I think so, but I will have to look at the money situation when we get back to the dealership, just to make sure the payments are something that I can afford."

"They will be," he reassured, as he reached over to tenderly squeeze her shoulder. "Up ahead take a right," Luke pointed out.

Emma looked at the sign and it said *"dead end"*. "The road ends ahead. Are you aware of that?"

"Yeah... I know it does," he suggestively winked. *"I thought I would take you somewhere private. Are you okay with that?"*

"Sure. I'm okay with that..."

Emma took the road, crossing over a few potholes in a road that needed to be repaired, before it turned entirely to gravel. It gave way to a densely covered area of trees that ended with a small park in the distance - filled with several picnic tables and barbeque grills strategically placed by each one. She stopped the car, putting it into park, now curious and glancing around at her surroundings. *"I have never been here before. Where are we at exactly?"*

"Just a hidden little gem that I've known about, and fortunately for us, many others do not," he explained in an eager sort of way, implying so much more.

Emma's pulse began to quicken. She remembered Luke was a part of that *"hunkie guy, stud group"* from Williamsport High School and beyond, that came with a reputation of *"love em and leave em"*, not caring what hearts were broken along the way. "You've obviously been here before," she stated clearly, making direct eye contact with Luke now.

"Maybe..." he teased, unbuckling his seatbelt in the process, leaning across and placing a hand on her knee.

"Luke, I'm not so sure that this was a good idea after all."

He looked confused, wanting the amorous *"willing vixen"* back in his arms from the parking lot of earlier. *"Why not? I thought you were all in on this."*

Emma shook here head, as she continued to clutch the steering wheel and keep her seatbelt securely attached, with the motor still running. "My heart is saying go for this, but my head is telling me to beware. *Why do I want to go down the same path as my best friend Zoe?"* she pleaded, with confusion in her azure blue eyes.

Luke removed his hand from off of Emma, resting it in his lap instead, as he stared out of the window for a moment and then returned his gaze back to her. *"I am not Noah Clark! Plain and simple. He fucked up by breaking up with Zoe, and I detest him for doing that to her! We were all friends, and he busted up the group. I never directly hear from the bastard, ever! Do you know how that feels when he was like a brother to me for so many years?"*

"That is so hard to believe. You guys were best friends. Are you telling me he has been totally silent with you since he left for England?"

"Honestly, I would say 99% yes. I heard from him once in the beginning. As I mentioned to you before, the only information I have gotten about Noah is second hand from his mother to my mother. Emma, I am not the same guy I was in high school. Please believe me when I'm telling you this!" he pleaded, desperately wanting her to trust him.

"Yeah, I get it, but remember I was around, and your questionable behavior continued throughout college too."

Luke shook his head in frustration, knowing he wasn't winning the war with her concerning the present subject matter, realizing his blemished reputation may always follow after him where Emma was concerned. "I guess we should get back to the dealership then. If you would like to buy the RAV4, I will take good care of you with the financing and make sure the payments are to your liking."

"Well that is decent of you, Luke, after that intense kissing we just shared," she replied with a sarcastic lift to her voice.

Luke began to laugh, still finding Emma irresistible. *"Come on, Em, lighten up some. We are two consenting adults here, and I think you have finally figured out that I do want you badly, and I think you want me too. Please stop allowing those people surrounding our past - which I realize we consider to be some of our closest and dearest friends – to define us and what we could potentially become together as a couple – especially since they are no longer dating anymore.*

Emma undid her seatbelt and turned off the engine, turning then to gaze at Luke. *"Please kiss me again, before I change my mind and want to leave this place, because I honestly don't want to deny how I'm feeling about you any longer."*

"Absolutely…" he agreed whole-heartedly, taking her in his arms for another passionate, soul-searing, series of kisses - that left them both unable to do anything else, but be lost in the moment.

Chapter 15

Emma lay entwined in Luke's arms, in the folded down backseat of the RAV4. Their clothes had been discarded and lay in a mixed pile, being now used as pillows behind their heads, as their ragged breathing took on a more normal pace again. Emma smiled pleasantly, as she realized her new car had been officially christened, not with a bottle of champagne - as some do on a virgin voyage of a ship - but with an amazing penis that rocked her insides until she exploded into a million butterflies of a blissful orgasm, like none she had ever experienced before.

"I hope no one comes by here for a picnic, right about now," she mentioned with some concern, looking over at Luke who was half-sleeping, with his eyes closed contentedly.

He opened one eye and turned his head, only with the purpose of answering Emma and easing her fears. *"Em, who really cares? All I want to do is fuck you all over again, before I gotta get back to work,"* he confessed passionately, finding her waiting lips that were ready to receive his tongue, along with her intimate opening that took his cock easily from the moistness of their recent lovemaking.

"Oh my God, Luke! I'm already coming!" Emma yelled out for the whole woods to hear, as he mutually climaxed, shaking and collapsing on top of her afterwards. They were both drenched in sweat, from the vigorous workout, finding the whole sexual experience mutually satisfying and fulfilling. Luke was in no position to return to work without a shower, but it was happening anyway. He rolled off of her, pushing his wet blonde hair away from his face, knowing he needed to get back to the dealership soon or Serena would be calling him.

"Sweetie, that was amazing! I guess you can see this new car of

yours has a big enough trunk for more than your business catering needs!"

Emma began to giggle, propped up on one elbow, looking around. "What about your work? It's obvious we have been gone a long time. Some there may wonder if we were preoccupied, doing things other than *"test driving"* this vehicle.

"Maybe so, but it was worth it. Don't you think?" he dared, nibbling on her chin. "And I felt the *"other test drive"* was necessary too, before we both signed up for anything more."

"Did I pass the test?"

"With flying colors!" he grinned, looking around and trying to sort out their clothes. He slipped on his boxers, slacks and then his dress shirt, fastening each button slowly as Emma eagerly watched, totally turned on by his muscular physique. *"You planning to get dressed anytime soon, Em?"* He taunted playfully, now noticing her lack of enthusiasm to get motivated.

"Oh my word, I'm just so relaxed, and I don't want to move," she said in way of an excuse, feeling half-embarrassed now that she was the only one who was currently nude, as she slipped into her own apparel.

"I get it and I feel the same way, but we don't want them sending out the troops to look for us. We have been gone for over two hours, in case you didn't know."

"No way!" Emma exclaimed, looking at her cellphone in disbelief. She returned to the front seat after they secured the back one into its original position, reattaching her seatbelt and then trying to smooth out her hair as best she could. Luke attempted to do likewise, pushing his blonde locks into place with a dab of spit, adjusting his shirt into his pants, and then sliding his belt around his waist afterwards.

"Do I look presentable?" he inquired of Emma.

"I guess so..." she giggled, finding the *"spit in the hands"* maneuver somewhat comical and gross. "Yes, you look just as handsome as ever!" she consoled, trying to ease his concerns.

They drove back to Taylor Toyota, continuing to give heartfelt glances along the way. Luke rested his hand lovingly on Emma's shoulder, just quietly lingering and lavishing in the passionate afterglow moments of what they had just shared, wishing it wasn't over yet. Now, all that remained were the pleasant memories of their first sexual encounter together - out in the deep woods - in the back of Emma's new SUV.

Emma steered the RAV4 in front of the sales office building, as per Luke's request, as he departed from the vehicle first. "Just pull over there in that parking space and I will get your paperwork started," he smiled tenderly and instructed. "See you inside."

"Sure thing, Luke..." Emma answered, feeling totally depleted from the vigorous romp in the back of the car that was still clearly etched in her mind. She parked and walked into the building, with her purse bouncing freely off of one hip, ready to transition into the next activity of buying a new car. She walked past Serena who gave her *"the evil eye",* obviously sensing that Emma was *"the one"* that Luke was romantically choosing over her.

"He's in there waiting on you," Serena commented dryly, not going out of her way to escort Emma into Luke's office, as she normally would be doing with other customers.

"Thanks!" Emma replied with a big victorious grin of satisfaction, assuming that the *"hot sleazy girl"* wanted him too.

Luke looked up from his laptop, grinning at Emma who stood in front of him with her arms crossed, looking somewhat perplexed. *"Please pull up a seat, pretty girl, but close the door behind you first,"* he whispered seductively.

"Don't get any ideas," Emma whispered back over Luke's desk for "his ears only" before taking the seat across from him, and moving it in closely.

"Oh, you mean in here? I'm not even that daring!"

"I'm not so sure about that!" Emma retorted back with a daring laugh, enjoying the frolicking exchange between them immensely.

"Here are the figures I came up with for you. Your SUV retails at $30,350, since it has the XLE premium package. I am selling it to you for $4000 less, which is the same price as the basic model, placing the price at $26,350."

"Can you actually do that?"

"What? Change that price?"

"Yes."

"Well, my dad won't be too happy with my decision, but as far as I'm concerned you are my new girlfriend and what is he going to say if he has to *"eat"* one deal?"

Emma sat in silence, staring at Luke. *"You really feel that way?"*

"Sure. I can definitely reduce the price for you."

"No, silly, not the price of the car – which by the way, is super sweet of you to do so – but what I mean, is what you said about me. I must ask, do you extend that same discount to all your *"girlfriends"*?"

"Never! Not even one time, Em. And I *sincerely* mean that!"

"Well, then I guess I should feel special, but the truth is, Luke, you haven't officially asked me to be your girlfriend."

Luke swung back on his desk chair, with his hands now clasped behind his head, feeling amused by Emma's fishing expedition, insisting on clarity from him. *"If you are wanting me to declare my undeniable devotion for you, announcing that I will exclusively date you and see no one other, than yes... that is what I am offering to you today – if you will have me as your boyfriend."*

Emma's eyes began to mist over, still absorbing all that she was hearing, finding it so hard to believe that it was actually coming true. When she was only a young girl, she had pretended that Luke Taylor was hers, roll playing in her bedroom that she was a bride - ready to marry him. Emma had went to school with Luke from kindergarten through her senior year of high school, having a *"head-over-heels"* crush on him from the first time she had met him on the school playground, even though he had barely given her the time of day. *"Yes, I will have you Luke, and yes, I will be your girlfriend!"* she announced passionately and proudly, meaning every last word of it.

Luke walked around the desk, not caring if prying eyes were peaking through the small glass partition on either side of his door, wrapping Emma in his arms and kissing her soundly once again. *"I know it's too soon to say this, but I love you, Em. I've known it for a long time, but tried to deny it, but I won't be denying it any longer."*

"I love you too... Luke," Emma conveyed back timidly, repeating the same amazing message back to him, feeling like she was having the best dream of her life and didn't want it to ever end!

He smiled at her, not desiring to change directions, but knowing he needed to if they wanted to get the deal done. "We should get down to business and talk about this loan and what the payments will be. I figured five years - interest free - if your credit is okay - which I'm assuming it is?"

"Yes, Luke, my credit is perfect."

Thirty minutes later, Emma's words were confirmed, and all the paperwork was processed and completed. A nice down payment was given, and Luke was able to get her car payment down to four hundred dollars a month, thrilling Emma greatly with the outcome. She cleaned out her Camry, saying her final goodbyes with a few photos that she took - especially for her mother's benefit – repositioning everything that she had removed from the old car into the RAV4 console box between the two front seats. Luke stood outside, patiently waiting until Emma had completed the task, with Serena noticing again the obvious closeness of the pair as she watched from the glass wall of windows in the sales building.

"Are you pleased with all this?" Luke asked.

"The SUV – absolutely – but you, even more so," she gushed, feeling giddy and numb from it all.

Luke's lips came down to rest on top of Emma's, confirming Serena's suspicions. The receptionist turned and walked away quickly, not wanting to see the obvious any longer, as she shed a few tears in the privacy of the woman's bathroom, out of the sight of everyone else's vision.

"I feel the same way, Em. You just bought a car, but more than that, you won my heart," he confessed. "I just remembered something, you don't even know where I live at anymore, do you?"

"No, I guess I do not...."

"I live off the Dual Highway in Londontowne Apartments."

"Why did you move away from your parents' beautiful house? I still live at home," she confessed, feeling not uncomfortable in saying so.

"I moved because I felt it was time, and I wanted to be closer to work. My brother has also moved out, so it's only my sister Charlotte that is still at the house with my parents."

"I love living at home with my mom and siblings! And I've saved a lot of money in the process, not having to make an outrageous rent payment every month."

"Good for you," Luke answered, not really caring in the least, as he pulled Emma in closer and pressed her up against his semi-hard penis, ready to begin kissing her again. *"So how about coming over tonight after I get off of work, and we can go "at it" again in a real bed instead of a cramped up trunk of your new car?"* he invited seductively, waiting on the answer.

"I would love to, Luke, but can I beg off for another time soon?" she replied with a sweet bat of her long eyelashes. It's been a long day and I know my mom will want an explanation about my new car, and I promised to hang out with my brother and sister tonight. They are always at my dad's house when I'm typically off of work, but tonight is the exception."

"What is your cell number so I can put it in my contacts?" Luke inquired, as he continued to hold Emma close.

"It hasn't changed since high school."

"Neither has mine," he grinned.

"I honestly would have loved seeing you later if I could have made it work out..." she explained, trying to make things clear. I just never thought any of this would have happened like this today."

"I get it. No worries."

One more series of kisses and a squeeze to the toosh, and Luke walked away, with Emma's head swirling in delight at the pleasantry of it all.

Into the driveway of her home in Williamsport, Emma drove her new RAV4, honking the horn the whole way until her family finally appeared at the front door, wondering who the heck was making *"all* that racket". *"Hey, you guys, get in!"* she yelled from her downed window, with the three trying to figure out the mystery.

"Emma, is this a loaner car that you are using while yours is being fixed?" Margie asked in confusion, as she jumped into the front passenger's seat, and Owen and Reagan took to the back of the vehicle.

"No loaner, Mom. I just bought this baby!" she announced proudly.

Chapter 16

"You actually bought this car?" Margie asked, reacting with shocked surprise.

"Well technically, I just bought a SUV! The Camry needed a new engine and it wasn't worth the money to replace it," Emma explained, as she pulled from the driveway and instructed her siblings to *"buckle up"*.

"Well, Emma, I understand your logic behind all this, but since the car had been mine initially, maybe a courtesy call would have been in order before you made such a dramatic financial decision on your own."

Emma glanced at her mother, as she pulled out onto Virginia Avenue, heading towards The Desert Rose. "Seriously, mother, you signed the car over to me a couple years ago, and unfortunately it is old and breaking down now. It was a great car while it lasted, but it was the time to replace it since the engine needed an overhaul. I got a great interest-free loan for five years, and yes, I can afford the monthly payments – if you really need to know these additional details."

"I guess you can afford the loan payments since you don't give me any money towards rent every month," Margie answered stubbornly, hurting Emma's feelings in the process.

Emma pulled into an available space near The Desert Rose, idling with the motor still running. "I can't believe you just said that! I thought we had an agreement that this was your way of helping me out with my new business venture. Plus, I do a lot cleaning and yard work, and also help you out with the kids whenever I can."

"Are you guys fighting?" Reagan begged to know, interrupting the mother-daughter debate in the front seat that was actively taking place.

Both ladies turned around as Margie provided Reagan with the answer. "No sweetie, everything is fine. Emma and I are just making sure that this car is the right one for her. That's all..."

"Doesn't sound like that to me," Owen interjected, looking at Emma now for answers.

"Hey, let's go inside and get a bite to eat, and maybe afterwards we can get some ice cream for desert. *How does that sound?*" Emma heartily suggested, trying to ease the tension and lighten the mood.

"Yeah, ice cream! That sounds great!" Owen yelled back.

"Dinner needs to be eaten first!" Margie insisted, holding on to her irritation from hearing about the new SUV, as she reached for her purse on the floor.

"Yes it does, and it will be eaten!" Emma tossed in, conceding to her mother, as she unfastened her seatbelt and waited on everyone to join her. She pressed her key once and locked up her vehicle, to a pleasant sounding beeping noise that was different from the Camry's. "By the way, my treat tonight."

"That works for me!" Margie replied with an edge, happy that Emma was even willing to do so, as they made their way into The Desert Rose, ready for an early dinner and then some *"hoped-for"* desert afterwards.

Luna's had been steady the majority of the day, with lots of towpath traffic coming up to dine after their hiking and biking stints were completed. Autumn was upon them and the air was now crisp and cool, actually increasing the foot traffic on the C&O Canal. The employees that worked at the C&O Canal corporate building, also frequented Luna's regularly, having become the consistent *"mainstay diners"* which the restaurant relied on for daily business and revenue.

Mason had just showed up, actually for a second time, hoping to grab some dinner and see a glimpse of his *"favorite lady"* from Williamsport. Zoe was truly amazed at his loyalty to the place and his determination to pursue her. *"I'm here again, sweet... heart,"* he announced with his best southern drawl spewing forth, setting her heart to flame.

"You know I won't be disappointed if you choose another restaurant once in awhile," she expressed with a roll of her eyes, as she escorted him to his *"regular"* table that should have had his name inscribed somewhere on it.

Mason began to laugh. "I am fine right here, little lady. I couldn't ask for more in way of menu selections, and of course the *"eye-candy"* in the place keeps me coming back for another look!"

Zoe shook her head, knowing what he was referencing. *"So what would you like tonight?"* she inquired, ready to write down his choice after watching him glance quickly at the menu in front of him.

"I would like a Yuengling and a cheeseburger with fries."

"Again?"

Mason slid the menu in Zoe's direction. "There are two things I can't get enough of... a good burger and you."

Zoe's face reddened, still trying to get used to his forwardness and ceaseless flirting. *"If you say so,"* she answered with a roll of her eyes, walking away with that saucy sway of her hips that kept Mason begging for more.

Ava was in the kitchen, preparing a salad for a customer, as Zoe entered and punched in Mason's meal choice into the computer, barking it out intensely to Dennis at the same time.

"I assume Mason is back?" Ava comically remarked, topping off the salad with a few cherry tomatoes and sweet onion rings.

"How would you know that?" Zoe grilled intensely, waiting on her friend for the answers.

"Well, for one thing, you typically just enter an order in the computer without telling Dennis about it, unless Mason is here, and two, you don't act so *"hot and bothered"* unless he is in the building."

"Is it that obvious?" Zoe paused to ask, with everyone mutually in the kitchen replying back with a – *"yes"*.

Ava began to laugh and walked over Zoe to give her a warm hug. "It's okay girl. I am so happy for you that you have a new beau."

"I'm not sure if you can call one date a *"new beau"* situation."

"So make it two dates, Zoe. He's a *"hottie"* and if you don't grab him, someone else in this small town sure will. Its not every day that a single guy who looks and acts like Mason Jones shows up in Williamsport, Maryland."

Zoe walked outside, behind the restaurant with Ava for moment, just to breathe the air, before the *"evening rush"* was upon them. "Ava, I'm trying my best to get over Noah, but unfortunately for me, it still feels like a very short time since we broke up. I hate to admit this, but my heart is trying to catch up with my head."

"I get it, but I don't get it. I found someone, as you know, and I'm going after happiness - no matter what. Noah Clark is your past. Let Mason be your future!"

"Thanks, Ava. I will try my best. And I'm happy for you that you are dating Philip. I guess this restaurant has become a meeting place for potential romance."

"Maybe we should advertise that!" Ava giggled.

"Maybe you are right!" Zoe agreed, locking arms with her close friend.

The cheeseburger and fries were waiting as Zoe and Ava reentered the back door of the kitchen, with Dennis scolding her that *"the food was going to get cold if she didn't serve it soon"*. With the tray held high, Zoe slid it off expertly onto the awaiting stand, and then placed the plate in front of Mason afterwards, along with his beer. "Anything else?"

"Yes, there is."

"And what would that be?"

"I need to file a complaint about this establishment."

Zoe looked somewhat puzzled, thinking Mason was always thrilled with everything about the place. *"Has the service been lacking in some way?*

Mason laughed, reaching over to touch Zoe's arm. "No darling... The only thing that is lacking is my time alone with you. That is my only complaint... This place holds you hostage and I honestly just want to see you again," he explained affectionately. *"How about tonight after work? Can you slip away and just hang out with me for a bit?"*

Zoe laughed and took a seat close by Mason, leaning in for his ears only. *"You scared me there for a minute. I didn't want to have to fire someone. What did you have in mind if I agree to see you after work?"*

"Maybe a walk around town and then we can head to The Third Base for a drink afterwards?"

"Wow, I haven't been there in a while."

"Then is it a date?"

"I should go home first and change out of my work clothes, but I guess I can meet up with you afterwards."

Mason shook his head, sensing that she was trying once again to keep space between them. *"Why don't you let me pick you up this time? I promise I won't bite!"*

Zoe smirked, knowing he was obviously on to her and aware of her tactics to maintain some distance. "There is really no sense in resisting your charms now, is there?"

"No there isn't, dar... ling, and I'm glad you are finally coming to that realization, because I have no plans of giving up."

Emma, Margie and the kids sat in a table in the back of The Desert Rose feasting on steamers and the *"soup of the day"*, with Owen being the only exception, ordering chicken tenders and fries instead. *"What do you say about ice cream now? You guys still up for that?"* Emma offered excitedly, with a loving grin directed at her siblings only, glad they had finally finished their meals.

"I want a cone with chocolate ice cream and sprinkles," Reagan announced.

"I want a banana split!" Owen chimed in.

Emma began to laugh. *"Seriously, Owen, where do you put it all?"* she asked with a shake of her head, very aware - from working there in the past – that this selection of a banana split was the biggest desert that The Desert Rose had to offer. Three large scoops of vanilla, chocolate and strawberry ice cream, a banana sliced in half and placed on both sides of the dish, several different toppings, nuts, whipped cream and maraschino cherries placed over the top, were the list of ingredients included in the grand finale ice cream masterpiece.

"He is a bottomless pit right now, Emma. You certainly should realize that!" Margie sighed, having added more money to the food budget recently because of her growing children, without an increase in child support from her ex.

"Whatever he wants! As long as he finishes it," Emma retorted, still on a *"high"* from being with Luke, as well as the excitement of owning a new car.

The kids got their choice and Margie decided on a small dip of vanilla in a sugar cone, with Emma selecting a small dish of pistachio – which was her favorite. The family took a leisurely stroll together around Byron Memorial Park, as they enjoyed their desert and the last lingering rays of sunlight, before heading back to the house for the evening.

"Get your baths now!" Margie barked out to the younger two, as they piled through the front door. "You have school tomorrow, so after your baths it's time for homework and then it's off to bed! *So no getting sidetracked! Do you hear me?"*

"Yes, Mom!" They both yelled back, with the sound of bedroom doors slamming at the same time in unison.

Emma sat at the bar in the kitchen, waiting patiently on Margie to join her. She could overhear her mother in the hallway, like she did most evenings, yelling loudly and repeating her same bedtime demands on the kids. *"I wanted to speak with you about something…"*

"Is it about your new vehicle again?"

"No mom, it isn't. It's about something else."

"And what would that be?"

"Well, I wanted to share with you that it's been a day of several wonderful surprises for me. I got a new SUV, as you already know, but something else amazing and unexpected has happened today."

"Well tell me… the suspense is killing me," Margie answered somewhat skeptically, making direct eye contact now with her beautiful daughter.

"I guess I don't need to be doing those dating sites that you suggested after all. I have a new boy friend," Emma beamed happily.

"You do?" Margie responded with a level of surprise.

"Yes, I do."

"Well, don't hold back, who is he?" She asked with a pleased smile suddenly radiating all over her face, wanting to hear all the details.

"Mom, it's hard to believe, but actually true. It's Luke Taylor."

"Luke Taylor? Your childhood friend whose family is wealthy from owning a car dealership?"

"Mom, that is somewhat rude, don't you think?"

"How so? That I'm concerned about your well-being and want to see you happy and successful in life? And if a man is the means to that end, than so be it!"

Emma shook her head, not wanting to be an opportunist like her mother obviously was, where men were concerned. "I like Luke for Luke, not for what he has financially. We have been friends for years – basically starting out in elementary school – and I guess we got closer when Zoe and Noah were dating and we all started hanging out together. We never pursued things with each other then, probably because our friends were dating, but now that their relationship has ended, we have decided to see what could happen between the two of us."

Margie's face lite up like someone had turned on a bright light. "I couldn't be happier for you, Emmie. What a perfect choice for you in a man! He's handsome and rich! Why don't you invite him over for dinner this week?"

"Slow down, mom. Seriously! This is just all beginning to unfold between Luke and I, and I don't want to scare him off by you overwhelming him with our family life. If we are *"meant to be"* he will be here at our house sharing meals soon enough. *Can you try to deal with that?"*

"Of course... " Margie conceded, reaching over to give Emma a warm hug.

Reagan ran out to the kitchen with a towel wrapped around her middle, as a trail of water droplets kept hitting the floor off of her wet, disheveled hair. *"Mom, I need some clean pajamas from the dryer! Can you get them for me?"*

"Oh my word, my dear, you are getting the floor soak and wet! You could have yelled from the bathroom for a set of pajamas!"

"I was going to, until I heard you guys talking about Emma's new boyfriend, so I decided to come out here and ask you for myself."

Emma began to laugh. "I guess I can't keep anything a secret around here."

"No, you can't!" Margie countered. "You definitely can not!"

Chapter 17

Zoe showered and changed into black leggings and a long-sleeved navy blue sweater that featured a plunging neckline, before styling her long brown, honey kissed hair into curls like she used to wear it when she was dating Noah. It felt odd to be doing so again, and this time for a new guy whom she was hoping to impress, still having a tough time with it all. She applied her makeup expertly as Emma had taught her years earlier, and then slipped into some black flats, applying a dab of her favorite perfume behind each earlobe and also on her wrists, hoping Mason would like the scent. A diamond, heart-shaped necklace that Nana Ruth had given her for a birthday not so long ago, was secured around Zoe's neck, which she felt was the perfect finishing touch.

"I guess I'm passable," she assessed with a smile, as she looked at Luna who was settled in on top of her bed, silently giving her *"the eye"* and watching her every move until she was ready to leave.

The kitchen was a clamor of activity, as Zoe joined the noise-filled room where cooking on the stove, news on the TV, and laughter was all taking place. Bryan had invited Kelly over for dinner, and he was busily serving up the spaghetti and meatballs that he had prepared, already placing the salad and garlic bread on the table.

"Well, don't you look exceptionally pretty!" Bryan praised, as Zoe made her grand entrance in front of the pair.

"Thanks, dad. I have a date tonight."

"Who's the lucky guy?" Kelly inquired with some interest, as she twirled her pasta on a fork and spoon.

Zoe paused, not sure she wanted to divulge the information, but trying her best to get over her apprehensions. "Someone new in town that is here working for the C&O Canal."

"*How did you ever meet him?*" Kelly continued pleasantly, doing her best to make conversation with Zoe as she sat at the table eating.

"He's a regular at *Luna's*, and I guess we have been *connecting*."

Bryan stopped what he was doing at the stove to turn and study his daughter. "*Didn't you already mention to me that you had a date with him a few days ago?*"

"*Am I being interrogated?*" Zoe shot back, feeling somewhat defensive now, finding the whole discussion a bit uncomfortable.

"Honey, I'm sorry. I wasn't trying to step on your toes," Bryan consoled, coming around to stand beside of Zoe where she was waiting near the door.

"It's fine. Sorry I'm a little jumpy, but I just want things to go smoothly. Yes, it is our second date, but I'm not rushing into a new relationship with him."

Kelly and Bryan locked eyes, silently reading the other one's minds. "*Is he a gentleman, Zoe?*" Kelly prodded gently.

"He has been nothing but a gentleman."

"*Well consider that to be a good thing, because a gentleman will never rush you into a relationship until you are ready. Always remember that!*" Kelly expressed with some sound wisdom, remembering a different place and time when she and Bryan had just started dating and were going through the very same process.

Zoe's phone began to ring, with Mason doing the calling. "*Hello?*"

"*I just arrived. Do you want me to come to the front door and scoop you up?"*

Zoe's slightly cocked her head, confused by the expression. *"Scoop me up?"*

"Yes, silly, come to the front door and escort you to the car."

"No, that's fine, Mason. I will be right out." She disconnected the call immediately, giving Luna a secure hug before releasing her pet to her father's care.

"His accent and sayings can be so strange at times."

"Where is he originally from?"

"Texas... Austin, Texas - to be exact. And he wears cowboy boots too!"

Bryan and Kelly began to laugh. "Well, that's a big change from what you have been around in the past."

"Don't you know it!" Zoe said with a sigh. "There's no need to wait up for me. I'm not sure what time I'll be home."

"Wasn't planning on it, my dear. Have fun!" Bryan wished, as Zoe went out the door to meet up with Mason. He was standing by his Land Rover with his arms crossed in front of him, looking as handsome as ever in his tight jeans and his white dress shirt that had one too many buttons undone, showing off a slight fringe of the hair on his chest.

"Well, don't you look as sweet as sugar, dar... ling!" Mason belted out all southern like, as Zoe walked in his direction, with his words making her giggle.

"And you look like a guy from Texas!"

Mason began to laugh. *"Teasing me again, huh?"* he asked while opening the front passenger's door and helping Zoe in, with a slight lift to her elbow.

"Maybe..." she teased back, as they pulled away from the house, assuming that Bryan and Kelly were peaking out from behind the curtains, taking it all in.

"Well, he definitely has one thing going for him. *He is quite handsome!*" Kelly mentioned, as they walked back to the kitchen, away from the living room curtains where they were spying on Zoe and her date.

"Oh, you think so, do you? More handsome than I am?" Bryan enticed, grabbing her around the waist and pulling Kelly in closely as he nuzzled her neck, making her laugh from the non-stop tickling he was giving her.

"Bryan, I can't breathe!" she begged, doing her best to pull away. "Of course you are more handsome than that Texan, my love. No one can compare with you," she offered, cherishing every moment with her wonderful, kind boyfriend. "For Zoe's sake, though, I hope things work out with him. She deserves a good-looking, nice guy who can make her forget about that past relationship with Noah Clark - that insensitive jerk who broke her heart!"

Bryan took his seat again at the table, finishing up his plate of pasta. "I liked Noah. I know he did Zoe bad in the end, but I honestly feel he didn't have the maturity level to continue in the relationship. He wasn't ready for an engagement and marriage, and I bet he was feeling the pressure from Zoe to think about such things."

"God, Bryan, I hope you haven't been that blunt with Zoe concerning her breakup. What you just said would crush her... you know. I would think for the majority of women, they dream about an engagement and then finally a marriage in their lives. Four years is a long time to be dating someone without taking it to the next level. *What do you think she should have expected from Noah after four years of dating him? I get it, why don't you?*"

Bryan shook his head and carefully considered his words before continuing, thinking back to his first marriage and the early years with Cynthia, and how things had gone wrong. Women mature faster than guys do. That is a known fact. Imagine if Noah would have asked Zoe to marry him and then they would have gotten married soon thereafter. Of course they would have had a big event with everyone present, and all of Zoe's fairytale dreams would have come true that day. Or so she thought…. living together, working, bills… you name it… would have been added to the mix of this new beginning of their lives together. She is no longer at home and neither is he. They probably would have been living in an apartment or house that they really couldn't afford at that time. Noah didn't have a job, so that would have been something that needed to be figured out to keep harmony in the relationship. Talk about pressure! Honestly, I could have seen them separating within the first year of marriage if they would have kept going the way they were."

Kelly got up from the table, placing her hands on her hips, taking a defensive posture. *"My word, Bryan, that kind of negativity is horrible concerning marriage!"*

Bryan stared at his beautiful girlfriend, trying to read between the lines. This behavior from Kelly was not normal for her. She was the *"laid-back"* type that didn't take offense to many things, which he had discovered in the time they had dated. He rose from his seat, joining her where she stood, wrapping his arms around her once again. "Darling, I am not a young man like Noah is. I know the difference between frivolous dating and serious dating. Let me get one thing perfectly straight, I love you and this relationship is serious for me. I want only you, and I have no plans of breaking this relationship up – ever!"

Kelly's eyes began to mist up. "Thank you, Bryan, for explaining that to me in such a nice way. I love you too, and I feel exactly the same way."

"Well that's good to hear! How about we clean up this kitchen and then depart to the bedroom, after I take Luna outside for a quick walk?

I think we should take advantage of our *"alone time"* while Zoe is away on her date."

"How about you walk Luna *now* while I clean up the kitchen by myself?" Kelly challenged and teased, reaching up to kiss Bryan passionately on the lips, feeling the sudden need to be satisfied.

"I guess I can make that happened," he seductively enticed, while rubbing up against her for a few seconds more.

Bryan removed the leash from off the hook on the wall, and snapped it into place on Luna's collar, with the Lab being more than ready to go outside and get in her time with the male member of the household. "I think Luna is anxious for her walk."

Kelly laughed, "Yes, I would say you are right!" she agreed, as Bryan walked from the house with the canine glued to his side. She loaded the dishwasher quickly, putting the remaining pasta and sauce away in the refrigerator, wiping everything off afterwards with a sanitizing spray, feeling anxious for her boyfriend's speedy return. It was a silent thought that she kept well hidden, but she too hoped that one day a surprise proposal would be forthcoming, and that it would happen sooner rather than later. A lovely wedding would then be planned out with the man of her dreams who had won her heart – Bryan Carter – her best friend and lover, and the one that she desired more than anything!

Chapter 18

Mason drove around the block, trying his best to find a parking spot, with the realization that parking was at a premium in front of The Third Base Bar. "I hope you don't mind walking," he mentioned casually, as he helped Zoe down from the passenger's seat, lifting her from the waist.

"I thought that was our plan anyway. I wore these flats so that we could walk a little. *That is, if you would still like to?*"

"Your call, my dear. I know you have been on your feet all day at work."

Zoe looked at Mason, realizing he was always kind and considerate, never missing a beat at being mindful of her needs. "If you don't mind, I think going right to The Third Base and trying to find a place to sit, may be the best thing - instead of taking a leisurely stroll tonight. I can already tell that it's overly crowded inside, since all the parking spaces have been taken up in the front of the building."

Mason smiled, reaching for her hand. "Lead on, beautiful!" he grinned, as they walked together the several blocks to their destination.

The bar was crowded, just as Zoe assumed, with wall-to-wall people all around. There was barely a place to sit except for a random seat or two, but unfortunately not any that were together. *"We don't have to stay here!"* Zoe shouted in Mason's ear, over the loud booming of a country song that was being played through a large speaker system.

"Why not, dar...ling? *I don't mind standing. You can have that seat,"* he offered, pointing in the direction of a vacant barstool. "I'm sure another one will be available real soon, as soon as someone decides to leave." Mason glanced around the room as Zoe was trying to make up her mind whether she wanted to stay or not, taking in the overall atmosphere of the place. "The crowd is here because of the football game that is being broadcasted," he explained, seeing a large group positioned at several tables that had been pushed together, in front of over-sized television screen, hooting and hollering and high-fiving after every touchdown was scored for their particular team.

"Yes, that is always the case during football season. Are you sure you are okay with being here?" Zoe asked one more time, still not wanting to make Mason stand.

"Absolutely, I'm sure! You grab that before someone else does, and I will get us a couple of beers in the meantime. Or would you like something else to drink?" He asked politely, not really considering what Zoe drank besides Margaritas from *La Paz*.

"Beer is fine," she smiled. "I drink Yuengling just like you do," she confessed. "See if they have Oktoberfest though. I love that variety this time of the year."

"Will do!" he answered, walking away from her at a fast clip towards the bar. Mason returned with an Oktoberfest and a Black and Tan, placing the requested one in front of Zoe and taking a swig of the other he still held in his hand. "Are you hungry, because the selection is pretty much limited to just pizza and pretzels. *Are you aware of that?"*

"I am now," she giggled. "Honestly, I forgot that what they primarily offer is alcohol and snacks. Typically, I didn't come here in the past for a meal."

"I'm fine with the *"bar grub"* if you are. After all, I get my fill at lunch when I eat at *Luna's*," he smiled reassuredly, trying to take the pressure off of her for something better.

"That works for me too," she agreed, feeling suddenly content and relaxed after drinking half of the beer.

Mason rested an arm on the back of Zoe's barstool, just as the front door swung open again to the establishment. Three females entered, all dressed in trashy looking clothes, with overly made-up faces and hairstyles that demanded to be noticed, obviously trying to gain some attention from the males that were present. They all wore very short dresses that over-accentuated their breasts with plunging necklines, choosing 4-inch stacked high heels - all similar in style and height. Zoe glanced over in their direction, realizing that one of the worst possible scenarios was suddenly playing out. It was Sophia and *"her posse of bitches"* from high school, all obviously out for the evening and trying to play the part and pimp out the guys at The Third Base - or whatever other bar they had already strolled into - while making the rounds.

"We don't have to stay here, Mason, if you truly want to leave after this drink," Zoe interjected nervously, trying to hurriedly finish her Oktoberfest now and get out of the place unscathed.

"Is something wrong?" he questioned, seeing her sudden change of mood.

The question was answered as Sophia and *"the squad"* walked over and made their outrageous appearance, attempting to place themselves right up against Mason in the overly crowded room that had very little space left in it to move or breathe.

"Well hello there, Zoe. What brings you in here tonight?" Sophia asked, as she fluttered her lashes and looked over every square inch of Mason, undressing him in her mind from head to toe.

"I'm out for the evening with a friend..." she muttered under her breath, wishing like anything that Sophia would just leave and crawl back into the pathetic hole that she came from.

"Do I know you?" she purred, while thrusting her breasts forward towards the handsome Texan, trying to conveniently rub up against Mason's side, waiting on the answer.

Mason glanced at the *"harlot-looking"* females and then at Zoe, realizing they were making her feel very uncomfortable. *"No, I can't say I know you,"* he answered bluntly and somewhat rudely, turning his back away from Sophia, and focusing his attention entirely on Zoe again, trying to avoid the intrusion and gain a little more space as he moved in closer towards the barstool.

Sophia proceeded to make her way around to the other side, trying to gain Zoe's attention once again. She did not care in the least about the discomfort she was causing, as she kept her eyes glued on Mason the whole entire time. *"Have you heard from Noah?"* she yelled out over the loud blare of the music that continued to play in the background.

Zoe's eyes widened in disbelief, realizing Sophia was doing her best to ruin the date she was on with Mason. *"No, I haven't heard from Noah! You know that it isn't a secret, Sophie, that we broke up! So why are you asking me such a ridiculous question?"*

Sophie pouted up her lips, acting if she were hurt by Zoe's reaction. *"Zoe, how was I supposed to know if you and Noah had made up or not? People do change their minds all the time about breakups."*

"Does it look like Noah or I have changed our minds?" she retorted angrily, standing now beside of Mason, wrapping her arm around his waist in way of a silent message to her *"female arch enemy"* from the past, hoping she would back off.

Mason took Zoe's lead, wrapping his free arm around her waist also. *"Darling, let's get out of here. It's time to leave so I can have you all to myself,"* he expressed with his best Texas twang springing forth, as Mason immediately came down on her mouth, planting a lingering kiss fully on her lips - just to give all three of the *"barflies"* that were taking it all in - a memorable eyeful.

Sophia and her friends were salivating and hungry for the answers, eyeing the scene like a porno movie playing out in front of them.

"What's your name, hot stuff?" Sophia called out loudly, as Mason and Zoe walked hand in hand towards the front door, ignoring the outburst entirely.

Zoe turned with a laugh, looking back at the desperate trio who could only dream of having someone as desirable as Mason to hang out with. She waved at them mockingly, almost as if she were on a float in a parade, bidding them farewell and departing once again to the outside world of The Third Base. Immediately, Mason and Zoe began bursting out laughing, realizing it was a comical moment they had just mutually shared between them.

"Wow, who the hell were those *"skanky looking"* women?" Mason questioned, making Zoe laugh all over again.

"You think they are skanky looking?"

"Let's just put it this way – Not anyone I would want to be seen with. They all look as if they've been fucked *"one too many times"*, if you ask me!"

"Oh my word, Mason, I never heard you speaking like that!"

"Sorry, Zoe. Maybe it's the beer doing the talking."

"It's okay," she giggled. "I actually find it hilarious that you feel that way. I have known Sophia and *"her girls"* since high school. She has always done her best to get to me with her cruel insults. I will be honest," she added as they continued to walk down the street a couple more blocks, "Sophie dated Noah – my ex – in high school before I started dating him. I don't think she ever got over the fact that he chose me over her. I mean, come on... we are lunar opposites. I'm sure you can even see that."

"It's obvious why he chose you over her."

"Why is that?" Zoe replied, suddenly curious and standing now to face him, wanting to hear his take on things. "You are naturally

beautiful and real, and she is fake and superficial, having to work a lot harder at impressing a man so that he will take notice of her. No comparison at all, Zoe. You are *"a ten"* and she is at best *"a five",*" he added sincerely, while bending down to kiss her again, but this time for her eyes only, without anyone else in the barroom nosily taking it all in.

Zoe broke free after a few moments, looking up at Mason's handsome face. "There is another place right down the street that you may like. It is called the C&O Grill and Pub and I know for a fact they do serve good food, and it's more than just pizza and pretzels. What do you say, should we attempt to go to another place and keep our fingers crossed that Sophia and her gang won't show up there too and stalk us?" She lightheartedly suggested, feeling free to joke around with Mason now.

"Sounds like a plan, but only if I can have one more delightful, passionate kiss out of you, before we make our entrance."

"You don't have to ask me a second time," Zoe answered, while being wrapped securely in Mason's embrace, lost to his touch and his magical tongue that was enchanting her, making her forget the name Noah Clark – at least for a few amazing moments.

Chapter 19

As promised, the food at the C&O Grill and Pub was more to Mason and Zoe's liking, each choosing a grilled chicken sandwich and fries. Sophia and her *"girls"* did not venture into the place, probably already hitting it up earlier before they made their appearance at The Third Base. Zoe was relieved and actually began to relax and unwind after having another Oktoberfest, realizing she had Mason finally all to herself.

"Are you ready to leave or would you like something else? Maybe more to eat or another beer perhaps?" Mason inquired sweetly.

Zoe looked at her cell, eager to know the time. "It's almost eleven and unfortunately work beckons early in the morning. *I'm ready if you are?"* She smiled, as Mason reached over to squeeze her hand lovingly, wishing the date wasn't ending quite yet.

The bill was paid as the two made their way from the establishment, with several eyes following them out the door as they departed. Zoe was well known in Williamsport now, along with her sad story concerning the breakup with Noah, and no one other than Mason had attempted to date her with her *"up-tight, pissed-off"* attitude she always exhibited. She had become angry with men, and the guys at the bar were fascinated that someone would be brave enough to even attempt to be around her.

As they walked towards Mason's Land Rover, he wrapped his arms around Zoe's waist, pulling her in closely towards him. *"I have a question to ask of you."*

"Okay?"

"I would love for you to see my place before I take you home.

Would you be willing to stop by just for a short while?"

Zoe hesitated, searching Mason's eyes. *"If this is your way of getting me in your place just to have sex with you, I'm not ready for that yet, Mason,"* she state clearly, uttering a staunch warning.

Mason began to shake his head and chuckle. "Zoe, that is not my attention at all, although, please don't get me wrong, I would love for that to be happening at some point! After all, I am a man and you are one hot, beautiful woman who is very desirable. I promise to be a total gentleman though, until you tell me otherwise," he added tactfully, staring into her questioning eyes that only wanted to trust and believe in him fully.

"Where do you live exactly?"

"So is that a yes? You will come to my place?" he asked with excitement.

Zoe paused to study Mason one last time before answering. "It is a yes, but if anything happens that makes me feel even slightly uncomfortable, it will be our last date. *Is that understood?"*

"Totally!" he countered quickly.

Mason drove to his apartment complex at Springfield Farms - which was a short distance away - parking in his reserved spot and then walking around and helping Zoe from the vehicle.

"I've heard about this apartment complex, but have never been here," she casually mentioned, as they climbed the steps to his unit. As Mason unlocked the door to his apartment, Zoe's anxieties began to take hold, having thoughts of why she was even willing to venture into his residence in the first place. *"Maybe this wasn't such a good idea after all,"* she said with panic-filled eyes, showing some hesitation to enter.

"We don't have to go inside, Zoe, if you have changed your mind, but I am a man of honor and I'm telling you nothing is going to take place in there unless you want it to. You are in charge and calling the shots, dar... ling," Mason expressed sincerely, locking his darker green eyes with her lighter ones.

Zoe could feel her resolve relaxing once again. Mason's *"East Texas" accent* always did that to her, and for some uncanny reason she felt safe and secure when she was around him, not having to fear the unknown. "Okay, lead on... I'm sorry Mason, to be acting so overly cautious. A bad relationship can do that to you."

Once inside, with the door closed behind them, he turned to look at her. "You aren't the only one who has gone through tough times when a relationship goes *"south"*. It isn't only females who get emotionally crushed and cast aside, you know. I am rather private about my past, but I went through something similar with someone, just like you have."

Zoe looked at Mason with a new sense of curiosity from hearing this discovery about his past, as they paused in what appeared to be a living room that opened up into the *"open concept"* kitchen-dining area, a short distance away. *"May I ask what exactly happened, if you don't mind telling me?"*

"I was engaged for a couple years, and then my girlfriend changed her mind about the engagement and broke things off with me."

Zoe looked shocked, not expecting that sort of revelation from him. *"Oh my word, Mason. Why would she do that to you?"*

He walked away before answering, switching on the lamp that was positioned on an end table right beside of the sofa, returning to Zoe afterwards. "I'm not totally sure what brought the whole thing on, but I feel she was seeing someone else on the side. I was busy with my job then, and she spent a good amount of her free time at the gym when I was working. A mutual friend told me it was a guy she had met there, but she denied it, only saying she wasn't ready to settle down and be married any time soon. We had already started the beginning stages of the *"wedding planning"*, but it all came to an end after that, along with our relationship. I tried to tell her we could keep dating and put the marriage on hold for however long she chose, but she didn't want any parts of it."

Zoe wondered about her name and maybe even more sorted details of the supposed betrayal, but didn't feel it was her right to ask any additional questions at that time. "Wow, I'm *so very* sorry, Mason. She definitely gave up a good guy when it comes to you."

"You think so?" he smiled, enjoying and needing her praise.

"Yes, I do… I guess we both have suffered things that are unfair in our love lives, and it does take some real effort to move on."

"Yes, you are right about that, but I am a little further along in the process than you are, Zoe. I've been broken up with Linda for over a year now, and she actually does have another boyfriend. "Hey, enough of this seriousness! Let me give you the promised tour of my apartment!" Mason grinned, grabbing her hand and leading her down the hallway. "The place isn't super big, but hey, I'm only one guy and how much space do I really need?"

"I agree!" Zoe replied, letting Mason lead her then from room to room, as she noticed his sparse furnishings. She took in every detail of the bedroom especially, taking a little extra time to linger there. *"You have a king-sized bed?"*

"Yes. Is that an problem?" He joked pleasantly.

"No, I guess I just didn't expect a king-sized bed, that's all."

"I'm a tall guy, Zoe, and I enjoy stretching out."

She giggled, understanding his logic. "Well you are from Texas where things are done up in a mighty *"big way"*.

"You got that right!" he answered, patting her slightly on the backside as they left the bedroom, making her react and jump once again with his advances. "I'm sorry, Zoe, it was an honest mistake," he shrugged, making her laugh.

"It's okay, I think I finally realize you are harmless."

"Well, I'm glad you have that figured out! Can I get you something to drink?" he offered, after walking into the small kitchen with her.

"No, that isn't necessary. Unfortunately, it's time for me to go home though. You have a very nice apartment and thank you for showing it to me, but it's quarter of twelve and I must definitely be going."

"I understand," Mason replied with a knowing smile, as they walked back down the steps and towards his vehicle, ready to be driven home.

"I had a nice time tonight."

"Me too," Mason agreed, as they pulled into Zoe's driveway. "I would love to see you again, if you are willing?"

Her heart was resisting, but her head was telling her to go for it. "Yes, Mason, I would like that very much."

"Then lets make it happen as soon as you are free again – and hopefully that won't be too long, because I definitely have been enjoying your company," he confessed with his strong Texas draw declaring his desires.

Zoe smiled, taking in the tenderness and sincerity of his words. "I will be free again in a couple of days once I can get evening coverage at *Luna's* taken care of."

Mason leaned over and found Zoe's lips that were eager for a goodnight kiss. It was all that she had longed for, the entire time they were at the apartment, being honestly surprised that he hadn't put the moves on her there. Several moments later, the *"make-out"* session with its series of tantalizing kisses, came to an abrupt end. All that remained afterwards was the sound of heavy breathing. It was obvious that things were intensifying between them, but the future and what would happen next was still to be determined.

As Zoe lay in her bed, with Luna taking her normal sleeping position beside of her, a text message came through from Mason with a *"beeping"* signal that woke her from sleep.

Made it home and I can't stop thinking about those last amazing kisses that we just shared. This isn't going to be easy, keeping my word and remaining that gentleman that I promised you I would always be.

I understand…. And perhaps I don't want you to remain that gentleman much longer, she typed out timidly.

Zoe, are you saying what I think you are saying?

Maybe… please give me a couple days to think about things before we see each other again, and then I will let you know.

I'll be dreaming about you.

Me too… she ended, silencing the phone and not waiting on his response.

Mason lay in his king-sized bed, with his hands clasped behind his head, with an *"erection"* that was just begging to be satisfied, remembering the kissing and every other detail of the date. He was excited about the possibility of making love to Zoe, if what she was implying in the text was true. For now though, his desires would be fulfilled through his sexual fantasies, as he had already imagined numerous times over since meeting her, knowing that in time the "real thing" would be so much better and worth the wait.

Chapter 20

"Hey, what's up?" Emma asked of Zoe. She was deep in thought, looking over the restaurant's spreadsheet of expenditures that was on her computer, not paying anyone that was present in the kitchen much mind.

"Just making sure we can survive here - minus Pappy Joe and Nana's Ruth's help any longer. I thought it was sure thing, but we have been down with the numbers the last couple of days."

Emma shrugged and shook her head, while grabbing a chair and bringing it in closer towards the desk where Zoe was working and evaluating. Chef Dennis was nearby preparing a *"soup du jour"* for the lunch crowd that would be showing up in only a few hours, tuning everyone out also. *"Such a worry-wart, my dear friend. You know we are fine,"* she offered, with kind reassurance in her eyes.

"You seem to be especially cheerful today," Zoe observed, pausing from her work. *"What going on?"* she asked with interest, knowing her best friend well and the different moods that she displayed.

Emma's face lit up, beaming with utter happiness, standing to make her profound statement and point known. *"I have a new boyfriend!"* she exclaimed with much enthusiasm and zeal.

Zoe's eyes widened with the news that she never expected to hear as of late. *"Well, when did this all happen, Em?"*

"Honestly... probably around the same time that you started to see Mason."

Zoe looked somewhat confused. "Slow down a moment, Emma. I've had a couple innocent dates with Mason, and that's all it's been.

I'm not sure that qualifies as *"us"* actually seriously dating or that we are considered to be *"boyfriend and girlfriend"*."

"If you say so," Emma barked out sarcastically with a roll of her eyes, not paying Zoe any mind.

"So, Em, who is this mystery man that you have not told me about?"

Emma stalled for a moment, not typically being one to hold back, but considering how this information could affect the close relationship that she had with her friend and business partner. *"He is someone you already know."*

"Oh my God, Em, just tell me who he is, for heaven's sakes! I got a busy day ahead and honestly don't have time for all these silly childish games!" Zoe expressed in earnest, rising from her chair and shutting off her computer in the process, with Dennis now looking on at the two females that he greatly admired, silently taking in their drama-filled lives yet for another time.

"Can we walk outside and talk in private?"

"Of course," Zoe agreed, finding the whole situation to be a painful distraction, but obliging her friend never-the-less.

Out back, and with the door closed, no one was there to hear the conversation - just as Emma had requested. *"Zoe, my new boyfriend is Luke Taylor."*

"Huh?" Zoe answered, not grasping the reality of the situation. *"Luke, as in Noah's friend, Luke?"*

"Well that is a peculiar way of saying it, but yes, Luke Taylor, the friend of Noah's – whom, if you recall, we all used to hang out with together."

"I can't believe you are seeing him!" Zoe lashed out in disbelief.

"Why would you do such a thing to me, Emma?"

"Do such a thing to you? Seriously, Zoe! What gives you the right to dictate who I should be dating?"

Zoe paced nervously, walking at a fast clip away from the back-end of *Luna's*, heading down Potomac Street and towards the C&O Canal, with Emma right on her heels and close behind her. "I think I need some space, Em!"

"Well, you are not getting it right now!" She yelled out in her direction, trying to keep up with her hotheaded pal who was on a mission to get away from her and the situation that she didn't want to deal with for the moment.

Zoe headed towards the Conococheague Aqueduct, with Emma continuing to squawk in her ear, trying to justify her dating decisions. "Emma, please go back to *Luna's*. I just need to be alone for awhile," she pleaded in earnest, as she looked out over the Potomac River, almost at the very same spot she had said her final goodbyes to Noah - several months earlier - giving him *"the middle finger"* in a fit of rage and denial over their unanticipated breakup.

"That is always your way, isn't it? To cast aside someone when you are feeling vulnerable and upset?"

"I do not cast people aside! They cast me aside!"

Emma stood silently, studying the *"hurt inner child"* of Zoe that still had not put the past to rest. *"I honestly feel sorry for you. Do you know that? Life is too short to not get over the bullshit of someone who has affected you in such a negative way! I know your mother screwed you over when you were a young girl, and then Noah came around for round two and only added insult to injury, but I am not one of those bad forces in your life that has tried to destroy you! I am the person who has always been there for you since day one of us meeting. Don't you realize that?"*

Zoe began to cry, with a steady stream of tears now cascading down her face. "Emma, I know what you are saying is true, but I can't always be the strong person that you want me to be, as hard as I try. I realize that Luke has treated me well in the past, but remember that you were the one who always told me that he was no different than Noah, and that they were all nothing but a bunch of *"players"*."

"Yes, I did tell you that, and I guess I was wrong... Luke isn't Noah. He is settled in his life with a good job, and he claims he has always had an interest in me, but kept his true feelings to himself because of you and Noah dating."

"When did you figure this all out?"

"I just bought a new car and Luke helped me with the purchase. We did a lot of talking while I was at the dealership and we were alone together, and the truth finally came out then."

"Just like that?"

"Yes, Zoe, just like that. I am not you, always over-thinking things so much. I have always liked Luke, as you are well aware, and this time I am taking a chance at love – no matter what the outcome!"

Zoe shook her head in disbelief, returning her line of vision to the river in front of her, taking in several kayakers down below who were enjoying their morning activity, as they floated by peacefully. "If he makes you happy then I am happy for you..." she breathed out quietly, resigned that she needed to accept what was happening, hoping to end the painful conversation quickly.

Emma reached out to hug her, with Zoe pulling back slightly, still being on guard. *"Thank you, my friend, for supporting me in all this."*

"I'm trying to be supportive, but you must realize that it may take me a while to get totally on board. I need to see if Luke remains consistent with you."

"He loves me, Zoe."

Zoe began to laugh and shake her head again. *"Does he now? He went from not dating you to telling you that he loves you? Don't you see that as a major red flag, Emma?"*

"We made love, Zoe. It was wonderful and I may be a naive fool, but I'm not putting up barriers of any kind with Luke! I love him too, and love sometimes doesn't have a long, drawn-out time table like you think it should have."

Zoe was totally shocked by what Emma had just disclosed, feeling like she was in the midst of a bad dream that she could not wake up from. Everything she was hearing and seeing - including the location of the very spot she was standing on and revisiting for the first time since her breakup with Noah – was too much to bear.

"Let me get this straight, you are dating Luke now and have already had sex with him, and you even have a new car on top of all of this?"

"That about sums it up," Emma tossed back at her without care, not really *"giving a shit"* how ridiculous it all sounded to Zoe. "And he is renting an apartment near his work!" Emma added, wanting to share all the exciting details of her new relationship.

"Did you see his place yet? Is that where you had sex with him?"

"No, actually I haven't seen his place yet, and to answer your question honestly, we had sex in my new car - out in the country and in the woods."

Zoe placed her hands on her hips and stood glaring in disbelief, looking her friend over from head to toe, trying to focus in on the madness she was hearing. *"My God, Emma, have you lost your frickin mind? This isn't like you to be so frivolous and carefree in your behavior!"*

"Yeah, I know it isn't, but Zoe it feels damn good to be this wild and adventurous of a person. I regret nothing and will do it all over again if Luke asks me too."

"I must say I'm shocked, but will try to believe the best, even if it is difficult for me to do so," Zoe conceded, feeling concerned and suddenly nauseous, hoping that her best friend didn't end up getting hurt like she had, once Luke tired of her.

"Thank you, Zoe," Emma answered, feeling relieved that the news was finally out in the open, as they turned to walk back to *Luna's* together. Zoe was no longer resisting, desiring only to be left alone at the canal to ponder things over in her mind, which was a major turning point for her - giving Emma some peace of mind. "So how are things going with Mason? Are sparks flying in the *"love department"* for you guys as well?" she grinned, locking arms with her *"bestie",* happy for a few additional moments of *"alone time"* with her.

"I like him a lot and he likes me too. I did get to see where he lives, unlike you, who only ventures out into the woods to do the unimaginable," she teased, suddenly lightening up in her mood and attitude.

"So where does he live?"

"He lives here in Williamsport - at Springfield Farms - in a one bedroom apartment. Which was honestly quite nice."

"You saw his bedroom?" Emma joked back good-naturedly.

"Yes, I did, but I will add that there was no irrational, not-thought-out, sexual escapades occurring there. *That is... at least... for now."*

"You see - you do like him!" Emma exclaimed happily, as they made their way back inside the back kitchen door of the restaurant.

"Glad you two decided to make your presence known once again. I did try to call both of you on your cells, but no one answered. We have less than an hour now until we open and someone already called in here, trying to make a reservation for over lunch."

"It's not the weekend, Dennis. I hope you didn't give in and tie up any of our available tables for today. You know our policy on this," Emma reminded him gently, grabbing a water bottle from the refrigerator and tying an apron behind her, ready to begin working.

"I didn't forget, and no, I didn't agree to do so," Dennis answered, returning to his task of stirring the large pot of Maryland *"red"* crab soup that featured a hearty array of vegetables, chunks of fresh lump crabmeat and Old Bay seasoning, with a dash of Tabasco sauce besides. But to give you the *"heads-up"* the caller did say a large group of fourteen will be here right at eleven-thirty. Something about *a special meeting that they wanted to have here for the C&O Canal Trust that Mason Jones was involved with.* I told them first come, first serve!"

"Well that changes things considerably, since Mason Jones is involved!" Emma shouted out sarcastically, already grabbing plates and utensils, with Zoe jumping in right behind her, ready to assist. They quickly pushed three tables together, placing each plate, napkin, utensil and water glass in place, making sure there was ample room for fourteen guests. "Sounds like they will be getting their way after all, since a *"special person"* is involved."

"Emma!" Zoe snapped back with a false sense of protest, suddenly feeling much happier and better, knowing she would be seeing Mason very soon, as she pushed in the last of the chairs.

Chapter 21

Mason made his way into *Luna's* with his co-workers standing right behind him, as Ava greeted all that were present. *"May I help you?"* Ava asked, surprised by the large amount of people coming in all at the same time.

"We will need seating for *four... teen, ma'am,"* Mason explained with a pleasant grin, and his strong southern twang doing the announcing.

Ava gulped, suddenly feeling unprepared and slightly overwhelmed. We will need a few minutes to arrange that amount of seating, sir," she offered, having just walked in the door herself right before the group arrived, with Zoe approaching now quickly, trying to set the record straight.

"It's okay, Ava. Emma and I already took care of all this before you got here. The tables are set up in the back and ready to go!" she informed pleasantly, as Mason was enjoying the mild confusion, glad to see Zoe taking charge – which was a major *"turn-on"* for him always. "Right this way, folks," Zoe directed politely, with the outstretching of one arm, taking the pressure off of Ava to wait on such a large group over lunch all by herself.

The board members followed behind to an area of the restaurant that was somewhat secluded, away from the gaming area tables, where things could get quite noisy. "I will be assisting you today with your selections," Zoe stated proficiently after returning back to the group, pulling the pad of paper and an ink pen from her apron, ready to take down their numerous orders, after giving them a few minutes to look over the menu.

"What are your specials today?" A middle-aged woman asked, dressed in a matronly black dress, with a white and black scarf wrapped stylishly around her neck.

"We have an amazing Maryland *"red"* crab soup, and a pressed sandwich of turkey, provolone, bacon and avocado with a special *"house-made"* dressing, besides all the other regular selections on the menu."

"That sandwich sounds delicious!"

"Yes, it definitely is delicious!" Zoe confirmed. "Our chef Dennis comes up with some inventive dishes along with some creative twists on the traditional fare that we offer, which by the way are some of my grandmother's recipes."

"Have you worked here long?" A male inquired with some interest, almost in a flirtatious sort of way. "Why would they use your grandmother's recipes?"

Zoe nervously laughed at the handsome, thirty-something year old, finding his questions somewhat disconcerting, locking eyes then with Mason who seemed to be enjoying the exchange. "I own the place... and the restaurant is fairly new. So no, I haven't been working here long... but neither has anyone else that is employed here," she added notably, as she stumbled over her words, ready to hand part of the task over to Emma or Ava, who were now busily waiting on a few other tables in the restaurant.

Each meal that was chosen by the attendees was expertly written down, as Zoe disappeared into the kitchen, imputing every item into the computer along with any special requests that were to be passed on to the chef, venting out afterwards to Dennis and Emma who were both in the back. "Chatty and demanding bunch out there. We will never get them served at this point, if I'm the only one servicing those tables."

"I can run interference for you, Zoe," Emma jumped in saying, unless we can free up Ava so that she can help out also."

"She's over her head at the moment with everyone else who has just showed up. It may be time to add a second server over lunch if this continues."

"Ava won't like that, you know. I have spoken to her in the past about adding a second server, and she insists she can take care of everyone, which she typically does a great job of as long as Philip doesn't show up to disturb her. It's honestly all about her tip money. If we add someone else to the staff over lunch, it will cause a major hit to her income. We don't want to upset her and then she quits on us."

"That won't be happening, Em! Maybe we will need to increase Ava's wages to keep her happy, if we decide to hire a second server over her shift. At this point, it's just something to be considered, so enough talk about it for right now. We have more important things to think about, so let's just get this large order ready and out on the table, before I have to answer more uncomfortable questions from Mason's colleagues that he seems to be getting a kick out of."

"What an ornery devil he is!" Emma joked, grabbing a large tray and filling it full with piping hot bowls of crab soup that the C&O Canal Trust attendees were just eager to sample. *See you out there!"* she yelled over her shoulder to Zoe, as she placed the serving tray high, walking through the swinging kitchen doors to the hungry group waiting on the far side of the dining room.

The lunch was served and then the meeting began, giving Zoe and Emma a chance to walk away and take a much needed break, while the members that were present began their exchange in earnest. Zoe stood with Emma by the hostess stand, taking in the progress of the whole thing, seeing Mason in a different light as he led the group, handing each one a neatly stacked and stapled set of papers, that were presented for their review and consideration.

"He certainly seems to know what he is doing," Emma commented casually, as she sipped on a sweetened iced tea.

"Yes, he does," Zoe replied, as she tried to listen in on the presentation, since they were a distance away, impressed by Mason's professionalism and expertise in leading the group. *"Hopefully, he is getting whatever he wants out of them."*

Emma glanced at her friend who was intent on watching Mason. "Maybe he wants to convince them of something important, but he probably desires more from you too. And what I mean by that is in the way of intimacy, as much as he shows up here to dine and then lingers afterwards, always wanting to be near you, and hoping for just a few minutes of your time."

Zoe realized Emma was doing *"her thing again"* by not holding back and saying whatever came to her mind. A wave of a hand from one of the board members, desiring a refill on her chosen beverage, took center stage as Zoe glared at Emma before walking away, wishing you could continue on with the conversation. *"We will discuss this later!"* she warned, giving Emma an *"eyeful"*. Mason stopped speaking for a few moments, as he watched Zoe refill the glass with sweet tea, smiling and making direct eye contact with her in an obvious, lingering sort of way, before his speech resumed again. She turned, being somewhat embarrassed, hurriedly grabbing a busboy pan nearby, ready to assist Ava with a table that had just been emptied of its patrons, hoping that those at the meeting didn't notice Mason's questionable actions that were intended for her.

"You don't need to help me," Ava insisted, wanting to put up a good front of being capable of *"doing it all"* around the place, not wanting to give Zoe an excuse to hire someone else during her shift.

"Well, I know that, Ava, but everyone can use some help from time to time, including me!" She answered, trying to put her friend's mind at ease.

"About that... there is a rumor you may be hiring a second server for the lunch shift during the week. *Is there any truth to the rumor?"* She inquired anxiously.

"Ava, I won't ask who is filling up your head with such meaningless gossip, but your income will not be affected if Emma and I make the decision to hire an additional server. You do an excellent job keeping up with the mid-day shift, but on a business standpoint, we don't want to turn customers away either, if we are getting too overwhelmed and busy. Don't you agree?"

"Of course I don't want to see you lose business, Zoe, but I think I have been keeping up with all my tables for the most part."

"Yes, you do. I have had no complaints whatsoever."

"So how would you accommodate me if I lose out on money with the addition of someone new coming on board?" Ava probed, desiring more information and not wanting to let go of Zoe's promise so quickly.

"We would pay you more on an hourly basis, but Ava that would only be for us to know and for no one else in here to find out about, or we may have a mast uprising on our hands about wages, and then the whole staff will want to quit unless I pay them more also. I would only do this for you as an exception since we are good friends, because I wouldn't want to lose you if things changed drastically with your income - from a lack of tip money."

"That's sounds fair, but please just know I would never take advantage of you or Emma and ask for something additional, if things remain the same with what I'm bringing in."

"We know that, Ava, or you wouldn't be working here," she confirmed with a smile, giving her a warm hug in the process. Now lets get these dirty dishes to the kitchen before the next group of bicyclers walk in, wanting immediate service, as they seem to be demanding all of the time lately."

"You got it, boss!" Ava joked lightly by saluting her, before taking the tub of dirty dishes to the kitchen to be washed.

"Mason is asking for you," Emma hesitantly mentioned as she walked over to Zoe and gave her the heads up, still remembering she had ruffled her feathers somewhat. She was in the midst of redressing a few tables with fresh place settings and silverware - acting put out and bothered - as she breathed heavily from the intrusion. *"The C&O Canal Trust group is ready to leave and I think he just wants to say goodbye."*

"Well tell him I'll be right there!" Zoe dismissed, still irritated with Emma's outspokenness, as she finished what she was doing and made her way back up to the front. Everyone in the group had departed, except for Mason. Zoe paused, realizing how handsome Mason looked, dressed in his khaki pants and a plaid dress shirt, along with his signature cowboy boots, that she had not taken the time to notice when he first walked in the place. He smiled broadly once she was near, happy for one last opportunity to converse with her.

"Lunch was great! The crab soup was a big hit with everyone!"

"Thank you. I will let the chef know."

"I think the message was already passed on to him, but let him know again personally from me – job well done on lunch! Couldn't be more pleased with the outcome, and in the future we will be back for more additional luncheon meetings!"

"Well that is very kind of you, Mason, and I will definitely share with Dennis your additional comments."

"How about tonight? Can I convince you to come over to my place and maybe watch a movie with me later?" he whispered for her ears only.

Zoe's heart began to race, thinking about Emma's words earlier at the canal concerning the *holding back of her emotions*, unlike what she was personally doing by taking a chance at love – no matter what the outcome. *"Sure, Mason, we can get together later to watch a movie, but I must go home first and freshen up, and take care of my dog, Luna, before I come over."*

"Feel free to bring Luna with you, if you would like," he offered sweetly, much to Zoe's surprise.

"Aww... that is very nice of you to offer that, but I think tonight she can stay at home with my father. He also enjoys her company."

"I'm really looking forward to seeing you in a few hours," he expressed whole-heartedly, leaning in to kiss her lightly on the cheek. *"See you soon, sweetie."*

Zoe blushed, realizing that probably more than a few sets of eyes were upon them, including Emma and Ava's, and maybe even those that were part of the kitchen staff, along with few random customers who were all watching and observing, but for some strange reason she no longer cared.

Chapter 22

Zoe knocked on the door of Mason's apartment, tapping lightly several times. *"Com... ing!"* she heard him yell from the other side, once again with his strong East Texas twang coming through and resounding. He opened it, smiling from ear to ear, looking her over from head to toe in the process. *"Well don't you look as pretty as a bouquet of beautiful sunflowers!"* he complimented, inviting her into his place.

"Mason, sometimes I'm at a loss of words when I'm around you. Do you know that?" She giggled, always humored by his accent and the endearing *"southern statements"* that he rattled off so effortlessly.

"And why's that?" He questioned pleasantly, as they made their way towards the kitchen where he had a cinnamon apple scented candle burning.

"I love your compliments, but it just takes some getting used to. Northern guys aren't so colorful in the way they say things, you know."

"Glad to hear that I stand out from the rest," he grinned, wrapping her suddenly in his arms, planting a light kiss on her lips that she welcomed.

"What would you like to drink? I have beer and wine, and I thought I would pop some popcorn, so that we can share a bowl during the movie."

"Wine sounds perfect!" Zoe answered, still finding the newness of being held and kissed by Mason somewhat strange but nice, after experiencing the same with Noah for so long. She pulled away slightly, waiting for him to comply, gaining just a little more space and time - in whatever was to come next - before the evening was over.

Mason opened a cabinet, reaching for the only two wine glasses that were present, taking them down from the top shelf. "Sorry, but these glasses need a washin'..." he apologized, cleaning both with a sudsy sponge and then rinsing and drying them off with a tea towel until they were spotless and clean. "I must admit I rarely drink wine and haven't done so since I moved in here," he admitted candidly, locating the bottle of Merlot in his pantry that was there for a while.

The wine was uncorked, with a generous libation being poured into each glass, with on being handed to Zoe, and the other one attended for Mason. "To you, dear Zoe, and to a wonderful evening ahead. Cheers!" he offered, clinking his glass against hers, before they mutually drank from the *"fruit of the vine"*.

"Umm... I love the taste of this. Where is it from?" Zoe inquired.

"Believe it or not, West Virginia. Not bad, if I must say so myself."

"I need to talk to Emma about this particular brand. We may just need to add it to our wine list at *Luna's*. Our clientele seem to love the locally made beers and wines that we offer."

"Glad to help out," Mason grinned, as he dumped the microwave popcorn that he had just popped into a large bowl. *"Ready to pick out a movie?"* He asked as they made their way to the living room together.

"Sure. Whatever you choose is fine with me."

Mason flipped on his Netflix, settling on a romantic comedy starring David Spade. "Someone at work told me this is a funny one to watch, even if it's been out for awhile."

Mason flipped off the lights as the movie began, wrapping his arm around Zoe's shoulder and pulling her in closely by his side. The wine was relaxing her, as was the humorous flick that she found entertaining and yet shocking, with some of its outlandish scenes – discovering that she was actually enjoying herself. Zoe sipped from her wine glass until it was empty, placing it on the coffee table in front her, before resuming the position in Mason's embrace.

"Why don't I get the rest of the bottle so I can refill your glass?" he offered, looking at Zoe for some guidance.

"Only if you will join me," she replied with a smile.

"That was the plan," he grinned, rising from the sofa to retrieve the wine bottle off of the kitchen counter. The glasses were refilled for a second time, with the bottle now being empty. Each drank deeply as their eyes met, trying to read the mind and emotions of the other. He took Zoe's unfinished glass, placing it on the cocktail table along with his own, leaning in for a long passionate, tongue-kiss, as the movie continued to play on in the background, with the script not being followed by either one of them now.

They reclined deeper into the sofa, as Mason reached for Zoe's one breast, massaging it through the outside of her clothes. She moaned slightly, not resisting his advances, granting him permission to *"proceed forward"*. The kissing intensified, along with their mutual touching and exploration, with only the outfits that they wore being the barrier now between them.

"I want you, Zoe," Mason confessed with a seductive raggedness to his voice, as he waited for her response.

"I want you too, Mason," she in turn responded back, surprised by her answer and willingness to take it to the next level.

He stood from the sofa, reaching out his hand and pulling Zoe to her feet, escorting her to his *"still-lit"* bedroom - without a need to ask why. She willingly complied, wanting now to be with him as badly as he desired to be with her also. Mason unbuttoned his shirt in front of her, slipping it to the floor, as Zoe took in his bronzed, muscular chest that was beyond her hopes or expectations. Her breath caught as he pulled her down on the bed and he cozied up beside of her, resuming the passionate kissing and the continuous rubbing of both of her breasts now. His hands began to wonder as the heated *"fore-play"* session continued, venturing beneath her top and then inside her bra, extracting one breast fully to his view that he nuzzled and licked until the peak stood up firmly - under his masterful control.

"God, Zoe, you are so damn beautiful!" he whispered ardently, as he helped her remove her top and bra. Free to gaze and play upon Zoe's upper torso now, Mason suckled each breast at his leisure, tempting and teasing with his mouth and tongue, returning to her luscious lips, not wanting to neglect them either.

Zoe felt conflicted – resisting the urges that were buried deep within her, wishing she could just break free and completely respond to Mason's advances, but finding it very difficult to do so. She realized that Noah was purely at the root of it all – now feeling shy and undesirable after his rejection. But she lavished in what Mason was doing to her - reigniting her body and soul – suddenly and totally being turned on – hot and heated and ready - willing for whatever he offered.

Mason unzipped her jeans, allowing his hand to wander inside of her underwear, finding the intended goal that was now wet from the continual thrusts of his fingers. She climaxed, yelling out her sweet release, much to Mason's delight, as his penis was now pressing against his own jeans, begging to be freed and inside of her. Clothes were hurriedly removed by both, with no thought of nakedness or observation, as Mason climbed on top of Zoe, positioning a condom quickly over his shaft before thrusting deeply inside of her several times. He exploded violently with a scream that she swore had that same *"twangy"* accent coming through it as his words, as she climaxed for a second time – accepting the gift that was bestowed upon her.

Mason is more than adequate in size, and just as adept at sexual mastery and satisfaction as Noah ever was, Zoe discovered, now having the distinct advantage of being able to compare them both, being the only two sexual partners she had experienced. It suddenly made sense that there was a life beyond her *"first love"* after all.

"You okay?" Mason asked, propped up on one elbow, stroking lightly over Zoe's one breast, while trying to calm his breathing to a more even pace.

Zoe turned to look at the man she had just made love to. "I am more than okay, Mason. I suddenly feel *"alive"* again," she confessed, with a warm smile radiating from her face.

"Well, I'm glad I could *"service you"* my lady and make you feel so good!" he grinned, teasing her as he nuzzled into the side of her neck. Zoe giggled loudly, turning away from the tickling.

"Mason, I'm going to pee myself if you keep this up!"

He pulled Zoe to her feet, slapping her backside playfully in the process. "Use the bathroom before that happens, silly girl!" he laughed and directed, as he hugged her tightly, before releasing her to pick up her cloths and have some privacy.

Mason had redressed, reappearing in the living room where Zoe was sitting on the couch waiting on him. She smiled, as he sat down beside of her. "I think it's time to leave."

"You don't want to finish our movie before you go?"

"Not tonight... although I really enjoyed it and thought it was funny."

"Well, let me walk you out to your car," Mason offered as he slipped into his cowboy boots. The two stood by Zoe's car, as he wrapped her one last time in his arms and kissed her tenderly. *"I loved our evening together,"* Mason confessed passionately, meaning every word of it.

"It was amazing, Mason," she responded back, agreeing with him totally.

She pulled away, with glimpses of Mason still smiling and waving in her rearview mirror, finding herself happier than she had been in months, glad she had finally listened to her wise and caring friend, Emma - just when she needed it the most.

Chapter 23

"Hello?"

"Em, are you awake?" Zoe questioned at 1 o'clock in the morning.

"Well, I am now..." Emma groaned out quietly, turning over towards the sleeping form of her new boyfriend, Luke Taylor. *"Hold on, Zoe. Let me get up so I can speak with you,"* Emma whispered, as she slid from the bed, trying her best not to rouse Luke. She wrapped the throw from the chair near by, around her nude body, ready to escape to Luke's living room so that she could talk more freely.

"What's going on?" Luke asked in confusion, suddenly waking and wondering what all the commotion was about, as he attempted to sit up and focus.

"Need to take this call, sweetie," Emma answered softly, smiling at Luke fondly. *"Please, go back to sleep, and I will be back to bed in a few minutes to snuggle with you again."*

"Okay..." Luke replied sleepily, not needing much encouragement to do so, after their lengthy *"romp in the sack"* just an hour earlier.

Emma walked into the living room, planting herself on Luke's cozy sectional. *"So what's going on?"* she asked, trying to get warm under the inadequate throw that was only half covering her and not doing the job.

"Oh my word, Emma, it's obvious that you are with Luke and I'm disturbing you! We can talk about things in the morning. I'm so sorry for waking you up."

*"I'm wide awake now, so you might as well tell me what's on your

mind, or I will just stay up all night wondering if you are okay."

"Well since you put it that way, I guess I will share with you what's going on. I went over to Mason's apartment tonight to watch a movie, and things progressed beyond the movie."

Emma sighed, feeling tired and wanting to return to the comfort of Luke's warm bed and his strong arms again. *"So are you telling me that you finally had sex with him?"*

"Yes, we did, Emma!"

"So how was it?"

Zoe shook her head, knowing her best friend never held back, always being very transparent. "It was honestly amazing. I didn't know what to expect after only having Noah as my sexual partner, but Mason is a fantastic lover."

"Thank God, you have come to that conclusion! If you told me *"Mr. Cowboy"* looked that good, but his dick didn't match that outside package, I would have felt badly for you. So I'm happy that things have all worked out for you and him in that way."

Zoe began to laugh, as she pulled into her father's driveway, and considered what was just said. *"Em, you do have a unique way with words, do you know that?"*

"I try... Hey, Zoe, can we talk some more about this in the morning? I'm beat and sitting here nude with only a small throw over me, honestly freezing and wanting to get back to bed. I'm hoping that Luke will want to *"do me"* again before I need to leave for work in the morning."

"You're spending the night with him already?"

"Umm, ye...aah. That's what typically happens when you decide to date and have a significant other. As I told you, I'm not holding back in any way with him. I am all in - no matter what!"

"*Obviously so,*" Zoe answered, with some surprise. "I will talk to you in the morning, and Emma I am happy for you and Luke."

"Likewise - for you and Mason. Now, it's time to say goodnight, Zoe. We will discuss all of this later, after a good night's sleep."

Emma returned to the bedroom and tossed the throw on the chair again, as she slipped beneath the covers and rubbed her breasts and bottom up against Luke's backside, taunting him to wake up for another time. She reached around to grab his penis, massaging it until the shaft was rigid and hard, only desiring that it were back inside of her again.

"*Umm... that feels good, Em. Everything okay?*" he inquired, willing himself to wake back up again and turn around.

"Just Zoe needing a listening ear and some sound friendly advice. That's all," she replied, wrapping her arms around him tightly as their genitals mutually touched and came alive, yet for another time.

Luke began to kiss her passionately, ready to please Emma all over again, pausing and breaking free for a few seconds more. "*She is definitely fine, right?*"

"She is definitely fine, Luke. Matter-of-fact, Zoe did the very same thing as we did tonight. Had incredible sex for the first time with her new boy friend."

"*Oh... really?*" Luke answered, with his interest suddenly piqued, as he propped up on one elbow, wanting to hear the details. "*Zoe has a new boyfriend?*"

"Yes, she does, and I couldn't be happier for her. It seems like we have all taken a positive step forward in our love lives recently. *Wouldn't you say so?*" she teased, as Luke reached for one of her breasts and nuzzled it, thrusting the nipple into his mouth with his tongue, making it respond and stand up firmly, under his skillful touch.

"I can't speak for anyone else, but I know I'm where I've always wanted to be. I'm very happy and content with what is happening between us."

"For me too, Luke," Emma exclaimed sincerely, with her words then being silenced, as desire and yearning took over for another glorious, lustful episode of passion - throughout the early morning hours.

The alarm blared out repeatedly at 6 a.m. as Zoe pressed the snooze button for fifteen more minutes of sleep, placing the pillow over her head and only wanting to shut out the reality of another early morning wake-up for work. The shrill sounded repeatedly again, with Zoe silencing it for good this time. *"That was no fifteen more minutes, Luna,"* she said as her feet hit the floor. *"I'll walk you after I take my shower, sweetie,"* she explained to her precious pet as she dragged herself to the bathroom, hoping that the hot water would do the trick and wake her up.

Zoe slid from her pajamas, welcoming the pulsating water that was now pleasantly massaging her back. She hadn't bathed after being with Mason, and now any remaining intimate contact with him was being washed away down the drain. She thought of the night previous and how romantic things had been between them, wanting a repeat of the same very soon, but still feeling apprehensive and scared. She dried herself, lingering on her most private parts between her legs, knowing that Mason's fingers felt so much better than any contact the towel was now giving. Luna still rested on the bed as Zoe dressed in her work attire – blue jeans and a *Luna's* t-shirt – which her closet held many of both, finishing off with socks and sneakers. She was ready to run the restaurant floor from the back kitchen to the front dining area, waiting on the tables inside and out - where there was additional seating consisting of patio tables with multi-colored umbrellas.

Zoe leashed up Luna, being greeted by her father in the kitchen, smelling the scent of coffee brewing and bacon and eggs cooking. *"Aren't you working today?"* she asked in confusion, surprised that her father was going to so much trouble to make breakfast, since that task was normally only undertaken on the weekends when he could do so at a more leisurely pace.

"No, I'm not working today," he answered, somewhat with a serious tone. *"Walk Luna, and then we will talk about my plans."*

"Okay?" Zoe questioned with uncertainty, wanting to understand the mystery. Luna was quick to cooperate, as if she understood the hidden meaning behind Bryan's words. She shivered a little as she came back inside, unhooking Luna and immediately dishing out some of the kibble into her bowl close by. "It's really starting to get cold outside and this light jacket isn't sufficing anymore for Luna's morning walks."

"Yes, it is. We're almost in November, so it's that time of the year."

"So what's up?" Zoe asked, as Bryan placed a generous portion of bacon, eggs and toast in front of Zoe, and then joined her at the table with his own plate.

Bryan locked eyes with his daughter, not sure how to proceed. "Zoe, I just got a call from Nana Ruth at 3 a.m. today."

"Why did she call so early? What is going on?" She asked, pushing the plate back after only a few bites, looking confused and concerned - all at the same time.

Bryan gulped and paused, suddenly not feeling hungry anymore either, taking a deep sip of his coffee before beginning. *"Pappy Joe had a massive heart attack last night and they are not sure he is going to..."*

"Oh... no...!" Zoe yelled out with her hands now covering her mouth in shock, breaking into Bryan's explanation, not wanting him to continue.

"Zoe, please let me finish," he insisted, reaching out for the top of her arm, trying to steady and comfort her. "I knew this would upset you, but now is the time that we need to remain calm and exhibit rational behavior. I need to be a strong supportive force for Pappy Joe and Nana Ruth both, and it's not going to be easy if something happens to your grandfather."

The tears were now streaming down Zoe's face, as hard as she tried to gather her wits, finding it impossible to do so. "I'm so sorry, dad, but Pappy Joe is more than just a grandfather to me. You know how I feel about him."

"Yes I do know, Zoe. My father, and your pappy, is a very sick man right now. He needs surgery, but his age isn't something that he has going for him. The surgeon is concerned he may not make it through the operation, and if he does, he still may not survive afterwards during his recovery period. They think he has around an eighty percent blockage going on with his heart."

Zoe shook her head in confusion, feeling very overwhelmed and in denial. Any wonderful pleasant thoughts of Mason and what had just occurred last night between them, were now suddenly erased with the tragic news that needed to be immediately dealt with. "I want to go and be with them."

"I knew that you would respond this way, but you have the restaurant to think about. I already called the plant and put in for a week of vacation time, which I will be spending in Fort Wayne with my parents. If need be, I will even take off longer, but for now - one day at a time."

"To hell with the restaurant! Emma and the other staff can watch over things until I get back! I wouldn't even have *Luna's* if it weren't for Pappy Joe and Nana Ruth. If something unfortunate would happen, I would never forgive myself that I hadn't taken the time off to be there for him. *Please understand my feelings on all this!"* Zoe exclaimed, with pleading in her eyes.

Bryan sighed, wiping his eyes in the process, feeling his own sense of despair that he was trying to keep in check, especially in front of his daughter. "I get it, Zoe. Make the necessary arrangements with your work, and then we will pack up the car and be out of here within a couple hours. *Can you make that happen?*"

"I will be ready in an hour," Zoe answered without hesitation. *"Whatever I forget to pack, I will just buy out in Fort Wayne."*

"Understood..." Bryan agreed, as he stood up and took both of the barely eaten plates away, throwing what remained in the trashcan.

Chapter 24

Zoe hurriedly packed two bags, taking only a week's worth of clothes based on her father's allotted time off of work. She also gathered Luna's things, which included the leash, a bed, two dog bowls and a big bag of kibble, waiting on Bryan to return back to the house. Emma was contacted next, knowing by now she should be at the restaurant, busy with the morning prep.

"Running a little late this morning, aren't you? Did you decide to go back and meet up with Mason at his apartment for another go round?" Emma laughed and questioned playfully, with Zoe having no time or patience for her twisted sense of humor.

"No, Em, I didn't go back to Mason's place," she replied gloomily. "Something bad has happened, and that is why I am calling you."

Emma was silenced, now with her mouth hanging open, walking out the back door of the kitchen so that Dennis and the others present didn't overhear the conversation. *"What's going on, Zoe? This doesn't have anything to do with Noah Clark does it? Did he reach out to you?"*

Zoe shook her head, feeling exhausted and put out by the assumption. "Oh my God, Em! Of course this has *nothing* to do with Noah, but everything to do with my Pappy Joe!"

"What's going on with Pappy Joe?" Emma questioned, suddenly realizing this wasn't a joking matter, as she took a seat at the picnic table, where the staff ate and also grabbed a cigarette on their breaks.

Zoe began to cry all over again, wishing Emma was with her now, ready to provide some comfort and a big reassuring hug, letting her know everything was going to be alright even if it wasn't. *"He had a massive heart attack last night. The surgeon isn't even sure if he'll make it through the operation - with his age and all."*

"I'm so, so sorry, my friend. What can I do to help you?"

"I want to join my father – starting today. We will be leaving soon and driving out to Fort Wayne, Indiana so that we can be there for my Pappy Joe and Nana Ruth."

"Of course, Zoe! There is no question that this is the right thing that you should be doing. Stay as long as you need to. I will handle things on this end."

"What about the daily numbers, payroll and the bills? You know that is normally my responsibility to take care of that part of the business."

"I can handle it, and you can take your laptop and I will follow up with emails on our daily numbers and how everything else is going. If I have any questions as to how I should be handling something, I will not hesitate to get in touch with you. And don't forget that Dennis can lend a hand too, since he has been in the restaurant business for many years."

"Well, it sounds like you will have things covered on your end," she admitted somewhat skeptically. "But remember, I also assist with waiting on tables and prepping food, even helping Dennis with the making of some of the easier dishes from time to time. What will you do about all that?"

"Hire someone else. We have talked about it doing so. Remember?"

"Yes, I remember, but I also remember our talk about Ava and that it would upset her if we did so."

"Zoe, you have enough on your plate to think about right now, other than the *"drama-filled"* females around this place. Let me manage things and deal with the day in and day out operation. I promise you things will be fine! Just do your best to take care of Pappy Joe and Nana Ruth, and *Luna's* and everything else in Williamsport, will be here waiting on you when you return."

"Thank you, Emma."

"You are welcome, and I will be praying for Pappy Joe and the rest of your family. Everything is going to be okay."

"I hope so, Em. I wouldn't know what to do if I lost my pappy."

"I get it…. He's a very special man. I will never forget how he *"stepped up to plate"* to put us in business. Now please get off of here and deal with getting on the road. I love you girl!"

"Love you too, Emma."

Zoe hung up with her friend, pacing the floor, waiting on her father to return from gassing up the car and saying his goodbyes to Kelly, which he promised to do within the hour. She assumed he was getting in a last minute *"quickie"* with his *"beloved"* before he got on the road, after convincing her to slip away from work and meet up with him at her house for an early lunch hour. Zoe thought of what was ahead, feeling scared and vulnerable with the uncertainty of things, but somewhat sad to be leaving her life behind in Williamsport, which involved her career and a new potential relationship with Mason.

Mason Jones had just returned to his office, after just being out on the C&O Canal towpath with a couple of the park rangers and a maintenance crew, reviewing the plans for some major tree removal. A recent storm had passed through the area, creating major damage with downed broken limbs that were now covering the pathway in several key locations, where hikers and bikers were constantly traveling through the area. It was deemed dangerous, until the debris could properly be cleared, so *urgency to do so was considered essential*. Mason communicated that message to the team, with the work already scheduled to begin that very afternoon.

"*Hello?*" he greeted, beaming with a pleased smile, delighted to see the familiar endearing name and number of *Zoe Carter* that he had added to his contacts, *"starring it"* to the top of the list.

"Hello, Mason. It's me."

"Hey, you. How is your day going so far? I was planning to stop in for lunch today, so I can see your beautiful face again," he flirted, hoping for some more sex in the next day or two, but at the same time just honestly desiring to see her.

"I won't be at *Luna's* today, Mason," Zoe replied emptily, with a hint of melancholy etching her voice. "And for that matter, I won't be there for the next few days…"

"*Why not, my dear? Is everything okay?*" He asked in alarm, suddenly realizing she didn't sound like herself, hoping she wasn't having regrets about the night previous and the intimacy they had just shared.

"Mason, I am going out of town for awhile. My grandfather had a massive heart attack, and my father and I are leaving within the hour to drive out to Fort Wayne, Indiana to be with him and my grandmother."

Mason silently shook his head, as he looked out of his over-sized window towards the Cushwa Warehouse that actually predated the canal, being built in 1790, and was now a museum and a visitor center for the town of Williamsport. It was only a short distance away, where many chose to relax and fish by its water basin, being much easier to focus in on with its pleasantries than the severity of Zoe's words that he was now hearing. *"Wow… I'm so sorry for all your family is going through right now. Is there anything I can do to help you out?"*

"No, there isn't… other than maybe pray… for my grandfather…

that he makes it through his surgery. He has a 80% blockage... and at his age this operation is a very serious undertaking," Zoe explained rather sadly, with her voice breaking with emotion - throughout each word spoken.

"I will be praying, Zoe... and maybe I shouldn't be saying this at such an unfortunate time, but I sure will be missing you, dar...ling," Mason confessed with his strong Texas twang resonating throughout each word, filled with total sincerity and compassion. "It's much too soon to be saying goodbye to you already, after the *"amazing thing"* that just happened between us last night."

"I know.... I know, but I need to get through this hurdle first with my grandfather, before I can think about anything else... and unfortunately that includes whatever has started between you and I also," she stated realistically, feeling miserable, wishing there was no need for the explanation.

"Safe travels to you, Zoe, and text or call me when you get the chance."

"I promise I will, Mason. Thanks for understanding."

"More than you realize, love."

Bryan pulled into the driveway of the rancher, idling with the phone still pressed to his ear. Zoe could see a somewhat pleasant smile on his face as he hung up from a call, leading her to believe that her suspicions were true concerning some last minute sex with Kelly. She tried to understand that he would want to see her, especially with the longevity and seriousness of their dating relationship, but there was a time and place for everything - at least that was the way she saw it – and now was not the time for such frivolities when they were in a hurry to leave and get on the road.

"All packed?" he inquired from the car window, now on a mission to depart.

"Yes dad, I've been packed and here waiting on you for some time now," Zoe whined, acting flustered, trying to press home the dual meaning of her statement.

He cocked his head to one side, sensing her irritation, trying to read her mind. "Zoe, if this is about me being gone for awhile so that I could say my goodbyes to Kelly, then I make no apologies for that. Our relationship is such that she *deserves* an explanation for why I am leaving town for an extended period of time."

"If you say so," Zoe said flippantly with a roll of her eyes. "You aren't married to her, and if you must leave town, why the need for a big explanation?"

"Please just get your bags and Luna, and we will discuss this further on the way!" Bryan exploded, as he went off on her, now no longer being in a good humor from the fantastic blowjob and amazing sex that followed afterwards, with *"the love of his life"*.

Zoe rolled out her two bags and the dog stuff, with Luna following behind on her leash, pausing to lock up the house before situating everything in the trunk of the car. *"Aren't you going to pray?"* she asked, looking at her father for direction, knowing that had always been the tradition to do so first before they traveled.

Bryan bowed his head, trying to refocus, answering her with the start of the prayer. *"Dear Heavenly Father, we pray for your hand of protection to be on us as we drive to Fort Wayne to be with our family at this very difficult time. I pray for my father, asking that you will be with him as he faces this difficult surgery that is necessary to save his life. I pray that you will keep us strong and help us to always trust you when we can't see our way through situations when they get especially tough. We pray this, in faith believing, that you hear and answer prayers. In Christ's name we pray. Amen."*

Zoe looked up at her father, feeling uncertain with his words. *"He honestly needs this surgery to save his life, doesn't he?"*

"Yes, Zoe, he does. So with that said, there is no time for trivial nonsense about things such as Kelly, and what she deserves or doesn't deserve in way of an explanation from me, before I leave town for an extended time period. Do you understand that?"

Zoe bent her head, not wanting to answer, before glancing at her father as he headed out of town on I-70 West. "I understand, but I can also clearly see where things are going with you and Kelly. What is going to happen to me if you two get married sometime in the near distant future?"

"Zoe, seriously, is that what you are concerned about?"

Luna huffed out loudly from the back seat, tired of the front seat debate that was occurring, desiring only quiet on the long journey out to the Midwest. "Yes, I am concerned about things. If you get married, then I will be sharing a house with you guys, or maybe you will even consider selling the house, and then where am I supposed to live?"

Bryan shook his head in disbelief, totally surprised by her irrational rambling. "I don't know if you are on *"emotional overload"* because of Pappy Joe, but for heaven's sakes, Zoe, you could have gotten married to Noah and left me too, you know."

"That was a little cruel," she chirped out, feeling somewhat hurt by his insensitive remarks.

"Not trying to be cruel, but no one is intentionally leaving the other one *"high and dry"* in this father-daughter relationship. I would never ask Kelly to marry me if it wasn't made clear to her from the start that you will always have a place to live with us. She seems to understand and accept this, and I also know that she does like you, Zoe, so a marriage would not change anything. I'm asking you to please stop worrying and concentrate on the important stuff that we can control right now in our lives."

"I wish that included this surgery that Pappy Joe needs."

"I know, honey. I only wish this was something within our control, but it unfortunately isn't. So we need to trust God that he will miraculously bring Pappy Joe through this difficult time, and he will have sound health once again."

Chapter 25

It was nine o'clock in the evening as Bryan pulled into the driveway of his childhood home in Fort Wayne, feeling weary and yet relieved that he was finally there. It was too late to go the hospital since visiting hours had ended several hours earlier, and he knew his mother should be at the house, waiting to greet them.

Nana Ruth had contacted her son during the drive, giving the details over the speakerphone to both Zoe and Bryan, filling them in as best she could about the surgery that would be performed the following morning on Pappy Joe. Zoe did her best to conceal her true emotions, not desiring to upset her nana if she heard an outburst of crying coming from her. With Nana Ruth repeating everything starting with Pappy Joe's heart attack and when it occurred, to him being rushed to the hospital by ambulance, and then finally the scheduled surgery for the next day and the seriousness of it. Zoe felt shock and overwhelmed, as she sat quietly in the car listening to her grandmother, but also a feeling of clarity, that she was no longer in the dark, with only sketchy information coming from her father.

The older neighborhood - where Joe and Ruth currently resided - was filled mostly with senior citizens now, after the majority of Bryan's classmates had moved away to other areas of the country, or stayed local and moved to trendier, newer neighborhoods that were slapped up quickly and cost a small fortune. This sort of development catered to a younger crowd of two-income workers, having kids who were out playing and riding their bikes on the safe streets of the community, being planned out to feature cul-de-sacs, walking trails and sidewalks, along with shops and restaurants – all located close by for their convenience.

It was quiet in the peaceful country setting of the Carter

household, where all was dark except for the faint glow of the streetlights overhead - that lit the way. Bryan and Zoe pulled their bags from the car, with Luna jumping down lastly, following up the steps beside them – glued as usual to Zoe's side. The place was familiar to the dog also, as she sniffed her familiar surroundings, being there only a few short months' prior when Zoe made the journey alone, with Luna in the front passenger's seat trying to keep her company. She had traveled out to Fort Wayne, for some rest and regrouping – seeking out the much needed advice of her grandparents concerning her breakup with Noah, and what she should do about going forward with the opening of her restaurant in Williamsport, Maryland.

Bryan rang the doorbell, hoping he wasn't waking his mother up in the process, which he doubted since she had planned to stay up until they arrived. *"Bryan, Zoe!"* Nana Ruth greeted pleasantly, grabbing each one for a sound hug. Luna barked in Ruth's direction, not wanting to be left out of the initial welcoming. *"Well, come here, girl,"* she offered tenderly, reaching down to hug the dog's neck, as Luna fondly rubbed up against her legs afterwards.

Ruth was dressed in her pajamas, with a housecoat wrapped securely around her waist, having her gray hair tied up on top of her head in a bun, which was her normal look before going to bed in the evening. She led her family into the house with all of their belongings that they had brought from the car. *"Is anyone hungry?"* she inquired. "I have a pot of vegetable beef soup on the stove simmering, and I just baked an apple cake that should still be slightly warm. "The vegetables and apples are from our garden!" she announced proudly. Zoe was honestly amazed that her grandmother would still want to cook at such a difficult time, knowing she wouldn't have it in her to do the same under similar circumstances.

"Mom, I will take the suitcases up to our bedrooms and then join you and Zoe for some soup and apple cake afterwards. I wish you wouldn't have gone to so much trouble for us," he smiled knowingly, realizing that this was his mother's way of keeping herself occupied, and not having to overthink things too much about the inevitable that she was facing the next day.

"It was no trouble at all," she smiled, as Bryan was already on his way up the steps. "Honestly, I made the soup yesterday right before Joe... had his heart... attack..." she stumbled out with her words, feeling her resolved crumbling under a flow of tears suddenly, as her hands went up to her face, trying her best to conceal the obvious.

"Oh, Nana Ruth, please don't cry!" Zoe comforted, reaching out to wrap her arms around her grandmother. "Dad and I will be staying as long as you need us, and of course we will be here with you tomorrow during Pappy Joe's surgery. Everything is going to be okay. Pappy is a strong man, and I'm sure he will be back on his feet in no time."

"I hope you are right..." Ruth answered weakly, somewhat with a spirit of doubt that others rarely saw in her. She was feeling weak in her faith for the moment, trying to believe that God and the surgeon had everything under control, even though her fears were welling up and trying to take over.

"Where's my bowl of soup?" Bryan grinned, after returning to the females a short time later. "I just realized I am starving after the long drive, and there's nothing like your homemade vegetable beef soup to warm the body and soul, and give one a burst of energy."

"Coming right up!" Ruth answered with a happy smile, suddenly feeling better for having Bryan and Zoe there to lean on during such a difficult time. "I have saltines and butter also, to go along with the soup."

"Wouldn't eat it any other way!" Bryan agreed, as his mother placed a *"saltine sleeve"* of crackers on the table beside of some softened butter that was in an antique floral-patterned *"butter dish"* with a matching lid – which had been in the Carter family for years.

A chunk of beef was removed from the soup and diced up by Nana

Ruth, being placed in Luna's dog dish that was now sitting on the floor, as her tasty treat. The pooch heartily devoured the offering in several bites, licking the whole way around her mouth with her tongue afterwards, showing her appreciation.

"I would say Luna likes your soup too, Nana Ruth," Zoe giggled, taking in the scene in front of her. *"May I try some of your apple cake now?"*

"Of course you may, my dear," Ruth replied, getting up to slice her granddaughter and son a generous portion of the warm apple cake that was sitting on the kitchen counter close by, still cooling off.

"Please, Nana, let me take over that task! Relax, and let me serve the desert!" Zoe insisted, rising up to stand beside of her grandmother.

"Yes, Mom, let Zoe take over from here. Let's just sit and talk, and she will serve us the cake and coffee."

Ruth smiled at her wonderful houseguests, taking a seat at the table again, not one to be typically pampered, and usually the servant to all that dined with her and Joe at their home, and not the other way around.

Zoe placed the desert plates filled with warm apple cake in front of each one, handing out three cups of coffee afterwards, before taking her seat at the table again. She sipped from the hot brew, finding that it tasted much better than what she regularly drank back at the house in Williamsport, which never made any sense since they both used the same brand of coffee. Bryan had explained, after she had questioned him about the subject in the past, that it *probably had something to do with the differences in the water,* but the mystery still remained - to the truth of it all.

"I hope this doesn't keep me up all night," Zoe mentioned with some caution, as she continued to drink the coffee anyway, "because I want to be fresh and alert when we leave in the morning for the hospital."

"It's decaf, my dear," Nana Ruth informed, as she rose to remove the empty dishes from the table, placing them in the dishwasher. Zoe followed with the coffee mugs, handing each one to her grandmother as she loaded them also, desiring only to help her in any way she could.

"I'm going to walk Luna and then I think we should *"hit the hay"*. I'm assuming we need to be at the hospital early tomorrow?"

"Yes, Bryan. I want to be there by seven a.m. to pray over your father, and then wait in his hospital room until they come to get him around 9 a.m., which is when the surgery is scheduled. In case I haven't mentioned it to you, our minister has promised to be there at that time also – just to join us in prayer and lend his support for Joe."

"We will be ready, Nana Ruth, whatever time you want to leave for the hospital," Zoe reassured, realizing once again this was all happening and couldn't be avoided - no matter how many prayers were being prayed - by either them or the pastor.

As everyone said their goodnights and departed upstairs to each one of the bedrooms, which was always the same whenever Bryan and Zoe were visiting, the mood was somber and the house was especially quiet, with only the ticking of the Grandfather's clock being heard from the floor below. Bryan texted Kelly, just to let her know they had made it to Fort Wayne safely and he already *missed her.* Kelly in turn let Bryan know she was counting the days until she saw him again. Mason had reached out to Zoe, much to her surprise, once again reiterating that *anything he could do to help he was there at her service.* Zoe returned the text, expressing appreciation for his thoughtfulness. Emma had reached out too, letting Zoe know that everything was fine at work and to take her time coming back. Nana Ruth was the exception – not hearing the endearing words spoken of *"good night and I love you"* from her partner of forty-eight years – who had always shared that loving phrase with her before falling asleep, secure in the other one's arms. If something went wrong – the thought of being without Joe - was a cross she didn't want to bear.

Ruth pushed back the covers, and then kneeled beside of the bed, resting her palms on the top of the mattress that she pushed together in a reverent sort of way, beginning a fervent prayer with her head bowed. *"Dear Heavenly Father, I come to you again to plead for my husband's life. If it is your will, please spare him. This may be a selfish request on my part, but I can't imagine my life without Joe in it, so I'm asking for a miracle!"*

Ruth stood and found the bed once again, pulling the quilt back over her shoulder as she rolled over on her side. She lay there patting the empty side of the mattress close by, hoping that her prayer was heard and would be answered for what she had just asked. Tears spilled down her cheeks, landing on the pillow that she now clutched, as she finally drifted off to sleep, dreaming a dream and seeing a beautiful scene from her wedding day - many years earlier - of a handsome younger version of Joe, dressed in a black tuxedo as he held her hand, reciting his nuptials and promising his undying allegiance and love to his beautiful bride – *"from this day forward - until death do we part"*.

Chapter 26

Five-thirty a.m. and Nana Ruth was up, showered and dressed, ready to face the day and whatever came her way – with newfound determination. She had barely slept throughout the night, rolling and tossing with dreams of Joe and their earlier years together, which were pleasant – to say the least - but had left her tired and feeling somewhat drained from the broken sleep that she had experienced. Now, she was committed to doing her best, desiring to believe and put her faith in action, trying to be that pillar of strength and stable force once again for her family. Bryan and Zoe were soon to follow, descending the set of stairs, and finding Ruth in the kitchen brewing a pot of coffee, but this time the caffeinated variety, that they all needed and craved just to fully wake up.

Ruth smiled, happy to see them, the family that she cherished and loved dearly. Bryan and Zoe had also showered and changed into fresh apparel, ready to be by her side at the hospital throughout the day, hoping to be that pillar of strength that she needed. "I'm sorry I didn't make a hot breakfast," Ruth explained with a hint of an apology, but cereal and fruit will have to suffice, under the circumstances."

"Mother, cereal is *always* fine. You know Zoe and I don't expect anything special out of you - ever! It is only you that constantly puts that extra pressure on yourself to cook for us."

"Well, thank you for that, Bryan. You know though, that I do enjoy cooking for you, but today is the exception to the rule."

"Of course..." Bryan agreed with mutual understanding, pouring a bowl of raisin bran and then filling up a mug with coffee that he drank down rather quickly.

The door slammed a little too loudly as Zoe returned in from the outside, giving Luna a much needed potty break, knowing she would be alone for a very long time after they had left for the hospital. "I thought it was getting colder in Maryland, but this is another level of cold. If this keeps up you will have snow before Thanksgiving."

"Zoe, have you forgotten already? It's quite normal for Fort Wayne to get snow in November, even sometimes as early as the end of October."

"Yes, I guess you're right. I did forget about that," she confessed. "It's hard to believe, but dad and I have been living in Maryland for over five years now."

"Ladies, not to break up this discussion about the weather and where we are currently living, but I do think we need to get going if you want to be at the hospital by seven."

"I definitely do want to be there on time," Ruth answered, suddenly changing gears and rising to the occasion. Zoe quickly helped her grandmother put the cereal and fruit away, grabbing a disposable *"to-go"* cup and lid from the pantry, filling it to the top with coffee, knowing that the extra coffee would help her wake up.

"Be good, Luna, and guard the house while we are away," Zoe instructed, as they were ready to leave. She walked away with a huff, accepting the inevitable, and then plopped down on her large, overstuffed dog bed that was situated near the sofa, ready to fall back to sleep.

As they pulled into the entrance of the Parkview Heart Institute, Bryan drove right up to the front entrance of the building, trying to make things easier on his mother. "Zoe, escort Nana Ruth up to Pappy Joe's room. I will be there in shortly, right after I park the car."

"Are you sure, Bryan, that you don't want us to wait on you?"

"No, please go on in with Zoe and get yourself checked in. I will be right up after I make a few phone calls and take care of some things. I must make sure everything is okay at the plant, and I also want to call Kelly."

Zoe walked Nana Ruth into the hospital, making her way to the reception desk that was a close distance away. *"Hello, my name is Ruth Carter, and I am here to be with my husband Joseph Carter. He is having surgery today."*

The hospital greeter looked up the information, handing Ruth her visitor's pass, staring then in Zoe's direction for additional clarification. *"Are you here also for Mr. Carter?"*

"He's my grandfather. Yes, I also need a pass."

Then attendant was dull in personality, giving Zoe the necessary security badge, before turning his attention to the next person behind them. They turned and walked away, going in the direction of the elevators. *"So your father is obviously still seeing Kelly?"* Nana Ruth inquired, as the elevator doors opened and then shut behind them.

"Oh yes, he is, and I wouldn't be surprised if one day soon they do decide to get married," she commented distantly, still thinking about the strained conversation that led to some heated words between she and her father, which brought up her living arrangements once they were wed.

"Really?" Nana Ruth replied, acting somewhat surprised. *"I knew they liked each other a lot, but I didn't realize that things had become so serious between them."*

"Yes, Nana Ruth, it is that serious, but my father has assured me if they do get married, I won't be kicked out of the house, thank God!"

"For heavens sakes, Zoe, no one would do something that insensitive to you!"

"I hope not," Zoe grinned, grabbing onto her grandmother's arm and giving her a sideways hug, before helping her off of the elevator. *"So where is Pappy Joe's room at?"* Zoe whispered, as they walked past the nurse's station that was a flurry of morning activity.

"Right this way, child," she answered and then pointed, as they proceeded down the corridor to the last door on the left.

Joe Carter was propped semi-upright in his bed, looking slightly sedated, with several bags of fluid being fed through an IV into his arm, and oxygen being fed through his nose, staring at the television that was broadcasting the early morning news. *"Well hello there!"* he slurred out, trying to act pleasant. *"What a surprise to see you, my sweet Zoe!"*

Zoe began to shed a few tears, realizing her wonderful grandfather shouldn't be in the state he was in, but having no other choice in the matter. "Well hello to you too, Pappy Joe," she answered caringly, bending down slightly to briefly touch his hand. "Dad is parking the car, and will be up here in a few minutes to be with you."

"Has the pastor been in yet today - to visit and pray with you?" Ruth inquired anxiously, wanting as much praying done as was humanly possible, before the open-heart surgery was performed.

"No, he hasn't. He said around 8 o'clock he should be stopping by."

Bryan joined the group, breaking into the conversation. "Hi dad," he waved from the other side of the room. *"Who is stopping by at eight?"*

"Pastor Davis. He wants to pray for me."

"Good to hear!" Bryan answered simply, dealing with his own set of strained emotions for what the day ahead held.

A nurse and anesthesiologist entered next, checking on Joe's vitals and asking a set of standard questions. "Mr. Carter, just to confirm, no known allergic reactions to anesthesia in the past?"

"*Correct.*"

"No allergies to latex."

"*Correct.*"

Ruth looked concerned, feeling Joe looked pasty white, eager now for the operation to be over and done with, as the questioning continued and Zoe locked her arm in hers for support. *"It's okay, Nana Ruth, everything being asked is standard procedure. It's for Pappy's safety, so it's a good thing,"* Zoe added quietly for her ears only, smiling reassuredly at her grandmother during the whole line of questioning.

"We are going to start administering a drug to relax you and prepare you for surgery. Someone will be here to get you within the hour."

"Thank you," Joe replied, as he smiled serenely at the anesthesiologist. *"I guess I will be here waiting, unless my family has other plans for me,"* he ended with some of his humor that he was known for, trying to remain positive while facing the unknown.

"I hope Pastor Davis shows up soon," Ruth said, feeling the anxiety beginning to take hold of her once again.

Bryan looked at his watch. *"Mom, it's only seven forty-five. He's not due here yet for another fifteen minutes,"* he commented somewhat sternly, trying to throw out a subtle hint, hoping that she would calm down and not upset or concern his father with her needless ramblings.

"Did I just hear my name being mentioned?" The well-fed, pleasant acting, fifty-something minister asked, as he entered the room.

"Thank God, you made it!" Ruth breathed with a big sigh of relief.

"I'm a man of my word, sister Ruth. You know that about me," he grinned, trying to ease the worries and tension of the room.

"Yes, you are, and I'm sorry, Pastor Davis, for doubting that," Ruth confessed, feeling badly now for her foolish thoughts."

"It's okay, Ruth," Pastor Davis comforted, reaching out to touch her. "It's a difficult time, and most of us would be no different under the circumstances. So let's get down to business. I'm here to offer prayer for our brother Joseph, and I would like for all of us to join hands around Joe's bed and we will pray together for him. The group did accordingly, joining their hands high over Joe's heart and down around his feet, as a shield of faith before the Lord. *"The bible says where two or three are gathered in your name, you are in the midst, so with that said, we are offering our prayers before you today, dear heavenly father, for Joseph and for the surgery that will be performed on his heart very soon. We pray that you guide the surgeon's hands in a miraculous sort of way, and bring our brother Joe victoriously through this, stronger and healthier than he was prior to the surgery. We pray all this in Jesus name. Amen and amen!"*

Tears were shed by all present in the room, as hands were released and positions were resumed a short distance away from Joe's bed. In came an orderly with a clipboard in hand, who was required to check the hospital bracelet of the patient, just to make sure he was wheeling away the right guy. *"Are you ready to go now, Mr. Carter?"*

"Yes, I am!" Pappy Joe answered with somewhat of a peaceful glow now present on his face, looking at Ruth lovingly as he spoke. "If I don't see you again - this side of heaven - you know my final wishes. I love you, my dearest Ruth!"

"Now, Joe, I don't want to hear that sort of talk coming from you!" She insisted, reaching out one last time for his hand, giving it a comforting squeeze of reassurance. *"Everything is going to be fine and you will get through this! Remember, we just prayed and asked God to protect you throughout the surgery. We will be here waiting, Joe, and*

then you will see us again real soon - when you are finally in recovery," Ruth promised with a sheen of tears suddenly stinging her eyes, as she reluctantly released his hand - hoping beyond hope - that she would be able to hold his hand once more and her words would come true. The orderly proceeded to take Joe Carter from the hospital room, departing from the family and Pastor Davis, wheeling him down the long hallway, through a set of double doors, where he finally disappeared and was no longer in sight.

Chapter 27

The diagnosis of coronary artery disease was disturbing enough news for the family, but six hours later, after pacing up and down the hospital hallways, knowing that bypass surgery was necessary to divert the blood flow away from the narrowing veins of Joe's heart, they were still anxiously waiting on any word. It was even more stressful for the diligent prayers warriors than for the patient, who without them even knowing, was already out of surgery and in recovery, being closely monitored by a full staff of professionals. Joe Carter had made it through the first difficult hurdle of having the operation, and now it was over and done with.

Doctor Stevens finally walked through the doors and made his appearance, still being in his scrubs, wanting to share the details of the procedure with the family. *"Mrs. Carter?"*

"Yes?"

"I'm Doctor Stevens, your husband's cardiologist and surgeon. We did already meet, but I realize you were still dealing with the shock of your husband's heart attack, so maybe you don't remember me?"

"Yes, I remember you, Doctor Stevens," Ruth answered emotionlessly, still trying to mentally catch up and deal with the reality of what was the *"new normal"* for Joe.

"Well, that's good to hear," he replied with a kind smile, trying to be conscious of her fragile mindset, seeing it daily with the families and friends of his other patients. *"Are we free to speak in front of the others here present?"*

"Of course! This is my son, granddaughter and pastor."

"I wanted to share with you that the triple bypass surgery was a success. There was an eighty percent blockage to his heart as you know, but it is now repaired and the blood is flowing freely again. I was concerned with the fact that your husband is a seventy-year-old man, but he seems to be in fairly good health otherwise - putting the heart issues aside. I know he stays active with outdoor activities, and that probably has been a *"life saver"* for him. I must inform you though, that he will have a long journey ahead of him with his recovery time. He will need to remain in the hospital for a week, being monitored and evaluated, and then it is going to take another three months until he is fully recovered and functional again."

"Oh my... that is a long time!" Ruth gasped, not expecting the surprising news.

Doctor Stevens slightly frowned by her reaction. *"Are you concerned on the extent of the hospital stay or the healing time afterwards?"*

Bryan and Zoe looked at each other, both experiencing feelings of helplessness, wishing they could soothe Ruth's apprehensions. Pastor Davis was also nearby, remaining quiet, but ready to jump in if necessary with words of comfort and encouragement for his loyal church member in her time of need.

"I'm sorry, doctor Stevens. This is all so new to me and I honestly had no clue what to expect after this sort of surgery took place."

"That is totally understandable. I wish the nursing staff would have filled you in somewhat better - with our various informational brochures - but going forward, you will be prepared for what lies ahead with your husband's lengthy recuperation. But for now, when your husband is stable, we will allow one person at a time to be with him for a limited period. Someone from our nursing team will be out soon, to let you know when visitation with Mr. Carter is possible. "

"Thank you, doctor, for everything you did to save my husband's life."

Doctor Stevens was touched by Ruth's kind and considerate words, that he didn't hear that often coming from other patient's families. "You are more than welcome, but again, I must say this guardedly, your husband has a long road ahead of him in way of recovery."

"Are you saying that there still is a chance that he may not survive?" Zoe asked point blank, suddenly feeling alarmed by the way the doctor was stating things and repeating the same message.

Doctor Stevens paused, fully turning his attention towards her, thinking carefully how to answer the question. "Your grandfather is still in a crucial time period for his recovery, but with that said, he is where he needs to be, being monitored if something would go wrong - where we can resolve any issues very quickly."

"It's okay, Zoe. Pappy Joe is in good hands here at Parkview!" Bryan reassured as he hugged his daughter close, trying to take the interrogating pressure off of the doctor and provide her with some much-needed comfort in the meantime.

"I need to go now, but in closing and just to review again, I feel good about the success of the surgery and I want you to focus in on that, instead of what could possibly go wrong," the doctor concluded, looking once again in Zoe's direction as he expressed his final remarks.

Doctor Stevens walked away, leaving the family and Pastor Davis alone once again, now waiting on the nursing staff to show up with the good news that it was finally time to visit with Joe. Zoe resumed her pacing up and down the hallway, unable to relax, losing her ability to be patient any longer.

"Zoe, why don't you go outside and just breathe the air? Maybe call Emma or even Mason? You realize it's after 3 o'clock and you haven't had anything to eat, except for that bowl of cereal that you had at Nana Ruth's house this morning?"

"But I may miss out on the announcement from the nursing staff that Pappy Joe can finally have visitors," she insisted.

"Yes, that may happen, but I will call or come outside and get you - if when we hear something. Remember, Nana Ruth should have top priority to visit with him first anyway."

"You're right," Zoe conceded. "I could definitely use a quick break if you don't mind," she admitted, feeling rather weary from the long day already.

"Take a few minutes, because there is no rush. Pappy Joe will be in the hospital for a week and you will have plenty of time to visit with him. Coming out of anesthesia and being on pain meds, he probably won't remember any of us visiting with him today anyway. *Do you realize that?*"

Zoe began to cry, with fear now overtaking her. "The doctor acted as if he still might not make it. Of course I want some time with him in case something unforeseen happens, whether he remembers me being there today or not."

Bryan shook his head in a troubled sort of way, empathetic and relating to her logic and concern. "I get it, but we can't *"borrow trouble"* about all this right now. Pappy Joe will make it. Just believe in that and try your best to stay positive!"

Zoe walked out of the main entrance of Parkview, after grabbing a tuna fish sandwich from the hospital cafeteria, finding a park bench close by where she sat and attempted to unwind. The autumn sun was shining brightly and warming her face, as she took a few bites, downing it with a cold bottle of green tea afterwards. She looked at her phone, after turning it back on, realizing she had three missed calls - one from Mason and two from Emma - with two text messages coming through from the very same people that she needed to answer.

Call me when you get the chance. Concerned about Pappy Joe. Emma

Zoe, I hope all is okay with your grandfather. I said some prayers for him today, which is big for me - by the way - because I typically don't do that much praying. When you get a chance, call me. I just want to hear your voice again. Mason

Zoe smiled at Mason's message, reminded that he was a kind and considerate guy, still not totally grasping the concept that he was probably considered her *"new boyfriend"*. She dialed him first, wanting to hear his voice also.

"Hi, Zoe!" Mason enthusiastically exclaimed, relieved that she was finally reaching out. *"How is your grandfather doing?"*

"I guess as well as can be expected, after having triple bypass surgery."

"It sounds like you and your family are going through a lot. I could put in for a few personal days and come out there to join you and help out."

Zoe smiled, appreciating Mason's thoughtfulness. "That is not necessary. Please don't take this the wrong way, but my family hasn't met you yet - outside of my father - so it probably isn't the best time to be introducing you to everyone - under the circumstances."

"I totally understand. I meant no harm by the suggestion."

"I know you didn't, Mason, and I'm sorry if I was being a little insensitive implying you are not welcome. It's just that I'm touchy right now with everything that is taking place here. We waited for over six hours for the surgery to be completed, and now that it is, we are waiting again for the *"green light"* for my Pappy Joe to be able to receive visitors while he is in recovery. All I want is to do is see him, so I know he is doing okay."

"Wow, that is a lot of time to be waiting, and I totally get it that you are on edge! Well, I won't hold you up any longer, and I'm super happy that you called me back today, Zoe."

"That was very sweet of you, Mason, to call and check on my grandfather. That means more to me than you could possibly know. Let's talk again soon," she concluded, happy that he had made the effort to reach out.

The next call was to Emma, but with this one she received her voicemail, which didn't surprise Zoe in the least. She assumed she was very busy at the restaurant, probably *"knee-deep"* with customers, trying to get their orders straight and their meals served in a decent time fashion, and then attempting to the best of her ability - to keep things organized at *"Luna's"* - on top of everything else.

"Em, it's me. Pappy Joe made it through his six-hour surgery. It was confirmed that he did actually have an eighty percent blockage of his heart, which required triple bypass surgery to correct the issues. Three months of healing time is now ahead of him, and Nana Ruth will have all this to deal with after my father and I leave. I am overwhelmed, trying to figure out what I can do to help out, since I know I must return to Maryland soon. That's about it for now.... Just waiting to visit with him and let him know how much I love him. I miss you, my friend, and thanks for going the extra mile and holding things down at Luna's while I am away."

Zoe hung up, taking the last few bites of her tuna sandwich, with another text coming through immediately from Bryan. *It's time to come back inside. Pappy Joe can finally have visitors! Nana Ruth just went back to be with him, and then it will be your turn next.*

Chapter 28

A friendly nurse escorted Ruth back the long expanse of the corridor, on the way to the critical care recovery area of the heart center. *"Right this way, Mrs. Carter,"* she whispered, as she pulled back the curtain of the partitioned area where Joe was resting, revealing a *"shell of the former man"* that she was not prepared to see. Ruth's hands flew up to her mouth in shock, after seeing her husband pasty white, with tubes coming out of his arms that were hooked up to drip bags of fluid, a monitor that kept track of his vitals off to one side, and oxygen being fed through a tube which had been placed in his nose. His chest had been split open and he was now stitched back together, and his body in that particular area, was wrapped in a way that made him look somewhat *"mummy-like"*. He was barely conscience, but his eyes were blinking slowly open and then shut, providing Ruth with a sense of relief and reassurance that he was still alive.

She bent over his bed without touching him, leaning in closely by his face, with the nurse still in the room - a short distance away. *"Joe, I'm here, sweetheart,"* she tenderly announced for his ears only, as he attempted to turn in her direction. *"Please don't move,"* she begged, not wanting to cause him any additional pain, as he looked at her, seeking out the eyes of that *"special female"* that he adored. *"Joe, you made it through the heart surgery and you are now in recovery. I also wanted you to know that you have a lot of people praying for you at the church, darling,"* Ruth explained, as she gently brushed over the covers. Joe slightly nodded his head and smiled, fully aware of what she was conveying.

Ruth sat for the remainder of her allotted visitation time by Joe's bed, making small talk about life outside of the hospital and what they had to look forward to once he was recovered. The nurse reappeared fifteen minutes later, intentionally glancing at her watch. "Mrs. Carter, if you would like Mr. Carter to have additional visitation from the others that are also waiting, it may be time to make the switch now," she politely reminded, as Ruth rose to say her goodbyes. *"Honey, it's time for me to go now, but I will return first thing in the morning to see you again. I love you with all my heart,"* she expressed with full devotion, blowing her *"cherished spouse"* a kiss on the way out of the room.

Zoe was soon to follow, being escorted by the same female nurse back the hallway, being given a *"pre-warning"* as to the present state she would see her grandfather in, as well as the same reminder about the time allowance. The curtain was pushed back again, but even with what was described in advance by the nurse, Zoe was not prepared to see the dire picture of Pappy Joe lying out in front of her like he was. Her eyes began to immediately puddle up with tears, as she looked to the nurse with pleading in her eyes. *"Are you sure he is okay? He looks extremely pale and out of it."*

"All normal after heart surgery," she confirmed, as they stood a distance away talking. *"His vitals are in a good range, so he is honestly doing much better than we had anticipated at this point."*

"Thank God..." Zoe breathed, happy and relieved to hear those words.

"I will be right outside if you need me. Take some time to be with your grandfather. I'm sure he will be glad to know that you are here visiting with him."

Zoe timidly approached, not wanting to wake him. *"Pappy Joe... it's me, Zoe."*

Joe blinked his eyes, smiling slightly as he watched Zoe continuing to stand at the foot of his bed and taking everything in – looking distressed from witnessing it for the very first time. *"Come... around... here"* he weakly requested.

"I'm right here, Pappy Joe," she answered, as she proceeded around to the side of his bed, now in closer contact with him. "My dad and the pastor are outside in the waiting room wanting to see you also."

A grimacing look crossed Joe's face as he tried to shift his position, suddenly remembering that he had just had heart surgery, alarming Zoe in the process.

"Are you okay, Pappy Joe? Should I get the nurse for you?" Zoe urgently asked, not sticking around for the answer. She disappeared from the room, finding the nurse a short distance away, walking towards her at an accelerated pace. The nurse looked up from her cellphone, surprised to see Zoe in such a panic.

"My grandfather appears to be in pain. Please check on him!"

They quickly walked back to the room, as the nurse checked the monitor readings and Joe's vitals. "Mr. Carter are you feeling like you need additional pain medication?" she inquired, as she replaced the covers over his bandaged area.

Joe shook his head slightly – *yes* – as the nurse disappeared to contact doctor Stevens. Zoe returned to the side of the bed, with concern now etched on her face, impatiently waiting for help to arrive. "Just relax Pappy Joe. The doctor should be here any minute to check on you."

Dr. Stevens was paged and joined the group, being polite but ready to assess the situation, as he made his entry. He rechecked the monitor and vitals, looking over the incision area carefully. "Mr. Carter, I see nothing to be concerned about, but I do feel it may beneficial for you to put off seeing anymore visitors until tomorrow morning - at the soonest. I'm going to administer additional pain medication and a sleep aid so that you can get a good night's rest, and tomorrow should be a much better day," he reassured, trying to ease the tensions in the room.

"So he is fine?" Zoe intensely inquired.

"I see no cause for alarm. Please notify the others, that I think your grandfather just needs some additional rest before visitation can resume again tomorrow," Doctor Stevens rationally explained, knowing it was the best thing for the patient.

"Sure thing. I will definitely let them know, doctor Stevens," Zoe confirmed, still looking at her grandfather in a worried sort of way. *"Get some rest, Pappy Joe, and we will all be back in the morning for another visit. Love you!"* she chirped out emotionally with a few additional tears now forming, disappearing from the room. She walked to the end of the hall, opening the heavy set of doors to the visitor's lounge where Nana Ruth, Bryan and pastor Davis were sitting and waiting, ready to convey the doctor's message to all of them.

Bryan rose, stretching his arms overhead. *"Well, I guess I'm next,"* he smiled.

"No dad, not today."

"And why is that?"

"Pappy Joe seemed to be in a lot of pain, so the nurse contacted doctor Stevens and he just returned to the room to check in on Pappy. He ended up giving him additional pain medication, as well as some medicine to help him sleep."

"Is he all right? He hasn't had any sort of setbacks, has he?" Bryan implored, suddenly feeling concerned.

"Doctor Stevens doesn't think so... But he does feel that Pappy Joe needs to get a good night's rest before visiting can resume again tomorrow. I was instructed by the doctor to give all of you that message - in case you were wondering."

"Should we leave Bryan?" Nana Ruth inquired of her son, now uncertain about the state of affairs with her husband again, feeling suddenly taken back and worried.

"I would say it is okay to take off. If Doctor Stevens rechecked dad and gave Zoe the information to give to us, I am sure we are free to leave the hospital. Don't worry, I will bring you back first thing in the morning," Bryan promised, with his arm now wrapped around his mother's shoulder.

"I won't be able to return first thing in the morning," Pastor Davis informed. "We have a men's weekly prayer time and bible study tomorrow in the a.m. that will keep me occupied, but I will be here the first chance I get during the afternoon," he smiled and promised.

"Thank you, Pastor David," Ruth replied, as the group exited the building, pausing for a moment to stand in a circle and grasp hands yet for another time, for one final prayer that was recited by Pastor Davis *for Joe Carter's healing, as well as a for a peaceful night's sleep for everyone,* before they drove away for the evening.

Zoe rested her head on the back seat, as she took a few moments to close her eyes, still reeling from the day's events. She could hear Nana Ruth busily talking to Bryan up front, quizzing him for answers about Joe's recovery - which he did not have the answers to.

"Mom, I know you have so many unanswered questions now flooding through your mind, but honestly, doctor Stevens, or maybe even a nurse, are the professionals who need to answer those questions and concerns for you. I am probably the last person to ask about anything medical," he confessed, feeling like he was letting his mother down somehow, as he pulled into the driveway. *"I will let you know this though, I'm starving! Maybe another bowl of that delicious soup would be nice, if you have it?"* he grinned, trying to lighten the mood.

"Yes, there is some more vegetable beef soup, and if you would like, I could make some grilled cheese sandwiches to go along with it?" Ruth offered.

"No need, Nana Ruth," Zoe insisted. "I am quite well-versed in cooking now, since owning the restaurant." "Why don't you both freshen up and I will get *"supper"* on the table for us very shortly?

"You got a deal!" Bryan answered.

The three walked into the house, feeling somewhat weary, with Luna running to greet them. "We're back, sweetie!" Zoe gushed, wrapping her arms around her *"furbaby's"* neck, leaning in close to her side as she petted her. *"I needed this hug more than you could know,"* she confessed tenderly, as Luna gave her a lick on the cheek, almost if she understood her mistress, making Zoe feel slightly better in the process.

The mood was somber and quiet as they ate their leftover vegetable beef soup and grilled cheese sandwiches that Zoe had prepared. Conversation was difficult and strained, and no one wanted to say the wrong thing to upset Nana Ruth concerning Pappy Joe, before they headed off to bed. The table was cleared and the dishes were hand washed and then put away by Zoe, as Ruth and Bryan retired early for the evening, knowing the next day would be upon them before they knew it.

Zoe lay in bed, feeling totally exhausted, as a text message came through from Mason, tender and just as sweet as all the others. *Thinking about you and how much I wish I were there to hold and comfort you during this difficult time. I am praying for you and your family, and hoping the best for your Pappy.*

Thank you, Mason. You don't know how much those words mean to me. I trust that those prayers, along with many others, will be answered. Good night and sleep well. Miss you also!

Chapter 29

Doctor Stevens had made the right decision of not allowing any further visitors until the next day for Joe Carter. He had slept peacefully throughout the night, and no major setbacks had occurred. The family returned to the hospital, with visits now being made by all three in the early morning hours. Pastor Davis also returned to Parkview in the afternoon, after the morning men's prayer and bible study gathering had concluded. He not only had the time to check in on his church parishioner, but also once again offered an uplifting prayer of encouragement that made Joe smile and shed a few tears of joy, realizing that God had spared his life and brought him through the difficult surgery under the expert hands of his surgeon.

After one week of being at Parkview Heart Institute, Doctor Stevens thought it was in Joe's best interest to go to a rehabilitation facility ran by Parkview, for an additional couple of weeks, where he would begin a physical therapy program. It was a vital step in helping him regain strength, under the watchful eye of an expert team of physical therapists that would be able to monitor him continuously - twenty-four hours a day. Ruth insisted she could fully take care of her husband at home, driving him daily to physical therapy appointments, but Bryan jumped in and was the calming sensible force for his mother saying, *"this was normal protocol after such a major surgery, and she needed to take some pressure off of herself and allow it to happen"*.

With Joe finally situated at the rehabilitation center, the daily routine began, and was not easy at first, as he pushed through each exercise that was custom-tailored exclusively for him. Beyond the physical therapy sessions, he walked the hallways with willing volunteers from his family and also the church folk, each taking a turn to be by his side, encouraging him to be strong and tough as they made the daily stroll together.

It has been over three weeks now of being away from Williamsport, and both Bryan and Zoe knew that it was finally time to leave. Zoe was given a *"pass"* for however long she wanted to stay away from *Luna's,* with Emma claiming daily *"that the place was running well without her"*, which honestly troubled Zoe to the core. She didn't want to think that she was so *"easy to be replaced"* from a business that she had struggled so hard to put into being in the first. The power company was being especially accommodating to Bryan, even suggesting that he could take off more time under the *"Family Leave Act"*, but it would be without pay. Ruth and Joe overheard the discussion that Bryan was having with the plant's human resource director, as he stepped off to the one side of his father's hospital room, considering his options for staying there several weeks more. His parents insisted that it wasn't necessary for neither he nor Zoe to be there any longer, holding Bryan to a date of departure, realizing their *"good-will"* gesture needed to come to an end sooner rather than later.

A compromise was reached, that Bryan and Zoe would remain in Fort Wayne until Joe was released from the rehabilitation center and back in the comfort of his own home, just to make sure Ruth could truly handle things as well as she claimed she could. A network of generous and kind church members and neighbors, signed up to assist in any way that was needed - from home and church maintenance - that Joe was single-handedly involved in usually - to providing daily meals - whether Ruth protested or not. Rides were also freely offered, for transporting Joe to the rehabilitation center, which was actually a sense of relief for Ruth, even if she didn't want to openly admit it.

The bags were packed and Bryan placed them in the car, knowing Zoe was still struggling with leaving her grandparents behind. She sat in the living room on the sofa with each one by her side, cherishing the last few moments that remained. The room was filled with numerous beautiful floral arrangements that had been sent by the church, the employees at *Luna's,* the power company workers, Luke and Emma, and finally Mason - which totally surprised her that he would make such a charming gesture. "Pappy Joe, you guys should come to Williamsport for Thanksgiving in a few weeks," Zoe suggested with a tender, caring smile, as she grabbed for his hand.

"I don't think I will be released yet to make such a long drive, my dear, but definitely next year we will try to make it," he promised tenderly, with an equally loving smile confirming it.

"How about I drive, Joe, and try to make the trip to Maryland this year for Thanksgiving?" Nana Ruth suggested.

Joe shook his head, leaning forward some to look at his wife, who was positioned on the other side of Zoe on the sofa. "Now Ruth, you know that never happens on our trips. I am the one who consistently is doing all the driving."

"Well things are different now, Joe," Ruth insisted practically. *"We need to transition, as you can plainly see."*

"Then why don't we return here over Thanksgiving?" Zoe brightened and suggested, with the thought of doing so now planted firmly in her mind.

"That may be a little tough this year, Zoe, since it's less than a month away," Bryan interjected, knowing Kelly was anxiously awaiting his swift return, not wanting to admit she held some weight in his decision making.

Zoe looked somewhat puzzled, surprised by her father's response. "Well, then I will come back alone. It isn't that far of a drive."

Ruth reached out to pat her granddaughter's free hand that wasn't holding on to Pappy Joe's. "There is no need for that. You go home and get back to the restaurant and that new man, Mason that you told me about. I'm sure he can't wait to see you again after being away for three solid weeks. And besides, our church is hosting an event for the *"less fortunate"* over Thanksgiving that we will probably sign up for anyway. If Pappy Joe is up for it by then, I will be helping out with the cooking and Pappy Joe will be supervising everyone, *making sure we are all doing it correctly."*

The group began to laugh at Ruth's jovial humor, greatly lightening the mood. "It's time to go, Zoe. I don't want to be on the road too late," Bryan stated firmly, once again causing Zoe some angst and confusion.

"Okay... understood," she answered, as she stood up, along with her grandparents. *"I want to say one last prayer for Pappy Joe and Nana Ruth though, if it is all right with your guys?"* She asked, hoping to gain their permission.

"Of course, Zoe!" Pappy Joe replied, finding her willingness to do so, endearing and thoughtful.

All hands were joined, as they stood together in a circle, and Zoe led the final prayer before they departed, closing out the last three weeks of prayers for her grandfather. *"Dear Heavenly Father, thank you for bringing my pappy through this difficult surgery, and for granting him remarkable strides in his physical therapy that he has been going through. I ask that you will continue to be with him, allowing for his complete healing and recovery, returning him to his former self, but only a much healthier version. I ask for safety also as we travel home, and shorten the time until we can all be back together again as a family. Amen."*

Eyes were opened once again and each held tears that were not hidden from the other family members present in the room. "Zoe that was a lovely prayer and I appreciate it that you wanted to pray for me," Pappy Joe genuinely expressed, being very touched by the sentiment, as he wrapped Zoe securely in a big bare hug and held her close, not wanting to let her go.

"Be careful, Pappy Joe," she whispered into his ear. "Please don't hurt yourself."

Joe laughed, holding her now at arm's length, trying to get his message across. "I'm stronger than you give me credit for," he reassured, releasing her then to take the journey back home. A few additional hugs were shared, with more tears being added to the mix, as they all walked outside and Bryan loaded the suitcases into the trunk. Luna had her final *"potty time"* before jumping into the back of the vehicle, with Zoe taking the front seat positioned by her father, who had already started the engine and was ready to get on the road as soon as possible.

"I will call you when we're back in Williamsport," Bryan promised, as he gave a final lingering look of concern directed at both of his parents. He drove away, watching their ceaseless waving that he could clearly see from the rearview mirror, until they were no longer in site, left only then with his restless thoughts to guide him along the way.

"I hope we are doing the right thing by leaving. Pappy Joe could have benefited from our additional help if we would have stayed there a little bit longer."

"Zoe, it was time. Pappy Joe and Nana Ruth are very lucky to have their friends and Pastor Davis to rely on, unlike many folks who don't have a support system when they go through something similar. Everything has been thought out and put in place by the church and the neighbors, which is pretty impressive when you think about it," Bryan explained, as he focused in on the heavy traffic in front of him. "And honestly, we have our life back in Maryland with our jobs and loved ones who are waiting on us there."

Tell me this urgency to go home doesn't have anything to do with Kelly, does it?" Zoe questioned, acting somewhat irritated, feeling there was more to the story than he was telling.

Bryan briefly took his eyes off the road, turning to look at Zoe, glaring at her in the process. *"That was a pretty brazen question that you just asked of me, don't you think?"*

Zoe shook her head in frustration, realizing that the same determination wasn't in her heart to get back home to Mason. She cared about him, but not to the level of making him a top priority over her grandparents. "Not really... You miss Kelly, and I guess I can understand that, but I also know we won't get a *"do-over"* if a poor decision was made for leaving. Now is the crucial time for helping Pappy Joe and Nana Ruth out. I just don't like feeling that we have *"short-changed"* them somehow."

"For heaven's sakes, Zoe, they are my parents, and I would never do anything to make them feel like I *"short-changed"* them ever! I spoke at length to Pappy Joe while you were out walking Luna yesterday, and we both came to the same conclusion that it was time for us to go. Kelly is very special to me, but she did not pressure me in any way to come home!" Bryan glanced over at Zoe again at that point, looking somewhat hurt by her rude remarks. "While we are on the subject though, I would ask that going forward you take on a different attitude towards Kelly. I know you are civil with her, but I also feel like you are suddenly resisting the seriousness of our relationship, and you can get quite bossy and opinionated where she is concerned."

Zoe's eyes suddenly filled with tears of emotion, as she watched her dad driving. *"It's been almost 18 years that it's been only you and I. Do you realize that?"*

"Yes, Zoe, I do realize that, but Nana Ruth stated it clearly *that we need to transition.* This is just a normal progression of life - growing up, moving on, and getting into the next chapter of things. I haven't been married in years, and then only married for a short period of time - six years to be exact - the first time around, when I was married to your mother, Cynthia. Maybe I'm thinking and hoping I will be a married man again one day."

Zoe paused, studying her dad and then honestly considering what he was saying. "I'm sorry, dad, for what you lost because of being married to Cynthia. I guess I can understand that you are in love with Kelly, and want to go forward with her in a marriage. *So when is this all going to take place?"*

"*I was thinking maybe at Christmas? Isn't that the time of year when people get engaged?"* he grinned.

"*I guess so…. I wouldn't know,"* Zoe replied rather quietly, somewhat hanging her head, remembering Noah's rejection once again.

"Hey, I didn't mean to upset you. One day, someone special will come along and want to marry you too. You are pretty and have so much to offer, not to be a desirable catch."

Zoe smiled, with her mood suddenly lifting. "You have a way of setting things straight for me, dad. Thank you for saying that," she answered, realizing her attire, hair and lack of makeup had been less than attractive for the last three weeks, and didn't do a whole lot to pump up her ego.

"I meant every word of it, Zoe. How about a *"pit stop"?* I see a gas station up ahead and I wouldn't mind switching places with you for a *"little shuteye"."*

"*Absolutely!"* Zoe replied back eagerly, ready now to get home to Williamsport for a little romance of her own. She was suddenly anxious to see Mason again, and catch up where they had left off.

Chapter 30

Mason, I'm back home, Zoe texted, as Bryan pulled into the driveway of their rancher, right at seven o'clock sharp. He hurriedly grabbed the suitcases, calling over his head as he unpacked the trunk.

"I'm heading over to Kelly's house. I won't be home until tomorrow," he explained rather briefly, leaving Zoe stunned that he hadn't mentioned his plans previously in the car during the long drive.

"Sure..." she answered blankly, not even certain Bryan had heard her response. *"Have a good time!"* she yelled out, as he waved and went back out the front door, with one ear already glued to his cellphone, probably talking to Kelly.

"Well, now what?" Zoe asked of Luna, who was begging for a walk after the long car ride. Her cell rang as she made her first lap around the neighborhood.

"Hey, babe, you...are fin... ally home!" Mason exclaimed with his cheerful Texas twang.

"Yes, I am!"

"I'd love to see you to...night if you are up for it?" He threw out pleasantly.

Zoe considered the invitation, remembering the house was totally hers for the evening. *"Sure. Why don't you stop by my house? My dad went to his girlfriend's place for the night."*

"So we will be all alone?"

"All alone, except for Luna," Zoe giggled.

"I'll be there within the hour. Would you like me to bring some dinner?"

"I would love dinner."

"Pizza okay?"

"Pizza is perfect! Do you need a suggestion on a good place?"

"No, actually... I figured that out all on my own while you were away. I stopped by a place called *Tony's* and had a pizza and some beer one evening. Wasn't too bad! *Have your heard of the place?*"

Zoe shook her head with a roll of her eyes, always having to remember Mason was still fairly new in town, just like she had been several years earlier. "*Tony's* is a mainstay restaurant in Williamsport, and yes, everyone living here - for the most part - knows about *Tony's*."

"Ex...cept for me, obviously!" Mason openly confessed, with his strong southern accent coming through once again, humoring Zoe and reminding her why she had been so attractive to him in the first place.

"Well, now you know about the place. Let me get off of here and grab a shower before you arrive. And by the way, I like peperoni pizza - if it matters."

"Of course it matters, dar... ling. I will be there with a peperoni pizza and a six-pack of beer in an hour. Can't wait to see you!"

"Can't wait to see you too, Mason."

Zoe showered and changed, out of her overly worn blue jeans and sweatshirt of three days' use, choosing clean black leggings and a cozy warm, tan colored, turtleneck sweater that she wrestled with to squeeze over her head. She had washed her hair, having no time to curl it, styling it in a ponytail instead, with a few loose tendrils running down the sides of her face and neck. Makeup was applied, giving special attention to her eyes - with several different shades of shadows, eyeliner and a sweep of mascara - which finished off the sultry look she was trying to create. A touch of lip-gloss and blush to the hollow of each cheekbone, and Zoe felt she was now presentable, and hoped Mason would think so too.

The chill of November was now present, and Bryan had turned on the furnace before leaving for Kelly's place. Three weeks of being away, made a huge difference in the actual temperature of the house, and now it was only sixty-two degrees inside. The unpleasant odor of a startup *"burnt smell"* was present in the air, but as Bryan had stated in the past concerning this - when the subject came up every Autumn - that it would *"soon dispensate once the dust was off of the heating element"*.

The doorbell rang and Luna ran from Zoe's bedroom, barking the whole way to the front door. *"Coming!"* Zoe yelled, walking at a fast pace, with Mason not hearing a word of it. She opened the door to a pleasantly grinning, tall handsome Texan, dressed in tight blue jeans, a white dress shirt with the sleeves rolled up and an extra button undone - that revealed his masculine chest hair - and his signature black cowboy boots that he chose most of the time. He was well-groomed, looking like he had just had his hair cut and his beard trimmed, making Zoe warm all over by the alluring picture he was creating, standing there on the front porch with a pizza box in one hand and a six pack of Yuengling in the other.

"Well, look at you…. you're as pretty as a bouquet of freshly picked flowers," he complimented, stepping across the front door threshold into the living room.

Zoe laughed out loud, always entertained by Mason's lingo. *"You look pretty darn good yourself, cowboy!"* She teased, as Mason hurriedly placed the pizza box and beer on the sofa close by, wrapping Zoe in an intimate embrace as he rubbed passionately up against her, and tongue kissed her until she was breathless.

"God, I missed you," he breathed against her hair, as his erection grew firmer by the second. *"Maybe we can wait on the pizza and beer for a little while until we get reacquainted?"* he playfully proposed, as Zoe grabbed for his hand and led him back the hallway towards her bedroom. Luna was right behind them, ready to enter the room, as Zoe suddenly stopped, and directed the dog elsewhere.

"Stay, Luna!" Zoe commanded, putting a straight arm out with an up-turned hand in the dog's face. *"Go lay down,"* she added sternly, before slipping to the other side of the closed door with Mason. Luna's head hung in disappointment as she slowly walked back out to the living room, jumping up on the sofa, with only the pizza and beer to keep her company.

Clothing, shoes and cowboy boots were quickly removed, as the two collapsed together on Zoe's bed, still with the comforter in place and not bothering to fold it back. Mason's tongue traced a trail from Zoe's trembling over-kissed lips, to her neck, finally resting on a taunt nipple that was just begging to be nuzzled. She moaned out, enjoying the feeling completely, as Mason expertly spread her legs with his other hand, massaging her intimately until she orgasmed with a couple of his moistened fingers. Just as adeptly he placed his throbbing member deeply inside of her afterwards, riding her with a wild abandonment, much like a frisky, untamed horse - out in the Texas badlands.

"Wow, babe, that was amaz... ing," Mason panted out, still trying to catch his breath after such a vigorous frolic. He lay on his side, propped up on one elbow, taking in the sight of the beautiful woman that he was now totally captivated with.

Zoe smiled contentedly back at him, taking in the sheen that was glistening off his chest hair and forehead. *"Yes, it was... I could take a nap now, but I also want to eat that Tony's pizza,"* she grinned, leaning forward to peck kiss him, before rising from the bed and realizing she was suddenly starving.

"Do I get a say so in any of this?" Mason questioned casually, not ready to leave the soft confines of their *"love nest"* behind so quickly.

"I must be fed if you desire more of the same," Zoe tempted, as she slipped into her clothes again.

"Oh... I see how this all works," Mason answered, still nude and wrapping his now dressed vixen in his strong arms, not desiring to release her just yet. He leaned in still, placing a series of light kisses all over her face, making Zoe giggle as she begged for release.

"Mason, I'm going to pee myself if you don't let me go," she bantered in protest.

"Oh... okay.... I see how you are playing this," he joked and laughed, finally releasing her as she ran for the bathroom quickly. "I think I've heard that excuse from you in the past."

Zoe walked into the kitchen looking around for the pizza and beer, realizing it was nowhere to be found, remembering it had been left on the couch while they were distracted and making love. *"Oh my word! I hope Luna didn't eat the pizza!"* She yelled out, making her way to the living room and finding the pizza undisturbed just as it was left. She carried the items to the kitchen arranging them on the counter along with a couple of paper plates and napkins, grabbing for a bottle opener besides. Luna was stretched out on the floor, being more concerned about her big bowl of kibble that her mistress had just provided over the *"intruder"* who had now entered the kitchen.

"Ready to eat?" Mason asked, reaching for a plate.

"Yes, I am, and we are lucky to say we even have something to eat," Zoe pointed out, before taking several slices of pizza and then opening a Yuengling.

"And why is that?"

"Because the pizza and beer were left on the sofa, and Luna was a perfect puppy and didn't get into the pizza box and help herself to some of the pizza."

Mason began to laugh, stuffing half of a slice into his mouth and then chasing it down with a swig of beer. "If you wouldn't have dragged me back the hallway like you did, the pizza would have been left on the counter in the kitchen like I had planned. I guess that's what happens when you've been away for three weeks and you just *"had to have me"*, dar... ling."

Zoe's eyes lit up, finding him sexy and amusing. *"Oh, I'm the only one that was horny and wanted something, huh?"*

"I think you already know the answer to that," Mason challenged seductively, already desiring Zoe again, as he reached over and playfully kissed her, between bites of pizza.

All that remained were only two slices of the pepperoni pizza, but each bottle of the beer had been enjoyed along with some more vigorous sex afterwards. Mason slept peacefully, as Zoe slipped out quietly from the covers and opened the door to her awaiting pup. Luna noticed the additional body before jumping on the bed, planting herself between them anyway, ready to take her regular place beside of Zoe as she did every night, whether Mason was there or not. The loud thump and positioning of the furbaby, that had now created a barricade between the couple, awoke Mason, as he sat straight up and took in the scene.

"Luna's here?" He asked as he looked at Zoe, trying to get his bearings and figure out what was suddenly taking place.

"I hope you don't mind, but this is our routine every night, and I can't change it now because you are here with me," she explained sweetly, hoping that this part of her life was not an obstacle or concern.

Mason grinned, reaching across Luna to plant a sweet kiss on Zoe's lips. "Of course not, dar... ling. She is always welcome to sleep with us, that is at least until after we have had sex, not during!"

Zoe began to laugh, making Luna raise her head with all the sudden commotion. *"Mason you are so crazy!"*

"Crazy about you, Zoe Carter. Totally and completely crazy about you!" he confessed sincerely, planting one last tender kiss on her lips before the happy trio drifted off to blissful sleep.

Chapter 31

Mason left early, with no time to spare for another hot lovemaking session, since the alarm had been ignored and they had overslept. Zoe took a quick shower, dressing in her work attire, but ignoring her makeup and other frilly details. She barely even had time to do her hair, securing it on top of her head in a loose bun, hoping that the customers and staff didn't notice that she was not at her best. The door to the house was quickly locked, with no sign of Bryan coming home, as Zoe opened the car door and Luna immediately jumped in first, crossing over to the front passenger's seat where she always sat when it was only the two of them. *"It's back to our normal routine again, Luna girl,"* Zoe chirped out in baby talk to the animal, as she pulled from her driveway and headed towards the restaurant.

She called her Nana Ruth along the way, just to check in on Pappy Joe, asking about her also, knowing that she had it all on her now – for the most part - to take care of him. *Everything was fine*, Nana Ruth had reassured, stating that *Pappy Joe had already been picked up for physical therapy by one of the churchgoers.* Zoe was relieved that things seemed to be transitioning well after their departure, still feeling somewhat guilty for doing so.

She parked the Mazda CX-3 on Potomac Street, a couple blocks down from the restaurant in her *"regular spot",* allowing for some freed up spaces right out in front for the patrons, who she felt deserved them. The welcoming fall flowers that greeted her, were eye-catching and appealing - in an assortment of colors and varieties - featuring Chrysanthemums, Celosia, Blue Sedge and ornamental grasses. It was obvious that they had been professionally selected and planted in the showy oversized red clay pots that were now on display, having a border of Creeping Jenny in hues of yellow leaves, cascading here and there and down over the sides, adding to the final overall look. Zoe stopped to admire each one positioned near the front door of *Luna's*, feeling somewhat slighted that she hadn't been consulted about the cost for the *"eye-catching"* additions, having left town with a much simpler variety of pots and plantings. She realized though, that she had given Emma full reign in making business decisions while she was away, including how to decorate for the fall season, and it was obvious she had done a good job without her input or influence.

"Love the beautiful planters!" Zoe complimented, as she leaned in to hug Emma soundly and give her a kiss on the cheek.

"I was hoping you would like them!" Emma answered back with a relieved smile. "Rosemary's helped me out with everything! They claim they will last us until December if we cover the pots when frost is in the forecast."

"Makes sense, but why don't we just cover them up every evening anyway, and then we won't have to worry if it ends up being a night of frost or not?"

Emma stopped to take in her smart and practical friend – more than thrilled that she had finally returned. She was the perfect business partner that added her logic to the mix, whenever it was necessary. *"Why didn't I think of that?"* Emma considered, reaching out one more time to hug Zoe.

"Because you can't think of everything, Em, and I know you have had your hands full while I was away, whether you care to admit it or not."

"I can't lie to you, it has been overly busy around here. I even had Luke volunteer and come in to help me out, especially over homecoming weekend for the high school when you first left. Our place was in high demand after the football game on Friday night, and then again on Saturday with the parade and actual homecoming dance."

"Wow, I wish I would have been here for all that. It sounds like it was a busy but exciting weekend in Williamsport. *So you and Luke are still an item then?*"

"Stronger than ever!" Emma confessed happily, sipping deeply from her coffee.

"Why don't you take off for a few days? Maybe you and Luke could do something fun now that I'm back."

"Seriously, are you totally cool with this?" Emma asked in pleasant surprised way, now thinking about the possibility for the very first time.

"Of course I am, Em. Care and consideration for each other doesn't just run one direction. I am focused and ready to take charge again, and just like you having Luke volunteering his time, maybe I will need to do the same with Mason," Zoe considered, as Dennis the chef turned for a brief moment to wave and take in the girls deliberating, glad to see them back together again.

Emma nodded her head, putting two and two together, bringing forth the sarcasm she was known for. *"So it appears that I'm not the only one who has continued things with someone special, even though she was out of town for a while. Did you do the "nasty" last night all over again with Mason?"*

"Yes! Are you happy now?" Zoe laughed. "Saw him again last night, did the *"nasty"* and I guess we are exclusively dating! I will finally admit it! He also spent the night last night at my house, while my dad was at Kelly's place."

Emma's eyes lit up and she was thrilled with the news. "Well, that's exciting, my dear friend. I couldn't be happier for you!"

"So get me up to speed on everything else," Zoe requested, as they both took a cup of coffee out to the back of the building, sitting at the picnic table with their jackets still on, from the chilly morning air that wasn't warming up any time soon.

"Business is incredibly up. I even hired Lou Scally – the local DJ - to come out last weekend for a night of Karaoke. It was a big hit."

"Maybe we should repeat that, from time to time."

"That was what I suggested to him, and he is agreeable in doing so, every now and then, as long as his schedule allows for it."

"That's great to hear! So book him again soon - for over the holidays."

"Will do," Emma replied, going then to the next point. "Dennis, has added some additional *"comfort food"* items to the menu for the fall season that have become popular choices."

"Such as?"

"Chicken Pie, Hog Maw and Salmon Cakes."

"Hog Maw? Are you kidding me?"

"Yes, believe it or not, the tourists are fascinated with this stuff, claiming Williamsport is the only place they have ever heard of or eaten it!"

Zoe began to laugh, shaking her head from a past memory. "I remember the first time I experienced the mention of *"Hog Maw"*. My dad had brought a large portion of it home from a coworker who had given it to him at work. He wanted me to try it out and I resisted – never having the nerve to do so. Just the name itself grossed me out!"

"Try Dennis's version. You may change your mind once you tasted it."

"Maybe..." Zoe reflected, trying to act polite since it was obvious Emma had grown up on the stuff, being a local also. They walked back inside, finding their aprons and securing them behind their backs, realizing their workday needed to begin. *"Ava doing okay?"*

"Yes, she is. Her dating life is going well also. She really likes Philip."

"It's hard to believe how much has changed since we were in high school. No longer the nerdy girls, and now we all have boyfriends. We need to get in touch with Lillian and have a get together again soon, just like we used to do."

"I think she is dating also, but I don't think she has found *"the one"* yet. I see her on Facebook with posts about her hair salon and the different places that she goes to, but rarely do I see her with the same guy. She does appear to be happy though, and she's always smiling."

"You just reminded me I need to make a hair appointment with her and get a haircut. She probably thinks I don't want to do business with her anymore since it has been several months since I was last at her shop. I feel badly, because I never informed her about Pappy Joe's heart attack, and I haven't kept up with my social media lately like you have."

"Speaking of Pappy Joe, how is he doing?"

Zoe paused, thinking about the difficult situation she had left behind in Fort Wayne. "I honestly thought we were going to lose him, Em, but thank God he is healing and getting stronger every day. It was tough for me to leave him and Nana Ruth, but my dad felt it was time. The church folk and his neighbors are his rock, volunteering and taking over totally now that we are gone."

"You can only do so much. Three weeks was a lot of time to give to them."

Zoe's eyes filled with tears. "I don't look at it that way. They have given me so much in life, and I owe them so much in return. Think about everything they have done for us, Emma, because of my nana and pappy you are better off also. We wouldn't have *Luna's* without their initial backing, plus they believed in our *dreams* and encouraged us to be in the restaurant business. *Please never forget that*!"

"I haven't and I never will…. But, I just know you gotta live your life too, sweetie," Emma gently reminded, not wanting to upset Zoe by taking a firm stand on the subject matter.

"Hey, this *"girl talk"* has to end now! I need help with the morning prep, as you both are well aware!" Dennis scolded, turning their attention back to the opening of the restaurant in only two hours.

"Sorry, Dennis, just catching up with my *"bestie"*!"

"I know, Zoe. Welcome back and sorry about your grandfather," he added somewhat aloofly, not one for emotion, while dumping in a can of tomatoes into the pot of boiling hot, spicy chili with beans, that he was making.

"Thanks, Dennis, that means a lot. And I wanted to thank you and everyone else here at *Luna's* for the flowers. They were beautiful and my grandparents really appreciated the kind gesture."

"You can thank Emma for orchestrating all that. She called Rosemary's and they took care of it for us."

"Rosemary's again?"

"Yes, Rosemary's again. They have really kicked in and went the *"extra mile"* for us lately," Emma explained.

"I need to mail them a *"thank you card"* for the beautiful planters out front, and also for all the coordination of the floral arrangements that were sent to my Pappy Joe from folks around here. By the way, are you aware that Luke's name was also included in on the bouquet card that you personally sent?" Zoe asked of Emma, being somewhat confused, as she diced up a couple onions.

"I'm very aware," Emma grinned, since we purchased them together. "Not too much that Luke does anymore gets past me," she replied with a pleasant rise to her voice, as she finished arranging iceberg lettuce and tomatoes in a large container and then placed it back in the refrigerator.

"I feel like I am missing something here?"

"Maybe a little something," Emma giggled.

"What, Em, is going on?"

"I just moved into Luke's apartment. We are in love and I want to spend every waking moment with him, when I'm not working here."

Zoe's mouth dropped open, totally dumbfounded by the news. *"Why didn't you bother telling me this when I was away in Fort Wayne?"*

Emma shook her head and sighed. "I honestly wasn't sure how you would react, and I didn't want to upset you with everything else you were going through with Pappy Joe after his heart attack."

"I'm excited for you, Em. Can't say that I'm not a little surprised by this sudden turn of events, but if you feel you are ready to take that next step in your relationship with Luke, then I wish you both all the happiness in the world."

"That means so much coming from you, Zoe," Emma exclaimed with tears of joy now glistening across her eyes. "I'm glad you are okay with all of this."

"I'm fine," she reassured, placing the Ziploc bag of diced onions in the refrigerator beside of the salad. *"What about your mother though? Surely, she is a little put off since you were helping her out with things at home."*

"We had a fight about it, but now she's fine, after some consideration on her part about the situation. She's actually thrilled to think I am dating someone whose family has money and clout in the community," Emma admitted with a roll of her eyes, being put off by her mother's desire to be around someone who was wealthy and could possibly bring her prestige.

Zoe began to laugh, suddenly reminded of Margie's desires – not only for herself, but also for her daughter. *"So Luke Taylor is now in her good graces?"*

More than you could ever know. She has already shown up several times to our apartment with my sister and brother, and it takes several yawns and hints of the *"lateness of the hour"* to get her to leave."

Zoe continued to be amused with the ongoing story of Margie, finding the whole thing rather comical, as she diced up the last of the requested ingredients that Dennis needed for a few dishes, which he was creating for lunch. "It's time to open in thirty minutes and I want to make sure the tables are set up properly out front. Give it some more thought about taking off for a couple days, and see if Luke is willing to do something with you. It's a beautiful time of the year to get away and *you definitely deserve it, Em!"* Zoe added with a warm smile before walking away, out of the swinging doors of the kitchen, ready to get back in the action of *Luna's*.

Chapter 32

Having Zoe back was a relief and blessing for everyone at *Luna's*. Her presence was definitely missed by more people than just Mason who frequented the establishment everyday for lunch, and typically also for dinner while she was away. He had brought in his co-workers, and even organized one more meeting with The C&O Canal Trust board members, who readily agreed that they wanted to return to *Luna's* from their last delightful experience of eating there.

Zoe was exhausted after her first day back to work had finally come to an end. She walked to the front of the building and flipped the *"open"* sign to *"closed"* on the window, making sure that not a single customer remained inside of the place. *"Hey everybody, it's time to finish up your work and get outta here!"* She announced with a big yawn, appearing and acting depleted.

"Did the day kick you in the ass?" Dennis asked with a big grin, as he finished cleaning off the top of the grill with a scraper blade and grill cleaner.

"Yes, I must admit it did. I gotta get used to this routine all over again."

"Give it a week, and you will be fine," Dennis promised.

"You're right," Zoe agreed, taking the last swig of Shiraz from her stem glass, and then handing it over to the dishwasher who was busily finishing up the remaining pots and pans.

Emma entered the kitchen, untying her apron in the process, having just completed the vacuuming out front. *"You look beat, my friend,"* She observed casually, not realizing that the subject matter was already being discussed.

Zoe nodded and grabbed her purse, after finishing up the daily bookkeeping, glad that she was handed the task once again. "Yes, I will admit it, I'm more than a little tired. Matter-of-fact, I was going to see Mason tonight, but I am going to cancel on him, because I'm so tired. He will be disappointed, but if I went over to his place right now, I would fall asleep as soon as I sat down on his couch."

"He honestly may not mind that," Emma giggled, as Zoe leashed up Luna, being the final task that she needed do before leaving. *"Then he can have his wicked way with you any way he pleases,"* she continued teasing and whispering, with Zoe chucking and understanding the meaning. They walked to the front door together, locking it behind them, knowing Dennis would take care of the alarm system after he was finished and the last one to depart.

"Is Luke at home?"

"Yes, typically he is there waiting on me most evenings, unless he gets into something with his guy friends now and then."

"It sounds like you have a good thing going on with him, and I'm glad that it's all working out so well."

"Well, it's only been two weeks of living together, and that is way too soon to say we won't have our setbacks, but right now it feels totally amazing."

"Don't forget what I said about doing something for a few days with Luke. I will hold down the fort while you are away. It is definitely my turn to *"take hold of the reins"* around here."

"Thanks, Zoe. I plan to talk with Luke tonight about the possibility of a weekend getaway trip. I hope he can take some time off of work, but he always seems so busy with things at the dealership. I'm keeping my fingers crossed though that he will say yes, and I will definitely let you know the outcome after we speak!"

Zoe reached out to give Emma a warm hug before she got into her car. "Thank you for being there for me during Pappy Joe's surgery and for the additional time afterwards. I couldn't ask for a better friend in life than you, Emma Baker!"

"You are very welcome, sweetie," Emma replied, taken back by the endearing sentiment. "Get some rest tonight. If I do get lucky and convince Luke to go away, you will have to be back on your best *"A Game"* again, watching over the shop until I return."

"Already figured that out!" Zoe yelled back, as she pulled away down Potomac Street, heading for home. Her cell began to ring, as she answered the call.

"Hey dar... ling, will it be long until you get over here? I wasn't sure if you wanted something special to eat or drink?"

"Mason, would you hate me if I cancelled out for tonight? I am honestly dead on my feet after my first day back. I'm sure by tomorrow, after a good night's rest, I will feel a lot better and then I will definitely stop by your place after work."

Mason groaned loudly, resigning himself to not seeing her as he had hoped. *"I can't say I'm not dis... appointed, but I understand if you are exhausted, sweet... heart. I had hoped for a repeat of that a... mazing "X-rated" sex that we had last night, but I will just have to be pa...tient and wait until you are up for it again,"* he allured, with his strong East Texas accent getting his point across clearly.

"I promise tomorrow evening will be much different, and then I will stop over right after work once I drop Luna off at the house."

"Maybe spend the night?"

"If you're lucky!" She teased back, enjoying the exchange.

Emma pulled into her assigned parking space at the Londontowne Apartments, climbing the steps to the second floor of the building. She opened the door to the loud sounds of applauding and cheering, and Luke standing on his feet with his arms overhead, *"fake punching"* the sky in victory, focusing totally in on a Raven's football game that was being broadcasted on the television set in front of him. He turned to smile pleasantly at her, as he realized *"the love of his life"* was finally home.

"Come here, babe," he requested playfully, as she willingly made her way over to the sectional, immediately being wrapped in Luke's arms for a lengthy, passionate welcoming kiss. *"I missed you,"* he whispered against her hair, with a slight slur to his speech. She could tell he was slightly intoxicated, probably from seeing the four empty beer bottles that were sitting on the coffee table, instead of being tossed in the trash can that was near by.

"I missed you too," she replied back, with only adoration filling her eyes for the handsome man who had incredibly changed the course of her world within a few short weeks. They collapsed together on cushioned softness of the sectional, taking a few minutes for each other while the commercials were rolling. *"I know you are watching the game, but may I run something by you?"*

"Of course," Luke smiled pleasantly, grabbing for a boob, once again with the after-affects of the beer doing the majority of the talking.

"Seriously, Luke, I need to ask you something."

"Okay, I'm listening," he answered, in between kisses and fondling. *"What is so important that it can't wait until later?"* He questioned, suddenly pausing to take a break and listen to Emma, waiting to hear what was on her mind.

"Zoe has returned, as you know, and she offered to watch over things at the restaurant, just as I did while she was away in Fort Wayne with her grandparents and father for three weeks. She suggested that maybe we could take a mini vacation somewhere together for a few days."

Luke sat back, clasping his hands behind his head, trying to focus in on what Emma was actually suggesting, trying to fully pay attention now. *"Like, go away and not work for a couple days?* I would have to run that by my father, but yes, I think we can make that happen, since I rarely take off. *How about going to Deep Creek Lake to my parents' cabin up in the woods?* This time of the year is beautiful with the changing of the leaves and the coolness in the air. We could take hikes by the lake, cook together in the kitchen, and build fires in the fireplace - where we can make love on the thick shag rug that is laying right in front of it on the floor."

"Sounds very romantic," Emma answered, getting excited already over the possibility of it all. *"Can you ask your dad tomorrow? After all, the leaves will be falling off the trees any day now, and we will miss out on what remains of the autumn colors if we wait too long. And then I must make final arrangements with Zoe so everything is covered at work,"* Emma chattered on, wanting to cover every possible detail as quickly as she could before the game came back on.

"No need to twist my arm, beautiful. I want to go away with you as much as you desire to go away with me," Luke countered with every intention now of being amorous. He reached his hand down between Emma's legs, massaging her intimately through her jeans as he resumed kissing her without end. The game resumed, now in its last quarter, with Emma being turned on to the point of no return, wanting only to be undressed, with Luke's penis deep inside of her, riding her until she collapsed and fell asleep in pure delight. Her wish was granted as clothes were slung carelessly to the floor and Luke entered her, after some intense mutual oral sex, giving one final shout out to the television and then to his intense climaxing orgasm, taking Emma over the edge along with him. The Ravens won the game, scoring the winning touchdown in the final seconds, making for the perfect ending to a very satisfying evening.

Emma drifted off to sleep in Luke's arms, with only thoughts of Deep Creek Lake and their trip away together now etched deeply in her mind. If all went as planned, her getaway adventure with her *"special someone"* would be happening very soon!

Chapter 33

Emma finished the last of her packing, rolling the large suitcase out into the living room, where Luke was busily pacing back and forth and talking on the phone, commiserating with a customer who would not *"do the deal"* with a new sales person he was being tossed over to - on a three-row Land Cruiser – with all the upgrades - unless he spoke with the *owner's son first who he honestly preferred working with, not caring that he had gotten a promotion and was no longer a salesman.* The high cost was affordable for the affluent buyer from the local business community of the town, but for some in the area it was almost the same cost as buying a *"starter"* home, and the price thereof required justification. Luke was smiling triumphantly as he resolved the situation, closing the deal with free oil changes for the next two years and a higher trade-in allowance on his existing ride. He would toss the *"rookie salesman"* an insignificant penance, but for the most part - the commission was all his to enjoy.

"You look pleased," Emma noticed, cocking her head slightly with her one free hand now placed on her hip, and the other one glued to the suitcase handle that she kept holding on to. She gave Luke the signal that it was definitely time to leave, as she continued to stare at him, refusing to sit down and tapping her foot impatiently at the same time.

He walked over to Emma, bending down to kiss her soundly. "I am very pleased! I just closed a deal on a $90,000 Land Cruiser!"

"Who is nuts enough to pay that kind of money for a vehicle?"

"Don't complain, babe," he justified, now totally surrounding her in his embrace, as he kissed her more passionately. "Tickets like this one is the reason why we can go away and enjoy ourselves for a couple days."

Emma's pulse quickened, as she suddenly felt herself weakening, wanting to delay leaving and return to the bedroom for a *"second go-round"* of some delightful morning sex, feeling exhilarated and excited knowing they were actually going away to the mountains for a vacation. "Aww…. as much as I hate to say this, we should really get going and save our lovemaking for when we arrive at the cabin."

"You're right…" Luke whispered in between neck nibbles. "But the thought of going away with you and not working for three days has me all *"hot and bothered"*."

Emma giggled, enjoying the attention he was giving her immensely. "Me too… *But what are you going to do if someone else wants your undivided attention in the next few days like this last customer demanded?"*

"Keep my dick inside of you and talk to them, I guess, all at the same time," Luke teased, giving her a sexy wink and then a playful slap on the ass.

"I'm up for that!"

"My God, Em, why did you pack so much frickin' stuff? Luke asked, somewhat surprised, taking over the wheeling of both of their bags now, as they walked out of the apartment and locked the door behind them. "I know how you women are, feeling like you need to take a lot more than is necessary, but we are going to the mountains where jeans and a sweatshirt will suffice."

"Sorry, hon, I'm just excited. That's all. I wasn't sure if we would venture out to a bar or restaurant at some point," Emma justified sweetly.

Luke loaded their suitcases, along with the cooler and a few other essentials, deciding to take his laptop also, just in case the sales team did require his assistance. "Of course we can do that, if you would like," he replied, not giving it much consideration, but agreeing to do so now, just to keep Emma happy.

The two-hour drive from Hagerstown, Maryland up to McHenry, Maryland was picturesque along the way. The autumn leaves were still vibrant and colorful with hues of reds, oranges and yellows, and only starting to fall from the trees, giving the desired picturesque presence that Emma had hoped for during that first weekend of November.

Luke and Emma laughed and joked as the ride continued, feeling light-hearted and carefree for actually going away, reminiscing over an earlier time when they were still in college. Zoe and Noah had also made the journey then, as the four of them went to the cabin together, but at that time they were *"only friends"* and Zoe and Noah were *"the couple"*. The sleeping arrangements were somewhat awkward, as Zoe and Noah chose the Master bedroom, and the other two slept alone in two of the four bedrooms, in the spacious mountain vacation home that was referred to as a *"cabin"*.

"It's incredible how much things have changed for all of us. Don't you agree?" Emma mentioned, looking over at her hunky companion who was dressed in jeans and a form fitting gray sweater, focusing in on the mountainous road as he maneuvered his 4Runner.

"Oh yeah," Luke grinned, glancing at Emma. "You know that particular weekend when we all went up there, I almost knocked on your bedroom door."

"You did?" She replied, with her eyes wide with fascination.

"Yeah, if you recall we were all drinking a lot, and I could hear some loud sex going on in my parents' bedroom close by, and I thought, what the hell, Noah and Zoe are getting it on, why not *"hook up"* with Emma also?"

Emma was delighted with his confession, wishing he had made the effort, realizing it was a different place and time with her feelings. "I think we were both sorta seeing someone else back then, if I remember correctly, we didn't want to be unfaithful to either one of them."

"Maybe you felt that way, but I sure as hell didn't. I hate to say it, Em, but I was *"a pig"* when it came to being true to one person when I was in college. I guess I held off because of Noah and Zoe dating. It felt too close to home, and I wanted to venture out of that Williamsport *"social circle"* and do my own thing. It was less complicated that way. Noah was doing shit to Zoe behind her back, with other chicks that she wasn't aware of at the time. If we would have gotten involved, I would have felt conflicted, feeling guilty about what was happening to your friend and not telling you. Or maybe telling you, and then pissing Noah off in the process. Either way, it was more trouble than I wanted to deal with."

Emma paused, taking in her boyfriend and considering what he was saying, as he continued to make the journey. "The whole thing is so terribly sad... I hate to hear that Noah was doing crap like that to Zoe. She didn't deserve it! I get it why you kept your distance from me during college, but I will never get passed what Noah did to Zoe. He should have ended things right away, if he knew he couldn't remain true to her. She is too good of a person to have been treated like that."

Luke sighed deeply, wishing they were still joking around and not talking so seriously now. "Many guys in college acted like this. I'm not making excuses for Noah, but I wasn't much better myself. Look at me now, I'm like half married to you!"

Emma reached across the seat to place her hand on Luke's leg, giving it a light squeeze. *"You really feel that way?"*

"About being half married to you?"

"Isn't that what you just said?"

"Yeah... I did say it, and I meant it, Em. It may sound crazy, after being together for such a short time, but I love you more than anyone else I have been with in the past, and I can't imagine myself dating anyone other than you now."

Tears began to glisten in Emma's eyes, enjoying Luke's declaration as much as the scenery spread out in front of her. "It really is kinda amazing that things have progressed so quickly for us. Within a few short weeks, we realized we liked each other, and then in no time we are living together. *How did it all happen?*"

"I'm not sure why any of this should come as a surprise to you," Luke commented, as several deer jumped out on the road and ran across to the other side, with the need to suddenly slow down somewhat. "We were friends and got to know each other for basically four years while Noah and Zoe were dating each other. No pressure was put on us, and it was only about seeing you for what you truly were, and not a *"love interest"*, which can cloud one's judgment."

"Well, that makes perfect sense."

"It makes more than sense. In a way, we had been dating each other, just not with any intimacy involved. I always knew you were fantastic, Emma, and actually somewhat jealous whenever you would bring a guy around from Loyola."

"Yeah, I can relate. I always felt that way too when you had your *"hot girls"* from Frostburg show up at a party with you, when you were back home in Williamsport. I guess I always pushed it to the back of my mind, never believing that you and I could end up together."

"*Dreams* are made to come true," Luke said lovingly, as he laid his hand on top of Emma's, taking the turnoff and proceeding down the long, private gravel lane that lead back to his family's mountain getaway destination. He parked the 4Runner in the ample sized driveway, by the expansive, wood-sided house, that was situated on a *"much sought after"* lake front location of Deep Creek Lake, happy to be back at his old stomping grounds of his youth. For just a few priceless moments, Luke had rolled down all the windows of his vehicle, just to linger and breathe in deeply of the pungent, pine-filled air that was surrounding them now.

"It's so peaceful here," Emma said, interrupting the quiet and solitude.

"Yeah, it is, but only until a few power boats go racing by, blaring their engines at full throttle! Then everything changes."

"Until I hear that noise I will pretend otherwise," Emma giggled, breaking from her spell of *"hoped for"* peace and tranquility.

The car was unloaded and the bags and other essentials were taken into the elaborate dwelling, as Luke flipped on the lights. "I almost forgot to tell you, but my father had someone that he knows and relies on up here - who does all our yard work and other miscellaneous maintenance things - stop by and adjust the heat for us in the place. He wanted to make sure we had a good time," he explained.

"How thoughtful of him!" Emma gushed, pleasantly surprised by the kind gesture. "Is your mom and dad, or maybe even Evan and Charlotte joining us?"

"Not a chance," Luke answered, wrapping Emma again in a welcoming bear hug, as he grabbed for her boob. "I made it perfectly clear with my dad, that we desire *"no visitors"* this weekend, and that includes my brother and sister also! All I want to do is be alone with you, and make wild, passionate love by a roaring fire in the fireplace - over and over again," he declared, making Emma slightly blush at the shameless prospect of it all. *"Are you blushing?"* Luke asked in surprise, taking in her reddened cheeks.

"Yeah, I guess I am," she laughed and then confessed aloud, touching her hands to her face, trying to conceal the obvious. "I just can't believe it's all happening. It takes some getting used to, you know, but I'm up for the challenge."

"You better be..." he insisted, while grabbing her hand and leading

her up the steps to the second floor that overlooked the spacious lofted entry area, with its rustic knotty pine walls. *"This time there is no separate bedrooms happening here, babe,"* he mused, leading her to the primary bedroom – very ready to begin their vacation.

Clothes were tossed haphazardly around the room, as their nude bodies lay entwined together, fulfilled and well sated from the sexual experience that they had just mutually shared. *"Are you hungry?"* Emma asked, as she propped up on one elbow, staring at Luke and waiting on the answer.

"If you mean for more sex with you, then yes, I'm always wanting more when it comes to that."

"No, silly, I meant actually something to eat. I'm starving!"

"I knew what you meant. I'm just messing with you!" he quipped, jumping from the bed and grabbing his boxers. Why don't we make a sandwich, since I threw some stuff in the cooler before we left, and then for dinner I will take you out to eat somewhere nice? How does that sound?"

"Sounds great!" Emma replied, feeling blissful and very content, knowing she was dating the perfect guy that was always doing everything right.

Chapter 34

A vigorous three-mile hike was taken near the water's edge of the lake, with numerous intentional pauses being made for passionate kisses and to admire the scenery of the colorful foliage and wildlife that they crossed paths with. Typically, it was a few deer and squirrels that were darting here and there, and up and down the limbs of the evergreens and other trees in the area that they encountered. *"What if we cross paths with possibly a bear, a bobcat or even a snake?"* she asked, feeling somewhat concerned and fearful.

"I'm here to protect you," Luke answered, somewhat heroically, wrapping his strong arm around Emma's shoulder and pulling her in close. "A lot of animals and reptiles have already started hibernating, so I honestly think we are fine, love, but that is why I am walking with this large stick."

"I was wondering why you needed it? I thought you were using it just in case you lost your balance."

Luke shook his head and laughed, tickled by Emma's assumption. "I'm not in my seventies, with balance issues like my grandparents," he joked, as he helped her over a few fallen tree limbs.

"Stupid me. I guess I just had a moment..."

"Your moments are all wonderful," Luke expressed, embracing Emma once again for a lengthy tongue kiss, as he grinded into her hips. "It's after four o'clock already and it may be a good idea to turn back, if you want to get an early start on dinner."

"Are you sure that is the only reason?" Emma retorted with a teasing gleam in her eyes, feeling Luke's well-endowed *"hard-on"* protruding suddenly against his jeans, yet for another time.

"Guilty as charged. Yeah, let's get in the shower and rinse off, and then make love again before we go out to eat. All this fresh mountain air and hiking has me feeling alive and especially horny."

"Me too..." She confessed, as they picked up the pace considerably, and headed back towards the house.

Luke grabbed two beers on the way up the steps, handing one to Emma as they stripped nude and entered the steamy tiled enclosure. *"Shower beers are the best!"* he grinned, as they placed their half-drank craft variety on one of the ledges of the oversized shower. His lips locked with Emma's for another time, as he reached for her wet breasts, rubbing each one until firm peaks in the center of her areolas were summoned to attention for his bidding. Emma moaned out as his moist fingers slid between the willing folds of her flesh, rousing a heat deep inside of her private parts that even the water that was pounding off of her back would not extinguish. She reached for his shaft, giving it equal time and attention, making Luke shutter deeply, with a contented look of delight etched across his face. He turned his more than willing partner towards the wall, taking Emma from behind as he entered her fully, thrusting repeatedly with abandon until he violently cummed and she mutually climaxed along with him. The water continued to pour out from the dual showerheads, spraying down over the both of them as they continued to hold each, trying to come back down to earth again - after some majorly fulfilling sex.

Emma reached for a washcloth, squirting a generous portion of the mint and rosemary blend of bath gel on it, hesitating at first because it didn't belong to her. It had been purchased at a spa in Berkley Springs, West Virginia by Luke's parents, but he said it was *no big deal if she used it, and would probably never be missed with all the other bath stuff his mother had always bought.* Emma made a frothy foam lather, ready to wash Luke as well as herself. "Turn around, my love, and I will get your back for you," she suggested sweetly, as he obliged her and did what she requested.

"Umm... *that feels so nice, Em,"* he stated quietly, being under her spell, feeling totally relaxed and pampered.

She massaged his shoulders, working her way down to his buttocks and calves, turning him then around to wash his front with equal attention and detail, not forgetting to wash his face and massaging his scalp also. Luke stood still, totally washed from head to toe, with his senses reeling from the heady scent of the mint and rosemary, feeling like he could fall asleep. They stepped together from the shower, grabbing for the oversized fluffy white towels that were there to dry them off, refreshed and well sated.

Emma slipped into a form fitting black dress with a plunging neckline that only helped to accentuate her already ample sized breasts, pulling on some contrasting tights and knee high boots that completed the look. She flat ironed her light blonde locks and then carefully applied eye makeup to her azure blue eyes, finishing it off with a generous layering of mascara to her lashes.

Luke joined her in the bathroom, after changing into jeans and another sweater that equally showed off his muscular chest, but this time in black. *"I guess like minded people think alike,"* he grinned, noticing that they somewhat matched with their wardrobe selection. "You look amazing, Em," Luke sincerely complimented, reaching from behind and wrapping his arms around her waist, as they looked together at their reflections in the mirror in front of them.

"So do you, my very handsome man," she flattered, taking in his blonde hair and blue eyes that were similar to hers.

Luke smiled, reaching for Emma's hand. "I made a reservation for us and we need to get going, since our table will be ready in only twenty minutes."

"Oh? What place did you decide on?"

Luke smiled, pleased with his choice. "A special place my parents introduced me to, that I think you will enjoy also. It is called *Dutch's At Silver Tree* and its considered to have some of the best food and service in the area."

They drove to the restaurant, making it just in time, with Luke walking around to the passenger's side and escorting Emma from the vehicle. They held hands as they entered the building, being greeted by a middle-aged female hostess who seemed anxious to assist them. "Good evening and welcome to Dutch's," she smiled. "Do you have a reservation?"

"Yes, we do," Luke confirmed. "It's for seven o'clock and under the name of Luke Taylor."

She looked at her reservation list, glancing up afterwards. "Yes, I found it. Right this way," she replied warmly, grabbing two menus and walking the happy couple towards a table by a large area of floor to ceiling windows that held an especially nice scenic view of the lake - which Luke had requested over the phone. *Is this table acceptable?"*

"Very much so," Luke answered back pleasantly, as he pulled out the chair for Emma and then took his seat afterwards.

"Your server will be right with you. Enjoy your dinner," she explained and then wished, walking away at a rather fast pace, ready to greet the next group of six who had just entered the building and were now standing by the hostess stand.

"The restaurant is decorated so beautifully," Emma mentioned, taking note of the elegance of the place and the tables that were draped in linen tablecloths, being moved by his thoughtfulness to bring her there.

"You deserve this, Em. It's a special place that I wanted to share with you."

Emma was overtaken with emotion, slightly chocking up and

feeling tears glazing over her eyes yet for another time, still amazed that Luke was actually hers. *"I will never forget this evening, ever!"*

The male waiter appeared out of nowhere, standing by the table now, ready to begin his pitch. "My name is Jacob and I am your server for the evening. May I start you out with a cocktail?" he offered, as he handed each one a menu.

Luke smiled at Emma and waited for her direction. *"Maybe some wine?"*

"Here is the wine list," the server explained, handing if over to Luke.

"I'll take this one," Luke pointed out, choosing one of the best. "And maybe Scallops wrapped in bacon for the both of us? *Would you like an additional appetizer, sweetie?"* he asked, turning his attention back to Emma.

"No, scallops are fine."

The youthful server returned with the bottle of wine, pouring a sampling in Luke's glass first, waiting for his approval before he filled each glass afterwards. The sizzling scallops and freshly baked rolls were soon to follow, as he stood waiting for their dinner order selections, ready to write them down.

"I will have the crabcakes with a baked potato and a garden salad."

"And your salad dressing?"

"Ranch," Luke answered, with the server immediately notating everything on his pad of paper.

"And for you, miss?"

"Fried oysters with the same two sides," Emma added, trying to be especially kind to Jacob who was acting overly nervous. She assumed he was probably right out of high school, maybe even his first time being a server.

"*He's sorta jumpy, don't you think?*" Luke observed as he downed two scallops quickly.

"He is, but maybe this is his first night on the job. Who knows," she replied perceptively, drinking deeply from her wine. "*This wine is delicious! What is the brand?*"

"*Expensive is the brand!*" Luke teased, knowing it costs two hundred dollars.

"Luke, you shouldn't have," Emma answered, feeling somewhat embarrassed, but touched all the same. "You know you never have to do anything like this to impress me."

"I know, and I wouldn't be dating you if I thought you were any other way, but after my big SUV sale today, I think I can swing a decent bottle of wine," he grinned and explained, reaching out for her hand.

"*If you say so,*" Emma answered with a roll of her eyes, still finding the whole situation outlandish and extravagant, but enjoying the offering greatly, knowing it was the most expensive bottle of wine she had ever drank and the taste was worth every dollar that Luke had spent on it.

Their dinners had arrived, with the salads being served first, following fairly soon after the scallops were finished – with not much of a pause in between. "I forgot to ask you if you wanted tarter... or cocktail sauce," the waiter admitted, stumbling over his words.

"One of each would be nice," Luke replied calmly, trying to remember Emma's words of wisdom. "I will also have a Heineken."

"And for you ma'am? Anything else to drink?"

"Just the wine. I'm fine," she said while smiling politely, doing her best to put him at ease and live up to her words.

The room was filled with the soft hues of candlelit and easy listening music, and the view of the lake was spectacular and mesmerizing. The moon sparkled off of it, with majestic pines hugging the shoreline, being just beyond the glass that separated them from the great outdoors. *"Any desert? Everything here is baked fresh daily,"* Luke explained before the server returned.

"I would love desert, but I'm stuffed," Emma confessed, reaching in the direction of her stomach.

"Me also, and I don't want to be too full for making love again," Luke confided quietly, as he leaned in over the table, with a naughty flirty look on his face, that Emma quite readily agreed with.

The bill was paid, with an ample tip being left behind for the server, as the blissful duo departed back to the elaborate mountain home that was nicknamed a *"modest cabin"*, but in no way resembled one. Luke built a roaring fire in the stone fireplace, just as he had repeatedly talked about doing from the start of their trip, coaxing Emma, with a reach of his hand, to join him on the shag rug - that was well cushioned underneath with a rug pad provided for such purposes. More beer and tantalizing foreplay was to be shared, with amazing uninhibited sex that ensued afterwards - at their leisure and throughout the wee hours of the morning - until the fire went out and a noticeable chill was felt in the air.

"Luke, it's so cold in here!" Emma shivered, leaning in to his embrace, hoping to get warm after waking up, with a noticeable draft coming in from the open fireplace flue.

"Grab a cover off of the sectional," he suggested sleepily, still feeling the after affects of the alcohol that was keeping him fairly comfortable.

"Or go upstairs," she moaned and insisted, knowing that the simple

throw would not suffice.

    Luke willingly followed, as she pulled him to his feet, discovering an amazing foam mattress - like none other that she had ever been on - along with an equally incredible set of soft Egyptian cotton sheets. Beneath the king-sized, down-filled comforter, of the master suite of Ron and Theresa Taylor, Emma no longer shivered or felt cold in the slightest, as she lay wrapped securely in Luke's warm embrace, feeling totally loved and secure, without a care in the world, as she dozed off to the best sleep of her life.

Chapter 35

For two additional, glorious days, Luke and Emma stayed at Deep Creek Lake, relaxing and enjoying the Taylor mountain estate, with its luxurious king-sized bed that included the *"hotel-like"* mattress with its bedding ensemble, oversized shower built for two, fireplace with the thick shag rug, and even the gourmet kitchen - as they attempted to cook a few simple meals together. Music was chosen over watching television, from the vintage, prized record collection of Luke's father, Ron, who had made it his mission to find the most *"hard to get"* albums from past *"rockers"* while he was growing up. Luke and Emma danced the night away to the classic tunes, having a stack of albums ready and waiting, when the last song was played on the current record. It was bittersweet saying goodbye, knowing the weekend had passed by much too quickly, as Emma snapped the last few candid photos on her cellphone of the house, the lake and all the abundant wildlife that surrounded the place, wanting to share each and every photo with Zoe, bragging about her fun getaway adventure - once she returned back to town.

"Did you have a good time?" Luke asked pleasantly as they headed home.

"It was the best time! If I had only one wish though, it would be for it not to be over so soon. I was just starting to relax and unwind," Emma explained somewhat dismally, as she stared out the car window at the beautiful fall foliage that they were passing along the way, driving back to Hagerstown and their apartment.

Luke reached out to place a hand on Emma's leg, squeezing it gently as he spoke. "Sweetie, we can go up to Deep Creek Lake anytime you would like. Maybe not for 3 days like we just did, but even for an *"overnighter"* I can work it out on my end, if you can work things out with your schedule at *Luna's*. The place is rarely used anymore, and I know my parents don't mind one bit if we go up there."

Emma smiled, her sad mood suddenly lifting. "Well, that makes me feel better knowing we have that special place to retreat to whenever we can get away."

"And don't forget we have the house in Marlin Beach also. So whether you are in the mood for the mountains or the ocean, we always have a place to go to and enjoy. If you would like, we can even invite Zoe and Mason to join us some time also."

"That would be wonderful, but I doubt we could pull that off easily, especially with both of us being away from *Luna's* at the same time. We just don't have ample staff for that."

"I understand, but the offer is always on the table if you ladies can work something out, and it would be an opportunity for us to get to know Mason better also."

Emma laid her hand on top of Luke's that was still resting on her knee. "I think I am the luckiest girl in the world, having you as my boyfriend," she declared while smiling lovingly, meaning every word of it.

"I am lucky too, Em, that I have you in my life. I may have been blessed with a father who owns a successful car dealership - and all the frills that go along with having money - but those material things can't buy love. I can't say it enough - you make me happier than any of the other girls that I have dated in the past."

Emma became choked up with Luke's poignant words. *"Can we please return to the lake now?"* She sighed, finding his confession of love to be somewhat overwhelming and scary if he ever changed his mind and she lost him now. *"Obviously, it has brought out the romantic side in you."*

"Yes, I would say it has," Luke agreed, pulling into their apartment complex parking lot, taking the reserved space beside of Emma's new car. "Let's get the bags upstairs and then I want to get naked with you one last time before reality sets in for work tomorrow."

"Always ready and willing..." Emma replied saucily, wheeling her suitcase into the building beside of Luke's. With another interlude of steamy hot intercourse, that left them both breathless and depleted, they were dead to the world, falling off to sleep in each other's arms – only wishing to be on the floor once again, on a shag rug, with the fireplace burning brightly to warm them.

"You're back!" Zoe exclaimed happily as Emma entered the kitchen of *Luna's,* looking rested and beautiful, with her skin glowing.

"Yes, I am."

"The mountains seem to have agreed with you! I'm seeing such a healthy look on your beautiful face."

Emma patted her cheeks several times. *"I have a glow?"*

Dennis stopped what he was doing - stirring a large pot of ham and bean soup that he had prepared - just to see what all the fuss was all about, taking in Emma's appearance also.

"I would call it *"rosy glow". Is it from lots of outdoor hiking or is it from something else you would like to reveal?"* Zoe teased, which wasn't something she did that often with Emma, usually being the other way around.

"Come outside, silly, and we will talk," Emma insisted, locking arms with her best friend as they went out the back door of the kitchen, for some alone time and privacy before the daily grind of work began. They took their normal stroll together, heading towards the C&O Canal towpath, just to catch up from the events of the weekend.

"So how was your time? Please don't let any detail out."

"Absolutely amazing! Everything about our trip was perfect! The leaves were magnificent with the fall colors, and being at the house with the view of the lake was just so pretty and relaxing. On top of all that, we hiked and went out to dinner to a great place."

"What was the name of the place?" Zoe asked with interest, knowing when she went there with Noah it was typically *"bar grub"* at one of the local hangouts, and not anything special to write home about.

"*Dutch's At Silver Tree* was the name of the place. The food was quite good and the service was outstanding."

"I'm glad you had a good time, Em. You have been putting in a lot of hours at *Luna's* and you deserved some much needed *"R&R"*!"

"Had some great sex too," she giggled out in delight, changing subjects rather quickly. "Felt like I was away on a honeymoon or at a spa, with that amazing house of the Taylor's. The master bedroom is fit for a king with that bed and shower."

Zoe suddenly looked somewhat sad, remembering that area of the house very well when she visited in the past with Noah, having her own special memories of the primary suite – designed and outfitted especially for Luke's parents. "I guess we should be getting back to the restaurant. Dennis is probably needing some help about now," she interjected, knowing it was in her best interest not to focus in on *"what had been"* anymore.

"You're not upset are you? I'm sorry, Zoe, it just slipped my mind that you had been there yourself, staying in the master bedroom with Noah."

"It's ok, Em. I'm getting past all of this slowly but surely. I can't lie that it still stings when I think about things, or something is brought up like you just mentioned, but Mason is fantastic and I care greatly for him. Slowly but surely, I think I'm beginning to fall in love with him. We also had a nice weekend together, even with things being busy at the restaurant. He was so helpful around *Luna's* and I felt guilty allowing him to volunteer his services for free, but he kept insisting that it was okay, so I didn't try to fight him after a while. It was actually nice having another set of hands around the place while you were away. And the clientele seemed to enjoy his easy going nature and his Texas accent as much as I do," she laughed, walking back towards the porch and the kitchen door again.

"Well, it's nice to hear that your feelings are changing for him, and that he took some pressure off of you while I was away. You deserve happiness also, Zoe, and I'm glad Mason is the one providing it."

Dennis was pleased to see the two had returned, as they entered and donned their aprons, ready to start the tasks that he always asked of them in the early morning hours before *Luna's* was officially open for business. "Good to see you back, Emma. Hope the mountains were a welcome change from being here in Williamsport."

"I love Williamsport, Dennis, almost as much as I love you," she joked, as he shook his head, knowing her constant teasing was the enjoyable part of her nature.

"The vegetables that I laid out need chopping, and one of you needs to put together a few salads – starting with tuna and chicken."

"You work on the vegetables and I will get the salads," Zoe suggested to Emma, grabbing for a large can of tuna.

"Will do, and later when we get the chance, I want to show you all the pictures that I took up at Deep Creek Lake."

Ava entered, joining the others, getting in on the tale end of the conversation. "You're here early," Emma observed, as she sliced up some carrots on a diagonal.

"That's been the routine since you been away on your vacation. They needed my help. *How was your trip?*" she asked casually, finding and tying her own apron in place.

"It was great, thanks for asking, and I'm glad you came in early, but you can go back to your old schedule after today," she answered matter-of-factly, resuming the role of boss and owner.

"No problem, Emma. You know I'm not a morning person anyway."

"Yes, we all know that!" Dennis barked out from the other side of the grill, frying up several pounds of bacon in advance, for chef salads and sandwiches that would be ordered in only a few hours, by the busy lunch crowd.

The group all laughed, being both co-workers and friends, knowing it was all in good fun and not to be taken too seriously. The morning preparation was completed early, with Ava's additional help, as they took a brief pause to go out back and drink their coffee at the picnic table, and look over Emma's pictures of her three-day vacation at Deep Creek Lake. Everyone who viewed them was impressed with her amateur photography skills that were actually quite impressive, being taken from her new cellphone with its *"up-to-date"* camera that she had just purchased.

The up-close, zoomed in shots of the pristine glistening lake with it colorful fall foliage, as deer and other wildlife wandered by, was eye-catching and appealing for all that were seeing them for the first time. Then there was the dinner pictures at the four-star *Dutch's At Silver Tree* restaurant, that were taken by Emma, but also captured by Jacob, who took a few of them specifically at the table with Deep Creek Lake in the background, looking very much in love while they cuddled and held hands. And lastly, the inside interior of the Taylor's mountain estate and the outside candid *"selfie"* photos of Luke and Emma posing in a variety of poses and locations throughout the weekend, were admired by all - with *hopes and dreams* that something as wonderful could happen for them too, just as it was now taking place for Emma and Luke.

Chapter 36

It was Thanksgiving week and all who planned to host the special holiday event were making their yearly, *"overwhelming"* grocery-shopping trip that was typically necessary for cooking for such a large gathering. Pappy Joe and Nana Ruth were staying in Fort Wayne, as he continued to heal and make significant progress with his physical therapy, that he was involved in every day during the week. They planned to share their meal at the church with less fortunate souls, as they volunteered and helped prepare the feast with the other members of the congregation. Luke and Emma were having Thanksgiving at the Taylor's house with his parents and brother and sister, much to Emma's mother's chagrin. Emma promised that she would reserve Christmas Day for her mother and siblings, easing the current debate somewhat, even though it didn't seem to be helping much. Zoe was spending the day with her father and his girlfriend Kelly at their house, where she planned to do the majority of the cooking. Kelly had offered to assist and even bring a few side dishes, but Zoe had politely declined saying, *"It was not necessary"*. Mason was invited also to the Carter's place, and had happily accepted, knowing it was impossible to go home to Austin and be with his family in Texas, since several pressing work meetings had been scheduled – before, and then right after the holiday. His relatives were disappointed, but he had made up his mind, to stay in Williamsport with Zoe and her family, giving them hope that *next Thanksgiving would be different.*

The doorbell rang as Luna barked and ran around in circles, sounding the alarm that someone was at the front door. *"Dad, can you get that?"* Zoe requested loudly, while trying to lift the roasting pan, with a twenty-pound turkey, off of the counter and back in the oven, after basting it several times.

"Sure thing!" Bryan yelled back over the blare of the television, being settled in and cozy on the couch, watching the Macy's Day Parade with Kelly by his side. The door swung open with a smiling Texan standing on the other side, as Bryan was there to welcome him inside.

"Hello there, Mr. Carter. Happy Thanks... giving," he wished with a pleasant smile that displayed a full set of perfect white teeth, and his strong southern accent coming through very clearly.

"Please, call me, Bryan," he insisted again, as Mason entered the living room where the two *"lovebirds"* had been hanging out. "I'm sure you remember my girlfriend, Kelly," he cordially commented, as she rose from off the sofa to shake Mason's hand and greet him.

"Happy Thanksgiving."

"And to you also, Kelly," Mason replied, trying his best to be polite and courteous. "Something smells amazing in the kitchen, and I'm sure it leads to the trail of my girlfriend."

Zoe stopped what she was doing, wiping her hands off on the apron that was tied securely around her, accepting the warm embrace from Mason that he was now offering. *"Hello, beautiful. I missed you these last two days."*

Zoe sighed, gazing at her wonderful man, glad that he even cared. "Thanksgiving takes a lot of time and preparation, as you know," she reminded sweetly.

"I wouldn't have a clue, since I don't cook that much," he laughed.

"Yes, I know," she replied with an eye roll, knowing that he continued to eat the majority of his meals at *Luna's* ever since they had met. *"Would you like something to drink before dinner?"*

Bryan and Kelly entered the kitchen, joining the pair that was still embracing. "How about a beer, Mason?" Bryan asked, while reaching in the refrigerator to grab one for himself.

"Sure! Set me up there."

Bryan twisted off two caps, handing Mason a Cushwa craft beer that was brewed locally, before taking a big swig. *"Great taste, wouldn't you say?"*

"I must admit, it's some of the best I've had in the area."

"Can we get past the beer tasting analysis and get dinner out on the counter? I think everything is finally ready," Zoe firmly announced, making the other three present honor her request and *"snap to it",* and help line up the numerous casserole dishes on the trivets that were already in position.

Bryan carved the turkey, which made Zoe somewhat sad, realizing her Pappy Joe had been given *"the honor"* of doing so previously at all their prior holiday events. Now, he and Nana Ruth were not there to share in on Thanksgiving, which was Zoe's favorite holiday. As they filled their plates to overflowing, Zoe looked at the others who were sitting side by side around the kitchen table, already beginning to eat without giving it any thought. She did not do the same, having her hands folded in her lap and not picking up her silverware just yet, hoping they would take the hint.

"Can we please say a prayer?" She asked somewhat dramatically, as the three *"eaters"* awkwardly put their forks back down on the table.

"Of course, sweetie. Why don't you lead it?" Bryan suggested with a smile, now with his hands clasped also in his lap.

Zoe bowed her head, beginning the prayer, as Mason reached under the table and found her hand, holding it securely. *"Dear God, thank you for this food that you have so richly blessed us with. Please be with Pappy Joe, and grant him continued health and healing so that he and Nana Ruth can be with us again next year at this time. We thank you for the wonderful people that you have brought into our lives, and that they are able to share Thanksgiving with us today around this table.*

We offer this in your precious name. Amen."

Mason smiled warmly and looked at Zoe, impressed and touched by her endearing prayer and sentiment. *"That was very sweet,"* he whispered, kissing her on the cheek.

She smiled and kissed him back, stuffing a big bite of turkey and cranberry in her mouth afterwards, not waiting on the others. "You better start eating now or it will be getting cold," she teased, finally giving everyone *"permission"* to officially begin doing so by her *"go ahead"* gesture.

No one held back on having second helpings, as Bryan complained of overindulging afterwards, as he stood up moaning. *"Why do I do this to myself every single year?"*

"I guess that is why we take a walk on the canal afterwards," Zoe chimed in, hoping that he would be agreeable to doing so again.

"You are right!" Bryan answered, walking over towards the coat rack. *"Anyone want to join me for a walk down on the towpath?"*

"Absolutely, but why don't we help Zoe clean up first?" Kelly offered, surprising Zoe that she was taking charge and lending a hand.

"Well, thank you, Kelly. It will only take a few minutes to wrap everything up and load the dishes in the dishwasher, before we leave."

Mason jumped in, already grabbing the stack of dirty dishes. "I will load the dishwasher and you lovely ladies can put the food away. How does that sound?"

"And I will take Luna out back to do *"her business"*. Easier to clean it up here than down out the canal."

"That is for sure!" Zoe giggled, knowing the massive size of her dog's poops.

Within thirty minutes, the task was completed, and the group then put on their winter coats, hats and gloves after listening to the weatherman on TV, trying to get a gauge if they were in for the first snow of the season. *"It's cold with a hint of snow in the air, but there's no need for worry about any significant accumulation, and at best it will only be a slight dusting."* Mason drove to the Lock 44 parking lot, stretching and loosening up first after getting out of his Land Rover, happy now that he had worn his sneakers after all.

"Are we ready?" Bryan asked, heading towards the small Lock 44 Bridge and Gatekeepers house in front of him. "Which way do you want to go?" he questioned, looking up and down the towpath.

"How about to the left?" Zoe suggested, especially enjoying the panoramic view of the Potomac River, that was near the I-81 Bridge, when they walked that way in the past.

Mason grabbed for Zoe's hand as they headed off, with Bryan doing the same with Kelly. Luna strolled in front of the others, leading the way as Zoe held tightly to her lead. "I love this towpath. Sometimes I gotta remind myself that this is a job and not just for my entertainment - when I'm out here taking care of things."

Zoe smiled at Mason, relating totally to what he was saying. "You are lucky to have such a wonderful career like you do. Being out in nature and enjoying everything the C&O Canal has to offer, is a *dream* job for many."

Mason reached down to kiss Zoe lightly on the lips as her father and Kelly lingered behind, snapping a few *"selfies"* with the Potomac River on display right behind them, ready to post the photos on social media shorty thereafter, as Kelly always took the incentive to do. *"Those two seem very happy together."*

"Yes, I guess you could say that," Zoe agreed. "It has taken me a while to get used to my dad having someone like Kelly in his life, but I am truly happy for them."

"Well, you have some... one too," Mason twanged out lovingly, wrapping her warmly in his embrace. "Let's get this walk over with so we can go watch football and have some desert. *Didn't I see a homemade pumpkin pie on the counter?"*

"Yes, you did," Zoe giggled. "I baked it this morning, along with my special chocolate chip cookies, that I'm famous for."

"I'll be the judge of that!" Mason teased, giving her one last lingering kiss before both couples got down to some serious walking - picking up the pace again for a three-mile vigorous jaunt, with Luna continuing to lead the pack.

Chapter 37

Dinner at the Taylor estate was quite different from the down-home, laid-back version of the Carter's that began earlier in the day at noon. The Taylor's Thanksgiving meal was scheduled for five o'clock, with casual television viewing along with drinks and snacks being offered before hand, if anyone wanted to show up and just hang out until the feast was ready. Theresa had made it a point of telling all who were planning to attend her holiday soiree that suitable dress was required, and that casual attire such as blue jeans or sweatshirts would be greatly frowned upon, and not considered acceptable.

Emma chose the same black dress with the tights and heels that she had worn at *Dutch's At Silver Tree* when they were away at Deep Creek Lake, hoping it was appropriate and to Theresa's liking. Luke picked out clothing that mimicked his work attire with a button down shirt and tie, along with his khakis and brown loafers, not concerned whether his mother approved or not.

As the doorbell rang to the impressive spacious mansion, Luke hugged Emma in closer, as she stood shivering from not wearing her winter coat, with both hoping that someone would answer the door very quickly. Luke still had the house key of his parents' abode that had been attached to his key ring since middle school, never removing it after he had moved out their place into his own apartment, only keeping it there in way of a fond memory. He knew he could still use it if he so well chose, being given the freedom to come back any time he wanted, but never crossing the line to do so - since he no longer lived there. It was about manners and etiquette, which Luke's mother always expected and demanded out of the entire family, never desiring her wrath if he didn't say or do something just they way she wanted him to.

"*Well, it's about time you guys showed up!*" Luke's brother Evan teased. "There's only so much that Charlotte and I can do to keep mom and dad entertained, you know," he added jokingly, wrapping a free arm around Luke's neck and pulling him forcibly and deliberately away from Emma, continuing to escort him towards the kitchen, leaving Emma behind to fend for herself. She looked somewhat confused and unsure of herself, as she remained in the foyer, not knowing what to do next, until Luke turned and attempted to wave, motioning for her to follow.

"You *finally* made it!" Ron exclaimed, as he reached forward to hug his son, after Evan released him abruptly. Theresa was soon to follow, giving Luke a *"half hug"* as she stirred her gravy and focused in on the other items on the stove, knowing the final timing of everything now mattered. Emma stood off to the far side of the room, taking it all in, feeling suddenly timid and not able to move any further.

"Where is your girlfriend?" Charlotte asked, as she popped the last bite of Brie with hot pepper jelly - placed on top of a wheat cracker - into her mouth, that was being offered as one of the appetizers.

"I'm over here," Emma chirped out weakly, suddenly feeling like an outsider looking in, wishing now that she had spent Thanksgiving with her mother and the current Internet date that she was bragging about who could possibly be *"the one",* along with her siblings, which she always enjoyed spending quality time with.

"You don't need an written invitation. Get over here and join us, girl!" Evan barked out rudely, being slightly intoxicated already from the several gin and tonics that he had partook of throughout the afternoon. "Heard you two went up to Deep Creek Lake and used *"the cabin"* a couple weeks ago? *At least someone in this family is getting some use out of the bedrooms up there,"* he implied obnoxiously.

Luke glared at his brother, giving him a stern look of warning, knowing he had just crossed the line with Emma for a second time already. He walked over and grabbed her hand, leading her towards the others. *"Sorry sweetie,"* he whispered into her hair that was hanging loose, *"Evan is drunk and being a dick."*

Emma whispered back, with a pretentious smile of affectation, realizing it was in her best interest to maintain and not create a problem between her and the man she adored, since they would be gone and back home at their place in only a few more hours - if all went according to plan. "Yes, he is being a *"dick"*, but you are here to protect me now, so lead on, my love."

Luke escorted Emma over to the kitchen counter, immediately offering a glass of red wine, hoping to relax her and the embarrassing situation at hand, pouring an additional one for himself also.

"Got beer in the frig, son, if you prefer that over the wine," Ron Taylor offered, trying to act cordial.

"No, this is just fine," Luke answered with a warm smile. *"So what's cooking?"* he asked, turning his attention towards his mother.

"We have turkey and ham in the oven, and I made mashed potatoes, gravy and stuffing, with peas and cranberry sauce on the side. I also made a big casserole dish of mac and cheese, because I know you guys love that too!"

"Sounds amazing, Mom," Luke complimented, giving her a quick hug and kiss.

The food bowls and platters were carried to the dining room by the aid of everyone present, being placed down the center of the very large, oversized table, that had been decorated expertly for the festive season, with room to spare for additional guests. Theresa stood close by advising each one to *"sit in their designated assigned seats with the place cards"* that she conveniently positioned on top of each dinner plate, with no other option offered. Emma pulled out one of the overly ornate, tapestry-upholstered chairs, finding it quite heavy to even push back in under the table with the Taylor's seeming to take it all in stride.

Emma and Luke sat across from Evan and Charlotte, with the parents taking each end, all waiting quietly until Theresa announced it was time to partake of the meal. They ate mostly in silence, with a prayer not even being offered at the start, only hearing the echo of clanking silverware in the substantially oversized room, and not much more.

Emma was now aware of one huge distinctive difference between their two families, after experiencing this sterile, uninviting gathering that had left her feeling empty inside, even if everyone present at the dining table was now consuming the food. Spending Thanksgiving in a simpler sort of way with her mother and siblings was a lot more fun and carefree, instead of having to follow all these stringent rules that was demanded and expected out of everyone in the Taylor household. Emma's fantasy bubble concerning her *"perfect boyfriend",* who came with no flaws, was suddenly burst - at least where his relatives were concerned.

"I heard from Jessica Clark that Noah is dating someone seriously in England. He may even be getting engaged by Christmas," Theresa mentioned offhandedly to the group, being insensitive to the fact that Emma was Zoe's best friend. Emma hung her head, playing the part and acting disinterested as she continued to eat, trying to remain calm and unfazed by the conversation. *The jerk can get engaged so quickly, after dating Zoe for over four years and never asking her to marry him? It was all she had hoped for and dreamt about!* She thought to herself, with her blood now boiling, wishing that the evening would end sooner rather than later.

Luke sensed her aggravation, realizing his mother was acting as rude and inconsiderate as his brother had been earlier, both now showing little regard or respect for his significant other. *"I never hear from Noah, and what he does with his life has little impact on me now. We have gone in different directions, as do many others after high school and college are over. Mother, I find this conversation inappropriate since Emma and Zoe are best friends, and the breakup was not pleasant between Zoe and Noah - as you are very well aware."*

Theresa's mouth dropped open with her solid silver fork still in mid-air, looking quite shocked by her son calling her out in such a bold way, breaking from formality and correctness. *"Well I never..."* she replied, feeling somewhat dumbfounded, as she touched the corners of her mouth with her linen napkin and then excused herself, going off to the bathroom to *"powder her nose"*.

Evan began to laugh out loudly, while repeatedly slapping the tabletop, making the crystal glasses filled with ice and water jiggle, finding the whole situation hilarious, not caring in the least how he was coming across or if anyone else in the room was bothered or not. *"Well, you told her, didn't you Luke?"*

"And that's about enough out of you too, Evan! In case anyone needs a reminder, Emma is very special to me and we are sharing a place together now. She is the woman I love and you better get use to it. If you can't show her some common decency, than I won't be stopping by the house again any time soon!"

Ron stood up, trying to rein in his family and regain some control, as Theresa reappeared, dabbing her eyes with a tissue, as she took her seat once again. "It is Thanksgiving and a time to be kind and considerate to all those around us. We are sorry, Emma, if any offense has come your way today by those in this household. After all, we have known you for years, since you and Luke grew up together and went to school throughout every grade. We do truly like you," he expressed with a sincere smile, making her soften with his genuineness. *"How about a few games of pool and some desert? Do I have any takers?"*

Luke immediately lightened up, smiling as he leaned forward and kissed Emma openly on the lips, trying to make an obvious statement. *"You wanna stay a while longer and play some pool? It is a family tradition around here every year."*

"Of course we can stay! And yes, I would enjoy playing some pool!" Emma eagerly agreed, trying her best to *"go with the flow"*. "But let me help your mom clean up the dishes first, and then I will join you downstairs later."

"There is no need to help!" Theresa interjected quickly, still feeling stung by Luke's stern reprimand, not desiring any more negativity or embarrassment. "I am very capable of doing things all by myself around here. Please feel free to join the others in the rec room for some desert and billiards."

Charlotte shook her head and sighed, suddenly feeling somewhat sorry for Emma. *"I will help you, Mom. Don't worry about it, Emma."*

"Your help is not necessary either, Charlotte!" Theresa declared clearly, hoping to be alone for a few minutes in the kitchen, just to sulk and regroup.

Emma stood up, already gathering the fine china plates and silverware, trying to suck it all up - be the better person - and take the high road. *"It's time to get the coffee brewing, Mrs. Taylor, if we want to beat the others once it's our turn to play pool,"* she grinned. Emma turned towards Luke and winked, before heading towards the kitchen with a stack full of dirty dishes that were now skillfully balanced in her hands from working at the restaurant, hoping that the rest of the evening would be a lot more pleasant, and she could gain some much-needed favor with the Taylor family.

Chapter 38

Thanksgiving had come and gone and now it was the official time to herald in the Christmas season in Williamsport, with all its fun festivities and special holiday adornment throughout the town. The Byron Memorial Park employed a staff of maintenance workers, but volunteers were also welcome to help decorate the park with the famous light displays that were positioned over every square inch of available space. Once the displays were in place, a entrance booth needed to be manned for those driving through, with all involved hoping that ample donations would be given to offset the huge cost of electric that it took to run the yearly event for several weeks.

Zoe and Emma had always taken on the task of helping out, enjoying the camaraderie with their fellow townsfolk, enjoying hot chocolate and cookies that were served in the pavilion nearby, while everyone else was busily working. Now, they had signed up a few more willing helpers who agreed to assist, including Bryan, Kelly, Luke and Mason, promising a party to all the workers, paid and otherwise, to be held at *Luna's* afterwards - for anyone who wanted to attend.

Mason hammered in the last of the four stakes, around a Santa whose arm was in a waving position over his head. *"I think that looks fairly straight,"* Luke observed, eyeballing it from a distance.

"Good to hear," Mason answered as he stood up and stretched, just to get the kinks out of his back from bending over so long. "The maintenance workers are securing the storage door, so I would guess that this is the last of it," Mason observed casually, as he and Luke began to walk over in the direction of Zoe and Emma, who were arranging a couple of crosses and a nativity scene off to one side, along with Bryan and Kelly's help.

Zoe smiled as she saw the guys approach. *"You are done already?"*

"Yes ma'am, we are finished! Ready now for that beer and appetizers at *Luna's that you've been talking about*! I'm starving from all that hard work," Mason expressed with his strong Texas twang sounding off his desires to be fed.

Zoe giggled, always being pleasantly entertained by her sweet Texan. "I've already contacted Dennis and Ava, and they are in the process of organizing everything now. By the time we arrive, you will have a cold beer in hand and a plate of spicy chicken wings to sample. *How does that sound?"*

"Perfect!" Mason answered, wrapping his arms securely around Zoe's waist and pulling her in close for a public kiss, that he didn't care one bit that a large group of workers nearby were witnessing first hand. If there was any doubt in the town that she had moved on and was no longer dating Noah Clark, and had a new hunky boyfriend to replace him with, it was very clear now that she had done so.

Zoe broke free, loudly making an announcement to all present, with her hands cupped around her mouth. *"Please don't forget to stop at Luna's for free food and drinks within the hour. We purposely closed the restaurant early to allow for this today,"* she reminded again, hoping that those listening would take her up on the invite.

"Can I bring my wife and kids along?"

"Of course!" Emma tossed out, standing off to one side with Luke's arm draped affectionately across her shoulder, as she silently looked at Zoe then just to confirm it was all right with what she had just offered.

"Bring whoever you would like! It's the start of Christmas in Williamsport for a month, and the more the merrier!" She laughed, feeling very warm, happy and festive with the *"season of joy"* that was finally beginning in their cozy canal town.

The front of *Luna's,* as well as the inside of the restaurant, had been magically transformed with the help of a few local merchants. Rosemary's provided the greenery and poinsettias for the large entryway pots that were now minus their fall flowers, and also designed the swags and wreaths for the front door and windows. Cindy's Country Thyme showed up to decorate the primitive tree inside and adorn each dining table, and other tucked away areas of the establishment, with candles and cute tabletop accent pieces. Overall, *Luna's* looked amazing, all lit up with white twinkling lights – inside and out – providing the perfect romantic mood with the heady smell of pine and cinnamon candles cascading throughout the place.

The buffet line had been set up and also a complimentary bar featuring wine and beer that Zoe and Emma had set no limits on. Chafing dishes of two types of chicken wings – spicy and barbeque – were offered, along with steamers, macaroni and cheese and cole slaw. Hot mulled apple cider and hot chocolate were off to one side in two coffee urns, and homemade deserts that included cupcakes and cookies, were presented on cheery holiday Christmas trays.

The place was filled to capacity, with the maintenance workers and volunteers taking the female restaurant owners up on their invite – very much enjoying the free food and variety of beverages that were offered. It was obvious they had put out the word to family and friends, and maybe even a neighbor or two, with the amount of people that were present. Whoever could be reached at the spare of the moment, was invited to the *"completion of decorating"* party.

"Come this way," Dennis smiled, as the first group timidly approached the buffet line. "There is more in the back, so take as much as you would like," he cordially insisted, as he helped a small child with a scoop of requested mac and cheese that he had made extra rich and creamy by adding more cheese.

"This is so nice of you guys to do this for the community," Luke whispered to Emma as they stood in line waiting for their turn.

"We have made an amazing profit already this year, and it pays to give back to those who have been faithful in coming here regularly. And if they haven't been our regulars in the past, hopefully they will consider it now from the goodwill gesture."

"Does that include boyfriends?" Luke grinned, planting a light kiss on Emma's lips.

"Only if they are wonderful, which you pass that description like no other," Emma gushed, grabbing for a plate, and then the tongs - that was situated in one of chafing containers - selecting a few chicken wings of the spicy variety.

Luke filled up his plate, not holding back, hungry from the manual labor that he was just involved in. "Where would you like to sit?"

"Wherever we can find a space, or on second thought, maybe we should stand up to allow others to sit down," Emma suggested, not wanting to take up a seat if someone else in the room could use it. They grabbed two beers, heading towards the table that Zoe and her group were already sitting at, deciding to join them since a few other empty tables were still available.

Mason smiled, patting the seat beside of him. "Come on over here, Emma, I promise I won't bite!"

"That's not what I hear," she joked, sliding in closely beside of Mason.

Everyone at the table began to laugh, knowing Emma could be quite amusing when she wanted to be. "Hey, I told you not to tell that little secret," Zoe teased back, jumping in and adding to the good-natured, harmless ribbing at the table.

"It was a successful time down at the park," Bryan interjected, changing things to a more serious tone. "When exactly is it again that they officially begin to light things up?"

"Once they have the Christmas parade, with The Williamsport Blue Band performing, then they will light up the Christmas tree in the square. After that, everything else starts falling in place and happening around the town. The light displays will come on in the Bryon Memorial Park and the *"Charlie Brown Christmas"* will happen at the Springfield Farm Barn, which by the way - just went through a name change - now being called the *"Celebration Of Trees"*, but it will always be the *"Charlie Brown Christmas"* to me."

Mason looked confused. *"They have a "Charlie Brown" theme going on in the Springfield Farm Barn? I'm not getting this?"*

Zoe began to giggle and shake her head. "No, silly, it isn't a *"Charlie Brown"* theme going on in the barn at Springfield Farm. It's different groups and individual people putting together beautiful Christmas trees and other holiday related items, and also Mr. and Mrs. Santa Claus are there too, with a place set up especially just for them. The children get a chance to visit and pose with them, and then have a photo taken besides. It's free to take a tour, enjoying the festivities and seeing what each participant has accomplished with their own unique sort of decorating. It is quite impressive and something I try to attend every year, so why don't we go together and see it?"

"Absolutely! It sounds like a bunch of fun, and I wouldn't want to miss out on viewing trees that have nothing to do with *"Charlie Brown"*.

Everyone at the table began to laugh, enjoying Mason's humorous side immensely. *"Do you think you will ever get used to our town?"* Bryan pleasantly asked of the tall Texan, as Kelly sat close by, just observing and taking it all in.

"Don't get me wrong, I love Williamsport, it's just that it comes with a lot of newness that I'm still having somewhat of a time acclimating to... being my first year here and all. If you guys were in

Austin, Texas, where I was born and raised, you would see some subtle differences in things that we do there also. It would definitely involve some explaining, since you were not native to that area either."

"Hey, how about another beer, bro? Don't let anyone get into your *"headspace","* Luke laughed, getting up to make a beer run.

"We tease who we truly love," Zoe threw out whimsically, surprised that she made the impromptu comment after it was out in the air for all to hear.

"Does that mean you love me?" Mason questioned openly, putting her on the spot, as all eyes were watching her now and waiting for the answer.

Zoe gulped, trying to find her voice, looking at each of the others surrounding the table. *"Yes, Mason, I think I actually do love you..."* she confessed with a genuine sincere smile, surprising herself in the process, realizing he had replaced her sorrow with joy, and she felt alive and happy again.

"Grab me two, Luke – one for myself and one for my lovely lady!"

"Two for us also!" Bryan yelled out, over the noise of the room.

"I guess that means a round for the entire table!" Luke confirmed with an equally delighted smile, as he glanced over at Emma, knowing he was madly in love with her also.

Chapter 39

The earlier part of December flew by without anyone having a chance to even catch their breath and take notice. Party after party – that was typically work related – was booked for *Luna's* – being the new, popular *"go-to"* destination. Barely a free day was found in between the nightly holiday events that had been scheduled several weeks out in advance. Beyond that, it was a juggling act trying to accommodate all the party attendees, and also accommodate the other patrons who were free to come inside and dine, if a table was available. Zoe and Emma even had to hire several other waitresses, just to help out over the busy Christmas season, with Mason and Luke kicking in whenever they were free or felt like doing so.

Ava had just finished setting up the tables for the next party of the evening, along with Zoe's help, adding a festive display down the center that included sprigs of pine and lighted sugar cookie scented candles, intermingling it all with several strings of twinkling battery operated lights throughout. The intended group would be in the door in only thirty minutes, and each would be served a dinner versus getting up and going through a buffet line, which was considerably simpler to pull off.

"Sorry things have been so darn busy lately. I don't even think I will have time to do anything special at the house like I usually do with your girls each year."

Ava began to laugh, taking a walk down memory lane, as she walked with Zoe over to the counter at the front of the restaurant. "I remember when we were seniors in high school and you had your first Christmas party at your house. We had pizza with no alcohol to drink, and we watched a *"chick flick"*. None of us had even had sex yet."

Zoe eyes rose in merriment, recalling the earlier time, making her join in with the laughter. *"We were definitely a bunch of nerdy girls back then, but who cares, we still had a lot of clean, innocent fun!"*

"You got that right! And Zoe, it's a non-stop Christmas party in here most of the time lately, so please take some pressure off of yourself and realize that I don't feel slighted in the least, that you are not hosting an event at your place."

"Well that's kind of you to say so, Ava, but remember Lillian doesn't work with us here and I'm sure she would enjoy meeting up with the rest of us sometime over the holidays. *Don't you agree that it would be nice to set aside only one evening and not wait on customers at Luna's, like we must always must do - day in and day out?"* It would be so divine to just sit down and have an uninterrupted bite to eat. A house party definitely solves this dilemma," Zoe explained, now considering the possibility.

"Yes, it would be nice, but also on the flip side, all this additional business here at *Luna's* means money in your pocket, and I'm sure you and Emma need as much as you can get right now to pay the bills around here – especially with it being a new place and all."

Zoe felt somewhat guilty, realizing Ava had never been asked to be a part of the initial business venture of owning *Luna's,* as Emma had been offered, but at the time the deal was made, she was going in a different direction with things in her life. At least her part-time job that she had started out with when the restaurant first opened, was now a full time position, and Ava was making a decent income with good tips besides, which gave Zoe a sense of relief that she was doing okay.

"Yes, we do need the money - there is no doubt about it - since the goal is to break free from our reliance on Pappy Joe and Nana Ruth to financially back the restaurant."

"How is your pappy doing, by the way?" Ava asked, switching the topic of conversation, as they stood waiting on the guests for the next scheduled party.

"Surprisingly, very well. His doctor won't allow him to travel for Christmas, because of the long drive, but by the spring they should be able to make the journey to Maryland. If for some reason they still can't make it here at that time, then I will be the one making a trip out to Fort Wayne. It's tough being apart for so long. I really start missing them."

"You're lucky you still have your grandparents around. On my mother's side, they both passed away while I was still in high school, and even though my dad's parents are both still living, I rarely see them because they moved out to California. *Are your other grandparents still alive?"*

Zoe paused, trying to get on the same page as Ava, feeling somewhat confused. *"My other grandparents?"*

"You should have two sets, right?" Ava giggled, forgetting Zoe's sensitivity to her mother's abandonment and what it entailed.

Zoe shook her head silently, staring off in the distance, remembering that difficult time and place once again, which rarely came back to haunt her most days lately. "Ava, in case you forgot, my mother left me when I was only five years old. I barely remember her, let alone her parents. I have no clue if they are alive or dead, sad to say."

"Aren't you in the least bit intrigued that they may be out there somewhere and you are their granddaughter?"

"Why should I be? They knew about me and never made any inroads to reach out to me when I was a child. Even if my mother told them to never get in touch with me after she made her exit out of our lives, who would do such a horrible thing to their own flesh and blood?" she reasoned, with a pained look of despair suddenly crossing her face. "So the whole *"granddaughter thing"* has no bearing on me where they are concerned."

The front door swung open, with several happy smiling facing approaching the hostess stand, interrupting the strained and somewhat difficult exchange that Zoe and Ava were engrossed in. "We are here for the *"Roof Center"* Christmas party. *Has anyone else showed up yet from our group?"*

"*Not yet,"* Zoe smiled, trying to regroup and act professional. "But it officially doesn't begin for another fifteen minutes yet. Why don't I take you to your designated *"party area",* and you can choose a seat and order a drink, while you continue to wait on the others?"

"Lead on, young lady!" A boisterous male replied with a throaty laugh, trying his best to impress the small group that were already present with him.

"Zoe, you stay here and greet the other guests when they arrive, and I will take over from here," Ava kindly offered, ready to lead the *"merrymakers"* to their intended tables, hoping Zoe wasn't annoyed with her from the heated discussion about her other set of grandparents.

Bryan and Kelly had just finished decorating the tree in Bryan's house - after taking it out of storage in the garage and setting it up - knowing Zoe had never completed the task that she had promised to complete several days earlier. Christmas was less than a week away now and it was obvious that she was overwhelmed at the restaurant, always taking care of the holiday decorating inside and outside of the house - usually weeks in advance. They stood back while holding hands, admiring their handiwork that they had just completed. The soft glow of the white mini lights that were strung perfectly throughout the artificial tree, were blinking in an intermittent, chasing pattern, delighting them both as they watched.

"Did you *"poof out"* the branches enough?" Bryan asked of Kelly with a look of concern, not wanting Zoe to be disappointed in the slightest, at what she observed once she returned home.

"I guess so... didn't think too much about it – to be honest."

"It's just that Zoe is particular about such details, and always has this meticulous way of doing things that needs be followed to the "T", so that the branches look *"just perfect"* with the way she bends each individual piece of the branch. She never lets me assist with the task, insisting she is the only one who can truly get it *"just right"*, and to be honest, it does make the tree appear *"more real"* looking," Bryan added, trying to justify his reasoning.

Kelly refrained from answering, not desiring to offend anyone, but feeling like Zoe should have made the time to do the tree herself if she was *that damn picky!* "I'm sure she can tweak it some if it isn't to her liking," she smiled reassuredly, hoping for a glass of wine and some romantic cuddling on the couch before Bryan's daughter came home. *"Did you finish the lights outside?"*

"Yes, I did, and I also placed the wreaths on the doors and windows."

"Does Zoe have a special way of doing that also?" Kelly teased, somewhat mockingly.

Bryan eyed her, seeing if she were being serious or not. *"You're upset with me, aren't you, for saying what I did about the Christmas tree?"*

"Not at all, silly, but now that we are finished decorating, I would really love to relax and have a glass of wine - if you don't mind," she saucily suggested, with her hands perched playfully on her hips, trying her best to turn on her man.

"Your wish is my command, sweetheart," Bryan answered, leaning in for a passionate, lingering kiss before departing to the kitchen. He brought back two wine glasses that he had filled with Shiraz, handing one to the woman he loved, who was now unwinding on the sofa and waiting patiently for his return.

"Umm... good wine," Kelly commented pleasantly, taking a lengthy savoring of the special bottle that they had just picked up earlier at the Castles Liquor Store, situated near the house.

Bryan snuggled in closer, enjoying the light show and the excellent selection of wine also. "We probably have two hours to be alone before Zoe shows up. *Should we make the most of the time?*" Bryan hinted with a grin, with Kelly being very receptive and on the same page also.

"*Of course we should make the most of the time, but Zoe's not going to Mason's tonight as she usually does?*"

"She texted me – just to give me the heads up – that she would be coming home tonight instead of going to his place. Mason is out with Luke at a concert in DC that Luke unexpectedly got free, last minute tickets for, from a rep's hookup who had offered them to him when he stopped by the dealership today."

"*Emma isn't going with Luke to the concert?*"

"No, because they are swamped with all these Christmas parties at *Luna's,* that will continue through New Year's. It's *"all hands on deck"* to keep things operating smoothly right now at the restaurant. Luke was going to *"eat"* the tickets, but Emma insisted he go to the concert and take a friend. It made Zoe happy that Luke had actually chosen Mason, since he still hasn't made a lot of local friends and only hangs out occasionally with a few work acquaintances."

Kelly downed the rest of her wine, suddenly feeling especially horny, pulling Bryan to his feet. "Then I would say it's time to hurry up and *"do me"* before I have to *"do myself"*," she tempted seductively, greatly surprising and turning him on by her bold and enticing statement. She wasted no time running back the hallway to the bedroom, with Bryan not far behind, eager and very willing to fulfill her request.

Chapter 40

It was Christmas Day and everyone was home from work including Zoe and Emma, since *Luna's* was closed so that the staff could get a well-deserved break. As promised, Emma spent the entire day with her mother and siblings, with Luke deciding to split his time between his family in the afternoon, and Emma's brood during the morning hours.

Margie had been up since five a.m., trying her best to create appealing, gourmet breakfast fare that would impress Luke, even though Emma had insisted that the *"simpler the better"* was the best option when it came to his desires. As hard as Margie tried, no dating site had provided a companion for the day, so she was stuck with only her family to hang out with, which really didn't seem to happen all that often anymore.

Owen and Reagan were very impatient, wanting to open their presents, moaning and groaning and begging that they should be able to do so before eating breakfast. Margie was shouting a non-stop reprimand from the kitchen, as Luke sat with the younger members of the family, trying to keep them entertained with a classic Christmas movie that was being broadcasted repeatedly on the television set, not having much luck at keeping them focused in on the humorous plot about "*a kid wanting a bb gun and shooting his eye out*".

The brunch items on Margie's menu - that she had pre-written out on a piece of paper - were displayed on the refrigerator with a Christmas Santa magnet holding it in place, with each one being checked off once it was finished. The mother-daughter cooking team finally finished up the elaborate offerings, much to the relief of everyone present. *"Breakfast is served!"* Margie announced with a beaming smile, removing her apron first before taking a seat at the head of the table, being closest to the kitchen if anyone requested anything else.

Everyone shuffled around the dining room table, with Luke and Emma on the one side and the kids on the other. *"How about a prayer first?"* Emma asked, looking at her boyfriend whose parents' household wasn't accustomed to doing the same thing.

"Of course, sweetie. That would be nice," Luke answered, leaning in to kiss Emma on the cheek.

"Would you like to say the blessing, Luke?" Margie suggested, making him shift in his seat uncomfortably, suddenly not sure how to answer her politely.

Luke began to chuckle, turning towards Emma as he spoke. *"It may be a better idea for one of you lovely ladies to take over with a Christmas prayer this morning. Not my forte - if you catch my drift."*

Emma grabbed for Luke's hand, trying to take control of the situation. *"I will pray, okay?"* she said, glaring at her mother.

"I'm starving!" Reagan moaned out. *"Just do it, Emma!"*

"Go ahead," Margie conceded, giving her younger child a *"warning look"* probably for the umpteenth time already that day.

"Dear God, we thank you for Christmas Day and the food we are about to eat. Thank you for family and for those we love and hold dear," Emma added, squeezing Luke's hand somewhat when she got to the *"love part"* of her prayer. *"May we enjoy the rest of the day and make the most out of every moment that we spend together. Amen."*

Eyes were opened once again, after the prayer had been completed, waiting on Margie's direction to finally eat. "Please help yourselves to the buffet line that Emma and I have set up in the kitchen. Owen and Reagan, do not take more than you can eat. I do not like to waste food," she reminded sternly, knowing she had over-extended herself with the food budget that included smoked salmon, cream cheese, capers and an assortment of bagels, amongst many other things.

"I only want bacon," Owen insisted, as he grabbed his festive paper plate off of the table - with the holly berry pattern - and headed towards the kitchen, on a mission to get his way.

Margie rose up from the second-hand, antique dining chair with its striped fabric that desperately needed to be redone, suddenly realizing she needed to assist the younger two, ready to put out the current fire. *"I think not..."* she answered succinctly, scooping out a smaller helping of scrambled eggs and some cheesy hash brown potato casserole, adding it to the over-generous portion of bacon Owen had already taken. She removed a few pieces of the bacon, placing it back on the serving platter with her bare hands, as Luke took it all in, knowing his mother would never be caught doing such a thing, or even parole the food so strictly.

Luke filled up his plate next, not missing anything that was offered, hoping Margie wouldn't start placing things on and off his plate like she had just done to her younger children. *"Looks delicious!"* he praised, with some trepidation as she looked on from a safe distance, assessing the situation.

"Well, thank you, Luke. At least someone here appreciates my efforts."

"Mom, Luke and I greatly appreciate all your hard work, and we thank you for making such a nice Christmas breakfast for the family," Emma answered for the both of them, realizing her mother was now sorely getting on her nerves. She poured a Mimosa cocktail of orange juice and champagne, taking an additional one back to the table for Luke who had already started eating at Margie's insistence, feeling the need to unwind and hoping the drink would do the trick.

The dishes were quickly stacked in the dishwasher afterwards, so that Regan and Owen could finally open up their Christmas presents, with no further hesitation to keep them from doing so. Margie had chosen several of the toys on their *"wish list"*, but had been practical too, choosing clothing that would take care of them now and through the upcoming spring season. Luke took notice once again to the considerable differences between Emma's family and his own, finally piecing it together that *this was the world of a single mother who needed to pinch pennies for her family any way she could.*

Emma handed out the presents to her mother and siblings, having a budget of two hundred dollars each that Luke had also contributed to. Margie held up a beautiful sweater that she had just unwrapped, looking it over and eyeing it like one of her Match dates. "It's very nice, Em. Thank you for remembering that I like the color purple."

"Glad you like it," Emma said with a smile. *"It's from both Luke and I,"* she over-emphasized, hoping that her mother realized that Luke had been a part of the gift exchange also.

"Well, thank you, Luke," Margie beamed. "It was very thoughtful of you to think of me also."

"It's my pleasure, Mrs. Baker."

"Call me Margie," she reminded Luke again, feeling way older than she wanted to feel whenever he called her by her proper last name. Margie opened up her remaining last present – a special bottle of perfume - that had put her way over the present-giving budget that Emma had decided upon. "Oh my... Em, it's my favorite," she sighed, taking the time to carefully unwrap the plastic cellophane from off the box, before removing the bottle from within. She immediately took off the cap and sprayed some behind each earlobe, pleasantly smelling the air afterwards with a delighted smile on her face.

"I knew it was," Emma answered, glad that her *"hard to please"* mother actually seemed content with her presents.

The last of the gifts were opened, with Margie presenting Luke with a navy blue silk tie, and then giving Emma a monogramed apron to be used at the restaurant, that she had handmade for her eldest daughter, knowing she would never take the time to do so for herself.

"I must go," Luke stated matter-of-factly, rising from off the sofa after the *"gift exchange"* had concluded. Emma and the younger children were shoving the remaining ripped up, Christmas wrapping paper into a garbage bag, surprised that he was already leaving.

"So soon?" Margie whined. "I was hoping you would have stayed to play a round of Scrabble with us, and maybe had some Christmas cookies that I baked especially for the occasion?"

"Well thank you, Mrs. Ba... Margie..." he caught himself almost saying, as soon as the blunder was made. "But my mother is expecting me at noon and it's already eleven-thirty. But the good news is you have Emma all to yourself today, so take full advantage of it and play board games and watch holiday movies with her. Thank you for breakfast and the sharp tie. I will be wearing it tomorrow!" he pleasantly grinned, as Margie gave him a warm *"almost too close"* hug goodbye.

Emma's eyes began to tear up, missing her guy already. "And you have fun being with your family," she wished sincerely, honestly relieved that Luke was going over to their place alone, and not pushing the matter for her to join him. She had been forced to endure a miserable Thanksgiving that had never turned around as she had hoped, even staying longer and taking part in his family's pool tournament that unfortunately she and Luke's mother, Theresa, had lost.

They walked to the front door - hand in hand - disappearing from view as Luke rubbed up against her. *"I should be home by nine,"* he whispered against her hair, as he kissed Emma several times, not desiring to leave her quite yet. *"We still have our presents to open, you know,"* he reminded, peck kissing her one last time on the lips before releasing her.

"I'll be back at the apartment waiting," she promised fondly, suddenly looking forward to the gift exchange between them later.

Luke patted her playfully on the backside, as he was ready to leave. *"Try to let your mom win a hand or two. That would make her happy, you know."*

"I don't have to let her win, Luke. She typically beats me most of the time when we play a game," she giggled with a roll of her eyes and a shake of her head, humored by his assumption.

"I will see *you* at nine," he pointed towards her as a reminder, before departing out the front door, on his way to a wealthier neighborhood and a snootier lifestyle.

Emma paused for a few moments, leaning up against the inside of the door, imaging what Luke had gotten her in way of a Christmas present or presents. She had purchased him a few work outfits, but also bought a man's watch that was way too expensive, taking the plunge and doing so anyway. She felt Luke deserved it, since his current one needed a new watchband, putting the sizeable bill on a newly acquired credit card she had just signed up for at a jewelry store in the Valley Mall, which made it possible to make the larger purchase.

Emma thought about Luke's reminder to be home on time – right at nine o'clock, which wasn't like him to press her about such things. *"What if he's giving me an engagement ring?"* she said with a gleeful look on her face, before walking back towards the living room, fantasizing and dreaming about the possibility now, feeling somewhat giddy - only hoping that it was really true.

Chapter 41

Christmas at the Carter house was also in full swing. Unlike Emma, Zoe had no interest in being engaged to anyone - which of course included Mason – even though *"he was wonderful and would make a terrific husband one day"*, Zoe had decided. Kelly, on the other hand, was as persistent about opening Christmas presents as were Emma's younger siblings, asking several times now, making those that were in the house wonder what all the rush was all about.

Breakfast was a simpler variety than what was served at the Baker residence, with bacon, sausage, eggs and pancakes being the only choices offered. Everyone kicked in to prepare the meal or help out in some way. Mason set up the table with a festive tablecloth, plates, napkins, silverware, coffee mugs and juice glasses, pleasantly surprising Zoe that he even knew how to do so without her input. He then volunteered to take Luna on a walk around the block, hoping one less person in the small kitchen would make things more efficient, feeling like he was bumping into the *"other workers"* that were present.

Mason opened the kitchen door, unleashing Luna in the process, placing her lead on the hook close by. "Geez, it's cold outside… winter is definitely here! Almost feels like snow in the air. I know there's been a few false alarms so far this season, but this time it may be the *"real deal"* and actually happen."

"I certainly hope not!" Kelly complained. "I'm visiting with my family tomorrow," she reminded, looking at Bryan with some concern, knowing he had taken a vacation day off to be with her.

"It will be fine, babe. My vehicle can drive through any sizeable snowstorm if that were to happen, but the weatherman isn't calling for more than an inch or two."

"The food is getting cold, so grab your plates!" Zoe insisted, trying to change the subject and get back on track with the schedule at hand, waiting patiently for the others to go before her. Mason wrapped an arm around Zoe's waist, as she stood close by the counter, allowing her father and Kelly to make their selections first. "Our turn," she announced to Mason, as they followed suit and filed in behind the others, dishing out a healthy portion of everything.

"So where does your family live at again, Kelly?" Zoe asked, trying to remember, placing more syrup on her pancakes once she was sitting at the table.

"Some live right here in Williamsport, but I have others in Chambersburg, Pennsylvania. That is where your father and I will be going tomorrow," Kelly explained. "You and Mason are welcome to join us, if you would like," she offered with a kind smile.

"I must work, but thank you for the invite," Mason offered, with his East Texas accent and politeness shining through, after taking a few deep sips of the hot coffee in front of him.

"Back to *"the grind"* for me too," Zoe added realistically. "The day after Christmas is a busy shopping day, with people taking advantage of the *"after Christmas sales"* and returning things that they received as presents and were not to their liking. We expect to be busy tomorrow since everyone will be out and about."

"Is Emma working also?" Bryan inquired.

"As far as I know. We are all going to be there except for Ava. She has out of town relatives coming in tomorrow, and wanted the time off to hang out with them, since they are only here for one day- passing through the area."

Zoe's phone began to vibrate, realizing she was receiving a call from Cynthia that she had not anticipated getting, after not hearing from her for a while. She turned her phone over, not wanting to deal with the reach out, trying to act unfazed and joining back in to the conversation at hand. Mason noticed the maneuver, as the phone began to vibrate for a second time. *"Whoever is calling seems to be on a mission to reach out to you today,"* he stated casually with a playful grin, surprising Zoe that he would come to that conclusion.

She sighed, trying to make light of it, not wanting to admit to him that it was her mother calling. This was a subject that had never been opened up for discussion with Mason, and of all days, Christmas wasn't the time to start. The thought of conversing about such a serious and painful episode of her life, that she was trying her best to forget, could be postponed for another day and time – if the need to do so became absolutely necessary. *"It isn't my ex, if that is what you are inferring."*

"Honey, it's okay if it were. I know he's no threat to us since we have a good thing going on between us," Mason whispered back, being very comfortable in his own skin.

"Well... It wasn't him...." Zoe stated somewhat defensively, rising to gather the dirty plates. "I will have the dishwasher loaded in a few. Why don't you guys go into the living room and then I will join you for gift giving, as soon as I clean up the kitchen?"

"Are you sure we can't help?" Kelly asked, truly desiring to be let off the hook this time, only being focused in on opening her presents from Bryan.

"Absolutely, I am sure! Mason that goes for you too," she smiled and insisted, desiring to have a few minutes alone now to think about things.

"Sorry, babe, if I said something wrong."

"You didn't," Zoe promised, as Mason reached down for a tender kiss. "Just save me a seat," she winked, knowing they always chose the loveseat in the living room anyway, where Luna attempted to wedge in between them.

Zoe joined the others, as Bryan turned on the stereo, setting the mood with some light-hearted Christmas music that played softly in the background. The cinnamon candle was lit and the lights on the tree twinkled brightly in a flashing cascading pattern, as each one decided on the same familiar place on the upholstered furniture that was always chosen.

"Who wants to play Santa this year?" Bryan asked with a big happy smile, as he looked at each one, waiting for the answer.

"Zoe would make a cute Santa," Mason commented with his arm already wrapped around her, as they cuddled together on the loveseat.

"I second that!" Kelly interjected quickly, wanting Bryan to remain close to her side.

Zoe rose off the furniture, faking it that it took some effort. *"First I cook your breakfast and now I am handing out the gifts. A woman's work is never done!"* She droned on with her arms outstretched - just for a dramatic effect.

"Honey, I will do it!" Mason replied, feeling guilty now for suggesting it.

"I'm only teasing, silly! Of course I will hand out the presents!"

Zoe donned the Santa hat that was sitting close by, and positioned it on her head just like her father and grandfather had done before her, when they were in charge of handing out the gifts and being Santa, just to signify that she was taking the role very seriously. She handed a wrapped present to each one, putting hers off to the side for when it was her turn to unwrap one.

"Who goes first?" Kelly asked, anxious to be chosen.

"I guess you do?" Zoe answered somewhat sarcastically, knowing this was the only thing on her mind.

Kelly ripped into the gift-wrap, almost shredding it from the needless, over-abundance of tape Bryan had put on the package. She looked somewhat confused, realizing the small box contained some cute diamond earrings and not *"the ring"* she had hoped for.

"Do you like them?" Bryan inquired excitedly.

"Oh… yes… they are very pretty," Kelly replied, pausing between words, not sure how to respond appropriately and feeling slightly disappointed.

"Why don't you try them on?" Zoe suggested with a pretentious smile. She was attempting to delay things somewhat, and purposely attempting to get under Kelly's skin, since it was more than obvious what she was hoping for.

"Umm…. Maybe later? Since everyone else deserves a chance to open a gift?"

Bryan went next and then it was Mason's turn. Each man receiving a wool scarf from Zoe that she had ordered online, with claims that it was the *"finest wool in the world"*, that she made sure to note, as they admired the item.

"I love it!" Mason chimed in. "I actually needed a heavier scarf for the winter, and haven't taken the time to buy one."

"Yes, I know," Zoe laughed. "That's what gave me the idea."

Mason rose to take over the *"Santa role"* handing gifts out to all three, but looking specifically for those with Zoe nametags. "You've worked hard today. Take a break and open your gifts too," he insisted, as Zoe sat back down and gazed at him, realizing once again how loving and considerate he always was to her.

Zoe took the time to open each one, saving Mason's for last. "Thank you, dad. Love the earrings!" Zoe said, feeling like they resembled Kelly's to a degree, and he had probably bought them at the same time and at the same place.

"You are very welcome!" Bryan replied, smiling contentedly, relieved that he pulled that off and Zoe seemed happy with his selection. Shopping and gift giving was not one of his strong points, typically being done hurriedly and at the last minute, without much thought or consideration as to what he should choose.

Zoe opened Kelly's gift next, holding up a cute blouse and matching sweater jacket that was to be layered over the top of it, admiring how pretty the combo looked. It was more than she had expected, and was surprised that Kelly would have gone to so much effort for her. *"I love it, Kelly! You didn't have to do this for me, you know."*

"I wanted to..." Kelly answered sincerely, with slight tears now crossing her eyes. It hadn't always been easy dealing with Zoe with her up and down emotions, being an adult child that was still living at home with her father. She knew about the past, and what her mother had emotionally created by abandoning her, realizing that one day – hopefully, very soon - Zoe would be her future stepdaughter, so it was well worth the effort.

The remainder of the gifts were distributed, with Kelly also receiving a scarf from Zoe, Bryan receiving new bowling shoes from Kelly, and Mason getting a mutual gift from Bryan and Kelly both of a dress shirt and also cologne that had a masculine sounding name surrounding the Old West. Mason presented a gift card to the happy couple in return, letting them know that *"La Paz in Frederick was enjoyable when he and Zoe went there back in the fall"*. All that remained under the Christmas tree was one single gift with a label addressed to Zoe - from Mason.

Mason reached for the last present, handing it to Zoe. *"I hope you like it, sweetie,"* he wished with his charming southern drawl, as she ripped into the ample sized present with the metallic giftwrap and over-abundant sized bow.

Zoe's mouth dropped open, as she peaked into the gift box and saw a black, lacy *"barely there"* negligee with a matching *"see-through"* robe and stiletto heels, edged out in fake fur trim. *"Umm... wow..."* Zoe sputtered out in embarrassment, looking at Mason in disbelief, and then at Bryan and Kelly who were doing their best not to burst out laughing, after catching a small glimpse of the *"unmentionables"*.

"Do you like it?" He implored in earnest, with his eyes now beaming, thinking he had picked out the ultimate, sexy gift for her.

"Yes, Mason. The present is very nice," Zoe responded graciously, having mixed feelings about it all, trying to close the box quickly over the *"sleazy"* contents and place it with her other Christmas presents that were close by. She joined Mason again on the loveseat, trying to breathe and regain her composure, trying to turn the attention back to Kelly and her father.

"What a nice Christmas. Did everyone get what they wanted?" Bryan asked, while rising from off the sofa and staring down at Kelly, who appeared somewhat perplexed, as he waited on the answer.

It was mutually agreed upon by all that it was wonderful, with mixed feelings being felt by the females for sexy black lingerie's and the lack of engagement rings. Bryan excused himself to use the bathroom afterwards, returning in no time to be by Kelly's side again. *"You went that quickly?"* Kelly asked in confusion.

Bryan reached in his pocket without answering her, giving her the last remaining present that she had hoped for, and then sadly didn't receive - after every other gift was handed out from under the tree. *"Another for me?"* She questioned reluctantly, not desiring to get her hopes back up again and then be disappointed.

"Just open it and see," he replied, smiling warmly, waiting for her to do so.

Kelly removed the paper slowly from the small container, with her hands shaking ever-so-slightly now. Zoe was across the room filming the moments on her cellphone, anticipating what was about to happen. The black velvet box was revealed, as Kelly looked at Bryan with questioning eyes, not sure where things were leading.

Bryan rose from off the sofa, bending down in front of her on one knee, as Kelly opened the lid to the velvet box, revealing a one-carat diamond that was mounted on a simple gold band, glistening brilliantly in front of her. *"Will you marry me Kelly?"* he asked with a heart full of love, waiting patiently on her to answer.

Immediately, Kelly's hand flew up to her mouth, lost in the moment, staring at Bryan and then at the beautiful ring several times over, before she was able to speak. *"Yes, Bryan, I will marry you!"* Kelly cried out, feeling happier and more surprised than she could have ever imagined, finally getting the Christmas present of her *dreams*.

Chapter 42

"Give me a second to find it, but I think there is a chilled bottle of champagne hiding somewhere in the back of the refrigerator," Zoe commented, acting naïve to the truth, knowing her father had placed it there several days earlier, planning for the engagement celebration afterwards. The bottle was located and uncorked with a pop, as the bubbly contents spilled over the top and down the side. Zoe filled up four champagne glasses that had already been cleaned and concealed in an out-of-the way place, being placed in a cabinet above the double ovens, where Kelly would have never thought to look. *"To the happy couple! Congratulations on your engagement!"* Zoe toasted with her glass held high, glancing lovingly at both her father and Kelly, knowing she needed to accept the inevitable that was now being forced upon her.

"Cheers!" Mason added, as the group clanked their glasses together and then quickly drank down the celebratory offering. *"So when are you two getting hitched?"*

Zoe once again looked shocked for the second time in less than an hour, wanting to seriously kick Mason in the ass. *"They just got engaged, for heaven's sakes! Give them a little time to enjoy the moment!"* Zoe sputtered out, much to Kelly's surprise, realizing once again that the challenges with her new fiancé's daughter was not always going to be easy.

"That is something Kelly and I need to talk about and decide," Bryan interjected practically, looking at his *"intended"* that now had the sparkly diamond ring displayed on the fourth finger of her left hand, for all to see and admire.

Zoe broke free of Mason, leaning down to pet Luna. "I need to return a call and will be back in a few minutes," she quickly explained, not waiting on anyone to question her. She grabbed her winter coat and leashed up the dog, disappearing out of the house with her cellphone in hand.

"*Don't be too long!*" Bryan yelled out. "*We need to call Pappy Joe and Nana Ruth and wish them a Merry Christmas and tell them the good news!*"

The phone rang several times, before being answered. *"Hello?"*

"Cynthia?"

"Is this Zoe?"

"Yes, it's me. *Merry… Christmas,*" Zoe practiced saying, knowing it had not been said or wished for Cynthia since she was a child.

"The same to you. Have you opened your gifts yet?"

Zoe took a few seconds to think about the embarrassing situation with the unwrapping of the box with the black negligee that Mason had put her through. *"Yes… we have. I mean… I have,"* she clarified, not wanting to admit who was also present with her that day. *"And you? Have you opened your gifts?"*

Cynthia had excused herself, disappearing into the kitchen while her husband and Eddie sat in the adjoining living room watching TV, hoping to gain some space and privacy to speak with her daughter. "We just opened our gifts after having our breakfast."

"The same with us," Zoe revealed, now that Cynthia had spoken in the *"plural"* sense of the word. "So you left me a voicemail message, and I wanted to return the call and wish you a Merry Christmas."

"Well thank you for doing so, Zoe. That was very sweet of you. Before we say our goodbyes, I would love it if you could speak with your brother Eddie. It would make his day knowing he finally had a chance to actually hear your voice and have a conversation with you, especially on Christmas Day."

Zoe considered the request, assuming Eddie was as much a victim in all of this as she was. *"Are you sure he understands who I am?"*

"Of course he knows who you are, sweetie," Cynthia replied, making Zoe's skin crawl from the *"term of endearment"* that she so frivolously just threw out.

She sighed, not sure how to deal with the request that her mother was now forcing upon her. "Then, please... just go ahead and put him on the phone... if you must."

There was a period of silence for a few moments and then a simple mouthing of a quiet *"hello"* which could faintly be heard on the other end of the line.

"Speak up, Edward!" Zoe could hear Cynthia demand in the background to her son, hoping he would be more forthcoming and less shy.

"Hello, Zoe. I'm Eddie – your brother – I guess...?"

Zoe shook her head, reading the situation correctly, feeling sorry for the boy all at once. "Nice to meet you, Eddie. Yes, that is what I heard also... that I am your sister."

The two conversed for several minutes, talking back and forth about Christmas and presents, focusing mainly in on Eddie's new gaming system that he *"just had to have"* and how long he would be off of school for his winter break.

"It was great talking to you, Eddie. Call me anytime," Zoe cordially offered, amazed that she had actually been willing to open the door for any further communication with him.

"It was great talking to you too," Eddie replied, being scripted by

his mother, who was standing right beside of him, ease dropping and telling him what to say next, finally being allowed to hand the phone back over to her. Eddie ran from the kitchen, falling on the sofa beside of his father again, glad the exchange was finally done with his *"new sister"* and he could return to his TV viewing and game playing.

Cynthia cleared her throat, whispering quietly into the phone. *"Thank you, for speaking with Eddie. That truly means a lot to me and him as well!"*

Zoe shook her head, fighting the bitterness of doing her mother even the *"slightest of favors"*. "He seems like a nice kid. Glad we finally spoke," she responded somewhat coldly, not wanting to appear too fazed by any of it.

"I'm still hoping at some point, that we can arrange a visit. *Maybe in the spring... if that is workable for you?* It would have been nice if we could have arranged it sooner, but things have kept us rather busy around here," Cynthia explained, making excuses that Zoe seriously doubted to be true in nature.

"Sure. Let's try for that time," Zoe offered, realizing that sudden, unasked for change was coming, whether she wanted it to or not. Her mother was attempting to step back into her life, and she had a new brother who she was having mixed feelings about accepting. Bryan and Kelly were now officially engaged, and maybe getting married sooner than she had anticipated, opening the door to another female who would be dwelling in the same household with her. Every discovery of the day came with its own set of unique challenges; but for Zoe, she finally felt at peace, being resolved that in time probably nothing was impossible to deal with.

Emma had beaten Luke home, just as she had planned, staying at her mother's place until 5 o'clock, enjoying all the traditional festivities that they shared and repeated, each and every Christmas together.

Scrabble, Rummikub and even a round of Parcheesi were all played, before retiring to the living room for movie watching that involved *"rich royals and holiday house switching"*. Owen and Reagan were preoccupied playing with their new toys, as Emma and Margie took to each end of the sofa, absorbed in the made up fairytales that were larger than life, but still each believing that they were possible.

Luke opened the door to the apartment, slightly intoxicated but with a handsome grin that Emma could never resist or say no to. *"You're here…"*

"Yes… waiting on you," she countered – being right on point - happy he was away from the *"aristocrats"* finally. "Did you have a nice time with your family?"

Luke sat on the sectional, pulling Emma down with him, pulling her in closer for a warm embrace. *"Give me a kiss first and then I will tell you whatever you would like to hear,"* he challenged, as he slowly and seductively kissed her, rubbing one breast through her shirt, making one perky nipple stand up to his attention immediately.

Emma pulled back. *"Something obviously has you horny? What did you eat at your parents' house?"*

Luke laughed, flinging his arm over the back of the sectional. "Not oysters, love, if that is what you are implying. I'm just happy to be home, back in my baby's arms. I missed you today, you know," he confessed, snuggling up against her for another passionate tongue kiss.

She softened, always being pliable under his spell. "I missed you too."

"Should we do our gift exchange now or get a little action in first? You can guess what my vote is," Luke offered suggestively, locking his blue eyes with Emma's azure ones.

Emma unbuttoned her blouse slowly, taking her time as she

lingered over each one, driving Luke mad in the process. He bent down to pick her up in his arms, carrying her quickly to the bedroom, not even bothering to shut the door behind him. Clothes were removed - each one helping the other - as fingers and tongues prodded and touched the intimate places that were all so familiar now, thoroughly turning the other one on in the process. Luke plunged deeply, in and out of the wet vagina that he was totally hooked on, much like an addict is to his *"drug of choice",* wanting it to go on forever with the *"high"* that it brought – every night, and all night long. His resolve finally broke, sending him over the edge and releasing his sperm deeply inside of the willing cavern of Emma's feminine being, feeling like Christmas had finally arrived - and no other gift was necessary.

"That was absolutely amazing! Merry Christmas to me," Luke expressed passionately, wiping the sweat from his brow, feeling breathless.

"Yes, it was amazing…. But I still say that you must have eaten something that brought this all on," she teased, jumping up to depart to the bathroom. *"And now that we have had sex, I want to open my presents now!"* Emma insisted, making herself perfectly clear, before turning and slamming the door behind her.

Luke and Emma sat on the floor by their modest sized, artificial tree that was white in color, having only two varieties of ornaments - royal blue and silver – being simply adorned. Outside of the apartment, a wreath hung on the door in the hallway, which matched the same look as the tree. Nothing else was decorated or even mattered, to the *"power couple"* that was always consumed with their careers. Luke handed Emma her third present, the other two being practical in nature and for the kitchen that she had requested, feeling her heart race as the box this time was much smaller than the other ones. She gave him a questioning gaze, undoing the professionally wrapped item.

Inside was an obvious jewelry box, somewhat large in size for *"a ring"* she realized. Emma slowly pried it open, desiring to savor the final moments to the discovery of what was actually contained therein. Her heart dropped to her feet in a matter of seconds, when she realized it wasn't the *"hoped for"* engagement ring, but a necklace that contained an aquamarine stone with a splattering of diamonds in a trendy, contemporary setting.

"It's beautiful!" Emma purely exclaimed, as she tried to put forth her best front and conceal her true emotions. She honestly knew it was too soon to be engaged to Luke, only officially being together for a few months now. *We decided to live together almost immediately so why not get engaged also?* She contemplated frivolously, throwing caution to the wind. But Luke reeled her back in, planting her feet squarely on the ground again, jolting her back to reality that taking it to the next step with him may be a slower journey than she had anticipated.

"I had it designed just for you. I knew that was your birthstone and I think it turned out great!" he bragged, assuming she felt the same way.

"That was very thoughtful of you, Luke, to have someone create such a lovely piece for me. I will cherish it forever!" Emma offered, wanting now to believe her words too, as she leaned in to give him a sweet kiss. *"You have one other present also. Here, open it,"* She instructed, handing him his last gift that she had taken the time to wrap at work, buying it the last minute on a whim – just in case she received a costly engagement ring.

Luke tore off the snowman wrapping paper that matched the same generic color scheme of the tree, opening the oversized gift box that contained a new ski jacket and matching bibs. *"Wow, sweetie, this is great!"* He exclaimed with unexpected surprise, pulling the jacket and bibs from the box, as he stood up and held both in front of him, just to make sure they were the right size.

"Don't worry, Luke, both will fit. I checked the sizes of your old ski stuff in the hall closet and I made sure it was exactly the same for the new bibs and jacket, which honestly astounds me that you haven't gained a pound," she explained, wanting to gain his approval.

"I love it! And honestly, I needed a new set. I haven't had new ski clothes since the beginning of high school."

"Yes, I know," Emma teased with a roll of her eyes. "I saw a few holes in your bibs and I wouldn't want to be seen with you on the slopes looking like that."

Luke began to laugh, recalling now the memories of those earlier times, skiing with Noah and his siblings, not caring about the *"rough and tumble"* way he used to ski and snowboard down the snow-covered trails during the crazy days of his youth. *"I guess we need to get you some new winter gear also, for when we go to Whitetail or up to Wisp. What do you say?"*

"I'm fine, Luke. I barely have skied over the years, like you have, and I definitely do not have any holes!"

Luke reached out for Emma, wrapping her in his arms once again, as he leaned in to nuzzle her neck, which made her giggle from the tickling he was creating. "Oh, you definitely have holes my dear," he whispered enticingly. *"And in all the right places, that I love to poke and prod and ride until I can't ride them any longer."*

Emma could feel herself becoming aroused again, ready to *"do it"* wherever or however Luke so well chose, not caring in the least about the room location or how adventuresome he wanted to be with her. He was her perfect match, and even without receiving an engagement ring for this first official Christmas that they were together as a couple, she was content and things couldn't get much better.

Chapter 43

Spring had sprung and so were the beginning signs that it had finally arrived, with flowers blooming, leaves on trees reappearing, and the growing of lawns that needed mowing way too often. The C&O Canal was showing an increase in tourist traffic once again, with an over-abundance of bicyclers, hikers and even fisherman who were dragging out their boats after the long winter that was filled with too much snow, taking to the waterways in great number for a day of fishing and beer drinking.

Mason and Zoe had made it a ritual to go to the canal early, typically most mornings at 6 a.m., taking a three-mile hike on the towpath together before work, with Luna taking the lead as they strolled and conversed about the day ahead. Emma didn't seem to mind that Zoe had turned her in for a new walking partner, grabbing a few extra minutes instead of *"cuddle time with her man, Luke"* who she adored and was still going strong with.

Easter had come and gone and Pappy Joe and Nana Ruth did make the journey as promised, staying for nearly a week, before returning back to Fort Wayne, ready to take on the spring planting that was so much a part of their daily lives. Mason was included in on the Easter festivities, even attending church on Sunday morning with the whole family, which of course included Bryan and Kelly who were now planning out their wedding. Mason met Zoe's grandparents for the first time, gaining their approval for *being a good choice in a boyfriend,* as she later shared with him after they had departed.

Luna's had experienced a slight turn down in business over the winter months, being considered the *"slump period"* that was normal for the town. It was actually somewhat of a relief, to the overworked staff of employees that had given it their all, during the busy holiday season dealing with all the parties that the restaurant had hosted.

Now, it was a new year with a new direction and vision. The building next door had still not been rented, and Zoe and Emma had a renewed interest in it, wanting to expand out in some way. Zoe, though, did not want to involve her grandparents in the second faze of a business venture, after the poor state of Pappy Joe's health, deciding to consider another investor instead on the advice of Emma. Luke Taylor, along with his father, Ron, had a keen interest in backing *"part two"* of their restaurant franchise, encouraging the girls to consider making one of the buildings a *"sports bar"* themed hangout, even though Zoe wasn't being convinced that easily.

"If you say so," Zoe resigned in frustration with her arms crossed, shaking her head as she interrupted the speech of the corporate attorney who was currently orchestrating and explaining things - page by page – during the settlement process for the *"still to be decided"* decision if *Luna C's* was to be a new restaurant or bar. "I never wanted *Luna's* to be a sports bar. *You know that, Em!"* Zoe spewed out irately, trying to remind Emma to *"read between the lines"* about her feelings.

Luke looked at the women sitting across from him and his father, who had agreed to attend *"closing"* on this day and time in the conference room of Taylor Toyota. The contract for the new eating establishment was to be signed off on and ratified, being directed by the car dealerships' lawyer who was also present. Emma sat by Zoe - her best friend and sometimes hard to deal with business partner - who was currently throwing an unrealistic *"monkey wrench"* into the plans for *Luna C's* – the *"C"* being a play on words for the *C&O Canal*, with the assumption – as stated by the attorney - that it was going to be a sports bar.

Luke threaded his fingers behind his neck, as he leaned back in his chair, considering the situation at hand and how to resolve it amicably. "Excuse me for saying this, Zoe, but I thought we worked this all out already, agreeing upon the direction of the business and what it would entail."

Zoe stood up, surprising the occupants of the room, while pointing her index finger directly at Luke and waving it angrily in the direction of his face. *"You worked it all out with Emma, but not with me! There are a lot of bars already in Williamsport that cater to that sort of thing. I was trying to make our place stand out and be special! How dare you state it in the settlement papers that the place is definitely going to be a sports bar without confirming that with me first!"*

Luke realized the *"fur was up on Zoe's back"* and even after all this time, he assumed Noah was still behind her frustration. "Why don't we take ten minutes and come back with a fresh perspective, and maybe then we will be ready to make this happen? *Can we all just consider doing so?"* Luke offered, giving his most charismatic performance and pleasant smile that he could muster, hoping Zoe would bite.

"I guess... that works for me," Zoe resigned, looking once again at Emma who barely wanted to make any eye contact with her now, knowing when to back away from Zoe's fiery temper.

The room emptied, with Emma following Zoe from the building, trying to catch up with her as she proceeded to walk in the direction of her car, which she was heading towards rather quickly. *"You aren't leaving, are you?"* Emma inquired, fearful Zoe was making an irrational decision now and would be sorry for it later.

"Of course not, Em. I just wanted to be alone and maybe call Mason, and seek his advice on all this. He always has a way of calming me down and making sense of things," she explained, trying to finally act rational. She unlocked the door with a beep of her keys, ready to climb into the driver's seat.

"May I join you?" Emma hesitantly requested, trying her best not to inflame the situation any worse than it already was.

"Of course... Get in," Zoe stated, not standing on ceremony.

The car doors were shut as Zoe started up the engine, trying to bring some *"much needed"* cooler air to the unseasonably warm day and as well as her disposition, providing both of them with a chance for some quiet time and privacy. "I don't want you to do anything you are uncomfortable with, but we did go over the *"pros and cons"* of turning one part of the business into a sports bar - if you recall from our past conversations - and you finally seemed to agreed with the rest of us that you could see the wisdom in the vision."

"Yes, I know all this, Em, but now that it is in the final stages of the legal *"mumbo jumbo"* that involves our signatures, I'm not so sure I can go through with it."

"Why not? Is this about Noah again? That he wanted *Luna's* to be a sports bar and anything having to do with him has turned you off to a reasonable and profitable business opportunity?"

"Maybe it is! *I still fight this demon everyday of what he did to affect my life by the choices he made - when he broke up with me and left town."*

Emma sat staring at her friend, shaking her head sadly. "My word, Zoe Carter, I feel very sorry for you. Just let the past go and get over things, for heavens sakes! First it was your mother and what horrible things she did to you, and then it was Noah and how he screwed up your life even more so! You own a successful business, have an amazing *"salt of the earth"* family who always has your back - no matter what - and then you were lucky enough to have stumbled upon a new wonderful boyfriend who adores you, and finally you have me as you best friend in life - as well as the rest of the townsfolk of Williamsport, Maryland - who love, respect and admire you for all you have accomplished - in spite of your circumstances. *Please just be the strong woman I know you can be and make the right decision for all concerned!"* Emma yelled out, departing from the Mazda CX-3, slamming the door firmly behind her.

Zoe sat in her car staring in disbelief, as she looked out of her rearview mirror at Emma who had turned and walked away, and was heading back towards the car dealership without her. She bent her head and began to softly cry, considering the words of her friend who had never held back the truth, especially when she needed to hear it the most.

"Hello?"

"Mason, it's Zoe. Can we just talk for just a moment?"

"Aren't you in a settlement meeting right now, ready to close the deal on your second dining establishment?" He twanged out, confused with the call.

"I was… and then I stepped away from things, not sure I could resolve the apprehensions that I am dealing with, without talking to you first."

Mason took a few deep breaths, waving the Park Ranger from the room, which was sitting opposite his desk, mouthing the words that *"he wouldn't be long"*. "So let's talk and let me try to help you work through your concerns."

"It the *"sports bar"* thing. You know how I feel about it, trying to set a different tone for my restaurant, not wanting to compete against the other bars in town. I don't want a rowdy group who wants to only party and watch football games all night in my place."

Mason began to laugh. "Umm…. Zoe, that is what most of the male population, including me… dar… ling, along with a few females besides, are enjoying these days. And that group of people that you are referring to, will bring money to the table. No *"ifs, ands, or buts"* about it!"

"Yes, and trouble too, when the cops show up!"

"Calm down, swee… tie! Obviously, everyone else in Williamsport who owns a bar has figured out how to handle the drunks."

"Just something I don't need added pressure with."

"Remember, Luke and his father are now a part of all this. I'm sure they have *"the smarts"* to figure out security concerns. Let go and just trust them... they are reputable and established business people in the community, who have a vested interest in seeing *Luna C's* survive. I can't see anything but success going forward for both of your places. I have a very good feeling about all this for you."

Zoe took a deep breath, happy that she took a few moments to speak with Mason and hear his perspective on the matter. "Thank you, Mason. What you said makes perfect sense – especially the part about the Taylor's dealing with the security part of the business. I guess I better get back to the meeting now. I know they are all inside waiting on me."

"See you later tonight for a celebration dinner?"

"I wouldn't miss it!" Zoe exclaimed happily, suddenly feeling much better for speaking to him. "I will text you once everything is finished."

"I'll be waiting, honey."

The stuffy conference room was filled with the same participants, patiently waiting on Zoe's return. Emma breathed a sigh of relief as Zoe re-entered the room, sitting in her appointed seat beside of Emma once again. Zoe smiled, trying to silently mouth her apologies to her friend, as Emma nodded back in return, with both now having an unspoken understanding and agreement between them.

"Are we ready to sign the contract?" the middle-aged, graying in the temples, male lawyer asked with impatience. He directed his comments especially towards Zoe, as he made direct eye contact with her, feeling irritated and wanting to conclude things quickly so that he

could go to lunch with his wife.

"Yes! Absolutely!" Zoe confirmed, with a radiate smile now expressing her cooperation. The sudden, 180-degree change of attitude, was a pleasant, unexpected surprise, and noted by all in the room, as the contract for *Luna C's* was passed around the large conference table and signed off on, making it official and finalized.

The *dream* was now a reality for Zoe and Emma - of owning their second dining and drinking establishment in the town of Williamsport, Maryland, close to the C&O Canal, even if it now involved a *"non-family member"* who was doing the investing. Hands were shaken as the Taylor's lawyer shut his briefcase, standing to give his final departing words and well wishes. "I'm glad that this all worked out nicely for all concerned. I wish you nothing but the best with your new business venture, and don't hesitate to contact me if you have any further questions," he added, being professional and smooth in his style and presentation, sliding two business cards in the direction of the female owners, just in case they needed them at some point in the future.

"Thank you," Zoe and Emma said in unison, as the attorney departed and they were left alone in the room with only Ron and Luke Taylor.

"Now the fun part begins..." Luke grinned, standing and stretching his arms overhead, just to clear the kinks from his neck. "If we are finished here, I really need to get back to the sales team for a meeting that I'm late for," he explained clearly, looking at his father for any further guidance and direction.

"As long as Zoe and Emma do not have any other questions, I think we can all get back to our jobs and responsibilities. *Are you ladies good with things?"*

"Definitely, I am!" Emma replied.

"When will we meet up again to start making plans?" Zoe inquired,

still having unresolved questions, but delaying to ask the majority of them.

"Give us at least a week to talk to *"our people"* and then we will set up a time to meet and start tossing out ideas about the concept for the new place."

"Who is *"our people"*?" Zoe grilled with an intense look on her face, making Emma feel somewhat embarrassed, as she dismissed Luke's need to leave.

Ron chuckled, looking over at Luke before answering, not usually being interrogated as such by a female. "I have friends in the area in numerous construction trades, so I need to find the right architect, contractor and maybe even an engineer to oversee all aspects of the remodeling of the property. We definitely don't want to deal with any structural issues that could arise in the future - which should be resolved now."

"I understand," Zoe finally conceded, as they four walked from the conference room out into the main part of the showroom. "I'm sorry I was dragging my feet some... I promise I will try my best in the future to be more cooperative and a better team player," she resolved with a cordial smile, finally loosening up some now that the settlement was finalized.

"It quite all right," Ron countered. "You have all the characteristics of a astute *"hands-on"* business owner. I admire your drive."

Zoe was taken back by the compliment, never expecting it from someone like him. *"Well, Thank you, Mr. Taylor. That means a lot coming from you!"*

"You are welcome, my dear. Now please be happy about all this and try to enjoy your day, since you are now one of the owners of a building that will house a great new place in Williamsport!" Mr. Taylor encouraged, feeling like Zoe just needed to calm down and stop acting so edgy, as his cellphone began to ring and he conveniently walked away - ready to disappear and answer it.

Chapter 44

With the legal agreement now behind them, the real work needed to begin in making *Luna C's* an actual operating bar that was open to the public. Luke and Ron interviewed and hired a contractor from the area who was in charge of all the renovations, with promises being made by him *that by early summer all would be completed and the place would be ready for business.*

Zoe was beside herself, realizing she was out of the loop, unlike the first time around when she put her heart and soul into all aspects of designing *Luna's*. The architect, who was brought on board for the project, was feeling especially challenged on how the place should be laid out - asking for all owners and key personnel on the project to attend a planning meeting, which was scheduled exactly two weeks to the day that the property had been purchased. It was to be held at the actual location of the new bar, and he desired that everyone should come prepared with ideas and suggestions.

A semi-circle of folding chairs were positioned in the main room of the bar, with each owner as well as the hired renovation experts, being in attendance. It was overwhelming – to say the least - the massive amount of work that was ahead, and inspiration for ideas was not first and foremost on anyone's minds. No occupant had been there in several years, and in its place was dirt on the floors and cobwebs on the walls, and the exposed rafters showed evidence of the same on the ceiling. Luckily though, the electricity and water still were functioning, with only the need to bring them up to code.

As the architect took over with his part of the presentation, he began immediately, desiring a *"request for ideas"* on how the place should be laid out and designed. Zoe was the first one to respond, trying to get past the strong mildew smell that was heavy in the air, as she stood up, ready to get her main points across. "I have given this a lot of thought and I feel a historic presence should flow and radiate throughout the pub, making it almost like a museum with pictures and artifacts from the earlier years of the canal, when it was built and finally made operational. It would be interesting to mention several local families who lived on the canal boats and what it was like doing so, even detailing the actual cargo that was transported on the boats, while going through the locks."

"That is an excellent idea!" Emma praised, as the others present sat by quietly observing and taking it all in, waiting on her to continue. Zoe smiled at her friend, appreciative of her support, before resuming her speech that she had prepared.

"Beyond this, I think it would be noteworthy to mention the earlier presidents that had visited the town, along with several wars – maybe focusing in on the Civil War specifically - and how it affected the surrounding area and townsfolk. Lastly, I think the major hurricanes that have passed through the area, are worth talking about. How about pictures of the shocking *"after-affects"* of specific hurricanes that had flooded the town and canal? Maybe display a picture of the Cushwa Warehouse where the water lines are marked on the side of the building, which notates the name and date of each disastrous hurricane that affected Williamsport specifically.

Surprisingly, all were in agreement that Zoe's ideas were excellent suggestions; with the architect already noting the need for a historical expert who could provide accurate information in a written form, as well as contacts for acquiring the necessary items to adequately decorate the building with those relics from the past. Ron suggested recreating the look of a bygone era of a local pub with a simple planked wooden bar, barstools, rough-hewed tables and chairs of a similar fashion, desiring also to refurbish and make operational the large stone fireplace that was situated on the adjacent wall - close to the bar. Luke thought that bringing in local vendors of craft beers and regional wines might be an interesting offering that would cater to the local tourists, and Emma came up with the idea that dressing up the servers in *"period-style garb"* would be unique and add greatly to the overall look of the place. And finally, Zoe gave her additional two cents, tossing out a theme of *"turn-of-the-century"* dishware, metal mugs, fake flickering candles in every window, woven rugs placed here and there on the floors, and wrought iron light fixtures suspended from the ceilings - communicating with the experts that it would set the mood and create a lasting memory for anyone who patronized the quaint establishment.

A similar look could be found elsewhere in other historic regions, but not in the town of Williamsport, Maryland. The core group of owners – including the professionals that were hired - agreed it might just work. Zoe felt a big sense of relief, realizing now that she could return to focusing in on *Luna's* - where her heart truly belonged - leaving all the hard work of the construction and design to those who specialized in such tasks. The one last element of concern, was the operational aspect of *Luna C's,* but after hearing what Ron and Luke both had to say, sharing their leadership skills and strong vision, there was no longer a doubt in her mind or anyone else's that the bar may just be a success, with the Taylor family leading the charge.

As the weeks progressed, *Luna C's* slowly took shape, with not too many hitches coming up in the process. The building was quite sound on the outside, pleasantly surprising the financial backers that nothing was drastically wrong with the foundation, with the only decision being made for the exterior, to replace the old metal roof with a new one and paint the existing shutters. The anticipated changes to the electricity were conquered, with a few modifications being necessary for the plumbing also. A new sink was installed behind the bar, the bathroom had to be rebuilt, and then some minor upgrades had to be made to the modest-sized kitchen, with a new dishwashing station and commercial appliances being added.

The fireplace was probably the biggest of the challenges – bringing in a stonemason from the Gettysburg, Pennsylvania area who specialized in historic preservation of buildings, confirming that he could *mimic the look of the old grout, and at the same time gauge the safety of the chimney - fixing any and all issues that were present.* As the wood was stacked and lit for the very first time, with a swirl of smoke disappearing up the refurbished liner of the chimney, cheers and applause went out in way of celebration for the completion of the *"eye catching"* focal point of the room - that Ron Taylor had especially requested.

All that remained was the placement of the furniture and extras that Zoe had gave vision to - early on during the beginning days of the project. An amazing amount of effort and success had resulted in locating the historic memorabilia and photos, with half of it being donated by local families, after a reach-out had been done through the town's social media page.

The final night before opening *Luna C's,* the entire team of owners and workers came back together, positioning tables, chairs, barstools, rugs, dishes and metal mugs on hooks that were positioned over the bar. Also, the electric candles were placed in each window, and the pictures were hung on the walls, with the historic memorabilia being placed strategically throughout the entire place - not missing out on any detail in the slightest. Zoe gave an appraising eye, checking out each room carefully, as Emma and Luke walked beside of her, taking it all in from their own vantage point.

"The new staff knows they need to be here by 8 a.m. sharp tomorrow for bar training, correct?" Zoe questioned, pressuring Emma to write down one more thing that she needed to remember on the pad of paper she was carrying.

"Yes, Zoe, I have the whole group coming in at that hour - the three bartenders, four servers, and the two dishwashers - that we hired. Plus, I've included two more from *Luna's* that are also new and need some additional training."

"That was an excellent call, Em!" Zoe complimented, surprised she had the good judgment to do so."

"You can thank Luke for that," she grinned, looking at her boyfriend lovingly, who was typically always thinking and planning ahead, when it came to business decisions.

"Thank you, Luke. Glad someone had the good sense to be proactive in formulating that important *"opening day list"*," Zoe mentioned with a sarcastic tone, raising a knowing eyebrow at Emma who didn't seemed fazed in the least by her *"overly intense"* friend who was currently on *"high alert"*.

"No prob, Zoe, I am on it for tomorrow! We better get back out front to the others though. I know my dad is on a tight time constraint and needs to get going. He and my mom have tickets for the Maryland Theater tonight for some concert."

"Of course!" Zoe answered, as she stopped what she was doing and speedily walked out to the main part of the historic pub, with Luke and Emma by her side. She placed her hands on her hips, wiping back a tear. The place looks so cozy, warm and inviting. It's too bad that it isn't the time of year for lighting the fireplace, but other than that - everything is just perfect!"

Ron Taylor walked over to the fireplace, pointing a small remote at the recent insert that had been positioned behind the antique wrought iron screen, where the wood logs were once stacked on the hearth. A fake fire flickered and danced in front of them, minus the heat from a real one.

"Wow, where did that come from? It's lovely, but who made that decision?" Zoe asked, amazed at what she was seeing for the very first time.

Ron smiled, pleased with the sharp-looking addition that he had suggested to the contractor, knowing it was a surprise to the others.

"This, my dear, is the summer version for the fireplace that I chose. It is an electrical fireplace insert that looks the real thing minus the heat, or even vice versa, if heat is wanted and no flame. Once it is cold outside again, it will be removed and real logs will be added and lit for our guests."

Luke walked over, placing an arm around his dad's shoulder. *"I'm impressed, dad. Didn't think you had a decorating flair in you, but I guess I was wrong,"* he teased, admiring the ambiance of the flickering flame of the fireplace also. "Not to put a damper on all this, but you know you told me to remind you when it was time to leave. Mom is going to have a fit if you aren't home right on time. She even texted me about it just a few minutes ago."

"You know what they say – *"Happy wife, happy life",*" Ron quoted with a shake of his head, placing the remote on top of the fireplace mantel after turning it back off. "Yes, she is looking forward to seeing this Motown group that is performing tonight," he explained, grabbing his cellphone from off the top of the wooden planked bar, realizing he had four missed calls already from Theresa, and would better get a move on. "I'll stop by tomorrow night with your mother for our first official night of being open, and share a pint with you."

"Sounds like a plan," Luke answered smiling broadly, pulling Emma in close by his side, happy and relieved that the tough part was finally over.

Chapter 45

Luna C's picked up in popularity right away – being the missing element that *Luna's* had lacked. It was the right decision, being consistently filled with a steady stream of customers throughout the day and evening. The majority of patrons who entered for the first time, commented on the décor and how amazing and authentic the pub looked, feeling like they were stepping back in time to an earlier era. Photos were kept to a minimum, not wanting the *"feel of the place"* to be duplicated at some other bar or eatery who would desire to mimic the look. The wait staff could only do so much to control the policy of *"picture taking"*, so it had been decided by the owners - right from the very start - that no photos would be captured specifically of the historic relics that now defined the place, or of the rare images that had been donated by the local citizens and were hanging in exclusive groupings, scattered throughout, and hanging on every wall. It was common practice, that most bars were notorious for allowing customers to pose for *"selfies"*, with their glasses raised high, choosing noteworthy locations in the building to be flashed all over social media afterwards. *Luna C's* was the exception, group photos could be taken, but just not in front of the priceless memories of Williamsport's historic past.

Luke and Ron were thrilled with their decision to fund the new hangout, after seeing the overnight success on their return and witnessing the packed house first hand. They even made an offer to Zoe and Emma for additional funding for *Luna's* - if a future need ever arose. Zoe of course was the first one to take offense, claiming that *it would never be necessary under any circumstances!* What became apparent though - right away to the girls - was the bar had only added greatly to the overall business of *Luna's*, and didn't distract in any way, as Zoe had feared it would once *Luna C's* was opened. It was an added bonus that the construction of the establishment had been completed early and beat the expected deadline of the beginning of June, allowing for a soft opening one week sooner than was anticipated, still being in the month of May, and before the ushering in of the summer season.

Cynthia had picked up the pace of reaching out to Zoe almost weekly now, ever since the pleasant conversation they had shared on Christmas Day when she over-reacted to her dad getting engaged to Kelly. Eddie was also included in most of the time whenever a phone call was made, sometimes with Cynthia initiating it and other times when Zoe was so inclined to do, trying to plan it out when Eddie was home from school. He enjoyed sharing with his sister about his life, friends and video gaming, which Zoe had figured out *"the later"* was his main focus for living.

Routinely, Cynthia would make promises that a *"visit was now definitely in order"* and claimed that plans were being formulated as they spoke for the beginning of June - once summer school break was officially beginning for Eddie. The plan was for them to see and tour the town, canal, and of course Zoe's two businesses that she owned – insisting she was very proud of her daughter's successes. Two weeks prior to the trip, Cynthia unexpectedly cancelled, with an awkward excuse and explanation that didn't make any sense, which set off another tailspin of emotion and resentment in Zoe, with a day of tears that required much effort to get her out of bed and stop the *"pity party"*. She felt betrayed and let down once again by her mother, and Mason and everyone else who were close to her, did their best to be *"junior counselors"*, trying to ease her pain and convince Zoe *"not to take it personally"*.

Mason and Zoe had become even closer, enjoying the warmer days of late spring immensely and all that Williamsport had to offer, when the two weren't busy and consumed with work commitments. The C&O Canal was their constant *"go to"* destination for hiking, biking and fishing, occasionally spending the night in a tent somewhere off the trail and in the deep woods, with Luna always being included. They both agreed that the best part of the day was when it was finally dark outside and the campfire - that they built together - was lit, cuddling next to the other for warmth, while viewing the stars and moon overhead. Nothing beat the quietness and the smell of the logs burning, while listening to the soothing song of the crickets that gave chorus near by.

Luke and Emma were also at a good place in their relationship, still happy and continuing to keep their sex life exciting and creative. Memorial Day weekend had arrived and they were invited to the senior Taylor estate for a big party that Ron and Theresa were hosting. Zoe and Mason had tagged along, at Luke's insistence, saying that *it was okay and his folks wouldn't care in the slightest.*

The house was quite crowded, with a large group of Ron's business associates and their families milling throughout the inside of the place, much to Luke's surprise that his mother would allow such a thing and not be present to supervise what was occurring. A picnic in the back yard and a swim in the heated pool were being offered, as Lou Scally – the local DJ of choice - played one oldies tune after another, that the Taylor's were fascinated with, as they slowed danced and reminisced to an earlier time when the music first came out. Each guest stood waiting in the lengthy food line - catered by Leiter's - ready to fill their plates to overflowing, with all the fixing's which included their famous fried chicken. Luke and his guests wasted no time joining in with the others, knowing that the excellent food was what made the day so special.

The public pool has just opened at Bryon Memorial Park, with a group of brave swimmers taking to the frigid cold water – not caring that it had just been filled several days previous. A parade down the city streets had occurred earlier in the day, before the local Little League Baseball team played an exciting neck-to-neck game in the field close by, delighting those happy observers in the bleachers who watched and cheered enthusiastically for their team and maybe an individual player who they personally knew.

After the Taylor picnic began to wind down at dusk, Luke and his friends headed out to watch the fireworks, which was their yearly tradition, although something new for Mason. Parking was at a premium near the park where the fireworks were going on, and it paid to get there early if a good space was to be located. Only one spot was available on the street, being a few blocks away, as Luke grabbed for it before the car behind him did so instead. The group of four walked towards Byron Memorial Park, realizing now that they should have left the party sooner, with every square inch of grass being taken over with blankets and lawn chairs, and the people that were sitting on them.

"Now what?" Emma asked in frustration. *"I didn't think it would be this crowded."*

"I guess we can stand," Luke replied, as he continued to look around, seeking out any available, untaken area that was missed.

"Over there is a spot!" Zoe pointed out, with the rest of the group not hesitating to proceed forward with her at a rather fast pace, as they politely tried to avoid stepping on people along the way.

The blanket was spread out, with everyone claiming a spot before a few other *"late comers"* tried to squeeze in beside of them. Within a few minutes the first of many firecrackers were thrown up high into the air, to the oos and aas of all in attendance. The sky was without a cloud and there was no chance of rain, making for a perfect day and event, which was always an added bonus on a holiday.

Luke and Mason came to discover that they had many things in common, especially the sports that they were both consumed with watching. After the concert that they had attended together, they made a point of trying to hang out and watch a game whenever it was convenient, usually when both of their ladies were busily working at *Luna's*. With the ending of a fun Memorial Day weekend, Ed's Third Base was their final destination bar of choice, knowing that *Luna C's* was otherwise their normal *"hang out"*. A couple of drinks each were to be had, and promises were made that *more similar fun times would be shared throughout the upcoming summer season, and maybe even a vacation or two if possible.*

To the surprise of everyone – especially Zoe – Bryan and Kelly had made secret plans to fly off to Las Vegas and get married that weekend. Zoe assumed they were doing a *"weekend get-away thing"*, never thinking they would actually have a *"quickie"* five-minute ceremony in *"Sin City"* without informing her first. Plans had already been discussed for a church wedding locally, with the wedding dress and even Zoe being the *"maid of honor"* decided upon.

Even once they returned, Zoe was not told privately, but informed at *Luna C's* in front of a room filled with strangers that they had just *"gotten hitched in Vegas"*, with Kelly flashing both rings – waving them high overhead for all to see - with a huge triumphant smile on her face. Zoe was shocked, feeling like she was kicked in the teeth for a second time in a couple of weeks by a *"disappointing, piss-poor excuse of a parent"* who had little regard for her feelings, trying to accept the reality of it all.

Mason's apartment became Zoe's main abode for sleeping after that, avoiding her dad and his *"new wife"* as much as she could, having a hard time forgiving them after what they had pulled on her. Mason really didn't care that Zoe stayed there every night with him, but was concerned for the reason why, knowing it was better if she could work it out between her father and new stepmother. Zoe assumed, even if it wasn't exactly true, that it was Kelly pushing for the Vegas venue, with her insecurities surfacing, fearing that the wedding would never occur - since an official date had not been agreed upon yet, before they had left on their trip.

Pappy Joe and Nana Ruth had not returned after Easter, being busy with the gardening and also church activities that constantly surrounded their lives. Zoe had reached out to them after Bryan and Kelly married, being the first to inform them that they had chosen Vegas over a more traditional church wedding setting, asking for their guidance about the situation. The phone was set on speaker as both grandparents listened in and gave their loving advice that she sought.

"Now, Zoe, why don't you give Kelly a chance and see how things work out? After all, your father has always told you that the house is there for you to live in, no matter what. You are probably worrying about things that you don't need to concern yourself with," Pappy Joe expressed sincerely, trying to calm her down.

"I know you are right, but this whole thing has been rushed, and going to Vegas and getting married there, instead of here in Williamsport, just seems so insensitive to everyone concerned."

"When you are in love, sometimes you just don't want to wait," Nana Ruth interjected thoughtfully. "Your Pappy Joe and I went to the court house in Fort Wayne years ago to be married."

"You didn't marry in the church, Nana Ruth?" Zoe asked in utter surprise.

"No, we did not, dear child. It was a matter of finances, but when we knew we were in love with each other, we didn't want to delay things and be apart any longer."

Bryan and Kelly called Joe and Ruth shortly thereafter, within a couple days of the phone conversation with Zoe. There was no mention of the exchange, acting surprised and congratulating them all the same - wishing the very best for what life had to offer. Polite promises were made that a visit would be forthcoming sometime in the near future - on both ends - with the possibility of that actually happening being very unlikely, especially during the busy summer months when life pulled each in a different direction.

Chapter 46

July was upon them and so was an invitation to the Williamsport High School, Five-Year Class Reunion. Sophia Robertson, who had been the secretary of the class cabinet for all four years that she was in high school, had mailed them out and then sent emails with the announcement also. She wanted to know the *"head count"* in only a couple weeks, since she had fallen behind in doing the task, allowing only one additional guest per class member that wanted to join in for the special event.

Zoe read and then reread the announcement, turning it over while scratching her head with curiosity, just to make sure there wasn't anything additional on the backside that she had missed. It was to be held at the end of August at the Springfield Barn, being situated on the historic farm of the same name in the town of Williamsport, Maryland. *It is the chosen spot for many beautiful weddings and other special functions, and will serve nicely for a class reunion location,* she realized.

The invitation explained that it would be held on a Saturday, beginning at seven o'clock in the evening, with a meal and then dancing afterwards, and the recommended dress code was noted also for the attendees as – *"casual dress, but with nice attire"*. Zoe could see no reason not to attend, but felt it was in her best interest to review the invite with Emma first, just to make sure she was also going, not wanting to venture there alone - with only Mason by her side. Zoe dialed Emma, hoping to resolve the mystery quickly.

"Hello?"

"Em, it's me, Zoe."

"Yes, I realize that, since your name came up on my caller I.D.," she

giggled, still relaxing in bed, after Luke had already left for the car dealership.

"I just received an invite to our class reunion. Did you receive yours yet?"

"Umm... not sure. To be honest, I haven't checked my mail in a couple of days."

"Sophia Robertson must be in charge since she details that in the letter. She mailed me a copy, but I also received one by email. So would you please check your email and see if one showed up for you?"

Emma began to laugh. "Boy, you are on a mission to figure this all out, aren't you? It's hard to believe that it's already been five years since we have been out of high school. It doesn't seem possible."

"Yeah, I know what you mean..." Zoe answered, drifting off once again to another place and time from her past.

"I got the invite," Emma mentioned matter-of-factly, after toggling to her email while still on her phone. "I'm glad Sophie decided on casual dress. I'm surprised she didn't want the girls to show up in prom gowns and the guys in tuxes," she laughed, with Zoe also relating to the humor.

"That may come off as a little weird dancing in a barn."

"Many a formal event is held at the Springfield Barn, and actually, it's a popular destination for weddings too - from what I hear."

"Yes, that is what I heard also. So are you planning on going, Em? I need to know before I respond to my invite."

"Why the urgency if I plan to go or not?" she asked with keen interest, grabbing for her robe, as she tucked a breast back into her pajama top that Luke had been licking and playing with earlier during a frisky *"morning romp"*. She scooped out the coffee, placing it in a filter,

pouring water into the coffeemaker afterwards. She was in need of a strong cup of java to wake up with, before heading back to *Luna's* for a full evening of work.

"Because, if you don't go to the reunion, I don't think I want to go with just Mason. You know how intimidated I can get around some of our old classmates."

"Yes, I do, and honestly, Zoe, it's ridiculous that you feel that way! It was five years ago, and if I had to guess, you and I are just as successful as the majority of those we went to high school with."

"So are you planning to go or not?" Zoe asked again, feeling slightly irritated by Emma's lecture, just needing to hear a *"yes or no"* response.

"Yes... yes, I'm planning to go. I should confirm all this with Luke, but of course *"Mr. Popular"* will want to go... so I guess you have your answer," Emma added, while buttering a piece of seven grain toast that she had picked up at the bakery in Williamsport.

Zoe felt a sense of relief, realizing her *"partner in crime"* would be there to protect her if she needed it. The only possible threat she could imagine would be if Sophia, or one of her *"posse"* members, unloaded a negative comment at the event, directed towards Zoe and Noah and their breakup – which of course was now ancient history.

"Earth to Zoe? Are you listening?"

"Sorry, Em. I have a lot on my mind, and I drifted off there for a moment."

"I was saying that I already texted Luke, and he also received the invitation by email from Sophia Robertson. As I assumed, he will be there with *"bells on"*, reliving his *"glory days"* for just one evening with all his many admirers."

"It surely won't be that bad now, will it?" Zoe laughed, enjoying her friend's sarcastic humor on most occasions, especially when it didn't

involve her.

"It's a burden I must bare to be dating a *"hot guy"* who was considered to be one of the most popular in our graduating class, outside of Noah. So what do you think, will Noah show up from England for this *"shindig"*?"

Zoe hesitated, feeling her heart race from her best friend's probing question, not even considering the possibility in the slightest. *"Emma, you can't be serious? Noah would never fly back to Maryland just for our class reunion. I think we are safe to say that I will dodge that bullet, and he will remain in London where he belongs."*

Emma silently shook her head, feeling her friend was protesting a little too loudly, hoping and praying - for Zoe's sake – that her assumptions were true.

Noah Clark sat at his computer, in his rented flat in London, England, looking over the emailed invitation that Sophia Robertson had just sent to him concerning the Williamsport High School, Five-Year Class Reunion. He bit down on his thumbnail, considering his college schedule.

"Well, damn, I guess I could attend - if I really wanted - since I will be on a two week break during that time period."

"Who are you talking to, love?" A British accented, sexy looking vixen with flaxen blonde hair that hung down to her waist, asked of Noah. He was bent over his laptop, totally nude and sitting cross-legged in bed - focusing in on the invitation that was just sent to him by Sophie and what he should do about it.

He looked up and grinned with a playful, alluring smile that reflected his boyish good looks that equally complimented his model girlfriend, who he was newly engaged to. *"Priscilla, I was only talking to my computer screen."*

"Okay?" She replied somewhat confused, crawling back into bed beside of him, also without a stitch of clothes on, curious and glancing at what he reviewing.

"As I shared with you before, I grew up in a small town in Maryland, and my high school graduating class is having their five-year class reunion at the end of August. I'm considering going to it."

Prissy cocked her head sideways, trying to understand. *"We don't do such things here. Once we are done with secondary school we never look back. Our focus is on college and our careers,"* she explained explicitly.

Noah leaned in to give her a kiss on the cheek, always being intrigued with her alluring beauty and her unwavering, staunch British ways. "That's what you get when you date an American. Crazy rituals and sentimental bullshit! I am what I am, baby," he confessed seductively, while laying his computer on the nightstand close by, taking Priscilla in his arms as the foreplay and kissing began again, yet for another time, on a mission to fuck her until he passed out.

With a decent nap now behind him, Noah resumed with his laptop, as Priscilla continued to sleep, placing it back on his lap that was now covered over with a sheet. He glanced at his girlfriend, knowing there was no doubting her hotness, but sexually she was not at the top of his list for being one of his most *"satisfying of lovers"*. It was Zoe, who took that honor, no matter how many times he wanted to deny it, or not think about it.

Noah quickly typed out an email, reaching out to Luke first, before answering Sophie who had included a personal note *that she wanted to see him if he came back to town.* Noah knew what that innuendo was probably implying, whether she was dating someone or wasn't currently. It really didn't matter to Sophia. Some things never changed...

Hey bud, I guess you thought I disappeared from the planet, but here I am again, reaching out to you about our class reunion. I'm considering coming in for the prestigious event, and make a guest appearance. I thought it may be the opportune time also to bring my fiancé along with me and introduce her to my family, who by the way, is a beautiful fashion model residing here in jolly ole England. Just making sure you are going to be there, but either way, I guess I will show up - with or without you. LOL Hope all is well. Noah.

Luke heard his phone beep with the email alert, as he sat at his desk at Taylor Toyota, patiently waiting on a salesman to hand him over the packet of paperwork on a customer that he was currently trying to close a deal on. He looked surprised, as his eyes rose with the unexpected reach out from his old friend that had gone MIA on him. He reviewed the letter, fascinated by its contents.

"*Well, you dog you!*" Luke grinned and said aloud, while staring at his computer screen, trying to think how he should politely respond back to his pal from childhood. "*Already engaged in only a year of being away, and to a model – no less. Will wonders ever cease?*"

Noah's cellphone rang, with the familiar contact of *"Luke"* coming up on the screen, feeling caught off-guard, but pleased all the same, that he was calling. He slid from the sheets, placing the laptop again on the nightstand, trying to slip out of the bedroom without waking Priscilla up in the process.

"*Umm... what's going on?*" She questioned groggily, studying Noah with only one eye open.

"Go back to sleep, Prissy. Gotta take this call from back home."

"*Sure...*" she mumbled, still half asleep.

Noah grabbed for his boxers and jeans on the way out the door, saying hello to Luke at the same time, as he fumbled to get dressed. "Hey, bro, good to hear from you. This phone call was definitely unexpected."

"*I could say the same... about your email that is...*"

Noah sensed his mood, knowing him just as well as his sibling Lindsay. "Yeah, about that... I guess you are wondering why it has taken me so long to get in touch with you?"

"*Ya think...*" Luke answered, somewhat rudely. "It's only been a year now since we have had a decent conversation. I can't figure you out, Noah."

Noah walked over to the large expanse of the sun-filled windows that were situated in the kitchen, staring out over the busy city street below, taking in a tour bus that frequented the area several times a day. "*Yeah, what can I say? I'm an asshole who didn't know how to handle anything once I broke up with Zoe and then left town. Can you forgive me?*" He quipped indifferently, not taking too much to heart with his self-absorbed personality.

Luke stood up, shaking his head, as the young new salesman entered the room. *"I'll need a few minutes,"* he whispered, holding his hand over the receiver. *"Just keep them entertained, and I'll be right out,"* he instructed, as the nervous looking rookie left the office again, shutting the door behind him.

"Bad time? We can talk later if you need to get going."

"*I called you, remember?*" Luke reminded, trying to maintain his temper. "Noah, we've been friends, like forever. I will cut you a break about your poor decision making when you and Zoe split up, but that had *nothing* to do with you and I not communicating for a year. Hearing a message here and there - that was shared between our mothers - is no way to go about doing things. I haven't liked it at all..." he concluded sternly, wanting to hold Noah accountable for his actions.

"You are absolutely 100% correct! I cannot argue that point or deny it!" he conceded. *"But I would like to come home now and see you, and let bygones be bygones. Is that possible?"*

Luke sighed, knowing things were more complicated now on his end than when Noah had left, and he had some news of his own to share. Noah may have broken up with Zoe, but he was in it to for the long run with Emma Baker – the girl of his dreams.

Chapter 47

With the unexpected news that Luke had just filled him in on, about dating Emma and living with her also, Noah felt like he had been punched in the gut and was floored. He immediately sat down with a hard drop, leaning on the kitchen table with both elbows resting on it, as he ran his hands nervously throughout his unruly brown locks, having to consider how to respond. It was a sudden wake up call from back home, not wanting to think about it or even admit that he was slightly taken back by the revelation. *"It's difficult for me to think about you and Emma being together as a couple, after seeing you both as only friends for the whole entire time that we hung out. But hey, I'm happy for you, bro – if she truly is what you want."*

Luke began to laugh tensely, forgetting how callous and insensitive Noah could act in situations unrelated to him. He had no filter and was always saying whatever came to his mind, whether it offended anyone or not. "What I want, and have always wanted, was a decent girlfriend who was loyal to me and who was loving and kind. I have all that with Emma, and then more besides – since she now owns two businesses. So I got the whole package with her," he bragged and added.

"Two businesses? I thought she and Zoe only had one place together?"

"That has just all changed. She now owns a sports bar next to the restaurant. Zoe and Emma are partners in this venture also. The place is a big hit in Williamsport!" He explained, keeping his percentage of ownership, along with his father's, out of the equation.

Noah returned to the sunny bank of windows again, knowing he needed to get to class soon. "I will make my plane reservations later today and maybe we can share a beer at Emma's new bar once I get back home. I guess I will need to witness all these interesting changes," he admitted somewhat convincingly, being surprised by the major updates - after only being away for a little over a year.

"Remember, the bar isn't only Emma's, but Zoe's also," Luke clarified. And while I am talking about what is different now since you left, I might as well get the biggest one out of the way, beyond Emma and I being an exclusive couple."

"What's that?" Noah asked, popping open a beer without any concern that he would be in a classroom soon, not sure he wanted to hear or deal with anything more at the moment.

"Zoe has a boyfriend."

"Why wouldn't she? I expected that to happen sooner or later," he replied coolly, taking a big swig, trying to numb out his senses. "She's a great person and deserves a happy life. I'm actually glad she is with someone."

"He's not a local, Noah. Came here from Austin, Texas and works for the new federal headquarters of the C&O Canal that is now based in town. He's a friendly and nice guy, and to be honest, I hang out with him a good bit too."

"Didn't know you swung that way, my friend," Noah teased, trying to make light of the situation. "What can I say, life goes on for all of us... Hey, I gotta get off of here. Class is in a few..."

"Yeah, I need to get going too. Good talking to you, Noah."

"Same back atcha, brother. See you in a few weeks."

Luke disconnected from the call, of exactly twenty-three minutes, feeling like a missing part of him had just been given back after not hearing from Noah for so long. The contract that needed his approval, was gone over thoroughly, and then a few more lucrative ones were signed off on besides, before the dealership closed up shop for the day, making for a very profitable Saturday at Taylor Toyota - after the daily numbers were reviewed. Luke placed a few additional contracts in his brief case that required a second peak at the finance options, and then headed back to the apartment. Emma was working late at *Luna's* and wouldn't be there to greet him as he wished she would be, after the challenging phone call from Noah.

A few beers later and Luke was out cold and snoozing on the sectional, as the door opened and then shut to the apartment, announcing that Emma was finally home. She tiptoed over to the sectional, smiling down at the sleeping man that she loved with all her heart, taking him in from head to toe with a happy grin. *"Catching up on some zzz's before we have a night of lust and passionate lovemaking?"* She tempted and teased.

Luke rubbed his eyes, sitting up for a warm *"welcome home"* kiss that his girlfriend always offered. "Not sure if I have it in me to go *"all night"*, sweetie, but I will give it my best shot!"

Emma sat beside of him, after pouring herself a glass of Chardonnay, ready to relax and kick back also. "The crowds kept growing at *Luna's* today. I know it's tourist season, but if I had to wait on one more person, I was going to blow a gasket! We need to slip off to Marlin Beach for a few days," she suggested with a sigh, feeling entirely worn out, drinking deeply of the wine in her stem glass.

"That can be arranged," Luke voiced quietly, wrapping a free arm possessively around his woman's shoulder, as she snuggled in closer into his embrace. "But with a new place I thought you said that wasn't happening for a while?" he reminded, resting his chin on the top of her head.

"True, I did say that, but I'm also exhausted from everything, and feel like I deserve a *"much-needed"* break, even if for just a couple days."

Luke sighed, not wanting to change the subject, but knowing he needed to if he stood a chance at getting a decent night's rest, desiring only to have some peace of mind. *"You will never guess who reached out to me today."*

Emma turned to study Luke, trying to read his mind. *"No clue. Who?"*

"Noah Carter."

"No fucking way!"

"Em, such language!" Luke commented, half in jest, always taken back by her sudden outbursts and trashy way of talking.

"Sorry, hon, but that's about the last person I would have guessed called you. I can't believe he had the actual balls to do so, after all this time of ignoring you."

"Yeah, you and me both, but he did. It was about the class reunion. He wants to come home and be there for that, and he will probably be bringing his fiancé along with him also."

Emma eyes opened wide, considering the possibility. *"So Mr. Noah Clark is coming home with his fiancé? Well fancy that! If this isn't about the worst news you could have shared with me this evening!"* She remarked intensely, on a mission now to go to the kitchen for some more wine.

"I know, babe, and I'm truly sorry, but I wasn't going to keep this from you."

"The irony is that Zoe and I were just talking about the reunion today, and I said that maybe Noah would come home for it, and she said that it would never happen. Now you are telling me it's going to happen. She will be dumbstruck with emotion when she sees him walking into the Springfield Farm Barn with another woman who he is already engaged to. It has only been a year, for heaven's sakes. *What a bastard he is!"*

Luke downed the last remaining swigs of his warm beer from the bottle that had remained on the coffee table for the past few hours, not wanting to share any more of the details, but knowing he needed to. *"Not just any woman, but a model from England whom he claims is quite the beauty."*

Emma rose, swinging her wine glass from side to side as she spoke, suddenly acting quite infuriated with what she had just been told. She paced back and forth in front of Luke, splashing some of the contents out on the area rug, without much regard that she was doing so. "Well doesn't that just *"take the cake"*? The prick will now be rubbing that in her face also! Maybe we shouldn't go, and when I think about it, maybe I will discourage Zoe from going also. *Why don't we get out of town and go to Marlin Beach that weekend with Zoe and Mason?* Then the problem of Noah coming to the reunion will be easily resolved."

Luke studied his uptight girlfriend, who he could tell was trying to devise a sudden plan of attack to protect her best friend, so that she didn't have to endure any more emotional pain at the hands of her ex. "Em, I understand your concern for Zoe, but she is a grown adult and has the right to decide what she wants to do about the class reunion. If she desires to go out of town to avoid Noah and his fiancé, then sign me up and I will miss our five-year class reunion also. If it comes to that, I promise we will have a wonderful, stress-free vacation with our friends in Marlin Beach, but I still feel the decision should be hers totally to make."

Emma returned to the sectional, doing her best to calm down and refocus. "Okay, I hear you. Please just let me think about things and talk to Zoe before you mention anything to Mason first."

"Of course, Em. I never considered anything but that option."

"Thank you, Luke," she replied, with a sense of relief.

"Now about that lusty sexual interlude you just promised me. Why don't we take this to the bedroom and make it happen?" Luke tantalized, while pulling Emma to her feet, nuzzling both breasts with his mouth through her top.

"You don't... have to ask... me... a second time," she answered, barely able to catch her breath - ready and willing - and desiring him just as badly.

Advanced Economics class was completed for another day, as Noah made his way back to his flat. Priscilla was patiently waiting, watching a British soap opera and filing her nails, having no commitments of her own to speak of, other than to hang out with her handsome fiancé, who in all reality could be a model also if he desired that sort of lifestyle. She smiled, as he walked over to the sofa, planting a sweet kiss on her lips that had been injected with *"a filler"* several days earlier, just to plump them up. *"Are we heading out to the pub now, love?"* She purred out pleasantly, anxious to get out of the building and do some socializing.

Noah smiled, wanting to accomplish a few things first that were weighing heavily on his mind, before they did so. *"Not quiet yet. I need to know if you are joining me in America for my class reunion next month, so I can wrap things up?"*

Priscilla sat quietly thinking, mulling it all over, staring at her modest-sized engagement ring that Noah had claimed would be *made much larger once he had finished Graduate School and got a decent job.* "If I choose not to join you, does that mean you will still go without me? She asked, fluttering her fake eyelashes at him, hoping to convince him otherwise.

"Yeah... I guess it does... I want to go home for a few days, before I'm back in school for the next session. I've been away for a year and I think it's time to visit with my family. *Wouldn't you like to meet them since one day we will be married and then they will be your relatives?"* Noah questioned, not liking the way Priscilla was suddenly coming off and acting.

She flashed at him a fake, pretentious smile, trying her best to draw in her prey, grabbing for Noah's hands – just for added affect. *"Of course I would like to go with you to America and meet your family, darling, but I must make sure I don't have any upcoming photo shoots scheduled for that time period. I will have to double check with my agent first."*

"Then I would suggest you do so now," Noah answered back firmly, breaking free from her constraint. "I need to book the airplane tickets and let Sophia - the secretary of my high school class who is organizing this thing - know if it will only be me coming alone, or if you will be joining me also – making the headcount two. After you figure this all out, then we can go to the pub."

Prissy pouted up her plumped up lips, realizing she wasn't making any headway with the subject matter, doing her best to act out the part and change Noah's mind. *"There is the also cost. I'm not sure I can afford to pay for all this."*

Noah began to laugh and shake his head, knowing his girlfriend was without money issues as he sometimes was, coming from a wealthy British family in the area, with a trust fund that she dipped into regularly without much constraint. *"Then maybe you just shouldn't go,"* he replied rather bluntly, not caring if he hurt her feelings or not.

"No, no, it's fine. Somehow I will manage…"

"Great! I will be done in a few minutes with everything, so why don't you get ready?" He offered with his signature, winning smile, already retreating to the kitchen table with his laptop in hand.

The airplane tickets were purchased for the end of August,

departing on a Thursday and returning on a Sunday, after Priscilla confirmed she was *surprisingly available,* not fooling Noah in the least - as she had hoped. He then reached out to Sophia afterwards, sharing with her the good news of his return.

Hey, Sophie, long time no talk. Hope all is well with you. Surprise of surprises, I'm coming home for our class reunion. Count me and one other guest on your "yes list" of attendees. Looking forward to it! Fondly, Noah.

Sophia received the message immediately, jumping up and down with excitement with the news that she had hoped for. "I wonder who the *"guest"* is?" She contemplated for a moment, tossing the thought aside just as quickly as it entered her mind. *"Who cares? Noah is coming home, and that's all that matters!"*

Chapter 48

It was Sunday and the day for most to be relaxing, except for Emma who only had the class reunion on her mind. Six thirty a.m., and she was already up, calling Zoe who was still sleeping and snuggled in beside of Mason. They had skipped their canal walk that they normally took together, because it was raining steadily outside and they knew the towpath would be muddy.

"Hello... Em, everything all right?" Zoe whispered, trying to get on the same page with her and wake up. Mason groaned and rolled over, now also awake from the early morning call, trying to figure out what all the commotion was all about as he yawned and stretched.

"Yeah, I'm fine, but is it possible to meet for coffee? I have something sorta pressing that I wanted to discuss with you."

"Are the guys invited?" Zoe asked, bending down to kiss Mason sweetly on his bearded cheek, as he grinned up at her pleasantly, liking the gesture.

"No, I prefer that it be only us. I know we are both off today, and it's important and can't wait until tomorrow when we are back at *Luna's* trying to work. I won't keep you long. I promise."

Zoe got up and reached for her robe that was hanging behind the bedroom door, securing it tightly around her waist as Luna jumped down off the bed, ready to go outside for her morning walk. *"You want me to take Luna out?"* Mason offered, braced up on his elbows now, trying to do Zoe a favor.

She covered the phone, addressing Mason before leaving the room. *"It's fine, honey, I will deal with her. I am going to get dressed and meet up with Emma for a little while. She needs to talk to me about something important that she wants to discuss in private, and it can't wait until tomorrow."*

Mason was up in a flash, with his *"morning wood"* noticeably popping out from his boxers, as he followed Zoe from the bedroom. *Get ready and I will deal with Luna,"* he insisted, grabbing for the leash.

"Are you sure? I know you wanted to sleep in since we skipped our walk," Zoe consoled, with Emma still holding on patiently, taking in the discussion between the couple.

"Yes dar... ling, I'm definitely sure," he replied, with his Texas drawl taking center stage, always being the heaviest in the morning for some reason.

"I'll meet you at The Desert Rose in twenty minutes. *Does that work?"* Zoe inquired of Emma, finally free to talk.

"I'll be in the back with two cups of coffee."

Zoe entered the restaurant, saying her polite hellos to Rose and Ted who were busily waiting on the Sunday morning breakfast crowd, not either one having a moment to spare for idle chit chat. She walked back the hallway, of the familiar hangout and place she used to work, taking a seat opposite her best friend, as Emma slid the coffee in her direction.

"It's just the way you like it," Emma simply explained.

"Well, thank you," Zoe answered, looking at her somewhat confused. *"This isn't like you to be so focused in on meeting, especially this early in the morning, and never on your day off. Is everything okay with Luke? Your family?"*

Emma silently shook her head yes, not honestly knowing where to begin, happy that only one other group of diners were sitting close by, hoping that Zoe wouldn't lose it and explode in front of them.

"Emma the suspense is killing me. Just to tell me what's on your mind!" Zoe insisted, with her arms now crossed on the table and leaning forward to hear the urgent news.

Emma gulped down a few swallows of coffee, trying to get her nerve up, hoping for the best. *"Remember our conversation about the class reunion the other day?*

"Yes, I remember."

"Do you also remember that I brought up the possibility of Noah coming home for the class reunion and what you said?"

Zoe shook her head *"yes"* while agreeing; suddenly not liking the way the conversation was going and beginning to feel her heart race. *"I said he would never show up. Emma where is this all leading?"*

"Noah reached out to Luke yesterday, and he is coming home... for the reunion... after all."

"Nooo!" Zoe yelled out at the top of her lungs, rising from her seat in shock, with her hands now covering her mouth, trying to silence her outburst any further as the onlookers turned to see what all the fuss was all about.

"Sit down, Zoe!" Emma demanded sharply, patting the table for added affect. *"Before Rose shows up and kicks us out!"* She threw out also with an intense serious scowl, knowing that would never happen.

Zoe complied with a few tears now forming and running down her cheeks freely, as she stared at her friend, feeling and looking grim. *"Why would he come back here?"*

"For a very legitimate reason. He wants to go to the class reunion. Just like you and I want to do so also. So here's the deal... If you can't handle the thought of seeing him at the class reunion, then I think I have a solution. Last night, Luke and I discussed this and he has agreed to lend us his support, if necessary. We will go to Marlin Beach that weekend with the guys and get out of town, and then you won't have to see Noah."

"You and Luke would do that for me?" Zoe asked, feeling touched by their loyalty.

"Of course we would do that for you, sweetie," Emma replied with a sincere smile of compassion and concern, as she reached across the table for Zoe's hand, making an effort to comfort and reassure her.

Zoe sighed, breaking free and sipping deeply from her coffee, trying to regroup and think things through more clearly. *"Why do I even care? I have Mason now in my life."*

"Exactly!" Emma agreed, *"high fiving"* her. "He is amazing and we all love him. You will invite him and then your problems will be solved! It's okay that you are upset. I would be too, since you didn't expect any of this to happen."

"Yes, it's definitely coming as quite the shock, but sooner or later it was obvious that he would return at some point. Maybe never to live here in Williamsport again, but certainly for a visit - since his family is still in the area."

"Now your are thinking straight!" Emma agreed, realizing she needed to go on in the conversation and broach the next difficult topic - whether she desired to do so or not. *"That isn't all of it, Zoe."*

Zoe looked confused, tilting her head to one side. *"Noah is coming home. I get it. What more is there to say?"* She asked, downing the rest of her coffee.

Emma whispered, leaning in for Zoe's ears only. *"Please control yourself before I begin. The room is now completely filled with additional people, and if you can't handle what I am going to say next, then maybe we should discuss it out in my car."*

Zoe crossed her arms defensively in her lap, sensing the second option may be in her best interest. *"Where are you parked?"*

"Around the corner. Follow me," Emma simply instructed, taking the lead and saying her goodbyes to the still busy, *"co-workers from the past",* who were slinging out breakfast quickly, trying to accommodate an *"at capacity"* crowd of diners. The girls climbed into Emma's new RAV4, as she started up the engine and adjusted the controls – hoping to circulate some fresh air and calm the heated tension that was present.

"We are alone now, so tell me whatever else you feel I need to know."

Emma looked at her friend, not ready to break her heart for another time, fearful that she wasn't strong enough to handle the news. "Zoe, as we know, Noah doesn't always use the best judgment when making decisions in his life. He is coming home for the reunion, but he is also bringing someone along with him from England as his *"plus one"* for the event."

"Okay? And why wouldn't he? We are also going with dates."

"He is bringing his new British fiancé with him!" Emma hurriedly tossed out in rapid succession, relieved that the deed of telling her was finally done.

Zoe's mouth dropped open in shock, staring at her best friend in disbelief. *"His fiancé? Seriously? He has only been gone for a year and he has a fiancé? I patiently waited for four fucking years to get engaged to this asshole, and he now has a fiancé already? And she is from England, no less?"* Zoe gritted out, feeling totally pissed off now with what she was hearing.

"Get a grip, Zoe! It's obvious you aren't over the jerk! Poor Mason! I don't know who to feel more sorry for – him or you. Would you want him to hear you reacting like this right now?"

"Probably not..." she answered quietly, feeling somewhat guilty as she hung her head, attempting to re-center her thoughts and act sane again. "It isn't a matter of how much I care for Mason, but how badly things ended up with Noah and I. Just when all seems right with my world, I'm having to be around him again and the British *"fiancé"*. *Can't you just try to understand that?"* She pleaded, with pain-filled eyes.

"Zoe, don't get mad – get even! I want you to go back to your apartment and ask Mason to accompany you to this affair, and then I want you to plan to look better than you ever have looked in your entire life! You have time to find that perfect outfit and you will get your hair done up by Lillian. I know you can finally do your own makeup, but if you would like my help, I will gladly roll over to your place and help you with it. Give Noah an *"eyeful"* and remind him what he has lost out on, when he said goodbye to you."

"You're right. That is what I will do. I will go to the reunion and my handsome boyfriend will be joining me. *We will all be sitting together, right?"*

Emma felt relieved with the new mindset, as she reached over to pat Zoe's hand. "Yes, my friend, we will all be sitting together. I will make sure of that. Ava and Lillian and their dates will be there too, filling up the table so that no one else can sit down with us. Sophia likes a great spot when she shows up at *Luna's and Luna C's*, so I will remind her of that, just to make sure our table placement is secured at the reunion. *Trust me on this. I got it covered!"*

"Thanks, Em. You are the best!"

"I try. Now get going and ask your boyfriend to be your special date. *There is a fringe benefit to bringing Mason, you know?"*

"Why's that?"

"He will blow Noah away with his good looks and Texan charm, and now that he and Luke are good buds, it will make an impression on him even more so, watching them hanging out at the reunion together."

"If that even matters," Zoe grinned, knowing that it really did.

Zoe returned to the apartment, finding Mason sprawled out on the sofa, taking in a golfing event on the television. *"I didn't know you liked golf?"*

"Not in particular, but I recognized the course. It's down in Texas."

"Oh... I see..." Zoe answered, taking a seat on the sofa beside of him.

"Everything okay with you and Emma?"

Zoe smiled, suddenly remembering that Mason had been left without a clue. "Yes, things are fine with Emma. She just had a situation that she wanted to review with me now, instead of when we were busy at work tomorrow."

"That's what I figured," he grinned, wrapping her in his warm embrace and then kissing her tenderly. "Since it's raining what did you want to get into today?"

"Maybe a movie at the Valley Mall?"

"Before or after we make love?"

"Afterwards... Of course..." Zoe answered with a challenging, wicked smile filled with sexual intention, as Mason turned off the TV, now focusing in on a different course – that didn't involve a golf game in Texas.

Chapter 49

The plans had been made and Mason had agreed to attend the class reunion with Zoe, proud to be her escort, only requesting that he be allowed to wear his cowboy boots which she wholeheartedly agreed to - knowing they were a big part of what defined his style and personality. She and Emma went dress shopping, venturing down into the Washington DC area, after several failed attempts to locate *"the perfect outfit"* anywhere closer. It wasn't easy finding just the right look, that breathed casual, but with an air of sophistication – that would be considered appropriate for a barn party in Williamsport.

Emma ended up with slinky black, satin capri pants that hugged her perfectly, having diamond rhinestones outlining each pocket on the front and backside of her derriere. A loose fitting spaghetti-strapped top, with rhinestones that matched the capris perfectly, completely incrusted the blouse and made for a sparkly statement. Black sandals, with 3-inch spiked heels were also chosen, that she found quite sexy, but somewhat hard to walk in. Her long blonde hair was worn stick straight, with her azure blue eyes being highlighted out with just the perfect shades of eye makeup that she had applied. The finishing touch was an assortment of bangle bracelets that Emma had placed on each wrist, varying in design and sizes, making her look somewhat free-spirited and gypsy-like.

Zoe chose a knee length dress that plunged in the front, in the shade of emerald green. It was slim fitting and emphasized her ample breasts perfectly, requiring only a simple necklace and bracelet as a finishing touch, which had been given to her on one of her birthdays by Nana Ruth. Emma had insisted that Zoe purchase a pair of black stiletto heels that somewhat resembled hers, after going shoe shopping together and then trying them on at the same time. Her long brown, honey kissed hair hung loose, being styled all over in a soft array of curls. Lillian unfortunately was busy with a full schedule of other clients that day - which had already previously made their appointments - having no additional time to fit Zoe in unfortunately. The decision was then made, to do her own hair and makeup, not admitting it to Emma who would insist on helping her out, ignoring her own needs in the process - of getting ready for the reunion.

Mason picked everyone up in his Land Rover, arriving especially early at the Springfield Farm Barn, only because Zoe insisted that *they needed to do* so *to get a good parking spot.* He helped her from the vehicle, just as Luke did likewise with Emma, as they stood close by to the action, staring at the decorated barn and surrounding grounds in front of them.

"Wow, they did a great job making this place look sharp for the party!" Mason expressed, while taking notice, with one arm securely wrapped around Zoe's waist. He was dressed in black jeans and a white shirt that had a button undone, revealing a fringe of his chest hair that always turned Zoe on. He wore his black cowboy boots in a reptile skin and chose a belt that matched, looking acceptable and alluring with his perfectly cut hair and beard that had been trimmed up at a local barbershop earlier that day.

"Yes, they always go all out. They are the experts at pulling off amazing gatherings for their clientele," Luke explained, looking equally as put together as Mason, being dressed in black slacks and black dress shoes, with an appealing button down shirt of light blue, that Emma had decided upon and purchased especially for the occasion when she and Zoe were out shopping.

Not many others were there yet - since they were an hour early - as they proceeded to stroll around the grounds, realizing that there was no need to sit at their assigned seats quite yet. Emma noted the historic features of the property, as they walked, educating them to the significance of what they were seeing. *"This barn was built in 1755 by*

Otho Holland Williams, the founder of Williamsport, and it is one of the largest barns in the state of Maryland. Battles that were fought during the Civil War, went right through this area, and trees are planted here in dedication to the fallen soldiers of that era."

Luke looked at Emma in surprise. *"Damn, Em, you could be a tour guide for the place!"* He exclaimed in amazement, making the others laugh.

"If you were paying attention, we did learn all this in middle school when they took us on a field trip here."

"I think I had other things on my mind, sweetie, besides barns at that time."

Emma rolled her eyes, knowing what he was implying. "Yeah, well I obviously wasn't one of the *"chosen girls"* back then."

"You definitely are today," he said, nuzzling her neck, with Mason and Zoe looking on and taking it all in. "And just to set the record straight, you are the only *"chosen girl"* in my life now, if we want to get specific."

"Enough with the mushy talk," Zoe tossed in, feeling her nerves getting the better of her, knowing the place would be filling up very soon with her classmates. Mason sensed her uneasiness, pulling her in closely to his side, trying his best to keep things carefree and fun for the evening.

"I bet that bar is finally open. Why don't we go inside and grab a couple beers?" he grinned, with his Texas drawl coming through and doing the asking.

"I think I would like something a little stronger," Zoe admitted sheepishly, feeling her stomach doing somersaults and only desiring to relax.

"Whatever the lady wants, the lady shall have," Mason answered,

trying to be cute and entertaining, while holding Zoe's hand and walking inside the barn, on his way to get the drinks.

Strings of party lights were strung from the ancient rafters, casting a romantic glow throughout the room. The band was setting up and the bartender was ready to greet customers as Mason came up to the counter. "I will have a Yuengling and my lady here will have a...?"

"I will have a rum and coke – with an extra shot of rum," Zoe clarified without hesitation, as Emma observed and took it all in, fearing the worst may now happen.

She walked up to her friend, whispering in her ear, hoping no one else that was standing close by could hear what she was saying. *"You may want to go easy, if you plan to make it through the night without saying or doing something you may regret later."*

Zoe whispered back. *"I get your point, but I seriously need a good stiff drink to unwind. I will go easy after this. Promise!"* she smiled and reassured, looking Emma over from head to toe. *"I know I told you earlier, but you look amazing."*

"You do too, sweetie. Anyone who sees you here tonight will realize that also."

The girls continued to converse as Luke and Mason drank their beers, happy to hear the first sounds of music being played from a band that had been brought in especially from Baltimore. Sophie had insisted upon them, remembering the band from when she was in college, when they played at a frat party on campus.

A much too tight and revealing prom gown - that was outfitted on Sophia Robertson - was an intentional, sexual display of hot pink, satin madness. She stood out like a sore thumb – just needing to be covered up in some way. It was impossible not to stare, as she attempted to approach the four, already *"wasted"* and hanging on to a chair, situated at one of the tables, for support. She took in the guys especially, only addressing them, and forgetting the ladies who were obviously there also – making a spectacle out of herself.

"Wow, wow, wow... I'm here for *any... one* of you guys who wants to dance with me," she announced with a slur, pointing at Luke and then pausing as she stared a hole through Mason. Her blonde hair was half pinned up with a few sparkly barrettes, with a few strands now falling in front of her face - definitely requiring a *"do-over"*.

"Maybe you should sit down and drink some water," Luke suggested with some concern, looking at Emma in desperation.

Sophie belched unladylike, laughing also during the process. *"I can't do that, Lukie boy... cuz I'm in charge of this amazing affair, and I must get up there on that stage and welcome everybody here to our class reunion!"* She pointed, towards the place she needed to go.

Emma began to shake her head in disbelief, feeling embarrassed by what was occurring, as a large group of people started coming in and milling throughout the barn, trying to locate their seats. She grabbed Luke, trying to speak over the music that was now at full volume. "Go over there and get *"her squad"* to rescue her! I seriously don't want to deal with Sophia Robertson tonight and have our evening ruined by all her crazy antics!

"Calm down, Em. I will take care of things. Why don't you guys find our table and grab a seat, and I will be back in a few minutes?"

"I'm holding you to that," Emma answered sternly, giving him *"the eye of warning"*. If you aren't back in five minutes, I will take matters into my own hands and pour the water down her damn throat for her personally!"

"That won't be necessary, Em," Luke replied, trying his best to be the peacekeeper. He looked at her with a handsome smile and his kind blue eyes that were locked with her own, as he bent down to kiss his hotheaded girlfriend and ease her concerns, understanding that she had a right to be upset over Sophie's obnoxious behavior.

The designated table was found as Zoe, Mason and Emma joined Ava and Lillian and their dates, with Luke not being far behind. *"Is everything okay now, brother?"* Mason asked, being somewhat out of the loop, and not knowing much about the *"drama-filled"* flamboyant woman name *Sophia Robertson*, other than what he heard about her from Zoe in the past.

"Oh... yeah... That's Sophie Robertson, the secretary of my high school class. She always has to make a splashy entrance with everything she does. Unfortunately, tonight is no exception to the rule. Her friends just returned with a large coffee from the Sheetz Convenience Store down the street, and they are forcing her to drink it. I think she will be up for making the announcements, as long as they are there to hold her up and keep her from tumbling off of the stage."

"No matter where one grows up there are always similar types of people trying to be *"showboats"*. I knew a few just like that in my high school also."

"It can be guys too, you know," Zoe added with pursed up lips, suddenly taking offense, and thinking about Noah Clark who would be showing up at any moment, more than likely.

Mason cocked his head off to one side, trying to read Zoe's mind and figure out why she was acting so uptight. "You are absolutely right, dar... ling. If my memory serves me correctly, I do believe I didn't imply male or female, but if you took it that way, I'm very sorry," he soothed, leaning in to kiss away her worries. Zoe downed the rest of her rum and coke, and then glanced over at Emma who still had a continued look of worry outlining her face.

Sophia walked up the steps to the stage, escorted on either side by two of her *"gal pals"*, who were doing their best to keep her looking presentable. She grabbed for a microphone situated near the band, tapping it three times, just to make sure it was working. *"Is this thing actually turned on?"* She slurred out, with everyone yelling back a loud *"yes"* in her direction. *"Welcome, Williamsport High School Graduating Class of 2016!* It's hard to believe, but it's been five whole years since we graduated. Thank you for showing up, and here is the order of things tonight. We have a buffet line over there," she flimsily pointed to several times, "and I personally know the band and they are amazing, and of course they will be performing throughout the entire evening, so hopefully you will get up and dance. In case any of you have forgotten my name," she said while grinning at both of her girlfriends, who looked embarrassed trying to deal with it all, "I am Sophia Robertson, your secretary from our class. I put this whole thing together for a night of reminiscing and having fun. *Now have a good time, people!"* She shouted out loudly, trying to act cool.

Just as Sophie concluded, and was ready to be helped from the stage, a couple that had arrived late, silhouetted in the large double door opening of the barn, was on display like a perfect pair of mannequins in a department store, outfitted for some festive event to be held in any other city or state than Williamsport, Maryland. A flurry of whispering and comments could be heard, buzzing from one table to the next like a hive of bees, realizing who had just shown up. It was Noah, with his British model and fiancé, Priscilla, ready to make their grand entrance and grace everyone with their fascinating presence.

Chapter 50

Zoe looked on in shock, not fully understanding what was occurring. To describe Priscilla as pretty would have been an understatement. She was stunning and probably the most attractive woman she had ever seen outside of someone on television or in a magazine. Her body was utter perfection, although somewhat on the thin side, but with each curve being of proper proportion and placement – the definite look of a fashion model. Priscilla's skin was light in coloring, without blemish or flaw, and the long blonde hair that she was blessed with, shimmered in the moonlight as did the perfectly appointed makeup that had been applied to her angelic face. She was arrayed in a very short designer dress of embroidered gold sequins that she honestly looked poured into. High-stepping, strappy sandals of a complimentary luminescent color, wrapped half way up her lower calves – as if to claim her as their own. A solid gold pendant swung from her neck and two-inch similar *"danglies"* hung from each earlobe. She was on display with her priceless good looks, perched on Noah's arm, and eager for an audience.

Noah matched her fabulous vibe, looking as if he had lost ten pounds since being away, but still athletic with the same muscular build. He was dressed in a meticulously tailored, three-piece, pinstriped suit – that featured two different tones of gray - with an even lighter gray shirt underneath, all fitting him like a racer's glove. A gray and gold paisley silk tie was chosen to play off of Priscilla's dress, and handmade, Italian leather loafers completed the look of perfection. As Noah possessively held on to Priscilla's hand, a random gold cufflink could be seen, attached to the bottom of one of his shirtsleeves. It was all planned out and coordinated by his model girlfriend so that he would look impressive and striking to anyone who had the privilege of viewing them together, being the style of European men's ware, and not what one would typically see on a male in the Williamsport area. His hair was as Zoe remembered it, brown and wavy - but in a controlled sort a way - probably with the aid of a styling product to keep it in impeccable form. He was breathtakingly handsome, and she honestly thought she was going to pass out if she looked at him for one moment longer, as her pulse ran out of control, overwhelmed with her emotions and scattered thoughts of why he had decided to come to the reunion in the first place.

People at the tables began to scatter, with some going towards the buffet line, the bar, or even the bathrooms. Noah had become a focal point too, with a group of his old teammates finding it absolutely necessary to greet and welcome him back home immediately, and check out the *"hot girl"* that he had brought to town. Zoe felt lost, not knowing what to do since her friends at the table had decided that it was their turn to get up also, ready to indulge in the food or get another drink, whatever was there preference. Mason looked down at her, confused with what she was doing by remaining seated. *"Aren't you hungry, babe?"* he asked.

"Of course she is!" Emma answered for her, reaching out to pull Zoe to her feet, whether she wanted to or not - not giving her any choice in the matter.

The buffet line was crowded, as Emma stood right in front of Zoe – trying her best to shield her. *"You never told me she was gorgeous and looked like a fashion model,"* Zoe whispered directly into Emma's ear.

Emma sighed, knowing she had left that small detail out of the mix. *"She is a model. I didn't have it in me to tell you that,"* she confessed, feeling guilty now.

"So you told me that Noah is engaged to her, but you couldn't tell me she was a model?" Zoe replied in utter disbelief, shaking her head, feeling somewhat hurt by Emma's omission. *"I suddenly can't wait until this evening is over. Maybe we should have gone to Marlin Beach, after*

all..."

Emma wrapped her arm around Zoe's waist, pulling her in closely as the guys disappeared, going in the direction of the bar, ready to grab another drink, instructing them to *"hold their places"*. "Well now it's all out! He is engaged and she is stunning! What the fuck, Zoe, get over it! Mason is a hunk too and you aren't too shabby yourself!"

Lillian and Ava walked towards Emma and Zoe, reappearing from the bathroom, after leaving their men to get refills on their drinks also. *"Who isn't too shabby?"* Lillian asked with curiosity, getting in on the tail end of the conversation.

"Zoe!" Emma exclaimed over the booming blare of the band that was now playing a *"dance worthy"* tune. *"She is beautiful, and if I were a guy - I'd be all over that!"* She conveyed lightheartedly, trying her best to pump up her ego.

The girls all laughed, never hearing Emma speaking about her best friend in such a way, amusing Zoe somewhat in the process. *"Same back atcha!"* Zoe replied light-heartedly, feeling somewhat intoxicated, knowing Emma was just being silly. Suddenly, she didn't care so much about Noah, since he no longer resided in Williamsport and had gone on with his new life in England, obviously a very different guy than the one she had dated and remembered. What truly mattered most were Mason and her good friends – who lived in the area and were loyal to her no matter what.

To the amazement of everyone, Sophia did not disappoint with the buffet. She had chosen chicken, fish and steak, with sides of mashed potatoes and broccoli, adding in a tossed salad and dinner rolls too, with most being amazed that she even had *"the smarts"* to figure it all out. As they sat eating, Zoe kept her head somewhat bowed, trying her best to avoid direct eye contact with Noah, only glancing up slightly when someone else at the table addressed her.

Mason leaned in, sensing something was just not right and was weighing heavily on Zoe's mind. "I wish you would tell me what is bugging you? You aren't acting like yourself this evening," he expressed tenderly, giving her a gentle kiss on the cheek.

Zoe gulped, resisting the urge to admit the truth, but realizing it was for the best if she told him. She looked at Mason, locking eyes with him, knowing she could tell him anything and without the slightest judgment. "My ex is here from England with his fiancé. I haven't seen him in over a year since we broke up."

Mason gently squeezed her hand, kissing her on the lips. "I am here to support you, along with everyone else sitting at this table who cares and loves you. Sooner or later this was bound to happen. Sorry it had to be at your class reunion though. *Why don't we dance and forget about all this?*" Mason suggested with a warm smile, trying to ease her worries.

Tears glistened in Zoe's eyes, as she realized once again how wonderful and amazing Mason was, never acting jealous or insecure when presented with a delicate situation, such as what she was going through. "Sure, sweetie, let's dance," she agreed, while being led out on the dance floor by Mason. They slowed danced to a romantic tune that was also being played five years earlier, taking another walk down memory lane with everyone else present, while dancing and mingling in the Springfield Farm Barn.

As Mason held Zoe close and moved intimately to the beat of the music, he spun her around slowly, coming in direct contact with Noah who was now only inches away, holding Pricilla in a similar fashion. His fiancé's hand rested on the top of his shoulder, with a glimmer of a diamond engagement ring being present that sparkled and reflected off of the lights that were strung above. Zoe immediately realized what it was, with panic now crossing her face that Noah could clearly read, remembering that same look from when they were last together at the C&O Canal aqueduct. He smiled, trying to put her at ease, but without any success as she immediately walked off the dance floor, with Mason following after her.

"Every... thing okay?" Mason asked, while leaning in towards her, with his East Texas accent coming through strongly, as they returned to the table.

"I need to use the ladies room," she announced, being determined to leave.

"Would you like me to walk with you?"

"No, I am fine," Zoe reassured with a sweet smile. "Just stay here, have a beer and enjoy yourself, and I won't be long."

The bathroom sat in a separate building outside of the barn, and the pathway leading to it was well lit with more strings of party lights extended overhead. Pretty planters filled with summer flowers, were bursting forth with color and variety, and had been perfectly placed along the way for all to see. An extensive line had formed, being intermingled with both guys and gals, with all deciding *"to go"* at the very same time.

"Hello. How are you?" Zoe heard the familiar words spoken, as she turned with a start, not expecting to see Noah standing right behind her.

Zoe was silent, just taking in his presence for another time, feeling torn with a mixed set of emotions wanting to resurface. *"Where is your fiancé?"*

"Back with Sophie and her friends, being interrogated about life in England," he laughed, making light of it.

"Did you follow me here?" Zoe gritted out in mild confusion, trying to understand the details of what was happening.

"Actually, I did. I saw you leave by yourself and I thought it was an excellent opportunity for us to talk."

"Well maybe I don't agree and feel the same way!" Zoe shouted out, causing a few others in the line to turn around and stare at her from the outburst, with several now recalling that they had been an item and dated in the past.

Noah reached out, placing an arm on Zoe, trying his best to calmly diffuse the situation. "Please, let's just talk. What is the harm in it? All I'm asking is that you join me for a couple minutes, and then you can go back to your boyfriend and I will return to Priscilla afterwards."

"I don't even know why I would be considering this, but okay, lead the way," Zoe reluctantly answered with a sweep of her arm, as the two walked around the barn to the backside of the building, where some historic objects from the past were being displayed. A bench was also positioned there as Noah sat down, requesting that Zoe do the same with a light pat to the seat.

"I'm sorry that things ended up as they did before I left for England. I was wrong to do what I did that day at the C&O Canal, and also, I was wrong to not *"man up"* and reach out to you after that."

Zoe began to cry, trying her best not to do so. "Why, Noah? That is all I wanted to know then, and still do today. Was I that bad of a girlfriend that I didn't deserve something better than that horrible ending, after being together in a relationship for four years? I had *dreams* and you were a part of them. I had to go on without you in my life after that, and open *Luna's* with only Emma by my side."

Noah hung his head with his hands clasped together between his legs, feeling very guilty all at once and not sure how to answer, as he turned and just stared at her for several moments. "What can I say? I'm a fucked up guy who never deserved you in the first place. But if it makes you feel any better, I realize that now."

"No, it doesn't make me feel any better, Noah! You are not getting off the hook that easily! I was in love with you and you broke my heart, but of course you can't relate to any of this, since you never experienced a broken heart of your own."

Noah sadly shook his head side to side, wanting to confess the truth, but resisting the urge to do so. "In case I forget to tell you, Zoe, you look stunning tonight," he smiled and confessed, wishing like anything he could reach out and kiss her until she was breathless and lost in his arms.

Zoe stood from the bench, staring down at the extremely handsome man with his sexy brown eyes that always pulled her in, knowing that he used to be hers, suddenly recalling the passion that they had shared. "I saw Priscilla. There is no need for false compliments just to make me feel any better," she replied bluntly.

"And I saw the guy that you are here with. He's a good-looking dude! What is his name, by the way?"

"Mason... His name is Mason and he treats me wonderfully!" she defended a little too dramatically, almost as if she was trying to convince herself of the same.

Noah studied her, doubting her sincerity, laying an arm on top of her own. "I'm really happy for you, Zoe. You deserve only the best in life, and that of course applies to any romantic relationship that you are involved in."

Zoe nervously laughed, removing Noah's arm and placing it back in his lap. "I'm sure everyone is wondering what is keeping us so long. If we're not careful they will send out a *"search party"* to find us, and that may not be a good thing if they discover us sitting here together," she mentioned with certainty, thinking about the wrath of Emma being upon them if that were to happen. "I wish you only the best as well, Noah, and now I must say my goodbyes," she articulated without wavering, not allowing him to detain her any longer.

Zoe rose and looked down at him one last time, as he stared back at her sadly, looking like he had lost his best friend. Suddenly, she didn't want to leave and everything felt frozen in time, knowing there was no other choice but to bid him farewell. She turned without a word and walked away, hoping and praying that Noah wouldn't follow after her, going once again in the direction of the ladies bathroom - where the line was still way too long.

Chapter 51

"You're finally back!" Mason yelled out, happy to see that Zoe had returned, already having another rum and Coke waiting for her at the table. "I was ready to start looking for you."

Her heart raced anxiously, considering the possibility of Mason's words that she had luckily dodged. "Yeah, the line for the bathroom was way too long," she tossed out in way of an excuse, with Emma looking a little doubtful with the explanation, after seeing Noah heading in the same direction minus his girlfriend, and then reappearing shortly thereafter, once Zoe had resurfaced again.

It was a circus act watching the old classmates flocking around Noah and Priscilla, wanting to know all the sorted details of their lives that they shared together in England. Sophia and her friends were treating Noah as if he were *"celebrity like"* as they gushed at his feet and begged for a dance, which he reluctantly agreed to, after getting permission first from his fiancé. Prissy didn't really seem to care that much, since a few guys had asked of her the same favor, having no issues with gracing them with her presence. Zoe took it all in, shaking her head in disbelief as she downed her third rum and Coke, with a few special fruity flavored shots to follow, even with Emma's warnings of keeping her head on straight and not *saying or doing something she would regret* by drinking too much.

Noah was also observing what was taking place across the room, seeing the table that was full of some of his former friends and new additions that he didn't recognize. Zoe was with her special group of girls that was constantly a part of her social circle, cozied up to her new boyfriend that Noah had to admit was *"striking"* in his own right. Luke was in the midst of the group also – which still took some getting used to that he and Emma were actually a couple and now living together.

He caught Luke's attention, waving at him to come over to where he was sitting, with a hopeful smile, not having the nerve to go in his direction. He feared the unknown of what Zoe or Emma might say, and then there was the reality of having to come face to face with Mason – doing the *"meet and greet"* for the very first time. *It somehow doesn't seem fair. It should still be me sitting beside of Zoe, and not this new guy who has taken my place,* he had decided selfishly, knowing he had no one to blame but himself.

"I think Noah wants to catch up. Do you have a problem with me going over there and doing so?" Luke politely asked of Emma.

"I'm not your mother. You don't need my permission!" she spewed out indifferently, obviously tipsy like all the rest that were sitting at the table. Emma knew, even before arriving at the reunion, that it was inevitable that he would want to catch up with *"his old gang from high school"*, whether she liked it or not. It was just a *"necessary evil"* of getting through the evening and keeping him content.

Luke made his way over to his old group of friends, smiling as he reached out to give Noah a brotherly hug and pat him warmly on the back. *"Looking a little different there, my friend, with that fancy suit on, don't you think? Didn't you get the memo that it was supposed to be casual dress tonight?"* Luke teased, staring at Noah's suit at arm's length.

Noah laughed, enjoying the camaraderie. "This is considered casual attire for a party in England. I guess I didn't overthink Sophie's email that much, since I read through it quickly."

"Obviously!" Luke laughed, sitting now amongst the other jocks and female *"squad"* members who were also at the table, along with their significant others who didn't have a clue, if they hadn't attended the same high school with the rest of them.

"It's just like old times..." Sophie cooed, being lost in the moment, swinging her wine glass at a sideways angle, spilling some of the

contents onto the tablecloth. *"If only we could go back in time... back when you guys were playing football and soccer, and I was the head cheerleader at the high school,"* she reminisced with a sigh and a far-off dreamy look, making Priscilla question her somewhat melancholy mood - not understanding it in the slightest.

"Do you have class reunions back in London?" One of the guys asked of Prissy, looking her over from head to toe, while salivating and wiping his mouth with the back of his hand, much like an uncultured individual that she avoided at all costs.

"Not in a million years, darling," She muttered beneath her breath, finding him and the whole event distasteful and below her positioning in life.

"Well you're always welcome to live here and be a part of *"our posse","* another yelled out from the Williamsport football team of the past, making Priscilla gasp in disbelief, at the thought of leaving her beloved England, just to move to America and hang out with these drunken imbeciles that Noah had never bothered telling her about. She made her excuses and escaped to the bathroom alone, walking away much too quickly from the building, with all the girls at Zoe's table taking it all in with a smirk.

"So how is work at Taylor Toyota?" Noah inquired of Luke, intrigued to hear the whole story, trying his best now to catch up for a few minutes.

"I'm in charge of the sales team. My dad promoted me and things are only looking up with the business and also with my career."

"Of course that was *gonna* happen!" Noah grinned, slipping back into his improper English dialect, now that Priscilla was out of ear range and not listening in on their conversation. *"Still ever heading out to Marlin Beach and Deep Creek Lake?"*

"Every now and then - when Emma and I can go away together."

Noah studied his close friend, since their youth, still finding the whole concept of the two of them being together very odd and strange. *"You really like her, don't you?"*

"Emma? Yeah, she's the one," Luke grinned. "I'm sure one day I will ask her to marry me and then we will start having a small herd of babies."

"Wow!" Noah answered, feeling somewhat stunned by his unexpected declaration of love. *"Things have really changed since I've been away,"* he stated and also realized, glancing over at Zoe who was now wrapped in Mason's embrace, as he planted a lengthy kiss on her lips, feeling somewhat jealous from watching the outward display of affection.

"What did you expect? That time would stand still until you returned? We have all gone on with our lives, Noah, just as you have also done. You didn't waste any time finding someone else and getting engaged."

"Okay, I get it," He retorted back with a far-off distant look, trying to shake off the obvious, and not caring to deal with the apparent details any longer.

"When do you leave town again?"

"Tomorrow... late. I'm gonna spend a little time with my family and then we catch an *"overnight"* back to London. My classes at Imperial College will begin again Monday for the next semester, and Prissy has a modeling assignment scheduled for next week that she claims she just can't miss."

Luke shook his head, still finding it hard to believe that this was his best friend who he had grown up with in Williamsport, Maryland, now acting all big and bad and cultured - living and going to graduate school in a foreign country, with a model girlfriend who he was now engaged to. "Well it was great seeing you, bro. Safe travels and email or call me sooner than you did this last time," he joked, patting him firmly on the back, hoping it would actually happen.

Noah stood, giving Luke one last parting hug, before he returned to the table to be with Emma again. Zoe was watching Noah's every move as they were saying their goodbyes, and he was watching her too, wishing like anything he could be hugging her also, knowing it was just a foolish desire that would never become a reality. Priscilla returned, not in a good humor, sulking as she sat back down, reaching out and pulling Noah down with her.

"How long do we have to stay here in this town?" Priscilla asked, as she leaned in towards Noah with a miserable look on her face.

"Why, did something happen?"

"No toilet paper! That's what happened. It was undeniably disgusting in the *"loo"* and I had to ask someone in the other *"cubicle"* to spare a few, which she shoved at me underneath the door. And beyond that, the *"cubicle"* was not even the whole way to the floor or ceiling. I have never seen such a disgusting thing!"

Noah laughed, honestly starting to grow tired of Priscilla's *"high maintenance"* behavior that she was constantly exhibiting without end anymore, wishing that she were not there and suddenly back in England, desiring only a few, peaceful remaining moments to be around his classmates without her present. "Just maintain and we will be back at my parents' place within the hour," he promised.

"About that... is there any possible way that we could take an early flight out and leave for London yet tonight? And if not, maybe we can stay at a hotel that is close by the airport, and leave first thing in the morning?"

"You're kidding, right?" Noah asked in disbelief, witnessing her lack of sensitivity first hand that he was suddenly detesting.

"I am not kidding, love. I miss being at home in London."

"Obviously, but the answer is still a definite – *no!* I will visit with my family, just as we had planned before coming here, and then we will leave tomorrow – again as we had discussed and planned," Noah answered firmly, feeling totally irritated with her now. "And just so you know, I have missed my home also, so I guess we have something in common beyond having sex all of the time!"

Priscilla smoothed out her hair, flipping it playfully behind one shoulder. *"Darling, there is no need to be flying off the handle like this. Please calm yourself, Noah. There are people here who are currently watching us,"* she whispered, with her bleached teeth showing, exhibiting a plastic smile that was also displayed in front of the cameras whenever she was modeling."

"I don't give a rats ass!" Noah yelled back, while raising his voice, not giving in and allowing her to control him as she typically did - trying her best to get the situation back where she wanted it by using her good looks and flirtatious ways.

"Well, it's about that time," the lead singer of the band called out over the microphone. "There's one last dance for the *"Williamsport High School, Graduating Class Of 2016"* before your reunion comes to an end for the evening. So grab your special someone and get out here on the dance floor, and make some final lasting memories," he encouraged, as the band broke into a *"slow dance"* number that was also played as the final song at their senior prom, that most there remembered.

The floor was packed, as Zoe and Mason squeezed in too, along with the rest of their friends who had been seated around the table. The majority of the other classmates had lingered, relishing in the last remaining pleasant moments of the reunion with the barn doors fully open – taking in the balmy, cloudless, star-filled sky of summer that they had been gifted with. Zoe rested her head on Mason's chest, closing her eyes, hoping not to see Noah again or make any further contact with him, wishing like anything that he would just up and disappear, making things so much easier for her to deal with. But there he was... slow dancing close by once again, with Priscilla back in his arms, just waiting for Zoe to open her eyes, so that he could catch a final glimpse of the woman he still loved and wanted, even if it was never to be.

Epilogue

"How was the reunion?" Jessica inquired enthusiastically, as Noah and Priscilla returned to the house after midnight.

"It was a fantastic time!" Noah answered, only with a half-truth, knowing he and Prissy had just had another heated exchange out in the car in his parents' driveway. *"Where are dad and Lindsay?"*

"Your dad is in the basement, waiting on you, hoping to play a few rounds of pool, and your sister is sleeping on the sectional, but I'm sure you can wake her up," Jessica explained with a loving smile.

"No need for waking the sleeping dragon," Noah teased, recalling his sister's fiery temper. "It's hard to believe she is going to be a junior at The University of Maryland, actually with a boyfriend of her own, who by the way, appears to be a decent guy," he complimented, recalling the introduction of Dylan earlier in the day before they had left for the class reunion.

"Yes, Lindsay is a mature young lady now, and we do approve of Dylan."

Priscilla yawned as she glanced at Noah, placing the hand with the *"engagement ringed finger"* over her mouth to politely cover it. "Why don't you spend some quality time with your family, love? I think I will go upstairs and retire for the evening, if you don't mind? I think I am still suffering from *"jet lag"*, she feigned sweetly, with Noah having a difficult time believing anything she said now.

"Works for me," he replied back rudely, surprising Jessica by his demeanor and callous behavior.

"Would you like to take a cold bottle of water upstairs with you, dear?" Jessica inquired politely, trying to save face from Noah's lack of couth.

"No, I am fine, Mrs. Clark," Prissy smiled and pretended, wanting only to escape to Noah's room and text out a few messages on her cellphone to her friends and family back home in England.

Noah leaned in for a perfunctory kiss, not even offering to walk her upstairs. "I will see you later, or in the morning – if you are asleep," he stated vaguely, leaving Priscilla to her own vices.

As Noah and Jessica walked down the steps to the basement, she looked at her son, questioning the exchange. *"Is everything okay between the two of you?"* She asked with concern.

"To be honest, I'm not quite sure. This trip has opened my eyes to a few things. *Maybe I moved too quickly by getting engaged already,"* he whispered, not wanting the words to float up the staircase to the second floor where his model girlfriend-fiancé was now resting.

David smiled, seeing that Noah was finally home. *"Ready for some pool?"*

"You better believe I am!" Noah answered with a major grin, rousing Lindsay in the process, as he removed his suit jacket.

She sat up, rubbing her eyes with both hands, while trying to wake up. "I see that you made it back from the reunion in *"one piece"*. Where's Priscilla at?"

"Sleeping..." Noah answered. "I guess she couldn't keep up with the *"River Rats"* from Williamsport," he jested, making his family laugh.

Two a.m. the pool tournament was finally finished, with the winning team being Noah and his mother, and his dad and Lindsay only losing by one point. *"We've missed you son,"* David confessed, wrapping a free arm around Noah's neck, as the pool sticks were gathered and placed back in the holder attached to the wall.

"Yeah, me too. I won't be staying away this long ever again," Noah promised, as they retreated to the upstairs, sad to see the evening finally ending.

Priscilla pretended she was asleep, even with Noah's best attempts to wake her with a kiss to the neck and a fondle to her breasts, rubbing up against her with his *"hard on"* that was pressing up against her pajama clad ass, feeling horny and still thinking about Zoe, that he was desiring badly. He finally gave up, rolling over on his side, realizing he shouldn't be taking his sexual frustrations out on Prissy anyway, knowing it wasn't fair to fantasize about his old girl friend while screwing his fiancé. This was a first, since dating Priscilla, but seeing Zoe had reminded him what he had left behind, and it was weighing heavily on his mind now.

The alarm was set for 7 a.m. and repeatedly beeped, with Noah being too tired to turn it off, after fantasizing and making love to Zoe repeatedly in his mind, until three in the morning. He sat up and stretched his arms overhead, once again with a massive shaft, but not desiring to use it on the *"beauty"* that had disappointed him with her behavior. *"It's time to get up, Priscilla,"* he mumbled on the way to the bathroom, ready to grab a shower first.

A slight knock was heard on the fogged-up, glass shower door, as the *"pixie"* slipped in, joining Noah under the hot, steamy, pulsating flow of the water. *"Can I join you?"* Prissy beckoned playfully, ready for some hot *"morning sex"*.

"Of course…you can," Noah grinned, unable to resist the offer. He turned her to the wall, taking her from behind, seeing Zoe's pretty face again that had robbed him of sleep. *"Aww… ohh,"* he groaned out violently, as he pumped in and out of Priscilla a few more times, only wishing that it were the *"woman of his dreams"*.

Breakfast was waiting on the stove, as Noah and Priscilla's bags were wheeled into the front foyer. *"I hope you are hungry?"* Jessica offered with a hopeful smile, as the family sat together at the large island, already eating from the fare.

"I'm starving!" Noah answered, with Priscilla clearly displaying a look of total indifference, with not the slightest desire to join the others and partake.

"Grab a plate, dear, and help yourself," Jessica suggested, as Priscilla stood off to the one side – just taking it all in. "I'm sorry, but I don't typically eat *"eggs and bacon"* or drink *"coffee"*.

"So what exactly do you eat for breakfast then?" Lindsay grilled, with a look of displeasure, as she stared at her with a mouth full of bacon and toast.

Priscilla giggled, finding the whole family and situation amusing, just like those at the reunion that she was forced to be around, feeling superior to every one of them. "I drink tea and sometimes have a tad of unsweetened yogurt with some fresh blueberries."

Lindsay huffed, finding her quite aggravating, as she resumed eating without a comment, glancing briefly at Noah instead, with a look of disdain.

"It's time for us to leave," Noah announced, after finishing his breakfast and helping his mother clean up the kitchen. Priscilla had been waiting patiently in the living room, attempting to converse with David and Lindsay, as the morning news was being broadcasted, not having the slightest interest in any of it.

"Thank you for your hospitality," she offered superficially, happy that it was finally over and she could finally return back to the home that she loved.

"You are very welcome," Jessica and David answered in unison, as the family walked Noah and Priscilla out to the front porch. An Uber

driver sat idling in the driveway, ready to make the ninety-minute journey to the airport whenever the *"riders"* of his vehicle were ready to do so. Priscilla wasted no time as she wheeled her suitcase off of the porch and towards the car, not caring in the least about the final farewell with *"the relatives"*.

"I hope college goes well for you next semester," Noah offered to Lindsay, "And by the way, I like your boyfriend. He seems like a good guy," he grinned, missing his mouthy *"bratty little sister"* already.

Lindsay leaned in, hugging her brother goodbye. *"Wish I could say the same for your choice of significant others..."* she whispered, hoping he would listen and take the well-intentioned hint to heart. "Stay safe over there and good luck with your classes also," she added, before walking back into the house, not feeling the need to take things any further concerning Priscilla.

Noah reached out, wrapping both arms around his mom and dad at the same time, suddenly questioning his decision to return to England. "Maybe I shouldn't have come back home for a visit. Now it's not easy... to say goodbye to friends and family, and leave Williamsport behind again. *I think what I'm coming to realize is that where I grew up - is not such a bad place to be living."*

"We are always here for you, Noah. Just know that," Jessica emotionally replied, with tears now welling up in her eyes. "Hopefully, you will give some real thought to your future, and what you would like to do - in way of a career - once you graduate from Imperial College."

"Yeah... you are right, but as you know, I do have a year of school left, so I do have some time to think about all that," he answered realistically, knowing it was time to join Priscilla in the Uber, as his dad nodded silently in agreement.

Noah and Priscilla slept the entire way to Dulles Airport, with barely a word spoken between them, being finally woken and then dropped off by the Uber driver with an announcement *that they had arrived*. "Thanks, dude, for the ride!" Noah extended, putting a nice tip on the bill. They slipped away with their bags in hand, doing the necessary check-ins that were required, before locating their designated terminal that would take them back to London.

"I can't wait until I can take a bath again in my own tub," Priscilla whined, with her pouty lips pushed up. She fashioned her slightly damp hair into a bun, high on top of her head, before replacing her sunglasses that she didn't need to wear inside, trying to act like she was famous.

"Soon enough..." Noah answered with a frustrated sigh, doing his darndest to tune her out. He realized the flight to Heathrow was going to be a long one, and his only desire now was to be away from her.

About The Author

Roberta L. Greenwald is a romance writer who resides in Williamsport, Maryland. She feels fortunate to be living near the beautiful C&O Canal and towpath where she likes to ride a bike or take a walk, delighting in the spectacular scenery. She immensely enjoys her life surrounded by family, friends and her beloved pets – all making her life worth living! The next novel is always being thought about and written down, happy to share it with you – the reader.

Made in the USA
Middletown, DE
28 June 2025

77461029R00205